Dragon Dreams and Stranger Things

A Collection of Stories from the World of Maera

Denys James Browden

Want to experience more of Maera?
Visit www.maeraworld.com

This work is dedicated with thanks to all those whose contributions have made Maera come alive.

PROLOGUE

Maera was in the throes of wondrous days, turbulent days. In what many deemed the Age of Man, a dark sullenness had settled over civilization. As the world entered the thirteenth millennium beyond the sharing of the First Words, its peoples seemed plagued by a sickness of rage that few could fathom. Filled with greed and ambition, men bemoaned their short existence. Seeking to conquer the waves, they explored vast lands beyond the horizon while braving the Dragon Skies above. Unfortunately, these new lands did not satiate the ever-hunger of man. In their gluttonous sprawl, they went their own way, seldom seeking the close company or wise counsel of the elder folk. The deep knowledge of Maera largely passed beyond their ken.

While man's reach grew ever longer, their ways seemed ever darker. In time, many factions of men perceived civility as weakness. Eventually, fear eclipsed hope as the boldest of the gods grew ever more contentious in their machinations. Their worshippers fomented intolerance and aggression, forsaking many generations of acceptance and understanding. In the arrogance of youth, those burdened by Loekii with free will no longer sought peace for strength but war for gain. My people receded in the face of such aggression, seeking solace and isolation 'neath the verdant canopy of our silva. However, not all of us were able to turn away. Some looked on in stark horror as men began to bring doom first upon one another, and then the wide world.

—An excerpt from "Gaedennon" by Raegolin Maeracil of the Eldanae

*Want to experience more of Maera? Visit **www.maeraworld.com***

TITLES

Warning! Some of these tales depict mature themes. Please visit www.maeraworld.com for further guidance regarding the various topics in each story that readers may find distressing or offensive.

KINGDOM
of
JAPARAND

Havens of
Doom

BENTUA

Rablaus

ISLE of
RUMORGA

Ignaér

Verda

Bacile

Matrios

Saen

Calmaeres

Celaca

Vasta

KEDOK HILLS

LAND OF BAÉLTHAS

MOUNTAINS

BURNT LANDS

OF SHANDRAK

Flood Plain
of Badasl

SEA

R   I   S   N   A

E   L

Esta

IN

VILLAINS, ALL

Havoc and Kaen concentrated intently, focusing on their balance, breathing, and pace. They were moving quickly through the dark, processing the mixture of half-moonlight, scattered open fires and a few other sources of light from the street below. Intermittent clouds complicated matters, but experience aided them. The two roof-runners were in their element, trying to put a little more distance between themselves and their latest victim.

Havoc, the older of the pair, calculated that there was only a tiny chance that anyone would give chase at all. The proficient way they covered ground almost ensured that all but the most competent pursuit would fail. Speed and stealth were what they did, the skills they had plied since their childhood together on the streets as purse-cutters in the Deep End. Few played the game faster or with a harder edge than this pair. They stopped at the border of the First and Second Wards, catching their breath and watching for any sign of being trailed. It was starting to look like they would make it through another night in the Dark City.

The teens were human, and their appearance was unexceptional. Both wore a dark semble, a fabric face wrap worn over the bridge of their noses. Each was hawk-faced, with dark hair and eyes but pale skin, all common local traits. They were the unwanted sons of alley-meat, women brutalized by a cruel city, long since devoured by the hunger of the night. The pair's quickness, agility, raw speed, and eagerness to draw their weapons meant that they were a dangerous encounter. However, it was their unfailing partnership that had kept them alive while so many of their peers had perished alone. The two had made it through a shortened childhood and were independent, living by their own hand, beating the odds each day that they held onto their aether, Rhal be ever praised, while avoiding the notice of more sinister gods.

The Life, as they called it, was measured in meals, small quick bites, anywhere from one to four in a night. They had to eat to live, so their minds had become accustomed to surviving until the next chance to eat. Theft of food on the streets of Ithil-Bane was so common that vendors figured their certain losses into their pricing, for there was no stopping the quick fingers of the rabble of street urchins of the metropolis.

A favorable, guild-sanctioned customer-to-vendor ratio in the city ensured that most of the street operators would stay above water, even when crime cost their trade heavily. Most towns suffered some measure of thievery and even violence on their public streets. Many cultures allowed just enough of such activities to force its citizens to participate in local theft prevention, with the vigilance of its inhabitants being a primary deterrent to a town's street crime.

Ithil-Banians thought of grift, outright theft, and more than occasional violence as a part of their culture. Put enough people in one place, and maak is bound to pile, as is said. Simply put, their citizens were less concerned about common crime than they were about the higher taxes required to fight it. The locals of the lower wards of the town, at least, anticipated thievery much like they expected everyone around them to carry at least one blade. They accepted Ithil-Bane as she was, assigning a female persona to their home and thinking of her much like an untamed yet beloved mistress that they always forgave and whom they somehow couldn't quite quit.

Travelers often claimed that there was no other place like it, primarily those unaware of the continent of Provos to the north, where her twin city Raeleen, capital of the draevar nation of Saestis, sprawled. The original Haven of the Night, for millennia, Raeleen's draevar population had set the brutal standard for a cruel city veiled in the dark of night and ruled by fear. Their Overlord, the magnificent Arch-Daemon Jezrael, had ruled that nightmarish metropolitan jungle for more than sixty generations of her draevar, the pure raven-skinned humans of legend.

As the chosen people of Loekii, the draevar were the most feared flavor of human and were the embodiment of achievement in worshiping the evil Goddess of Chaos and Deception. Under a harsh enough ruling hand, it seemed that even the most audacious megalopolis, comprised of the most aggressive, unlawful, and malevolent citizenry imaginable, could not only exist but thrive without tearing itself apart under the sheer weight of its own brutality.

Ithil-Bane mirrored Raeleen's inky image as a place of black stone and metallic construction with intriguing vertical architecture. It teemed with commerce fueled by the nation's aggressive naval conquests and trade from distant lands. It was a burg that offered anything you could want and many things for which one should not wish. Made vibrant by a blend of locals and travelers from the world over, residents here sought a way to increase their chances of survival, wealth, or personal power. Everyone had an angle and the intrigue began when those angles intersected.

Ithil-Bane was a nation of great wealth but also a place of tremendous, systemic disparity in the distribution of those riches, ensured by wicked policies of wanton corruption that its noble class thrived on. It was a city of contrasts with magnificent buildings and many destitute, transient unfortunates that slept in its gutters and alleys. It was a town where anyone of means walked in public with at least one body-man, for bloodshed only incurred a fine if it became a public disturbance. The authorities did not involve themselves unless the person left standing did not mitigate their mess in some way. If groups were involved, the law provided the needed crowd control. As with many aspects of life in the mighty city state, this was excitedly, if inaccurately, depicted abroad, often portrayed as "anyone can kill anyone else they encounter in Ithil-Bane." The city residents rarely corrected such exaggerations when they heard them during their travels and seemed to enjoy such embellishment. It was fair to say that the cultural norms, political policies, and harsh laws of Ithil-Bane were infamous. They set the stage for much of the drama that played out nightly in what men often referred to as the City of Dreams.

The town was circular, its buildings taller and taller as you climbed further towards its center. The buildings of the Outer Ward were mainly a single story, while those of the Second Ward were generally two stories high, the Third three, and so on. The Twelve Wards of Ithil-Bane were estimated by some to hold over a million mortals, the majority of whom were human.

At night the streets of the Dark City teemed with life. In a threatening display of evident power, the Citadel, the central fortress of the town, rose above the rest, somehow malevolent and cruel seeming in its very existence. Its spires and sharp angles seemed to leer over the place, its apartments and balconies afforded a spectacular view of the wash of life that ebbed and flowed through the city's streets.

Havoc surveyed the streets below them while Kaen watched the rooftops behind. The pair had a routine for nearly any situation, a division of labor based on instinct and experience in self-preservation. Their backs to one another, they took stock of their status. Kaen's gaze strayed from the rooftops to the Citadel, as it often did. He had never noticed how often his eyes were drawn to that mighty edifice. It was looking up that, ill-advised though it was considered by so many, now saved them. As Kaen peered into the black sky, the moon broke free of its veil of cloud and the thief could make out the mass that was quietly swarming towards them. "Bats!" he hissed, his body now tense. Havoc spun in response and let out a low growl of assent.

"They're coming right for us! Are they hunting us?" Kaen asked.

"Over a purse?" Havoc countered. He could take no more time to think. It was already beyond the moment to go. "With me, street-low, NOW!" he called and was gone. Down he swung, under the eaves, clambering onto the sturdy drainpipe that gave a wall-climber like him an easy slide to a lower place nearby. He kept his second hand gloved and padded for such instances, for the pipes in the Dark City were often sharp-edged, barbed, or even razored against assassins and thieves. Property owners were also known to slather paralyzing agents or worse on these traps, but Havoc expected no such danger here. The off-hand grip strength of a street runner was a testament to the thief's experience and daring. Their second forelimb was often bolstered by some slender design of armor that locals simply called an "arm." Havoc hadn't had an opportunity to acquire an arm yet but intended to do so as soon as any chance presented itself.

They passed down from the Second Ward to the First, heading towards the thickest traffic, taking advantage of the city's design. When fleeing a foe or the law, it was common to race towards the city's outer wall, as the sheer press of bodies in the streets grew ever tighter as it neared. This tactic provided more ways to slip pursuers, making any chase more challenging. Conversely, as you approached the mighty Citadel at the city's center, the structures rose higher, and there was a subtle incline of the streets to match, ensuring sewage runoff to the lower regions of town. In the interior wards, there were more restrictive laws, proclamations, and declarations to make the areas progressively more exclusive. A policy of heavy visual profiling ensured that the authorities quickly encountered those inappropriately dressed or out of place, a thing to be avoided.

Ithil-Bane was particularly dangerous for youngsters or teens unescorted by adults. In the outer wards, at least, they were immediately assumed to be beggars, thieves, thugs, or worse. Any such children were typically detained, beaten, or at best, chased away. Treatment like this led to youths running in packs for protection in numbers, and they were often violent in their defense. Passing through any tight crowd was inherently dangerous for the roof climbers. While fleeing however, sheer numbers around them could aid their escape. Then again, a press of bodies would slow them down—too many eyes, hands, and blades. So, Havoc compromised, leading Kaen along the edges of public spaces. This made them vulnerable, as it increased their chances of being singled out. Thus, Havoc soon leaped towards an alley that had a large center channel for drainage, marking the meeting of the First and Second Wards.

Kaen would usually have stopped at the gutter, checked for danger, stopped again halfway down, and paused when his shoes hit the cobbles. But the emphatic "NOW!" issued earlier by Havoc meant that they must forgo standard precautions in favor of raw speed. The streets held hundreds of people on any given block. The pair disappeared towards the pitch of the passageway, barely turning a head in the nearby crowd. They had long ago mastered passing without a sound, audible to none but the most trained ear. Even while sprinting, they could keep well below the constant din of the crowd. Three paces into the alley, a family was huddled against the wall on the side of the First Ward, dividing part of a loaf between them. As the pair passed, Kaen produced his second blade. The large boy he had mistaken for a man saw the flash of an edge and gasped, putting up his hand to fend off a strike against those he squatted over. Kaen seized the good fortune of that tense gesture and gave the teen a substantial slash across his palm to make him bleed.

Haeffrin's summoned *Blood Bats* swept into the channel between the buildings and continued their chase. Then the intoxicating smell of fresh blood reached their senses and the swarm washed over the unfortunate family like an inky wave. As the two runners sprang down the alley and then around the corner back into the Second Ward, they did not look back. Had they done so, they might have noticed a single splendid raven that swept into the scene, landing on the cobbles. It witnessed the fate that befell the hapless family under the fangs of the bats and watched the runners disappear to the east. It gronked once, loudly, and then took flight, continuing to shadow the thieves as its master had ordered.

Eben had been bound to Haeffrin for over a year and had witnessed many things during that span. But few of these things had provided him with the tangible sense of raw amusement he had felt watching two young thieves get the better of the egomaniacal man he currently served. It was soon apparent that they were simply Lifers, two more of the vast, rudderless mob of children of the street, a massive and lost amalgam of mortals that struggled, suffered, and lived on a day-to-day basis while wicked men like Haeffrin trod upon them. Over the past year, Eben had born the indignity of his enslavement quietly, with little but his cleverness to entertain him. However, he was enjoying this night immensely.

The runners were adept and covered ground quickly and without wasted motion. They put several blocks between themselves and their unfortunate victims and concealed themselves beneath the alley doorway of a business that appeared to be closed. Eben had been flying above them and now landed on a nearby chimney. He watched as the two quietly worked out what had just happened. "It doesn't add up. Why waste a casting over a few slugs? I don't get it." Havoc, the slightly larger and much more talkative youth, pulled out the bag and poured its contents into his palm as he spoke. By design, the bag yielded just a few ragged coins made mostly of copper.

The purse was simple cloth, appearing ordinary in every way. "It's a light take," Kaen, the more diminutive lad, said. "It doesn't rate pursuit, let alone an attack! Unless …," Kaen's eyes widened with realization, "… unless it's something more—at least to the owner!" The wizard Haeffrin's avian familiar concentrated and his interest heightened. Then he could hear every word that passed between the humans. "Best result?" Kaen continued, "We're sitting on a fortune here!" As the words left his mouth, his partner realized their meaning. Havoc, not sharing his companion's growing excitement, seemed annoyed by Kaen's enthusiasm. The thieves stared at one another for a few heartbeats, their minds calculating a wide range of possibilities and consequences.

"Even if that's true, we'll never live to see it," said Havoc. "Think! Anyone who could tell us what it is, if we could even find such a person, would be powerful enough to take it from us. All we know for sure, in any case, is that the bastard we took it off is willing to kill for it." Havoc paused for a moment, growing stern. "Worst thought? The one who gave it up is tracking it. No, it's too dangerous! Too dangerous by far. Let's just be rid of it." And there it was! The human lad tossed the bag idly onto the cobblestones to his left, just past his partner. "Let's go!"

"Yeah, sure, you're right, of course." Kaen seemed to accept the reality of their situation with evident, disappointed resignation. At the same time that Havoc set out, the bird prepared to leap into the air and coast down to nab his prize. The return of the purse would surely earn him a special treat and perhaps a day's favor with Haeffrin. Eben watched in alarm as the second boy curiously eyed the small pouch and then looked to be sure his friend was not watching. The thief picked the bag up, placing it in the fold of his tunic. Only after he had secured it did he follow his partner. Kaen was the impulsive risk-taker and he had freed the purse. He wasn't about to leave their prize to the cobbles! As the raven stood stunned, the lad rushed to catch up with his partner. The act of Kaen taking the small pouch, known as a Moon Purse amongst spell casters, spoiled Eben's mood.

By Rhal and all that's shiny! Eben's mind raged. *What in the ever-frozen wastes of Hell just happened?* He was squawking mad and stamped his clawed feet angrily, rocking from side to side. The runners had disappeared down yet another alley, leaving the raven alone to rattle on in frustration. Quickly the bird calmed himself. The sun would rise soon and he had to at least follow the pair to see where they slept to report back to Haeffrin. Bad news was still news and better than no news at all. Once more, he took wing and quickly caught up to the thieves as they evaded the crowds, street-low. He made a mental note to offer Rhal the first bit of shiny he came across to regain the favor of fortune, as it clearly had left him.

The runners were more than mates, tighter than friends, closer than partners. They were like brothers and not like Hezric and Geiger, the Jaan twins who had long ago founded the City of Ithil-Bane and who had, in the end, killed each other over their creation. Havoc and Kaen trusted one another, literally, with their lives, which had saved them many times already and they were just thirteen years old. They had pledged with words, and each understood that they must follow agreed-upon strategies and tactics that maximized survivability and the chance for success in a generally lawless place seemingly always trying to end them. It marked the pair as different, and it had been proven to be a potent balm against the searing burn of the Dark City.

The two slept in many places but always together, always close. They looked for certain qualifying features when seeking a place to sleep, things that had made a difference. The Dark City was enjoying the moderate temperatures of the month of Waerm. Always, though, there was the threat of rain to be considered. The climbers preferred rooftop sleep, but finding a suitable perch was challenging. The two were used to physical contact while sleeping, so much so that either would have found it challenging to rest if they didn't touch. Experience dictated that they had multiple sets of sleep gear cached at various locations around the Second Ward, where they often slept. These packages were tucked away into a handful of hidey-holes where they'd be safe from prying eyes and snatching fingers.

The sky above was the safest exposure if one played the odds, which all residents of Ithil-Bane did. No matter that everything from dangerous parasitic insects to dragons used the skies above the city freely. Undoubtedly, the other residents of the town posed the most significant threat. They learned to sleep lightly, quietly, with one eye open if possible, and with a blade in hand. The two thieves slept back-to-back for safety unless the cold dictated otherwise. Their clever method of sleep was one of the things that set them apart from the alley-huddled masses.

Kaen, gifted with anything sharp in his hands, had learned to sew as a child. It was a relatively ordinary skill in a town where many couldn't afford a second set of clothes. One had to be clever and resourceful to survive long on the streets. After a magnificent haul had brought them an entire bundle of gray blankets, Kaen had sewn two together and added a robust and long strap to produce what would have been a useful carry pouch for a giant. The pair placed that strap around a chimney and took advantage of the close match of the fabric to the slate roof tiles that were so common in the Dark City. The satchel afforded cover from both sight and weather, adding a small measure of comfort to their rest. While peering from beneath the flap, they could keep a wary eye in both directions. Satchel-sleep was one of their best innovations, and they had used this strategy successfully for several years.

Neither of them noticed the raven flying overhead as they settled in for daylight's rest, still chewing the final bite of a meal they'd stolen on the way there. Eben spent the dawn curiously regarding the young men as they carefully prepared their perch for sleep. The two were impressive for a pair of lowly alley thieves, Eben had to admit that. He had landed to watch them, but that's all he would risk. Eben was wary that they might harm him if he tried to approach them. Ravens were held in ill repute in the Dark City as they were common familiars, associated with known extra-planar beings, as well as being among the favored of Loekii. The best way to keep all of one's feathers was to be constantly cautious and vigilant. The bird remained quiet until the pair settled in and then took wing. Eben circled once high above the thieves as the sun crested the horizon over the Great Eastern Sea. When the Horn of Dawn blasted its warning from the Citadel over the quieting city, he flew southeast and returned dutifully to his master.

Haeffrin Manefourt had come to Ithil-Bane trying to escape his past, like many others. He expected pursuit but if the private bounty on him became a public offer, the dog would go from bark to bite very quickly. His travel papers had been issued in Eglair, the Refuge, under false diplomatic pretenses and had cost him a painful measure of coin. However, the corruption of the Dark City was well known, which stripped him of any sense of security.

Haeffrin had believed that he might have a chance to start anew in this vast, threatening place. He had associated himself with a group of travelers on board the coast runner known as the *Thunder Tide* but things had gone to hell their first night in town. Foolish, hasty words after potent drink had worsened a misunderstanding with a new acquaintance that had threatened his intended business. Then the riches he had stolen in Eglair to fund his flight had been taken by a pair of street runners just a few hours later. It was inconceivable! Things would worsen if Eben didn't turn up soon with Haeffrin's Moon Bag. Where was that useless, thrice-cursed wad of feathers?

Just then, Eben landed on a cart a few feet away. Haeffrin could not sense his familiar approaching, a disturbing trend, yet another sign of their mental bond weakening. "Where in all the Frozen Hells have you been?" he demanded. He was careful to hide his rage from his companions but Eben sensed it. As he anticipated the hostility, the raven had not sought the wizard's mind as he approached. Eben croaked, then emitted a series of low, gurgling sounds from the back of his throat, varying in pitch, that those nearby heard as a "kraa-kraa" sound. To Haeffrin, it was as if the bird spoke a fluent dialect of the human tongue. His displeasure with Eben's report was hard to mask.

"I have confirmed that your bats succeeded only in taking inno-cent lives and alerting the thieves to our pursuit. They still have your purse, for I had no opportunity to retrieve it. However, they are now resting and I can lead you to them." The perfunctory response met Eben's sworn obligation to Haeffrin in his service to Aelar, Goddess of Magic. Eben had long ago stopped giving the man anything more. The wizard approached him, coming too close for comfort.

"You're more worthless to me every day. Did you even attempt to get it back? Do you realize what's at stake?" The human had lowered his voice until only Eben could hear it. The raven turned, purposely shat on the man's right boot, and took flight, croaking a few choice expletives as he did so. The human maintained his self-control but only through a considerable expenditure of effort. Biting laughter came from the viper amongst his fellow travelers.

"And he's your friend, eh? It seems that bird has better taste than we do, fellas," said Nellis, a thief and an unwelcome associ-ate of the wizard. Her presence was irritating enough. Her voice mocking him was intolerable. The caster decided to confront the surly brigand. In his hands, he silently pooled the energy required to deliver a brutal electrical jolt. He held back on the casting, preempt-ing an audible crackle or smell. He turned to face her, ready to take that next step.

"I'm sorry, what did you say?" he asked calmly.

"Don't step to me, ya' gash, unless you're tired of wearin' your skin!" the cutthroat from Bentua threatened. As she spoke, a dagger suddenly appeared in her left hand and she took a step forward, menacing the wizard with it by bringing the knife up and brandishing it between their faces. Her pale eyes flashed with an evident desire to draw blood and her grin spoke to her vicious nature. It seemed that a meal and a few hours to cool off hadn't assuaged the blade-tough's previous anger. The words used earlier still carried weight and it seemed that the two travelers would have a serious disagreement at some point.

"By all the bastards in Bedlam!" said Tollem. "Will you two stop?" The massive warrior had seen that Nellis' right hand was hovering over her long dagger. He knew it was a blade that she kept slathered with shaatra, her favored venom. Tollem pushed off the wall of the tavern and stepped up to the combative pair. Tollem's subordinate, a less bulky fighter named Adams, stepped with him. Adams stopped a pace behind and to the left of his sergeant. The soldiers were non-committal enforcers, motivated by any bit of shiny they could muster and, right now, their only source of that was Haeffrin. Their bond, earned in the crucible of combat, continued to serve them well. It was unwavering, the unspoken affinity between men who had bled for a shared cause and over the same ground. Tollem disliked having to speak at all, and Adams seldom did. But without the two, the others would have seen their dislike for one another through to whatever came naturally. Tollem wouldn't tolerate it, not today.

"The Horn of Dawn has sounded. We need to get inside. Scrape this horse shit from your boots! We've got business to see to before that hot blood between you two spills!" He was right, of course. Since they all knew it, his words did the trick. And so, the wizard

19

and the cutthroat both took a step back. Haeffrin didn't try to disguise his disdain for the ugly bandit. Nellis' eyes lingered overlong on Haeffrin's handsome face. She imagined it with swaths of skin missing and reclaimed a slightly better humor.

Tollem quietly studied the thief with whom he had adventured, catching a particular look in her eyes. He had seen that look before on more than one occasion and the silent message of that gaze couldn't have been clearer to him. *Soon*, it promised. Tollem had hoped the two would just kuet and be done with it. The warrior realized that the group had to conclude their proposed venture as quickly as possible. In the meanwhile, he needed to keep the wizard and thief apart.

Locals said that only fools and the blood-rich let their shadow touch the cobbles of Ithil-Bane under Aarn's light. The hearth house where the four travelers had eaten their fill was next door to the old inn where they had paid to bed. They had spent extra for a smaller-than-usual common room with just four individual slender wooden beds built with wooden slats beneath a padded mat to stretch out on with unaccustomed comfort. Their privacy was important but they had paid for protection from unwanted trespass. One had to be extremely careful in choosing where to lay one's head in a land where robbery and murder were more common than wind and rain.

Ithil-Bane was a dangerous place to be a familiar, and Eben found it stressful. He felt that he was under constant threat and the open hostility that Nellis had expressed for his master made him uncomfortable. She was just the type who would believe that hurting him would damage his wizard. Eben had a strong sense of people and typically knew who could be trusted, and that woman was mean. He knew that she had done terrible things in her life. Her presence made being near Haeffrin nerve-wracking, so Eben perched on the room's crossbeam where it met the western wall. His wizard sat beneath him on the edge of his bed as he faced Tollem.

The situation required action during the long hours of light and Haeffrin was fretting over the thought that he'd have to tell the party what had transpired. The wizard was sure that he needed the assistance of his group to regain the bag that held most of his wealth. His mind raced as he pondered what he should say to secure their help. Haeffrin just needed to explain that he had been targeted and robbed. It was that simple. It could have happened to anyone and did happen, to nearly everyone here, at some point. Then a clever deception occurred to him.

"Tollem, my raven has brought me important information we need to act upon. We must risk the day and take a meeting in the Second Ward. It will be a quick enough errand—but it must be handled delicately." Haeffrin ensured that both Adams and Nellis could hear him across the room. He had definitely earned the attention of the group.

"Did you really just suggest that we take a little stroll out under Aarn? Are you out of your soft, kueting head?" Nellis didn't disappoint him. He had only known the woman for a few days, but he could already predict her every action. It was Tollem that Haeffrin had to convince; Tollem decided matters for the three. Tollem's face spoke for him before he even opened his mouth.

"Showering sparks of Haemur," said the soldier, "That's a scary notion you've had there!" They had no papers to do so and unless the wizard had much more pull here in the city than Tollem had guessed, no such documents were coming. "The very last thing we want is to meet the Military Guardsmen out on the streets. Explain how we're going to avoid that." Nellis had risen to her feet while Tollem was talking but thus far, she'd done nothing else.

"This one's outside his mind!" Nellis declared loudly. "Who do you think you are, eh?" she directed at the wizard. She was openly afraid of the idea and skeptical that Haeffrin could manage any such scenario. "The bad men get to have their way with you if they catch you out there casting shadows!" Haeffrin felt relief.

Manipulating the group would be easier than he had hoped. The wizard, of course, had the answer they needed to hear to even consider such an outing. "First of all, it's cloudy today." That assertion incited Nellis' loud exasperated but inarticulate exhaling of breath. "But that doesn't even matter because we'll be invisible the whole time we're traveling." Haeffrin's promise brought the conversation back into the realm of reality. "We should be out and back without detection and in no more than an hour or two." The reassuring tone of his voice reflected Haeffrin's growing confidence that he had the situation well in hand. If he could get close to the thieves, he had a few ideas about retrieving his property with minimal difficulty.

Tollem had seen the multicolored gemstones that Haeffrin carried and, as far as he was concerned, the wizard called the shots. Sometimes it was a good thing to be a man of simple motivations. If the wizard needed to do this, they would get it done. Tollem made it plain how he felt. Nellis grumbled but soon went back to sitting on her bed. The group discussed their new mission until everyone was entirely on board. Haeffrin convinced them to follow his plan as the scenario depended on his powerful magic and the lead of his raven familiar. They left soon after that as Haeffrin felt that less time to think things through was a variable in his favor.

His comrades could have forgiven Haeffrin to some degree for thinking that his magic would be enough to facilitate a venture into the streets of Ithil-Bane in direct violation of martial law. *Unseen* is, after all, a tremendously effective casting when the wizard in question had any measure of fundamental proficiency. In particular, adventuring wizards used it regularly and relied on it to achieve the success to which they had grown accustomed. However, it might have occurred to anyone reasonable that the Military Guard of the Dark City, that daunting elite unit that enforced martial law, might be accustomed to such spell casting in the streets and thus be prepared for its use.

The four travelers, already *Unseen*, exited their first-story room at the inn through their western-facing window. The group moved slowly and with an agreed-upon cautious quiet. The four had decided to follow Haeffrin's raven to the location of the promised meeting. Haeffrin may have been used to the casting and was comfortable under its gloam but his three fellow adventurers were not. They had tied knots every five feet in a length of rope and looped one end of it around the belt of their thief, Nellis, who agreed to lead as she was the group's expert in the use of stealth. Haeffrin centered his casting on himself, a standard tactic when a wizard deployed any defensive spell. The rope kept them close together, within the radius of the spell's effect.

Tollem of Sedan followed immediately behind Nellis, and the wizard walked behind him. Adams guarded their rear. Nellis would set their pace while the spell caster kept in mental contact with his familiar, making sure that Eben was always close. Haeffrin, Nellis, Tollem and Adams had agreed that Nellis would tug on the rope once to warn when she was about to stop and twice before starting up again. Each man would pass that message back, hoping it would keep them from bumping into one another. It was a simple plan and although it proved clumsy at first, the group managed to figure it out during the first several minutes of their walk. At some point during that march, they each realized that the rope somehow made them feel like they were still visible. It was disconcerting but it helped them maintain their concentration, which was good.

Things went well for a while. The group crept near the walls of the buildings, even though the streets were virtually empty. The day was overcast and comfortable, with just an intermittent breeze. Any sound tended to amplify and echo. The Dark City's mighty Citadel caused an acoustic phenomenon that the populace dreaded. Locals declared that the city was a living entity. To their thinking Ithil-Bane had a heart and a mind, and a dark aether that was generated by some sinister magic emanating from the Citadel. Haeffrin had considered it nothing but an urban myth and laughable. He had to admit that once he had experienced the strange acoustics of the Dark City firsthand, there just may have been something to it. Locals often whispered, seldom shouted, and generally kept to themselves for they feared that the Citadel heard all. *Precisely the kind of frightening notion that a tyrannical government might spread,* thought the caster. Ithil-Bane had a turbulent magical presence that permeated every level of its culture more oppressively than in almost any other nation on Maera. This notion was enough to explain some of the high tension one could sense in the streets of the City of Dreams.

The party followed Eben, who had put aside any ill feelings and was in constant touch with his master's mind. He kept close to the cobbles, often perching on streetlamps and other low-lying terrain features of the streets to remain within the group's field of vision. Nellis was an adept professional treasure seeker and was on high alert. She'd been in Ithil-Bane before and understood the risk she was taking by simply being outdoors and walking the streets during daylight hours. The only reason Nellis was willing to do so was the promise of being staked by the wizard in a lucrative mission in the region. Nellis also had no intention of genuinely risking capture by the Ithil-Banian Military Guard and had sworn by all of the Thirteen Torments of Otten that she would save herself should things go awry. She was very confident in her ability to avoid detection and get out of the area, clear of trouble, if she had to run for it and leave the others behind. It wasn't part of the plan but if it came to that, so be it.

Tollem and Adams had recently been in Ithil-Bane after fighting as mercenaries for the city-state in the recent Fall of Harab. They had seen years of service together in the Sedan army, a nation that customarily executed its prisoners of war. The two veterans found the wartime behavior of the Ithil-Banian Marine Corps to be cruel beyond belief. The trooper's skin-shredding, face-taking and eye-collecting were just too much. They had enough coin to survive for a few months in the Dark City but were looking for a much larger score. Straight-forward shiny pay for daring ventures sounded good to them for the moment and Tollem was of a mind to risk much, if need be, to see such a venture through. The job had already begun, in the soldier's practical way of thinking. They needed to add an archer who could scout and perhaps a priest, and their group would be ready to go. Tollem was willing to stand with the wizard, whatever came their way. The spell caster had, thus far, backed up every bit of his talk. Adams would follow his lead.

Haeffrin was pleased enough with the veteran warriors from Sedan but the wizard did not feel he could mitigate his issues with Nellis. Tollem swore the thief would honor any standard venture contract but the Bentuan was a drinker and base. Apparently, she held wizards in general contempt, seemingly resenting Haeffrin in particular. Perhaps this was because he had the promised coin that would finance their venture and thereby could claim the position of leader and make decisions for the group. Haeffrin found motivations more challenging to weigh than threats, and there was no denying it. The two now had an intense personal dislike for one another that had become evident over their first night together in town. Nellis had poor control over her tongue and a threatening demeanor, while Haeffrin would suffer no physical threat. The spell caster thought the situation irredeemable and Haeffrin had no intention of remaining in the woman's company for even one more day. As they made their way through the streets, his mind worked darkly, spawning plans within plans.

The raven reached the rooftop where the pair of street runners slept in their pouch. The darkest alleys below had filled with the homeless who desperately sought to avoid the light of day. He landed quietly on the roof's chimney so then Haeffrin would be sure to see the thieves. It struck Eben as wrong to give the youngsters to the party, unfair somehow. After all, they'd gotten away with it clean. But he was indentured to the human and by Aelar's glittering gaze, he would not go against the word of his Mistress, the Goddess of Magic. He could not see the group in the light of day. Aarn limited his vision but his mind was in active thrall to Haeffrin's, so he knew where they were and as a result, Eben knew when the party stopped as they encountered an obstacle.

Nellis had come across the lone body of a man that lay on the cobbles, face down. The thief didn't smell anything nastier than what issued forth naturally at death and saw no blood nor any other evidence of violence. It lay directly in their path, so she gave the corpse a cursory check for shiny. As it was soon evident that the body had nothing of value, including its belt and shoes, she stepped over the unfortunate wretch. As she did so, she muttered under her breath, "Take the aether given up here for what awaits it. Let it not linger in this place. Your willing servant asks this of You, Mistress." Like so many others who swam in the darkness, Nellis cared only that the dead did not rise to hunt the living. The group passed over the body, each in turn acknowledging the loss of a life in their own way.

The four kept moving forward, approaching the building where Eben rested. The raven watched with sudden undesirable excitement as a small band of Military Guardsmen turned the corner and walked casually down the road—directly towards the group of wayfarers! The voice of one of them preceded the unit as it echoed down the cobbles.

"I don't care what Sestus says. He can talk all he wants but no man will back him if he makes that play." There were six of them, widespread across the cobbles. The man speaking was their leader, if you could go by headgear. To his right were three soldiers of low rank, each with a spear in hand. To his immediate left was a man in strange garb, some type of spell caster, Eben guessed. He wore black robes over a royal blue tunic and a black semble. Even with his face hidden, the man smoldered with menace. His aetheric radiance was strongly negative. Eben felt that he should warn Haeffrin of the sheer weight of malevolence he sensed around that dark man. He attempted to convey the sensation to Haeffrin through their bond of magic. However, the two were ill-paired, and the wizard had allowed their relationship to become one of servitude instead of cooperation. Haeffrin was unresponsive and Eben feared he was too fixated on the Moon Bag.

"Well, Thrace, what you say goes, until you're dead or replaced. How do we handle it?" The man replying to Thrace was the one to his immediate right. Just then, the group of guardsmen noticed that a body lay in the street to their right and perhaps ten paces further ahead.

The man in robes stopped walking. His compatriots followed suit and watched as the dark man muttered something and drew his hand before his eyes. He then looked around carefully as if searching and soon turned directly towards the party, staring right at them as if they were visible to him. The raven gronked a loud warning to his master. It was too late, as the dark man had started gesturing arcanely. Haeffrin's party had their backs to the guards and were crouched low, simply trying to keep quiet and go unnoticed. It was how they had agreed to deal with such an encounter but it didn't work. In just a few seconds, the dark man had completed his casting and the adventurers stood like fools, fully exposed, their invisibility dispelled. The warriors saw them and leaped ahead, striking a stance with their spears forward.

Master Sergeant Thrace's sword had sprung from its sheath and once he could see who he was dealing with, the man made his formal arrest announcement. "In the Chancellor's name, give yourselves up to his justice or you shall be declared enemies of the state!" Had he had a moment, Eben would probably have enjoyed the stunned faces of the party as they began to realize just how rotten things had turned for them. The pair in the sleep satchel were roused and starting to mobilize. He took wing to avoid the two below him and to lend his claws or beak if he must.

Haeffrin was the first to react as he felt his magic dispel before his sight registered it. As the Guard's leader spoke his demand, Haeffrin cast his new spell and gestured, finishing it quickly, with a throwing motion towards the two thieves emerging from their sleep. An extremely sticky substance suddenly manifested over the pair, still half within their satchel, fastening them, confused and utterly helpless, to the roof. Haeffrin smiled. He had completed his new casting before the sergeant had finished his speech. He hadn't disobeyed any order yet. The wizard assigned to the guard unit, menacing in his dark garb, had the adventurers cold. Haeffrin had only one spell that he could strike with quickly enough to have any chance of disrupting whatever casting the dark man already had prepared. As he conjured it, Nellis made her move, distracting Haeffrin.

The thief did quick calculations in her head. She was already further from the group of soldiers than anyone else and had cut the rope tether. Nellis reckoned their group had no hope of winning a straight fight. *Surrender, then?* she thought. The image of an Ithil-Banian cell in some dark hole was not appealing. Her choice was quick and easy. Nellis broke from the group, sprinting for the alleyway ten paces ahead. She was a speedster and she was there in seconds. As she entered the corridor, her boots splashed in the water of the shallow gutter and Nellis broke into her typical, confident smirk for she was but moments from escape. That lopsided, quirky grin became ironic as suddenly a tremendous electrical bolt of energy scorched through the thief's slender body, burning her flesh and tearing at the aether of her core. Clothing combusted, gear ruined, she was carried by the force of the casting into the alleyway, where she landed in a heap with a dull thud and slid to a stop. Her charred flesh was perhaps most identifiable by the slanted smile burned black into her ravaged face.

"May I speak?" Haeffrin asked the officer of the guard. The display of raw power by the dark wizard was impressive. The black smokey swirl born of his gestures, his command of the maegum tongue, the quickness of his casting, his control of it, were signs of tremendous prowess that Haeffrin could not ignore. The death of Nellis was a relief, at least. But all thoughts of an aggressive reaction had fled his mind. Haeffrin was sure to show that his hands were empty by opening his arms wide as he bowed, face downward, in an entreating gesture. He lifted his head slowly as his two companions stood frozen in anticipation, hands on their blade hilts. After watching the dark casting blast Nellis with a lightning bolt, the role of the supplicant came quickly to Haeffrin. The leader of the guardsmen let out a single heavy, exasperated breath.

"If you waste our time further, I'll feed you to my fastidious friend Vance there and let him play with you," Master Sergeant Thrace promised as he gestured to the man furthest to his right. Upon hearing that oath, the soldier smiled with such sadistic pleasure that it chilled Haeffrin. The man bore terrible facial scars that marked him as a survivor of brutal violence. He wore a shredder, which was an eccentric type of arm. It was made for torture, designed to shred the flesh of his victims. Haeffrin put the thought out of his mind and gave himself a moment to bolster his composure. Then he spoke with a tone of confidence and an air of equity.

"We recently arrived in the City of Dreams and I fear we know not how to secure the papers required for daytime public travel." He did his best to control his facial expression and body posture to help maximize how reasonable he seemed. "If I understand the custom and laws that apply, we need to seek them from Military Guard officials such as you?" Haeffrin paused to allow the sergeant's mind to marinate in the air of commercial innocence he had created. "It was on our way to acquire the papers that things went awry."

A verbose orator himself, Master Sergeant Thrace was enjoying the way the wizard spoke. He imagined the presentation culminating in a flourish that might prove lucrative, so he encouraged the man to finish his tale of woe. "Do continue, traveler," he said, gesturing placatingly. Haeffrin sensed that success was within his reach, so the wizard continued.

"Two street runners managed to extract my gem purse, using a clumsy hulking man as a clever, opportunistic distraction." He used the tone of his voice to convey the begrudgingly genuine admiration he felt for the sheer boldness of the thieves. "The vermin made off with a small fortune, forcing us to pursue them across the cobbles until we finally overtook the two on that rooftop just as you arrived." He pointed to the spot where the thieves were desperately trying to extract themselves from his webbing. In his mind, he sent a message of clear intent to Eben, who flew back to the pair, trapped like rats. He croaked at the two and cawed loudly to his wizard. "Give the raven the bag you took! I shall forget all else!" he shouted to the thieves, hoping the generous offer would set a standard.

Havoc was in a panic but before he could shout back that they no longer had the bag, Kaen stopped him. "It's right here," he told the ebony bird. Havoc cursed him for the fool he was while Kaen desperately tried to work his hand free enough to reach inside his clothing to retrieve the bag. The raven picked at the sticky mess with its beak, careful not to entangle itself, to cut a few strands of the binding stuff to aid the thief. After a short time, Kaen could, slowly and with great difficulty, extract the purse. The bird kept pecking for a few moments while the confused but grateful thief watched with bated breath.

Haeffrin continued his explanation while Eben was retrieving the arcane purse. "As you can see, we now have the thieves neatly trapped and my familiar will bring my prize to me as soon as he can." As they were awaiting Eben, who seemed to be taking his time, the commander spoke, anticipating the end of the story.

"And I suppose, once you have your bag back, you will suddenly have the funds to pay for proper papers of passage?" Sergeant Thrace said with a larcenous leer. Haeffrin smiled uncomfortably as they all continued to await Eben's anticipated arrival.

The raven picked up the bag in its beak and Kaen whispered, "May Rhal smile upon you!" Eben nodded his head several times as if in acknowledgment before flying off. He swept down to Haeffrin where he stood in the street, landing lightly on his shoulder with the Moon Bag in his hooked beak. Due to the raven's generous assistance back on the roof, Kaen had managed to free his second blade. His habit of keeping his knives razor-sharp aided his work against the sticky stuff. He cut at the webbing furiously while the men on the street below were still distracted.

As the raven finally landed on his shoulder, Haeffrin smiled graciously and said, "Just so, friend." The relief felt by Tollem and Adams, neither of whom had any idea what was going on, was immense and physically noticeable. Their bodies relaxed and their breathing changed audibly. Haeffrin grinned with genuine satisfaction. "Well done, Eben," he said. The raven dropped the Moon Bag into his master's open palm and continued resting on the wizard's shoulder as Haeffrin slowly walked towards Master Sergeant Thrace. As he did so, he asked coyly, "Now, if only you knew what the proper papers cost?"

Spears lowered and hands left sword hilts as Tollem and Adams cautiously approached the Military Guardsmen. Introductions commenced and the soldiers mixed as Haeffrin and Thrace continued their negotiations. Adams looked back, feeling at least some obligation to Nellis. Upon seeing that look, the soldier known as Vance smiled through his scarred lips and said, "Pay her no mind. She had already left you, so leave her to the street. It has a way of taking care of such things." Vance put his hand on Adams' shoulder, directing him forward, and they walked off together.

The dark wizard maintained the mystery his semble provided and walked silently along, slightly behind the rest of the group. He looked over his shoulder once and watched the pair of roof-runners slip away. In the alleys adjacent to the street, many eyes of the homeless mob of gutter sleepers silently watched as the soldiers left after the tense drama of the encounter ended. The young street thieves clamored quickly over the crown of the roof and were soon concealed by the crest. Havoc looked down to the alley below. "Fleshers!" he said, his voice full of loathing. "We run high. On me!" He led Kaen forth as they ghosted into the endless labyrinth of rooftops, alleyways, and clever hiding places that made up their world in Ithil-Bane, the City of Dreams.

In the yawning mouth of the alley, Nellis still lay, smoldering. She murmured a bit and then coughed weakly as her profound agony caused her to twitch. The rogue began to weep as she slowly comprehended the extent of her body's ruin. Nellis couldn't move, except to writhe in her body's blackened state of char. Pieces of what had been her skin broke off and floated away on the gutter water she soaked in. She tried to cry for help but it came out as a wet, inaudible gurgling. Aarn had not yet reached far into the alleyway. From morning shadows many hands slowly stretched out and took ahold of what remained of the hapless Bentuan. The stench of burnt human flesh poured from the husk of her body as she was unceremoniously pulled deep into the receding shadows of that corridor where she fed dozens of hungry mouths, giving her last measure of usefulness to the hunger of the night.

Omnipresent in all its immense size and menacing facade, the Citadel of darkness watched over and saw everything. Wicked

Loekii, as She ever did, found bountiful amusement in Her rule over the Dark City and those within—villains, all.

*Want to experience more of Maera? Visit **www.maeraworld.com***

A MAN THAT NEVER WAS

His was a humble home, the kind of place that went unnoticed—a small farm in a nondescript hamlet in a quiet corner of a peaceful kingdom. Gaereth Benton was a good man and kind. Everyone thought so, people said so, and his wife of many years took great comfort in her lovely man. Gaereth was taller, more handsome, and seemed cleverer than the other farmers in town. Even his beard was nicer. He was so well thought of, seemingly by all, that he was sent to the annual farm collective as their village representative.

There Gaereth did what Gaereth does. He pleasantly said his hellos. He smiled and nodded. He quietly sat and he listened long. He spoke when asked direct questions but his thoughtful, gentle manner and clever choice of words made him stand out amongst his peers. All that gathered were quite impressed with the shy-seeming fellow with the kind eyes and pleasant smile. Although his ideas were few, each was adopted by the collective. So it was that Gaereth greatly influenced the region to benefit everyone.

After the collective, Gaereth returned home to Lana, his rather charming and fetching wife. Word spread about his success in advocating for their small village and when they next attended church, it was evident that his favor and respect had grown. Indeed, in the days to come, Gaereth was approached more than once about becoming mayor of their town. It was a job he neither coveted nor would accept. It wouldn't be right. Gaereth politely eschewed such talk. In time, he returned to his duties around the farm in the peaceful quiet he so loved. He was a happy sort, content in working the gentle land under the warmth of Aarn and in the good graces of Celeste, who was the daughter of the aerth and sky, also called the Matriarch of Farmers.

Things could hardly have been better. The weather was truly kind and Gaereth's days were productive. He worked as hard as the farm demanded, often overcoming obstacles with his wit and creativity, introducing new methods that he taught others to their great advantage. He happily joined his neighbors whenever they needed extra hands and they returned such favors. The whole community prospered and years passed without grief or any measure of hardship. Gaereth and Lana had a great deal to be thankful for and they were. But even in these times of good fortune, the couple did have one glaring want, one stark exception to their happiness.

Gaereth was not from this town. He was found one day at the edge of a farm owned by a childless older couple. All at once, seemingly, he was standing there, watching the man working the field. He was clean, his hair combed, his clothes tidy, smiling passively. No tracks led to him, although the day's conditions were conducive. The farmer and his wife feared some traumatic event must have preceded the boy's sudden appearance but they took him in and gladly watched over the lad as discreet inquiries were made through their church.

Much time and effort were spent but the child could not be traced to any farm or family in the region. No explanation for his odd and sudden appearance on the Benton farm could be found. When questioned, the child seemed to have no memory of his life before he arrived in the field. The mystery was, in fact, never solved. The boy, and his abrupt appearance on the Benton farm, went without any explanation. Nobody ever came forth to offer any identification or knowledge of Gaereth, as the Bentons named him, at any time—no one, never, nothing whatsoever.

The Bentons had no children, although they had always hoped for them. The lad they had found was handsome and well-made. He was a quiet, respectful, and obedient child, evidently at peace. He seemed trauma-free and wasn't even distressed at his lack of memories before coming to them. The pair sought and received the local priest's blessing. So, Gaereth had a home.

It had seemed almost too considerable a measure of fortune to be true, for the boy was kind and gentle, clever and honest, a tireless worker who offered none of the challenges that children so often pose to parents. The couple counted their blessings and praised Daellus for the splendid occurrence. For quite some time, the incident brought great excitement to the community. Eventually however, the town continued with its simple, productive, happy existence. The Bentons finally knew the love of a child, which the quiet couple had sorely desired all their lives.

The pair agreed that their child was roughly eight years of age, so Gaereth attended school during the colder months when the farm chores were lessened and there was little else to do. He learned to read and write, skills that his parents did not possess. The boy did not seek mischief, and his teacher was pleased with his rare way of getting along with everyone. These traits made him an ideal student and Gaereth made his adoptive family proud and happy, even if he was a bit quirky.

Gaereth liked to be alone outdoors and took many long walks under the open sky. There was little odd about that. The way he stared at the clouds and spoke to himself was curious. When asked about it, he claimed to be talking with Celeste, the Wondrous Maiden. Farmers often prayed to Her for the excellent weather that favored their crops, a habit considered harmless and even admirable. Gaereth's enjoyment of time alone was a bit uncommon but not in any way problematic. Spending time apart from the community seemed to keep him out of the prying thoughts of others, which in turn must have contributed to his peace of mind. It certainly didn't keep him from his chores. Still, the Bentons awaited the day when Gaereth might become troubled over the circumstances of his life before he came to them, perhaps wishing to find his true family. They waited but that dread day never came. The lad never wondered aloud where he had come from and who had birthed him. It was a bit perplexing but the farmer and his wife knew not to question life when it went their way. They again praised Daellus, Lord of Peace, that they had been so blessed and that their boy was carefree.

Gaereth was, in fact, quite a boon to his parents as they grew older. A decade passed and they'd formed a happy little family. But time flowed on and kept flowing. Too soon, it seemed. Gaereth was working the farm alone, and one day, his dear father did not awaken. In the worship of Daellus, such a peaceful passing is considered a blessing. The most common guess in the community was that his heart had failed him. It was customary in such a situation to accept the grievous loss as the will of the gods. They buried him, following his wishes, on the farm beneath his favorite fruit tree.

After that, mother and son pressed on. Gaereth noticed that she had never seemed the same after his father had passed. Gaereth's attempts to comfort her were always appreciated but failed to assuage her grief. It was difficult for him to understand. Had his father not gone to Daellus, to whom his aether was promised? Gaereth noted that his mother seemed to mourn the loss of her husband's physical life more than she rejoiced in the translation of his aether to a higher state. As much as he missed his father, Gaereth struggled to understand his mother's overpowering sense of loss, even as he endeavored to empathize with her.

Her ongoing grief took its toll. Soon, it was as if her splendid inner glow was diminished. Her everyday life seemed almost too much to deal with and became difficult. It was then that Gaereth realized that what she had always worked so hard for was a life together with her man. As a result, his mother's longing and pain proved more difficult for Gaereth to bear than the loss of his father.

His mother seemed to break down physically once Gaereth's father was gone. Within a year of his father's death, she had had several episodes in which she fell unconscious. After each fall, his mother seemed weaker and her overall health suffered. The simple human worship of Daellus allowed for the most natural path of her mortal life to unfold. There would be no healing or intervention for her. Far too soon, Gaereth found himself caring for his ailing mother and working the farm. He bore his burden with quiet dignity. Gaereth proved to be a kind and gentle caregiver, which did not go unnoticed amongst the faithful in town. Even so, it was not long before his mother made her way through the veil to manifest her next state. Gaereth Benton had just entered his twenty-third year.

Gaereth inherited the Benton family farm and kept up his responsibilities to the small community that he called home. He was formally introduced as a prospective partner to a young lady named Lana while attending a service of Daellus. The pair already knew one another casually from school. She had always thought him to be quiet and good-natured if a bit strange. Lana's promised mate had tragically passed in a farming accident. While she'd spent an extended, appropriate amount of time mourning him, that time had passed. As they were both of advanced age for a union and he was alone while she was willing, the two quickly came together as a couple. It was thought to be a clever match and pleasing to the community. It manifested in a whirlwind of sudden romance that advanced speedily. Their Ceremony of Union was accepted and celebrated, and they happily took their place with a robust dedication to their future. All was well and the pair thrived in their new life together on the Benton farm. The next step was clear, logical, and, of course, expected by all.

That expectation went unfulfilled. The couple's love was passionate and active but they produced no offspring. Lana was twenty-one and of abundant health, and Gaereth was an impressive specimen. Their lack of children was unexpected and all manner of thoughts were expressed in town. The oddity of Gaereth's childhood, once seemingly somehow forgotten, was revisited. Some folks suggested that the Benton farmstead was somehow cursed, and that was to blame for the lack of children conceived there. In the end, such ideas were again put away.

Their infertility was chalked up to unfortunate circumstances, as the couple's charm seemed to win out over the wagging tongues of gossip. Children or not, they were valued members of the community, helpful and friendly neighbors, generous and good church-goers, and solid, patriotic members of their nation. The years passed and flowed over the farm like a warm breeze through the tall grass. Gaereth worked smarter and harder and achieved more success than expected. During those years, the kingdom knew great peace. Their ventures in agriculture enjoyed the blessing of continued fantastic weather and thrived. Their farm collective grew with new lands and farms, and all concerned met this news enthusiastically.

All the while, Gaereth and Lana enjoyed good health. Gaereth aged very well indeed. He stayed trim and fit but so did many who put in such hard physical days on a farm. His skin and face somehow seemed to remain very youthful, not in and of itself so unusual. His body was not affected by the stiffness, fatigue, or loss of strength and flexibility typically associated with aging. His hair remained a sandy blonde, and his teeth remained pristine as he lived through his forties.

By the time the couple passed the age of fifty, Lana had come to appear markedly older than her husband, and Gaereth's apparent youthfulness astounded his fellow churchgoers. Once again, the couple was the topic of much idle conversation, for it now seemed obvious which of them had been unable to produce a child. After all, just one look at Gaereth spoke volumes about his masculine energy and vigor. It was painful to bear the gossip of others, especially the fully-grown children of their peers. The Kingdom of Telemar was a nation of Daellus, and its people were good and well-meaning. While his continued youthfulness was indeed a sign of intense virility, it had never been more evident that there was something more than odd about Gaereth.

During the long months of Waestrel of that year, Lana fell ill and, although she certainly received fawning care from her husband, she could not fend off the long sickness that assailed her. When the weather finally broke, Lana gave up her aether to Daellus, and Gaereth was left alone on the aging farm. It was sad for the community to see him at church as he politely went about accepting his peers' condolences and well-wishes. Still, he handled it all with his customary calmness and kind demeanor.

Indeed, Gaereth went about the farm's business that year without a hitch, not letting any aspect of his work be neglected. The neighbors who brought him food and showed him kindness in other ways after Lana passed all reported that Gaereth seemed just fine when they checked on him. In fact, he appeared unchanged by the ordeal. Gaereth graciously rebuffed all efforts by the community to hold him closer, all gestures of deeper friendship extended to him. He instead embraced a life alone, kept to himself, and indeed seemed none the worse for that decision. The years passed freely through the hamlet like a stream bubbling past a stone. Gaereth thrived as he worked his farm, living alone without complaint.

One might imagine the surprise of Father Reagis, who had spent five long decades meeting the spiritual needs of his community, when, for the first time, Gaereth Benton came to the Church of Daellus seeking his help. The farmer explained to the priest that he needed to ask a favor of him. Gaereth had a sealed letter and asked the priest to safeguard it. He told the Father that he required his word that the letter would remain unopened and in his care until the day came when he would know to read it. The cleric agreed with a small measure of trepidation. He met Gaereth's gaze, looked deep into those kind and gentle eyes, and gave him his blessing of peace on the matter.

Gaereth spent one more day on the farm, alone with his animals, ensuring everything was in order. The next day he rose before the sun as always, made sure the animals were taken care of, and sat down to eat his breakfast. He enjoyed his meal and then cleaned up after himself. Then he went to his pantry. Gaereth stood in the center of the room, effectively a long closet, and recited ancient words in draegari, the language of his kind. Rising through the room's floorboards and then floating upwards to the farmer was a beautifully crafted rhoanswood box. Its wood shone red in the sunlight that crossed the kitchen and illuminated the pantry. It rose slowly upwards until it was waist high. Gaereth took the box, carried it into the kitchen, and placed it in the center of the table. He spoke once more in draegari, closed his right hand, and rotated it so that his palm was facing upwards when he opened it. A key appeared in his hand. Gaereth placed the key on the table, resting in front of the box, for Father Reagis to find. Then he went outside for one final stroll under the vast, open sky.

As he entered the furthest field on the farm, the same area where he had so suddenly appeared fifty years ago that day, Gaereth smiled a knowing smile. He strolled through the field, fingertips brushing the chest-high wheat. He heard Her voice, which always found him here.

"Are you ready to come home to us, my dearest?" She asked. That voice made him feel weightless, almost as if he were floating. It brought him great peace, and he looked to the sky and answered.

"I live, as ever, to serve you, Mistress. You have but to say the word and I shall join you aloft. How I have missed the skies." He stopped and awaited the command that would finally free him of the aerth. His heart leaped in anticipation. He spread his arms wide, tilted his head back, and closed his eyes. A breeze swept across the field, blowing his hair from his forehead.

"You have done well and served me brilliantly. Rise now, fly free, ride the winds and stretch your wings. Please return to us, for we have awaited you too long. Come home to us, beloved of the winds." With that, Celeste freed him of his charge and summoned him home. She watched from Her Cloud Island, high above the plains, standing at the edge of its eastern face as the inverted mountain rode the sky over Maerisna. From that great distance, She watched with indulgent pleasure and a subtle smile as Her servant departed the aerth.

Gaereth, as he would seldom be called again, began to rise above the green aerth slowly. His feet were together, arms spread, head back. With a look of true delight on his human face, he rose higher and began to spin. He spun faster and faster and then suddenly threw his chest out toward the blue sky. He burst from that tiny, frail form, which dispelled and dissolved like the season's first snowflake. He spread his wings for the first time in fifty years, surging further into the sky.

In due time word reached the village that Gaereth had not been seen in some days. Neighbors approached his farm, his fields were walked, and his name was called but as it was thought highly unlucky to discover a body, none were willing to enter his cottage. The local priest was informed of the situation and agreed to investigate. But first he took a few moments to gather the sealed letter entrusted to him by Gaereth mere days earlier.

The cleric politely called for Gaereth through an open front window. The current farm dog was at hand and seemed nervous, if not truly spooked. The priest slowly entered the home, closing the door behind him to any curious eyes. While he found no one at home, he quickly noticed a lovely wooden coffer resting in the center of the kitchen table. A simple metal key lay in front of the box.

The holy man sat himself down, having decided to use the key. He was an older man, nearly seventy now, and one accustomed to very little drama in his life. As he quietly examined the key, he couldn't help but ponder his relationship with the man the village knew as Gaereth. He had taken his final vows in the Church of Daellus mere weeks before being assigned as the new priest of a tiny hamlet in the vast Telemarian countryside. As he settled in at his new post, the first issue to face him was the sudden, unexplained appearance of a small boy on a local farm.

He marveled at how quickly fifty years had passed since that day and how he had effectively known Gaereth for most of his life. The man had been there every week for services. Gaereth had been a strong but calm and quiet voice in the community. He had served the farming collective brilliantly, and nary a harsh word had been said against him all that time. Yet, now that he thought about it, he pondered why he had never thought to examine Gaereth more closely. He could not imagine now, looking back, why he had never inquired, even informally, further into Gaereth's life.

What did he even know about this man who had spent a lifetime in his charge as a parishioner? How many times, he pondered, had they ever exchanged more than a few words or had anything more than even the most obligatory conversation after a service? Gaereth had always been reliable, robust, silent, and steadfast. The priest wondered at his failure to do his duty in the most basic sense. He had willfully taken the man for granted, thankful that he did not require his attention, was grateful that he never had to devote his energies to Gaereth or his household. He had failed to embrace a member of his church, a man who had, no doubt, neither sought nor seemed to require such a relationship. He had ignored a good man for a lifetime, given him virtually no thought, and never aspired to be a more significant part of his life. It had been easy to ignore his duty as Gaereth was so upstanding. He had never needed to counsel the man, who had never reached out to him for help. Now, here he was, due to willful neglect, facing a situation that made him feel ill-equipped. And that feeling was, undeniably, his fault.

The cleric placed the key in the box's lock and turned it. He lifted the lid and looked inside. The casket was lined with red cloth and held a palm-sized leather pouch, nothing more. He removed it and opened it. Inside were three round stones, red, blue, and green, each roughly the size of a large walnut. Next, he opened Gaereth's letter. It was short and to the point but created as many questions as it answered. Here is what it said:

"I thank you for your great kindness these many years. It was only with the thoughtful kindness of you and others that I was able to assimilate into your community. I have enjoyed the time I have spent living in this realm, and I feel that I have learned much about what it is to be human.

I have left you three enchanted stones to show my sincere gratitude to the people of the congregation, village, and nation. The stones are to be explicitly used as described to maximize their potential.

The Harvest Stone shall be buried elbow deep in the aerth at the center of the community. It will convey the blessing of benevolent harvests for all within the region for not less than fifty years. Once buried, it must never be disturbed.

The Sky Stone shall be cast upwards into the sky during the next soaking rain directly above the location of the Harvest Stone. It will mark the region as a place blessed by the sky for fifty or more years. The area will receive that blessing in the form of benevolent weather that will signifi-cantly assist farming and help ensure prosperity in the land.

The Blood Stone shall be ensconced in your most holy place for the next fifty years. During that time, you have my Blood Oath of protection over the community. I shall watch over you as my favored folk and be diligent in my guardianship of you and yours. I shall not fail you, and any foe seeking to do you, or the community, harm shall first face my righteous fury. Rest easy in knowing I am always with you, as you are in my heart and mind.

Once you've placed the Stones, keep this knowledge to yourself. Follow these instructions alone. Keep our secret, and you shall count yourself amongst those blessed by the Aeglain. I know that you will seek the guidance of Daellus and believe you will find Him supportive of this. If you honor my request, you shall not succumb to death for the next fifty years. You will no longer age and shall retain your current physical state and all of your existing mental faculties. Should you desire such a fate, and Daellus blesses your commitment to this path, remaining in the community for the next fifty years will amplify the power of the stones and further ensure the unending good fortune of the region.

You may explain to the community that you do not know who I am or where I have gone any more than you know where I came from, for is this not the truth? You will find the community is more accepting of this than you might imagine, just as they accepted my arrival fifty years ago. I will quickly fade from their minds now that I am gone. Please see that the Benton farm is useful to a young, deserving couple. The land will continue to be productive if it is worked diligently.

Thank you for your trust, guidance, and mentorship these many years. You have been more benevolent than you will ever know. I am and will continue to be your friend forever."

— R

It felt strange having read the letter. The priest found himself more than just a bit confused, and it felt quite odd. He reread it. "R?" Who was "R?" As he tried to focus on the information in the letter, he felt a tickle in his consciousness. He shook his head as if to clear it. Soon, it was as if a light fog had lifted from his mind. He blinked, then blinked again. He felt light-headed and concentrated on his breathing for a bit.

How did he feel about this new reality? It was too soon to say and he determined that he must pray on it. He placed the key in the box and closed it. He placed the letter back in his pocket, the stones in their bag, and then in another pocket. Then he stood up, carefully put the chair back in its place, and closed the open window by the door. The cleric took a moment to look once more around the kitchen. He noticed that the box had disappeared. He felt a strange tingling in his fingertips. He thought to search for it but somehow knew it was gone. He turned, and then he left the farmhouse.

He asked the neighbors that were gathered outside to please watch over the farm's animals, as he had not found a body or any clue as to where Gaereth was but felt confident that he would not return. There were questions, of course, and he tried to relieve their concerns but soon he took leave of them and returned to his church. The priest cloistered himself within the private library of his residence at the rear of the small church. He considered the situation he was in and prayed about it. Ultimately, he determined that he would do what was best for his community and swore to Daellus never to speak of the matter.

Raen-K'aer Rae soared above the aerth, reveling in the sheer physicality of flight. The dragon summoned his voice, and he cast powerful magic, rendering him *Invisible* to mortal eyes. He stretched fully with each stroke of his mighty wings, climbing higher. The rush of the air over his massive, outstretched body, the warmth of Aarn on his skin, the feeling of restored freedom after fifty long years bound to the aerth was nearly too much for him to process. Raen-K'aer Rae closed the nictitating lids of his eyes and gave himself over entirely to the experience, immersing totally in this reality, restored.

Raen had sought to fully engross himself in his mission during his time as a man. Such was his charge—seek to grasp what it was to be human. Although it took years, Raen had achieved his goal. But now that he had assumed his primary form, memories rushed back, and Raen suddenly realized how much he had given up over the past half-century. He stretched his back legs and flexed his toes and their talons. He inhaled deeply and filled his lungs with the free wind. It was such an astonishing thing, wearing his own skin and returning to the skies!

Waves of pure joy washed over him and he savored its simplicity. His heart pounded as he broke through the clouds, and his fully vertical body coasted slowly to a stop. As he peaked and rolled over into a dive, he enjoyed the long moment of equilibrium with gravity. He rotated his great head on his serpentine neck, engrossed in his physique's raw strength and proportions. He looked in all directions, and for as far as he could see, the clouds lay beneath him. He felt at one with the everlasting sky, once more in tandem with the wind. He slowly inverted, then plunged again towards the aerth, losing himself in the clouds.

He tracked ever east as he returned home to the Cloud Island. He easily homed in on the radiant energy of the Wondrous Maiden, which pulsed in his mind like a beacon of strength. In a few short hours, Raen had arrived. He marveled at the sight of the utterly massive stone island suspended in the sky, as he did every time he saw it from such a vantage. He tried to comprehend the power expended to create such a phenomenon. As always, he failed in the attempt. It was as if a mountain had been ripped from the aerth's bosom, flipped into the air, and suspended in the clouds.

The island was primarily flat on the top side, with a massive stone keep at one end. The towers of that structure stretched high, several hundred feet above the plateau, but the fortress was dwarfed by the underside of the massive mountain, which was roughly pyramidal. Raen dispelled his casting of *Invisibility*, sweeping up and over the polished plateau of that magnificent juggernaut in the sky. It was a large, open expanse, and at the far end stood the mighty Keep of Ethaerion, the home of Gaellus Gaeltharson and the Wondrous Maiden. And there, seemingly awaiting his approach, was no less than the Demigod Gaellus standing before the tall, ironclad gates of the keep.

Never before had Lord Gaellus spoken to him. Indeed, when He met the dragon's eyes, it was for the first time. The elegant beast concentrated on his landing, ensuring that fifty years away from the winds did not now embarrass him. He held the legendary, smoldering gaze of the enormous demigod and palm-walked towards the gates. The tales of the intensity of that stare failed to do it justice. The dragon felt vulnerable and exposed, held in that steely, piercing regard, and he wisely awaited whatever Gaelthar's eldest had to say. He did not wait long.

"Hail, Raen-K'aer Rae! You are most welcome in the House of Union. Come forth in favor, beloved of Celeste." The Demigod of Storms nearly staggered him, flattering him with such a greeting. If that were not enough, Gaellus lowered His head, bowing ever so slightly to acknowledge an honored guest. Raen gathered himself into his most formal posture and responded in kind, using his ancient native tongue as Gaellus had.

"Hail, Son of Gaelthar! You do me great honor. May the Eternal Sky ever guard the faithful!" He showed respect to the entire family of Gaellus thus, and his words were well received. Gaellus looked pleased and pivoted as He extended His left arm towards the mighty flyer.

"Come, for your Mistress awaits you," He said, in a measured, even, gentle tone. In both His word and demeanor, Gaellus signaled His approval. The mighty titan slowly strolled towards the gates, which stood open, awaiting Him. Raen accompanied Him, one stride to His left and two behind, being sure to follow the expected protocol.

Many stories describe meeting Celeste, Beloved of Gaellus Gaeltharson, known as the Wondrous Maiden, the Daughter of the Aerth and Sky. In these tales, She stood roughly fifteen feet tall in Her preferred form and appeared to be an exquisite female giant. Caramel, curling hair cascaded elegantly down Her back, shimmering in the flickering torchlight of the chamber. The great hall was awe-inspiring, with its vast marble floor under lofty rhoanswood arches. There were magnificent tapestries. Some depicted the Aeglain during their interactions with worshippers, including those of Gaelthar and His offspring. Celeste was resplendent in a form-fitting gown of a material that dazzled the eye. At first, it was a beautiful blue-green tone, but it seemed to be a different shade every time She moved. Her presence was intoxicating, and Her voice was melodic and delightful. She turned, cast Her eyes upon the dragon, and smiled while She crossed the room to greet him.

"Your return gladdens our hearts. Come and take your rest with us now. Enjoy the comfort of our abode and tell us, if you will, of your adventures among the humans. We have eagerly anticipated your return and have waited overlong to welcome you home." The affection in the tone of the Maiden threatened to overwhelm Raen. Her words were like a soothing balm to his mind. The dragon suddenly felt greatly fatigued and followed the titans to a grand dais, where the pair took their ease on the cushions of their matched, enormous stone thrones. Raen-K'aer Rae was attended by a young servant who invited him to lay atop a large pile of flat, tasseled pillows arranged on the floor beneath the dais. Servants entered the hall, seemingly from all directions, carrying drink and all manner of delicacies to eat.

"May I suggest that you assume your human guise once more? I believe that you will find it is to your great advantage to slowly, rather cautiously, again grow accustomed to your primary form. Taking food and drink for at least some short time should be done as a man." Celeste was careful with Her words, being extraordinarily genteel. She was reputed to be a kind, generous and graceful being who was also an excellent benefactor to many. She represented much more than that to dragon-kind. She was the primary manifestation of Her mother, Madrain, on Maera. As such, Her home was a holy place of elemental sky power, and all dragons not in the thrall of the evil gods saw it as such. In matters regarding transmutation, Raen would certainly trust Her experience.

"You will find that you are at great ease morphing into human form from now on. I would encourage you to do so daily to maintain your rare familiarity with those folk and continue to offer us all the usefulness of your abilities." The Maiden was right, of course, and Raen morphed easily into Gaereth's body once more. They took food and drink while the dragon relayed the personal accounts of his long years amongst man. Although he had reported almost daily while on assignment, Celeste now wanted his conclusions after five decades among them. Such insight as he had was thought to be essential, as all the powerful rulers of Maera desperately sought to understand human motivations and behavior, so they might better be prepared for the utter chaos that humankind spawned. Celeste sought to gain a measure of what good men were capable of, and Raen could help.

Raen was encouraged to start from the beginning. He was to take as much time as needed and include as much detail as possible. The amount of time spent and the intensity of the attention the two demigods paid to his efforts shocked Raen, who quickly realized just how crucial his mission had been. It seemed to him that time itself was in some way warped as he spoke, and he found that he could convey far more acute memories of the past fifty years than he had imagined possible. Celeste herself had morphed him into the body of a man-child on that fateful first day, and he now realized that he had been in Her thrall for the entire time he had been human. That thrall had affected him and those he met, so he was paid as little mind as possible, forgotten easily, and thought to be inoffensive. Indeed, he felt enthralled during the audience he had with Gaellus and Celeste, as it was inordinately long, and there was never once any deviation from the topic.

The pair hung on every word, leading him to focus on his report with great intensity. They sometimes asked questions, politely raising a finger to signal that they had a query. Most of their interruptions were requests for Raen to explain in greater detail the emotions humans felt and their effect on their behavior. Explaining human emotions proved a great challenge for the dragon. He often had to admit that even after five decades immersed in the human experience, he failed to glean as deep an understanding of human emotions and motivations as they desired to learn. While at first, he found his account lacking in this crucial area, he quickly realized that it was expected. He was not the first disciple to be sent out amongst the humans and certainly would not be the last. Interpretation of the human mental processes was beyond Raen, just as it was beyond the other observers the Cloud Island had sent out amongst them over the centuries. The most significant value of the information gathered lay in the overall insight these accounts gave Celeste and Gaellus, and the patterns they saw in the reports shared by the various witnesses that returned to them.

Their intelligence gathering was an expansive ongoing endeavor and was considered a tremendous challenge, even by these great beings who had put this complex plan into action. Immortals, however, excelled at such evolving and unremitting tasks. So it was a long-term undertaking but one that, over time, yielded the precious information they required. As they concluded the session, the Wondrous Maiden had a final line of questioning for the dragon.

"In your judgment, Raen, and based on your experiences, do you believe that humans are redeemable? Can their aessance truly overcome the sinister influence of their creator and the riotous chaos of their subconscious minds?" The flyer thought long and hard, taking a bit of food before he answered.

"I have seen them do wonderful, selfless things and make great sacrifices to serve an ideal. And I have also witnessed crushing weakness in them, seen them commit casual treacheries and manifest sinister motivations that brought to ruin all their gains and achievements. While they slept, I watched them, monitored their dreams, and recoiled from what I saw there. They are capable of such extremes that it repulsed me and yet I grew to love them. While they all do questionable things, the ones I met never stopped fighting against their own cruel and selfish nature. Yes, the answer is yes. I believe that humans are redeemable and worthy of effort such as I have put forth." With that, he fell silent while the titans exchanged meaningful glances. Soon thereafter, he was excused.

Raen-K'aer Rae was left intellectually drained and physically exhausted by his intense meeting with the demigods that ruled over the Keep of Ethaerion. When they were through, little time had passed in the House of Union. But in the mind of Raen, it seemed like many cycles of Aarn had run. He knew that he had been affected by some strong enchantment. It was as if time itself was somehow reckoned differently in the throne room of the mighty keep. But he was too tired and confused to contemplate a thing so obviously beyond his ken. And, so, Raen accepted the fact that the Aeglain worked in their own mysterious, marvelous ways that mere mortals, even dragon-kind, could not hope to grasp. He also took solace in quite a strong feeling that he had done very well in the service of the Wondrous Maiden and an accompanying sensation that that was enough.

"He has done a great service to our cause and shall be rewarded," said Celeste. "I say that we must keep him close to us as we continue to glean the benefit of his connection with humanity. He shall be given a permanent assignment gathering intelligence in our network. He should be elevated to the rank of Guardian. He shall be welcome in the Hall of Union and be one of the favored, agreed?"

"As you wish," Gaellus, the Lord of Storms and the Rage of Justice, quietly assented. He had found, over the centuries of their devotion, that agreement with His beloved was well-advised. Her decisions were habitually flawless, in any case, and unless the topic was warfare, Gaellus had no reason to interject. "I will take care of it after he has rested. We worked him hard."

The giantess nodded her agreement. "His insight is acute but his ability to earn the trust of humans is most exceptional," She said. "He may be able to serve a larger purpose than we ever anticipated. Much larger." Celeste already imagined a role for Raen-K'aer Rae that extended far into the future. Gaellus could see it in Her eyes. She was the far-seer, He the initiator of action. Her gentle, thoughtful ways calmed His storm and soothed His raging heart.

Maera was entering a dangerous time and the Cloud Island would play a critical role in the conflict to come. No one among the very wise liked the prospect of the humans playing a pivotal role in that struggle but neither did anyone deny the certainty of it. It was the role of Gaellus Gaeltharson to bring the forces of good together under the death banner of His father. Celeste had a role to play in helping that happen. He needed Her like few need another. Gaellus was not a gentle or kind being. But He knew how to fight, what was worth fighting for, and how to love. Perhaps, in the end, that would be enough.

"You have become adept at finding the best opportunity for our emissaries and adapting them to their assignments." Gaellus was not one to flatter or waste words. "You do masterful work, truly. But our dragon friends are far more like men than any of them see or would ever want to admit. They are perfect for this work but we must ever push them harder as the darkness draws nearer." Celeste knew that His words were valid but She was saddened at hearing them. Gaellus saw Her reaction and fell silent once more.

And so it was that Raen-K'aer Rae, Guardian of the Union, faithful friend of man, Highflyer of the Eternal Sky, spent the decades that followed above the human Kingdom of Telemar, watching. He watched as the humans lived their short, confused lives. He watched trouble brewing along their northern borders as the nation of Sedan pressed their kingdom in a bid for their land and resources. Raen watched their human warships sail the great Inland Sea and blockade the Badaal River. He watched the movement of troops of both nations as their forces built up and war came closer to fruition. He reported all he saw to the Wondrous Maiden, but Raen also kept a watch over the Benton farm and the town he had called home. Raen-K'aer Rae grew concerned as the march of war encroached on that peaceful place.

Raen's duties kept him increasingly busy, as he was a part of an enormous ongoing mission to gather reconnaissance on Maera. The sheer number of daily flights conducted on behalf of Celeste and Gaellus required a considerable number of dragons and a high level of coordination. Raen-K'aer Rae was fortunate to serve close to the standard flight path of the Cloud Island. It meant less flight time to and from his assigned recon route and more time to himself. It allowed Raen to enjoy the many amenities of the House of Union, which proved to be an exciting place full of intriguing distractions and fascinating encounters. It also allowed him to volunteer for additional duties and help wherever possible, ingratiating him with the Union. Raen had a purpose, was respected, and was counted amongst the favored of the Wondrous Maiden. Under the strict eye and unerring command of Gaellus Gaeltharson, he had learned the military discipline of the Eternal Standard and committed to following the Path of Righteousness. It provided a welcome structure to Raen's life and a solid moral compass for the faithful.

When war came to Telemar, Raen-K'aer Rae bore witness to its ravages on the land and its people. The Sedanites were cruel enemies, Aerdos folk who sent all they met to their Hell in the name of the Dead God to be the slaves they needed to have the power they craved in that next place. Men had free will, which dragons called aessance, with which they could choose their own way in this life, determining their entry into the next. But it seemed a disturbing percentage of men chose poorly. Humans could be gentle, kind, thoughtful, wise, empathetic, and caring. Raen-K'aer Rae knew this to be true, for he had experienced all these things himself while spending a human lifespan amongst them as Gaereth Benton. He had grown to love the humans in his charge and had promised to watch over them. There came a day when that promise was tested, as great peril found them amid the clamor of war. So it was that, in the fiftieth year since he had left the company of man, the dragon named Raen-K'aer Rae, a Guardian of the Union, dutifully approached Gaellus Gaeltharson, the immortal Lord of Storms, regarding the keeping of his word to humankind.

Father Reagis Maerin, High Priest of Daellus, had waited as long as he dared. It was fifty years ago to the day since he had buried the Harvest Stone in the aerth at the center of the Hamlet of Randell. Then he had cast the Sky Stone into the storm that passed through the area that evening. He had followed the cryptic instructions of the man he had known as Gaereth Benton to the letter. The Harvest Stone had never been disturbed where it rested, elbow deep, in the aerth. Father Maerin now wore the Blood Stone in an amulet around his neck. And he had never mentioned a single word to any other living being about the deal he had accepted five decades earlier. But on this day, that pact would end.

Indeed, the region had experienced fifty years of fabulous weather that resulted in thriving farms and a successful expansion of the community. With some difficulty, the priest managed to convince the leadership of the Church of Daellus that he needed to remain in his position in what was, at the time, a small farming collective near the northwestern border of the Kingdom of Telemar. He was now known to be quite anomalous, for he was miraculously unchanged in the last fifty years, both physically and mentally. He was still quite elderly in appearance but was one-hundred and twenty-one years of age, older by far than any other Telemarian had managed, to anyone's knowledge.

Father Reagis had lived an exceedingly long life, during which he'd made every effort to be a good and kind man. For many years, there had been quite a lot of fuss in the community about his longevity and mental fortitude. Still, that talk had mainly faded away, as those who remembered him as a younger man had passed into the aether. Those who lived in the community he served now seemed comforted by his presence, unchanging appearance, and steadfast demeanor. Although he did not desire recognition for servitude rendered, he had gradually, inevitably, been elevated in the Telemarian Order of Peace until he had been granted the title of High Priest. It felt wearily perfunctory at first but the designation did allow him to choose his career path without interference from above. It may have seemed odd to many that he decided to remain in Randell but he had made a promise, and now he had kept it. There was only one thing left to do, one duty left to perform.

Randell evacuated on orders of the military out of what seemed to be an abundance of caution. Father Maerin had sent his flock to the safety of the nearest fortress. Only the priest remained and spent the past few days preparing himself for what he did not know. All he knew was that the enchantment placed on him and this place was about to end. He had slept well and woken refreshed. He had eaten a good meal and ensured that his things were in order and that the rectory, and the church were well-cleaned.

Then Reagis stood where he had buried the Harvest Stone, elbow deep as instructed, fifty years ago. The exact spot where he had stood alone in the driving rain later that same day as he cast the Sky Stone into the air above him, from whence it never fell. Father Maerin stood alone beneath the overcast sky. He prayed quietly to Daellus, the Maker of Peace, asking that He preserve his parishioners' homes, crops, and animals. The armies of Sedan approached from the north, announced by the carrion birds that circled above them. Rolling smoke darkened the horizon. The priest waited alone as the enemy grew closer, knowing he faced death.

As the afternoon fled, the wind strengthened and changed direction. It began to blow from the south and east. That wind carried a rolling fog, and it thickened as it came. Behind that fog came a storm. The heavy mist reduced the lightning to mere flashes of light, oddly diffused bursts of a golden-white hue amidst the darkening, swirling sky. The priest had heard tell of such storms, of sudden maelstroms, the turbulence and tumult of which was legendary. Thus, he turned, the better to greet the storm and perhaps the creator of that tempest, which built to a loud crescendo. Father Reagis Maerin raised his arms to welcome the cleansing gale.

There was a sudden blur of motion above him, and a huge dark figure was barely discernible, so abruptly did it pass. The single glance Reagis was afforded promised a creature of vast proportions was on the wind. The cleric felt his heart leap in excitement, the like of which he had never known. He had spent untold hours imagining the true nature of his mysterious friend, Gaereth Benton. Could his wildest musings prove true? Suddenly, great flapping came as if some giant being had descended behind him. Reagis turned and a rush of air accompanied another blur of motion. He barely caught it in the corner of a glance that a vast, dark shape had condensed somehow into the man that suddenly stood before him—none other than Gaereth Benton.

The clergyman was amazed and stood with his mouth agape at the familiar and unchanged visage of this handsome man, who met his stare with a smile. "My old friend," said Gaereth, "How good it is to see you again!" Gaereth's physical appearance was uncanny and struck the preacher as odd. He reasoned that his reaction must have been like those who saw him after a long time. "I see that you have adhered to my instructions these many years. Well done!" As he spoke, his eyes fell unmistakably on the pendant around the priest's neck that carried the Blood Stone. "Now it is time that I honor my pledge to you, Father," said Gaereth. With that, he strode forward and turned, taking his place by the priest's side. "Let us watch together what our devotion has wrought."

Gaereth gestured towards the sky above them to the north, which was now dark and foreboding. There before them, manifest in its titanic impossibility and at a distance from them and the aerth that Reagis could not judge, was the legendary Cloud Island of Celeste! "By the gods above!" was all the cleric could utter.

"Indeed. The purpose of the Harvest, Sky, and Blood Stones has finally been fully realized!" answered Gaereth. "Behold the wrath of Gaellus that your foes now face! Marvel in the razing of the Sedanites from your lands! Retribution shall be had by the hand of Gaelthar's Son, at the behest of the Wondrous Maiden, and by my word of promise. Rejoice, Favored of Daellus, for your allies are truly great!" As he spoke, Gaereth gestured to the dark skies before them. As if in response to that gesticulation, the clouds broke for a few heartbeats and revealed many strikes of lightning forking down from the Cloud Island, as if that great, monolithic, inverted peak suddenly wished to be seen. It was as if the lightning sprang from the base of the very stone itself. It did not cascade wildly, striking randomly in all directions. It forked to the aerth directly, as if aimed with fell purpose, scarring the ground as it sought the foes of Telemar, who were reckoned now as the enemies of Gaellus.

The effect of the lightning was utterly devastating and the thunder shook their world. The armies of Sedan were caught in the open, confused by the fog, then left shelterless against the following downpour. When the lightning storm came, their army was helpless against it, and great gouges were shorn through their units, beleaguered as they were by the shock of the attack. For whom amongst them had ever faced such wrath? The very ground trembled under the onslaught. The mortals were ravaged, whole groups of them at a time utterly destroyed by the explosive power of the Aeglain, now so brutally aligned against them. Soon, the survivors sought the quickest retreat possible from that field, their ranks hopelessly decimated and broken beyond any command to stand further.

Later, once the armies of Telemar realized their great advantage, they sent units of pursuant riders that claimed many more victims. They rode down survivors, mere shells of men blinded by the flashes of lightning and whose ears had been rendered useless and bloody by repeated terrible roars of devastating thunder. Many who endured found themselves so downtrodden as to take their own lives, petitioning the Dead God to accept them still into that next place with His dark blessing. The day's slaughter would be recounted endlessly in song and verse, living on the silver tongues of bards for long-counted time, for that is how such things work their way into lore.

It seemed strange that the greatest marvels that Father Reagis Maerin ever witnessed came to him on the last day of a life so long. He felt that life was leaving him as the storm finally abated. So long had he stood and watched the storm, it felt like a natural weariness had come over him. He gasped quietly and would have fallen flat onto his back had he been alone but Gaereth was there to take him gently to the aerth.

All at once, the vast weight of his years was upon him. The priest breathed his last rather suddenly, with neither pain nor complaint. Gaereth, having fulfilled the promise he had made to their satisfaction, carefully removed the Blood Stone on its pendant from around the prone man's neck, ending their compact. He smiled sympathetically, addressing him one last time.

"Take your rest now, son of peace. Your home and people are again safe, for you have seen to it. You have been as good as your word and have served Daellus long and well. He now awaits your gentle aether in His golden realm." Then he turned away and extended his hand over the ground, palm down. The aerth was disturbed a few moments later as the Harvest Stone worked its way to the surface. Once it lay exposed, Gaereth closed his eyes and focused even more deeply. The Stone leaped to his palm. He placed it in his other hand, with the Blood Stone, and then turned his outstretched palm to the sky. After a few moments, his concentration was rewarded as the Sky Stone dropped into his hand.

He looked one last time upon the peaceful body of the cleric, placed the three stones in his pocket, and lifted his face to the open sky. It was then that it struck him, and he smiled as he realized it. "I never even gave him my name," he said aloud. Gaereth Benton raised his arms, tilted his head back, and rose from the aerth. He began to spin, slowly at first but then faster, arms outstretched. His chest out, Gaereth lifted further into the air as he turned, and there was a blurring of his body as he assumed dragon form. So it was that the great orange and red being rose higher and higher as he began to flap his broad wings. Upwards the dragon climbed until he merged with the clouds and vanished from sight altogether. And so, all knowledge of him was lost to the people of that time and place as Raen-K'aer Rae once more returned to the sky.

Although in days hence few knew its cause, a simple pledge of protection well-kept and given fifty years prior had provided an opportunity for profound change. The First Son of Gaelthar, supported by his beloved Celeste, Daughter of Madrain and Gaerd, had finally taken direct action against evil. Sides had been taken, choices made, and now consequences loomed. The Eternal Standard of Gaelthar had once again been taken up by Gaelthar's eldest, who stood proud in his stead. The alliances of the Aeglain had been restructured, and their plans were now finally put into motion. All this from a tiny spark, well-kindled and nurtured, finally brought to an open flame and fanned into a conflagration—a spark spawned by a bond between a quiet, unassuming man and a man that never was.

Want to experience more of Maera? Visit ***www.maeraworld.com***

THE HONOR OF BLOOD

Kurjen was all nerves and aggression as he tried to concentrate on the task at hand. His poor sleep as of late was taking its toll. *Too many dreams*, he thought. Collecting the take of his traps was a simple enough task but he was distracted by his thoughts and taking too long to do it. According to the teachings of his tribe, that was a sure sign that Kurjen lacked the discipline needed to be a warrior. Until he could better control himself, he would remain a cub and not be allowed to run with the wolves of his tribal pack. Little did Kurjen know that his habit of quietly brooding over such matters was precisely the trait that led others to believe that he was mature, serious, and ready to contribute more to the tribe.

Kurjen wore his long flaxen hair tied behind his head but his rugged face was hairless, for he was not yet a tribesman and therefore was not afforded the honor of a Zuentok's beard. He wore blood-dyed leather trousers tied at the waist with a short rope and soft leather boots. Kurjen used the stone knife of the baerbaraan, his stone spear lying on the grass beside him.

Kurjen went about his business bare-chested, as did all his brethren. The sun of the plains had long ago darkened his pale skin but he, as yet, bore few scars. Kurjen had just marked his sixteenth summer and already he was a tall, broad-chested, well-muscled specimen of his kind. Kurjen was a member of an elite tribe, the

Zuentok—the tip of the mighty spear of Aeres, God of War and Blood. They, amongst all the baerbaraan folk of the continent of Maerisna, were favored by their deity. Service as a warrior was expected in their culture but Kurjen was by no means guaranteed a place amongst the Proven of Aeres.

Kurjen used a weighted leather tether that he kept wrapped around his waist to tie up his catch, a few hares. He headed home, following the river on his left. Then he saw his younger brother, Urvaar, running towards him as if the wind itself carried him. Kurjen had two older brothers who were currently warriors of the tribe. The eldest of his siblings had given his life's blood for Aeres two years earlier. Kurjen had two younger sisters as well. Two more brothers had been lost as cubs to illness and misadventure. Urvaar stopped in front of him, panting and too exhausted to speak. So Kurjen walked past him, ignoring him, as he perhaps too often did. As he continued to walk, the youngster caught him from behind.

"Wait, Kurjen ... wait!" he managed to get out between deep gasps of breath. "They are asking for you at the tribal fire! Jaeger himself sent me for you!" Hands upon his knees, the youngster was finally getting his wind back. "This is it—it's happening!" Urvaar, in his twelfth year, could not contain his vicarious excitement. His older brother was about to become a Pack member, as he would one day.

"Calm down before you fill your pants," said Kurjen.

"Aren't you excited? Your day is finally here!" Urvaar was exasperated.

"We'll see, brother. Many my age have been made to wait," Kurjen said, walking at his usual pace, determined to maintain his self-control. Could this be his day? Surely Jaeger would not waste his time otherwise? "Walk with me, Urvaar, for if you reckon true, then this will be the last time we walk together as cubs."

The brothers followed the river's bend around a low flat hillock, walking side by side. Kurjen was determined to display the kind of temperament the Zuentok required for a cub to become a member of the tribe's Warrior Pack. When they saw the tribal fire, Jaeger was awaiting him and the tribal shaeman had joined him. Kurjen's heart began to race—this was happening! He again consciously exerted control over his emotions and gait. He would not act foolishly with the eyes of all his clan upon him.

Indeed, the members of his tribal band stood about and as Kurjen neared the central tribal fire, he felt the group studying him. They were looking to see if he was ready to run with the Pack. He handed the tethered rabbits to Urvaar and walked up to the Proven of Aeres. The tribal shaeman, Taevor the Elder, who'd lived through more than fifty winters, used his stone knife to draw blood from his own chest over his heart. He then stepped up and placed his hand on Kurjen's face, marking him with the *Blood Palm* of Aeres. The young warrior-to-be, eyes closed now, kept still as the shaeman asked for the favor of the God of War on his behalf.

"Lord Aeres, see this supplicant, whom we now deem amongst the Worthy—marked this day as Yours! The Zuentok tribe pledges that his blade, blood, and life are Yours! Command his courageous heart in the fury of battle and grant Your servant a death worthy of Your sight!" With that prayer completed, the shaeman removed his hand, leaving the bloody print of it centered on Kurjen's face for all to see.

Jaeger stepped forward next, a great honor for Kurjen, as the warrior had taken many skulls and was one of the most respected runners in the Tribal Pack. He had come to sponsor Kurjen as a new member of that pack, putting his good name on the line. So, Jaeger drew his stone blade and ran it across Kurjen's chest from left to right. Blood flowed from the slash. It would form an enduring scar to mark Kurjen as among the Worthy. The young warrior stood stoically, showing no outward sign of pain or fear, quietly enduring all willingly and with genuine enthusiasm.

"AERES, WE BLEED FOR YOU! SEE US!" Jaeger shouted to the sky and then made a vertical, slanting cut above the Blood Ritual scar on his chest. The slash was his third thus far, and he seemed excited to bleed with this new, young warrior. "Come, my brother in blood! Today you join the ranks of the Worthy!"

Now the thrill of the Blood Ritual was felt by all. The members of the tribe came forward and took their turn, smearing Kurjen's blood over his torso. Each, in turn, placed their bloody palm on their own face so then the new warrior would see his blood on them all and always remember that his blood served Aeres for the tribe. Aeres, the Zuentok, the Pack—this was to whom his life belonged.

The shaeman stepped forth again when this was done and he withdrew a handful of poxy from his waist pouch. He spread the white powder over the slash across Kurjen's chest, speaking his words of power and blood sacrifice, which staunched the bleeding to a large extent. Kurjen once again closed his eyes. The poxy took away the pain of that cut, numbing the area. The power words ensured that the wound would scar prominently. Kurjen had had his first heavy dose of poxy, the white powder made by stone-grinding the tiny, white, sun-dried blossoms that broadly grew on his homeland's great, grassy plains. Its liberal use was implicit in running with the Zuentok, who came to prominence mainly by controlling the supply of poxy on Maerisna.

Kurjen's mouth went dry and his chest tingled oddly. His blood surged through his veins, causing a rush he could hear inside his head. Kurjen realized that he was breathing in rapid, shallow pants, so he consciously inhaled through his nose and exhaled through his mouth. He opened his eyes for the first time one of the Worthy. Kurjen's heart seemed about to beat out of his chest and great pride rose in him from somewhere deep within. The confusion and doubt of that morning were gone as he felt a sudden intense rush of vitality and a flush of warmth.

All his young life, Kurjen's heart had only had one desire. Some on Maera wish for love, while others strive for wealth, fame, or power. Kurjen wanted to be a warrior, a simple thing, but an accomplishment that meant validation in a difficult life without the luxury of options. Baerbaraan cubs raised on the plains of the continent of Maerisna are bolstered by training to build strong bodies, focused minds, and hardened hearts. Finally, Kurjen was deemed mentally and physically ready to fulfill his one aspiration and become a cog in the Aeres war machine.

With his blood fortified by the poxy coursing through him, young Kurjen turned, found Urvaar nearby, and bent a knee before him. He took the leather thong from around his neck. Dangling from it was a claw from the bear that gave him his first battle scar. He placed it around Urvaar's neck and gave the now saddened cub a skull bump and a half smile. He then turned and walked away from his childhood forever. As the shaeman's exultations to Aeres resounded behind them, Kurjen and Jaeger first walked, then jogged, and finally broke into a sprint as they left the tribal fire behind, hurtling towards the future.

Three of the Pack had run to hunt, a smaller number than typical. But they were close to their camp and it had been days since their Pack had faced a blood fight. The three had been caught unaware, at no fault, as their foe was very fierce and cunning. Now two of his blood brothers lay slain, savaged by a single legendary creature that'd never been done justice in the tales told about it.

Kurjen recalled that he had first heard a tale of that feared beast around the tribal fire as a cub of no more than six years. Kellum the Elder was their clan's Chosen Voice at such fires and he seemed to know all their folk tales. But the story of the Roc-tuul had always been a favorite of the cubs, Kurjen included.

Bramblers, as the rest of Maera called them, were plentiful, living in the same grassy plains as the baerbaraan folk. The sheer number of bramblers, combined with the vast population of human baerbaraans indigenous to the plains of western Maerisna, were thought to be responsible for the virtual disappearance of wolves on the plains. They were still found on the continent and in the woodlands of this region where they thrived. Killing a brambler alone, with only a stone spear, a knife, and one's wits, was a rite of passage for the tribe's cubs who sought to run with the Zuentok Pack. Every warrior had a necklace made with the claws of a brambler, proof of their ascension to manhood.

But that meant almost every brambler story they heard was similar, usually a tale of a young warrior using stealth and cover or perhaps a trap to render the beast helpless or surprise it. The brambler Kurjen had slain a year earlier was full grown to be sure but an older, slower, one-eyed beast that he had been able to surprise in a job well done. How different it was facing a brambler in the prime of its life!

70

The three had entered the flat between hillocks, a sort of natural depression in the grasslands that was more than a spear throw wide and about four deep. They had awakened to the first bird songs and were running east as the dawn broke in front of them. A hazy morning fog clung to the aerth, thinning as the sun rose. None of them saw the dirty, shaggy gray figure blending into a rocky crest at the far end of the lawn in the glare of that sunrise.

Drool seeping from its colossal maw, its bulbous body rocking to and fro, its long slender arms dangling, the brambler was a big mature male at the peak of its strength and speed. It saw the lead runner, maybe even the two trailers that flanked him, as they entered the depression. The morning breeze had brought their smell far earlier, making the beast's stomach churn. Nothing about the humans registered as a threat. What the brambler saw was a meal.

It leaped from its perch, landing softer than any observer might imagine possible, its thin, almost spindly legs absorbing the weight of its spherical torso. Upon closer examination, its thighs suddenly widened as they neared the hip, thick with muscle. This fact was mostly obscured by the creature's overhanging gut, at least from the front. Once on its feet, oversized, razor-sharp black claws stood out, as did the bizarre predator's gigantic, slathering jaws. Half of its mass seemed comprised of its belly, mouth, and hanging jowls. Indeed, its thick, muscular neck could only be seen from the rear, as could its broad shoulders and sinewy back. The effect of this was that, from the front, the brambler appeared to be a fat and slothful creature. A sense of its massive power could only be readily perceived from the rear.

Now the beast began its famous bramble. It started to run towards the warrior named Kaesig in what seemed a staggering gait, clumsy, with its arms waving over its head. The brambler's joints were complex, and its elbows bent at freakish angles. While accelerating to a full sprint, it started to spin, lurching left and right like a top, at all times seemingly moments from sprawling on the grass. As it neared Kaesig, he stood still, gaping at the strange antics of the approaching brute. The brambler began to shriek in a piercingly loud, plaintive voice, gurgling, grunting, screaming, and growling as it spun closer and closer, now zigging and zagging as it rushed forward. Suddenly, in a great burst of speed, it was on Kaesig, who stood confused, as if in some kind of stupor.

In a heartbeat, it was over. The Zuentok warrior was reduced to a bloody heap on the ground, ravaged in a shocking explosion of gore. At that moment, Kurjen was on the beast's western flank, under ten paces away. He loosed his spear when his target moved the least—as it was murdering his comrade. The spear struck the beast in its left shoulder but passed through the muscle meat only, bloodying the beast and causing only a momentary cessation of its attack. The monstrosity turned and fixed its sights on Kurjen, bizarrely rotating its head vertically nearly halfway around, holding that gaze the whole time. Then it sprung back into action, making hideous noises and bounding quickly into its bramble.

Kurjen had stopped running and untied his waist tether with its dual leather-wrapped stones. He pulled it free of his body and quickly measured it out. As the brambler started to close the distance between them, zigging and zagging, he began twirling the weighted leather rope above his head. He said aloud, if only to himself, "Don't stare at it. Don't stare at it."

Kaarl, his other companion, bellowed a piercing war cry and attacked the creature from Kurjen's right. The yawping beast reacted with shocking speed. It lurched to the south, away from Kurjen, and placed its left hand on the grass. It then kicked its body around in a sweeping motion, using that same arm as a fulcrum and, with its legs extended, horizontal to the ground, it raked the charging warrior with its foot claws across his face and neck area. The claws of the great bloodied beast landed heavily against Kaarl's neck and skull, stopping his forward momentum while turning the baerbaraan's head completely around on his shoulders, his throat and face gushing great gouts of bloody horror. But in his moment of death, Kaarl had thrust his spear into the brambler's lower belly, tearing a brutal gash along the front of its left side. The next moment, Kaarl's body slumped, face ruined, to the aerth.

The brambler shuddered to a complete stop, clutching its bleeding abdomen with its left, clawed hand. It straightened up to its full height, a head taller than Kurjen. It tilted its head back so that its gaping, ravenous hole opened fully to the sky. As Kurjen flung his weighted tether, the wretched beast emitted a stupendous roar that seemed equal parts rage and agony. The rope found its mark, wrapping around the thin lower legs of the creature, if only loosely, as they were spread wide. Would that success give him the time he needed?

Kurjen sprinted, looping to his left, forcing the brambler to turn towards him as he accelerated. It stretched in a full layout, coming much closer to reaching him than he had thought it could. But he passed the monster as it crashed to the aerth. Three stone spears lay on the ground here now. The closest one was Kaarl's, which had landed past the brambler after slicing its belly. Kurjen reached it as his foe struggled to understand why it had fallen. As he picked the spear up and turned to face the beast, he saw that it could quickly slash through the leather tether around its shins with its black claws. As he assessed the situation and watched it slowly rise, Kurjen committed to his plan. Survival would come down to his athleticism and sheer nerve—in other words, his strengths.

The pair eyed each other, warrior and beast. The brambler was bleeding from two wounds yet it seemed to ignore them. It bobbed its massive head back and forth, left to right. It was making a strange noise, a faint low chittering with intermittent clicks. Kurjen held the spear in his left hand and drew his stone knife with his throwing hand. The noise grew louder and it started swaying left and right. He averted his eyes and stopped looking at it. Kurjen shook his head violently and snapped himself out of a sudden fogginess.

"Ah," he said, looking once again at the beast. "Even standing still, you can do that, eh?" He smiled widely, his upper left lip curling around the scar that ran through it. "Are we ready, then?" He prepared his blade, turning it in his hand.

The brambler seemed to realize that Kurjen had not succumbed to its ability to disorient and confuse a foe and it went into a rage, signaling its attack by letting out a throaty roar and leaning forward, bearing its claws. Kurjen threw his knife at the center of the monster's gigantic head. It was a good throw, and he knew it as the blade left his hand. That caused the brambler to step to Kurjen's right and gave him an extra stride as he broke left and ran east. The warrior's knife sank deep into the flesh of its face. The monster howled again in its fury, seemingly ignoring the strike. It then began its bramble once more, giving chase.

Kurjen knew he could accelerate fully before the brambler reached its top speed. Once it did, however, it would quickly overtake him. He also knew that he couldn't survive an exchange of attacks with the creature and that having the high ground was his best chance. So, he sprinted to the rocky outcropping at the far eastern end of the grassy depression where he would at least be able to use his spear to his best advantage. He could hear the creature coming up behind him and realized it was close. A year of running with the tribal Pack had conditioned him for such a situation. As Kurjen reached the hillock, he sprang up the northern side of it as the brambler bore down on him from behind.

The brambler was severely injured but it didn't bother to remove the blade so deeply lodged in the upper right side of its face. It was not accustomed to its prey resisting this way and it perhaps would have been wiser to break off its pursuit and return later for an easier meal. But, enraged as it was, the notion never even occurred to it. Instead, it plunged forward to attack, blood issuing simultaneously from three different wounds of varied severity.

Kurjen leaped deftly to the top of the rocky crest with the brambler scrabbling up the slope behind him. It didn't seem to handle the grade well, giving him precious seconds to spin and wedge the spear's fire-hardened butt into a crevice in the stone behind him. He put his weight onto the shaft of the spear, directing its head towards the brambler at a vicious angle. The oncoming fury of that horrid beast might have shaken another combatant but the young baerbaraan let loose his own furious bellow in the face of a hideous death. The beast was nearly horizontal to the crest as it launched itself at the human.

The spear entered the bulbous sac beneath its giant mouth, piercing the throat and then splitting the breastbone of the brambler. As his weapon impaled the monster, Kurjen let go of the shaft and dove to his left, throwing himself off the crest to the lawn below. The impact of the brambler's massive skull against his right thigh as he dove spun him in the air. As the warrior twisted hard to the right, the creature's bulk lurched to a stop. The spear had done its work.

The right arm of the brambler swept forward past its body, raking across Kurjen's chest as he spun through the air. He twisted as he fell, rotating in the air, falling short of his intended landing spot on the grass below the ridge. He hit the rocky slope hard, chest first, bouncing to the turf below.

It wasn't a purposeful attack but a death spasm. Still, it caught Kurjen flush enough to leave four gouges across his chest, half a finger joint deep and over a foot long. He had hit the turf with a dull thud, rolled onto his back, limbs flung wide, and succumbed to the inviting darkness. The brambler shook spastically as life left it. It gurgled its last breath, perfectly skewered on the spear. As it slumped on the shaft with its total weight, it swayed right, snapping the shaft of the spear with a loud "Crack!" It fell to the edge of the crest of stone, then rolled off the rock to the grass below.

Kurjen awoke after some unfathomable length of time, flat on his back. There was pain but more than that, there was a stench so amazingly foul, so offensive that it overpowered all his other senses. Upon its death, the brambler had splattered the entire area with its bowels' evacuation. It was as if that stink had crawled up his nose and wrapped around Kurjen's brain. He slowly tried to roll to his right side. Pain searing through him, he vomited.

The creature had fallen from the crest and nearly landed on top of him. Kurjen, still flat on his back, reached for his waist pouch. He used every bit of the poxy there to treat his wounds. His bruised right thigh ached, and even with a heavy dusting of the white powder, the four gouges in his chest still had a throbbing, burning life of their own. At least the poxy stopped most of the bleeding. He did his best to ignore the nauseating fetor of the carcass, now mixed with the reek of the former contents of his own stomach. The drug seemed to help with that as well. He fought to get to his feet, managing it only with great effort and suffering. It was immediately evident that he could not stand and he staggered several steps forward, propping himself up against the bare, exposed stone of the hillock. Kurjen put his back to that stone, slowly slumping back to the turf, his head spinning.

Kurjen spent an undetermined amount of time in a daze. The sun had burned away the morning mists and a clear blue sky invited mid-day. He fell in and out of consciousness, sweat running down his face and forehead. Kurjen didn't know it yet but he had struck his head squarely as he landed on the ground while leaping for his life. A rather impressive welt had already formed on the right side of his forehead. He was watching the carrion birds circle lower and lower when he came to his senses. He slowly rose once more, felt light-headed, stumbled once, and found his own spear in the grass. He nearly tumbled over as he picked it up but overcame his wooziness as he leaned on it.

He had some dried meat in his leather waist bag, took it out, and forced it down. Kurjen drank half of his water skin and poured the rest over his face with his head back. His beard and mustache wet, he walked slowly, purposely from the nauseating brambler and towards what was left of his running mates. Kaarl lay on his left side, legs together, right arm pointing away from his body. Kurjen looked at his ruined head, twisted backward on his shoulders. His face was unrecognizable, replete with minced gore. Kurjen took Kaarl's food, stone knife, weighted trip-thong, water, and claw necklace. He pressed his right hand into the blood pooled around that slashed face and then wet his palm with Kaarl's blood. He pressed his open hand against his face, honoring the life Kaarl had given in service to Aeres by wearing his blood.

Kaarl had died well in combat, aggressively attacking a superior foe. Fear had not kept him from his moment and in celebration of that death, Kurjen knelt, put his spear on the lawn, and carefully rolled Kaarl further onto his front. He took Kaarl's stone knife, and with it, from the lower back cutting up behind the ribs, the young Zuentok removed his friend's heart. Then Kurjen stood slowly, head lowered. With the smooth, blood-covered heart held in both his hands, he extended his arms above his head.

There was no burial for dead baerbaraan warriors, no wordy ceremonies, and no wet weeping of mates or breeders. He lifted Kaarl's core to the eternal sky, showing Aeres the heart of His warrior whose life had served Him well. Kurjen looked to the sky and turned in a small circle, presenting the organ to the heavens.

"Go then, brother, to that next place, where eternal strife awaits us all. Surely Aeres sees you now and will welcome you there." That having been well done, Kurjen took the time to wrap Kaarl's heart in leather. He would take it home to burn in the tribal fire, so all could feel him go. He owed him that much and more, as it was his spear that had saved him. But he left Kaarl's body to the beasts, for his blood no longer flowed and his spirit no longer dwelled there. It was part of the Zuentok way. Vultures need to eat, same as the vermin, and Kurjen would not feed a warrior's meat to Gaerd, God of the Aerth, who was worshipped by dwaerves and other foul races.

Kurjen returned to the brambler and examined his work. He often felt fortunate after a battle, thrilled to be alive, but rarely did he feel this lucky. The spear had pierced straight through the brambler's chest and was sticking out of its back. Kurjen cut open its grotesquely bulbous throat, slashing through thick layers of muscle and then a pearly-toned fibrous sac. His cut revealed a heavy, saliva-soaked wad of poxy paste nearly the size of his head. The ball of concentrated poxy would help him get home, being far more potent than the powder his folk produced. It was a grand prize that the Zuentok Proven of Aeres would celebrate together. He recovered his knife from the brambler carcass and retrieved only the front half of the spear, which proved difficult to dislodge in his condition. Kurjen claimed the brambler's digits, chopping off the fingers and toes to carry home. He'd prepare the claws later at his ease by the tribal fire. He would then fashion them into a necklace he'd wear with pride for the rest of his days.

Kurjen was feeling more vital, as he was already under the influence of the poxy paste of the brambler and felt fit to travel again. He would have impressive scars from this encounter and his life's story would grow amongst the Zuentok of Aeres. His stride was strong but he would not run, not yet. As he passed the ragged remains of Kaesig, he did not slow down, look at him, or acknowledge him.

Kaesig had died poorly, a weakness of his mind exploited by the brambler. His failing had put his brethren in danger, so his heart, weapons, food, water, and personal items stayed right where they were. As wasteful as that was, it was all part of the ceremonial existence of the baerbaraan. Taking anything from him, showing him any attention, might cost Kurjen the hard-earned favor of the Blood God. His story died with him and it would not be told. Aeres did not see him. Kaesig's blood had been wasted and he had not served the tribe in his death. His soul would not grant maena to Aeres. Kurjen's heart hardened but such emotion was a familiar thing and born solemnly. It would be helpful to the survivor in the coming years when he would genuinely need such strength.

As Kurjen strode west, his heart lightened. He reveled in his pain, which was surprisingly manageable now. As time passed, he began to anticipate the fire of his tribe, and he rejoiced in his heart, for he had slain a mighty foe and lived to tell the tale. He walked proudly, for indeed Aeres saw him this day. Kurjen once more strode into the future, knowing he held the favor of the Blood God and had surely earned great honor—the honor of blood.

Want to experience more of Maera? Visit **www.maeraworld.com**

THE AENGELS
OF OUR HEARTS

Benjamin took his time slinking through the streets. Out of habit, he stayed close to the walls of each building he passed. He was in the gloam of the *Invisibility* he so frequently cast to prevent being detected, for the large white cat was otherwise highly noticeable. It had been too long since he had been able to get away and he needed to relax for a few hours with a group of friends who understood at least some of what he went through in his daily life. Benjamin took an alley off Lake Shore Drive behind The Four Winds Tavern. As he approached the rear entrance, Benjamin saw a rat.

It was a slender, remarkably clean rodent of medium gray tone. It darted behind the barrel under the rain spout and Benjamin followed. An overflow channel ran behind the barrel, along the tavern's side, and the cat pursued the rat along that shallow gully in the alley towards a stack of crates and then behind them. It was a tight squeeze for Benjamin and while he might be notoriously lazy, the payoff would be worth the effort.

A horizontal basement tilt-hinged window had been left half open behind the crates and Benjamin stepped inside. The air in the room was stale and the rat was crossing the floor below, so the downy feline followed. The room was a wine cellar and the rat ran behind a vast wooden storage rack lining the wall opposite a large wooden door to his right. When Benjamin entered the space behind the storage shelves, he saw that the clever, nimble vermin had climbed up the back of the wooden rack to an opening high up on the wall behind it. Benjamin slowly climbed up the shelves and reached the opening, which had a small wooden door.

Benjamin scratched the door twice, hesitated a long heartbeat, and then scratched once more. He heard a quiet click before the door swung open to his right into the space beyond. Operating the door was a tiny humanoid, one of a race of the faerie folk known as the paelum. Standing slightly over a foot tall and looking like a tiny gnoam, the paelum smiled broadly as he swung the door open just wide enough for the cat to enter.

"Benjamin! It's good to see you! Come in, come in! You are most welcome!" the arcane being said enthusiastically, clearly pleased to see his furry guest. He stood on a wooden crate as he waved Benjamin into the room.

"Ah, Uerkel. How are you, my friend?" Benjamin replied. The two spoke maegum, the secret language of wizards and their familiars. As a rule, that ancient and arcane tongue was all that was spoken here in The Lair, as this crawl space was aptly named. Benjamin rubbed up against the tiny doorman as he entered, purring, and a jubilant welcome arose from those present. Uerkel scratched the cat's shoulders and head in response. The feline grinned. *Yes,* he thought, *this is precisely what I need.* The paelum closed the door behind him.

"There he is!" shouted Jeremy, the gray rat. "I thought you'd never catch up!"

"You look well, Jeremy!" answered the handsome tomcat. The rodent was the familiar of Lady Charlotte Gabain, a well-known and well-respected enchantress. He had served his mistress for many years, for a familiar was a gift from Aelar, the Goddess of Magic, not merely a creature imbued with magic over its short natural lifespan. Quite the contrary, familiars lived as long as their companions breathed and could have genuinely consequential power.

Benjamin went around the room and was greeted by each occupant in turn. While Jeremy was resting on a satin pillow on a rocking chair, sitting quite contentedly, atop a small keg next to him was a most robust toad.

"Reginald, how are you?" Benjamin queried. "It's been too long, my excellent friend."

"Very well, very well indeed. How is Maxwell treating you, Benjamin?" the large amphibian croaked. His skin was ever so bumpy and interesting.

"For all the chaos on the estate, things seldom actually change, and Maxwell perhaps least of all," said Benjamin. Reginald nodded his great head in understanding. "How are things in Castle Uriens?" asked the cat. Reginald was the familiar of Gasdad the Magnificent, the Wizard to the Court of Duke Leonard Uriens, and he was as impressive as his master.

"Well, the pressure is really getting ratcheted up around the place as the great anniversary approaches," the toad replied. "The short lifespan given to our humans seems to encourage them to cling to their traditions." With that said, he flicked his thick and heavy tongue, deftly snatching up a fly foolish enough to have landed near him on the keg.

"Indeed," Benjamin said with empathy. "At least Maxwell ages well. That aelven blood of his does come in handy." Reginald was referring to the upcoming celebration of the four-hundredth

Anniversary of the Coronation of the First King of Gindlorn. Each province was responsible for its own festivities and the cost of such things weighed heavily on those who wore a crown.

Next in line was Eva, short for Evangeline, a beautiful red fox. She was just as clever as lovely and a particular favorite of Benjamin's. Eva served Naevol Bettermon, a famous former resident of the Protectorate of Tharlas. Her wizard was a Naelen, who are famously short of stature but beloved in the City of Gaegen and he was perhaps the greatest spell caster his gentle folk had ever produced. He was a great friend of Maxwell's and a rather frequent guest at the manor.

"Ah, if it isn't the lovely Eva," said Benjamin with a flirtatious grin. "It has been too long since you and your Naelen have visited us!"

"Well, the view just improved in this place!" Eva said silkily. That remark was met with croaks, caws, chitters, boos, and other gentle expressions of complaint. "You need to get Mad Maxwell out of that big house of yours and come see us in the center of town," she said in that same smooth voice. Eva ignored the rest of the group and nodded towards the far end of the rectangular crate on which she curled. "Why don't you take your ease over here with me, old man? Uerkel was good enough to swirl a blanket there for you." They liked to tease Benjamin about his age, for he was the eldest of the compatriots that met in The Lair.

"Well, that certainly sounds good to me," said Benjamin. As he crossed the candle-lit room, he stopped to acknowledge the last two group members present, relaxing to his left.

"Clayburn, it's always good to see you," he directed to the shiny black raven roosting on the back of a wooden chair. Clayburn was companion to MaryAnne Devries, an elderly sorceress of true renown and possessed of a formal disposition. His lady was of noble birth, the previous King's daughter.

"Good evening to you, Benjamin. It would seem Sealon agrees with you on this fine night," quoth Clayburn, referring to the nearly full moon. He was a bit stiff at times but a reliable acquaintance.

"Very much so," Benjamin answered. "I see that the winds have been gentle under your wings since last we met. You look positively splendid tonight." The magnificent bird bowed low in response, which the cat mirrored.

"Chandra, I hope the evening finds you well." Benjamin had turned his attention to the last occupant of the room, a fire drake of exceptional quality. She was roughly the size of a large owl and currently presented a ruby red hue with fiery orange and yellow highlights. That meant that she had entered a rather tumultuous phase in her life. Their host Uerkel had a perch set up in a corner for her, and her physical presence was impressive.

Fire drakes, just like dragons, their larger cousins, changed colors throughout their lives based on their diet and other factors. Her bright and fiery hues indicated that Chandra had entered a reproductive stage. Another fire drake that saw her would know full well that she was ready to produce young. Likewise, their coloration would indicate whether they too were prepared. Any other fire drake was capable of impregnating her. If each were fiery in tone, the coupling might even result in each drake being impregnated, yielding two sets of offspring, for drakes and dragons possessed both male and female sexual organs. Hermaphroditism significantly increased the chance of finding a partner at the right time, thus enhancing the survivability of the races.

"I have indeed been extremely fortunate as of late, Benjamin," Chandra replied. "My Lady Aeleen sends her greetings to you all," she said to the room. Chandra served a renowned aelfhael, the Lady Aeleen Elmondae, also widely known as the Scarlet Lady of Gaegen. She was one of a few powerful wizards to have settled in Sudlund's capital city during its recent growth spurt. She was still young and many thought her rather beautiful. A measurable percentage of the populace of Gaegen already felt a degree of goodwill for her. She was very cunning and seemingly sought to wield political power in the province.

Chandra was the most recent addition to the group and there had been those that opposed her invitation. There was concern that she might share their private conversations with her mistress, which was greatly frowned upon by the companions. Chandra's greeting to the group from her mistress was precisely the kind of indiscretion that piqued such concern in The Lair. Since she had joined the group a year earlier, the group's eighth member, who was not present that night, had been attending their gatherings less frequently.

That member was one of the group's founders and one of its leaders. Her name was Daelia, and she was a gorgeous raccoon. She was the companion of Traemar Haggerty, a bright young star of the local Guild of Enchantment. She had openly opposed the fire drake's joining but while Benjamin voted with her, the count went four-to-three against her. Daelia's wizard was a rising member of the Guild here in Gaegen and his uncle Willem was a distinguished leader in that prestigious body. Daelia was one of Benjamin's most preferred companions, and the pair had been known to romp in town late at night.

Once, soon after the group first started meeting, Benjamin had tried a bit of fine Naelen nip that Uerkel had gladly procured for him. So that her friend would not indulge alone, Daelia had a saucer of Bentuan dark rum. The night quickly became a blur and before he knew it, Benjamin found himself helping the raccoon gain entry to a bakery where she was hoping to find some pastries in their refuse. Benjamin was at first a bit taken aback at the notion but there was a delicious feeling of mischief in the misdeed. The two succeeded and Daelia got her pastries, the fruit filling of which was of interest to the feline.

The next evening, having returned to a more ordinary frame of mind, Benjamin returned to the scene of their crime. He felt somewhat guilty about violating the business's privacy and was trying to find a way to repay what he perceived as a debt. As Benjamin climbed to the rooftop across the street from the bakery, he found himself face to face with Daelia, who was of a like mind. At that moment, the two became fast friends. They cast a little creative magic to ensure that the shopkeeper came out ahead as a result of the incident and went on their way, all the better for their adventure.

Uerkel excused himself for a moment, disappearing with an odd disturbance of the air. In mere moments he returned, blinking back into their secret room suddenly. He now held a platter with an assortment of foods preferred by his six guests and began to offer them to each in turn. There was a lovely bit of sharp cheese for Jeremy, mealworms for Reginald, hulled peanuts for Eva, Clayburn's favorite raw eggs, a salt lick, some spicy peppers for Chandra, and a lovely bit of mackerel for Benjamin. Their paelum host also produced a fruit-based pastry and a cup of wine for himself. Uerkel had all these items readily available as he lived in The Four Winds Tavern, owned by its proprietor Landrew Strangely, a semi-retired gnoamish spell caster.

Uerkel's gnoam was a wealthy entrepreneur who owned several businesses in Gaegen. He chose to live in the tavern rather than a private residence for unshared reasons. It provided a perfect opportunity for a quiet place in which the members of their group could meet. The Lair, as it was so practically named, was easily placed under a gloam of *Privacy*, assuring that nothing they said could be overheard, even by the property owner. This meant that the familiars could speak about the unique difficulties and stress they faced every day while trying to balance their service to their creator Aelar, the Goddess of Magic, and their spell-casters to whom Aelar, in her unsurpassed wisdom, had assigned each of them.

The relationship between a wizard and a familiar on Maera is complicated, for you do not simply summon a creature from the wilderness to serve your needs. Aelar recognizes exceptional achievement in magic by honoring a worthy spell caster with a great ally with whom they could form a nearly indomitable partnership that sets them apart from their contemporaries in both power and prestige. Through such a symbiosis, Aelar, in return, gleans real power from Her worshipers, advancing the influence of magic on Maera in general, for many relationships of this nature result in the creation of new spells, as well as improvements on older castings.

Wisdom dictates that familiars be respected as the powerful creatures they are, independent of their wizards. However, they should be genuinely feared while in the company of their partners because, as a team, they are radically more potent than when apart. Even as this remarkable symbiosis is recognized, it must also be acknowledged that familiars have their complaints and irritations, like any other beings. The difficulties inherent in their relationships were discussed at great lengths during the bi-weekly gatherings in The Lair.

For his part, Benjamin seldom added much to the conversation. He had few complaints, as his companion was famously serene. Maxwell, in fact, demanded very little at all of Benjamin and seemed genuinely more interested in his willful company. This dynamic was well understood in The Lair and his compatriots both accepted and envied it. Benjamin did enjoy hearing the others go on about how irritating their wizards were, in all their hubris and frailty. He found such tales somehow cathartic. His arrangement with Maxwell had spanned more than twice the length of the others' relationships, so they valued his perspective. His company was deemed priceless, as he contributed great resources and brought joy to their society of familiars.

The group noticed their friend Benjamin was conspicuously quiet but this was typical of late and they did not mind. Even though he was the eldest of the group and clearly the most powerful, Benjamin was perhaps the most emotionally fragile, and they respected and indulged his vulnerability. After all, his circumstances were unique and the particulars of his existence were quite sensitive.

The biggest complaint amongst the familiars was the rampant ego of their companions, who seemed to share the belief that what success they achieved was through their individual efforts and not wholly through the grace of Aelar. The non-human wizards were somewhat less guilty of this offense but the mortal intellect seemed unable or unwilling to grasp that magic was a gift of power directly from Aelar, pure and simple.

Benjamin devoted his attention to a rather lengthy self-cleaning as the group chatted. He even fell into a short slumber at one point, visibly twitching and gesturing in his sleep as he dreamt. They talked until the aengel hour and then the group began to break up. Uerkel used *Blink* to move several of them to the roof, where they could take flight toward home without undue exposure to risk. Jeremy and Benjamin left the way they came, accompanied by Eva. Reginald, the most physically vulnerable of the group, was blinked right to his doorstep as a courtesy their host was glad to provide. Another meeting had been scheduled for a fortnight hence, and all committed to trying their best to attend. Benjamin said his farewells and went on his way, returning to Maxwell's mansion with all due secrecy and caution and without incident.

He entered the property through the iron front gate, knowing that, even invisible, he would be detected by the excellent security on the property. As if on cue, as he trotted towards the mansion past the guard house, one of the humans stationed there called to him.

"Hey there, Benjamin!" It was Richard, an extraordinarily kind individual for a man who made his living wielding steel. Benjamin let out a cursory meow in reply. There was no reason not to be friendly. The feline strolled into the gardens flanking the main entrance and leaped onto a window ledge. The window was on hinges that opened by swinging outwards and locked by a latch inside. It had been left open for him by Maxwell.

Benjamin gestured with his tail while turning his ears and pointing his whiskers in a combination that cast a quick spell, rendering him *Invisible*. A second such casting gained him entrance to the otherwise trapped and impassible aperture. He was pleased to see that Maxwell was seemingly asleep in one of the tall-backed hardwood chairs with soft padded cushions of the type that the aelfhael so favored. The feline entered without so much as a whisper. The wizard opened one eye and spoke to the apparently empty room.

"Good morning, Benjamin," he offered in a low tone. "I trust you enjoyed your night out. How are your co-conspirators?" he queried playfully.

Benjamin suddenly appeared on the chair opposite the master of the house, lit by the lamp on the table between them. He sat up on his back haunches and cleaned his front right paw. He took his time responding, invoking the casual comfort between them.

"A lot of complaining, as always," he replied. "I hope you appreciate my attendance at such gatherings. While there can be no doubt that hearing about the wizards of my fellows makes our relationship seem much less arduous," he said unapologetically, "listening to their endless griping wears my patience thin." It was a remark that, while true, he made half in jest.

"Oh, I do appreciate it, I do," replied the spell caster. "And I hope you realize how much I cherish our relationship, my very dear friend." Maxwell was surprisingly kind in his reply and Benjamin certainly appreciated it. He really did love his wizard and was awfully glad to have such a comfortable home. He settled down, content to relax in Maxwell's pleasant company, which, after all, had always been enough. Benjamin soon napped, giving in entirely to a profound sense of well-being.

Maxwell observed his companion as he slept, for Benjamin's dreams were often quite telling. The spell caster had ample reason for concern, as the peculiar case of Benjamin was ongoing. Any visitor to the mansion would quickly realize that the master of the estate had quite a penchant for small animals. Birds of many kinds filled the trees on his property. A wide variety of frogs and fish lived in the ponds, and he allowed rabbits and mice indoors. All were welcome, and the wizard's friendly "conversations" with these creatures were one of his well-known eccentricities. It was also obvious that the luxurious white cat he called Benjamin stood out as his clear favorite amongst all the various inhabitants of the property.

Of course, it was much more than that. Maxwell was precisely the type of wizard that the Goddess Aelar would deem worthy of Her attention. His long and successful career as a spell caster had been highlighted by the creation of many new and unique spells, as well as clever alterations to several others. Having thus bolstered the strength of Maera's magic, the aelfhael was a perfect candidate to reward with the gift of a familiar. Maxwell had come to Aelar's attention, in fact, far earlier in his life. As part of his training as an initiate in the arcane arts in the aelven Kingdom of Golaidris, Maxwell was a disciple of Shaeyla Silverstalk, a mighty caster of far-reaching renown. The aelven beauty made quite an impression on his young mind.

As a daughter of the King of Golaidris, Lady Silverstalk was a proponent of the aelfhael and her support had meant a great deal to Maxwell. She dedicated herself to the worship of Aelar, and her devotion to the Goddess of Magic strongly influenced Maxwell. She was known for her profound love of animals. So fervent was it that, when her power and influence had grown to the requisite level, she prayed to Aelar and asked that the goddess not subjugate an animal as a familiar to her. Her affection for the wildlife of the aelven forest was an example that Maxwell heeded and one that helped him form the deep devotion he now showed to nature's creatures on his estate.

One day, years ago, a songbird he had playfully named Nathaniel came to Maxwell, as he had many times. The spell caster valued any chance to spend time with the tiny warbler, as he was so cheered by its clever songs. On this occasion, Nathaniel was in an excited state, agitatedly flitting to and fro. It was such a departure from their everyday interactions that the wizard was disturbed enough to follow when Nathaniel seemed to try to lead him away, even though he had been deeply intent on his work. And so, he had left his study through the open window and entered his backyard garden to follow his small friend.

Nathaniel led him to a drainage pipe that emptied rainwater collected most cleverly from the mansion's roof to feed the pond behind the house. It was his design and Maxwell was quite proud of it. However, this afternoon it was the source of some consternation, it would seem, for little Nathaniel led him right to it. Gaegen had seen some rather heavy rain earlier that morning, leaving the ground very soft. As he approached the pond, Maxwell was in a bit of a snit, what with his soft house shoes sinking into the garden soil.

"Confound it! Why did I leave my study without thought to proper footwear?" he muttered, nearly losing his balance as he tried to judge the best place to step next. It was then that he heard, or at least thought he did, a strange sound. It seemed to echo from somewhere nearby and, just as he said aloud, "Was that a cat?" he again heard a tiny meow, this time very distinctly. Nathaniel was darting back and forth above the end of the piping as it opened to the water. As Maxwell reached the opening, he again heard the plaintive little meow.

"Well now, what have we here?" he spoke aloud, in a gentle, soothing tone that all his animal friends knew well. "A small fellow has found his way into my pipe, has he?" It took several minutes, intermittent meowing continuing the whole time, but eventually and with no small effort, Maxwell extracted his arm from the piping. At the end of that arm, he had a handful of a soaking wet kitten. It was pure white, tiny, and just about the most adorable thing the spell-caster had ever seen. He was in just a bit of discomfort as its little claws were sunk into his hand. As he lifted it to get a better look at it, he rotated his hand, and it stared up into his calm, green eyes. It was at that moment that the two quite different beings connected.

"Well then, things aren't so bad after all, are they, my little friend?" Maxwell said. "How did you get yourself up in there, eh?" he asked the kitten, which meowed at him as if to answer. It was a meek and pitiful sound, but the wizard smiled widely. "You must be frozen half to death, poor thing," he said. With that, the kitten clamped down on his thumb with wicked little fangs, drawing blood. The wizard resisted the urge to drop the beastie, choosing to tuck it into his robes instead. *"This,"* he thought, *"is where trust begins."*

"Come on now. I have you. Let's get you inside and warm, shall we?" said the wizard, walking directly to the lawn along the pond's edge. Maxwell entered the back door to the kitchens where there would be warmth and perhaps a bit of goat's milk for his new charge. Maxwell Biptomen was always busy, as any highly proficient spell caster was. Still, he dropped everything to take in a tiny kitten. Its sheer cuteness and innocence were enough to secure the kitten a place in his home and heart.

Maxwell coddled that kitten, ensuring he was happy and safe and watched over him as he grew into a large, magnificent cat named Benjamin. The two were fast friends, and people who witnessed them together often said it was remarkable, almost as if they could understand one another. The pair shared many dramatic ventures around the mansion and its accompanying estate. Unfortunately, time can be cruel to such relationships, and the years flew by. As Benjamin matured and then grew old, the great wizard was pained by the deterioration of his beloved companion.

Having aelf blood is undoubtedly a blessing but one who lives for centuries must say farewell to many friends in their time on Maera. Maxwell had steeled himself to this reality. However, for some reason he could not quite explain, as Benjamin's time approached, it was somehow different. Staff, friends, and even his business contacts all noticed that Maxwell was not himself. It went on for some time as Benjamin's health slowly declined. So it was that, in the end, the sorcerer bent a knee, said a prayer to Aelar, and asked that She intercede on his behalf.

That night at the aengel hour, Benjamin passed beyond the veil while lying peacefully on Maxwell's lap. The wizard was broken-hearted and spent the night alone in his study one last time with his baby boy, whom he cuddled close to him. He had an awful feeling in his chest, as if it were physically compressed. His gut felt twisted and his very spirit ached. Maxwell had never felt so utterly alone. Finally, he nodded off, sitting in his chair, his reddened eyes swollen from tears, just before sunrise.

The morning had nearly fled when he awoke and Benjamin was gone. His body was simply not where Maxwell had left him and the wizard sat silently for a bit, truly distressed. It was then that he heard a familiar meow. There, sitting on the sill of the open window of his study, was Benjamin, or at least a cat that looked very much like him. Maxwell was confused but when the feline leaped down, crossed the room, purred loudly and rubbed against him happily, the wizard was thrilled. It was not only Benjamin but a young, healthy, virile incarnation of his beloved companion! Maxwell closed his eyes and said a silent, grateful prayer to Aelar. Benjamin leaped into his lap, demanding his favorite face rubs. It was at that rather memorable moment that the situation elevated.

"It's me, my friend," said a voice, clear as day. The wizard looked at Benjamin. His mouth hadn't moved but Maxwell could hear him in his mind. However, it was somewhat confusing, since it was a human-like voice speaking maegum. "Aelar has seen fit to answer your prayer. She has allowed me to return to you. From this day forth She would have us work together to advance your studies." Maxwell was stunned and it took a few moments for him to think it through. Benjamin seemed to sense Maxwell's apprehension, for the voice came again. "I can bite your thumb if it would make you feel better." The large cat squinted, grinned, and looked up at his old friend in such a way that it calmed Maxwell. Indeed, this was Benjamin!

It seemed that Aelar had granted Maxwell's wish. By sending his companion back as his familiar, She had extended Benjamin's life in an act of inspired expediency. While She would send a unique and magical being to other spell casters, here She simply enhanced an already existing being and tethered its lifespan to Maxwell's. Even as Benjamin discussed past events with Maxwell, giving voice to his perspective of their shared experience, a deeper understanding of this new stage in their relationship came to the wizard.

Maxwell realized that he hardly knew Benjamin at all. His senses, intellect, and comprehension were all quite different than Maxwell had imagined when he had even taken the time or made an effort to contemplate such things. The wizard very quickly concluded that for them to work together effectively, he needed to get to know his friend at a much more intellectual level than he had ever thought to hope for before.

Recognized throughout Maera and all the recorded history of magic therein, was the ongoing story of familiars and their very complex relationship with their wizards. Here now was a new variation of that relationship. Beings that had known each other, one of them throughout an entire natural lifespan, who now had the opportunity to come to a much greater understanding between them.

This closeness was aided by the unspoken bond that already existed between the pair for although Benjamin had not been able to speak with Maxwell, he had been able to convey many of his emotions and thoughts to his friend. Now that sense of extensive trust, the understanding that Maxwell had a genuine affection for him, made all the difference. Communicating at a new level with his friend allowed Benjamin to articulate that he understood and appreciated that Maxwell had always provided a safe place for him, had willingly given him his protection, and had seen to his comfort and needs throughout his entire lifetime.

Likewise, Maxwell could explain how Benjamin had touched his heart, kept him grounded, and made him a better person. It was now clear how, in his willing commitment to a tiny, stranded kitten, Maxwell had nurtured not just a creature of nature but himself. He explained how his time spent with Benjamin had fed the aengels of his heart, starving the daemons that dwell therein, and helped him become a kinder, better version of himself, one he now greatly preferred.

So, their collaboration became a real adventure, with Benjamin possessed of a voice and an elevated intellect, if not any Aelar-given maena, which is magic directed through the divine. He'd be able to cast conventional willful magic spells through rigorous study and practiced execution, like any other wizard seeking such power. Benjamin's limitations, having paws and therefore struggling to use many of the physical components of spell casting, were only exasperated by his standard nakedness. The cat had nowhere to carry spell components!

With Maxwell's considerable prowess and his long experience training disciples of the arcane arts, the two forged ahead into territory that had seldom, if ever before, been explored. Maxwell concentrated on modifying his spells, decreasing and, in many cases eliminating the need for material components. These modifications customized many of the castings to suit Benjamin and significantly increased Maxwell's power by reducing his casting time. If that weren't enough, the pair made a new and significant discovery while pursuing this work.

Benjamin began having dreams about future events that very often came to pass. Maxwell immediately recognized that this could be a manifestation of *Life Dream*, a potentially potent manaera discipline. Benjamin started to exhibit other manaera abilities which they were able to develop over time. It was ideal, for manaera is raw power requiring no incantations, gestures, or physical components. Manaera manifested in the caster's blood, and there were wielders of manaera that exhibited great power without ever having studied the arcane arts. All that was needed to master manaera was time, applied concentration, and intense effort to wield some of the most coveted personal powers on Maera.

Benjamin saw his opportunity to become something more, something no other being had a chance to be, as great as his friend Maxwell, greater even. After over a century of academic effort and engrossing commitment, he had grown into one of the most powerful familiars in the history of Maera. In his symbiosis with the aelfhael, having his length of life, the two truly became an unassailable force. As a team, they could only be matched by the millennium-old aelves that founded the great nations of those elegant folk.

Benjamin was also a cat, though, and Maxwell, his companion. The two awoke nearly simultaneously, as they often did now. As far as Maxwell knew, Benjamin had paid close attention to every word at the previous night's gathering in The Lair. Maxwell did not ask further questions in that new day's beaming sun. He felt he didn't need to. He was sure that, had anything significant transpired, he would have heard about it. Truly, Benjamin was keeping tabs on the group as always, particularly the fire drake Chandra, these days. As a matter of course, the feline would have briefed Maxwell had anything of actual interest been said in The Lair. His wizard and he, after all, shared a bond that even the oldest of married couples seldom shared, working together on all things. He was no conventional familiar.

Benjamin stretched and yawned, still lying on his cushioned chair. Maxwell stood and stretched as well. "Thank you for sharing your sleep with me," said the wizard. Although Benjamin had a habit of doing so, Maxwell didn't want to take it for granted. The extra hours of rest his mind and body gleaned from the feline allowed him to work more while sleeping less and was a unique aspect of the pair's symbiosis. Benjamin could also share Maxwell's hours of sleep, although he needed far less rest than he had during his first life as a cat. It was a gift the two had put great effort into and one that Maxwell deeply appreciated.

They were now striving to share Benjamin's manaera ability to *Dream Walk* and to experience *Dream Sight* so then Maxwell might share in the great benefits of the premonitions his familiar so enjoyed. In this way, Benjamin repaid his mentor's tireless reworking of many of his castings, reducing their requirement for material components. These incremental changes further fed Benjamin's growing powers and thus served their combined purpose. It was this way with nearly everything between them, share and share alike. Few, even amongst the wise of Maera, realized what wonders were transpiring in Biptomen Manor between wizard and familiar.

"Shall we get a start to our day, my boy?" asked Maxwell.

"Indeed. Let us visit the kitchens and see what they've prepared for us," replied Benjamin playfully. "I feel terrific and this is going to be a wonderful day!" he declared.

"Yes, yes … may Aelar be ever praised," Maxwell responded. Having heard Her name said in praise by a believer of consequence, Aelar smiled down upon the pair and saw them in their time stream, strolling down the halls of the mansion. The Goddess whispered aloud before giving Her attention back to the wondrous works in which She was otherwise engaged.

"Bless you both, my favored sons, as you continue to make me so very proud."

The pair reached the kitchen and greeted the staff, who were prepared for their arrival. Maxwell stood by the cutting table at the center of the large room, and Benjamin leaped up by his side onto the block. He rubbed against his mentor, who scratched his head and neck. The white beastie purred and leaned into the attention he still enjoyed immensely. As they took in all the delightful smells around them, Maxwell thought to himself, looking upon his most excellent pupil with evident joy.

Truly, this is the aengel of my heart.

Want to experience more of Maera? Visit www.maeraworld.com

THE BUBBLE SWAMPS
OF AENTHA

The thief knelt, taking in the terrain ahead. His group was about to enter the swamp proper—the point of total commitment. He had successfully sold his services to the group posing as an experienced Way Maker and now that lie was catching up to him. He didn't worry about it much though, as he'd made a career of negotiating difficult situations as they came and had few complaints. Loose and easy was his way. Besides, his companions had spewed plenty of maak in the days since they'd met at The Crossed Blades to plan this venture. He had quickly sized them up as the rum flowed. Out of the six of them, only their priest had let his tongue wag true, in his estimation. Thus, he was discovering the skills of his party members as they went along, just as they were weighing his actions now.

As their self-declared Aerth Walker, he had insisted that they travel as lightly as possible but several had ignored that advice. Likewise, no one else had procured a hefty walking stick as he'd recommended to any who didn't normally wield a staff. Now treacherous ground lay ahead and they'd done little to mitigate the inherent dangers. *Sealon's tides!* he thought. *Didn't I say we might face this? Didn't I predict the terrain would get nasty?* He may not have been a wilderness runner, but he could read a kueting map! *You can't force people to use their brains,* he thought. It was out of his hands now. If his party mates slipped and sank into the dank muck, it was between them and Rhal!

His job was to lead the group through the wilderness and swamplands to reach their destination. He had gotten them this far with ease by doing nothing more than following their map, but now what? Since he didn't know what way was best, he went with his gut as it had rarely failed him before, outside of romance. The rogue had always considered himself favored by Rhal and left regular offerings at the deity's shrines to ensure it stayed that way. He had promised one coin of every ten gleaned from this outing to Rhal's coffers once he'd returned safely. The thief fully intended to give so much that it hurt. "Risk is what puts the shine on coin," his running mate used to say. He felt confident the next few days would be shiny indeed.

"Here it is," he began as he addressed the group. "There are several ways to go. We can try to skirt the marsh to the south, along its edge. It looks to be rather a slender path though. There's a second trail north of the center but it appears to taper off and disappear about halfway through the swamp." He paused for effect. "This place wasn't always a fen. According to our wizard's research, it flooded sometime after the fall of the City of Aentha. The road that split the valley was a wide causeway built up for speedy travel. The central path seems to be that ancient avenue, although it's overgrown now." He paused again, looking to see if they were all paying attention. "It's still a ridge through this mire and is our best bet. We'll want to stay close together and be in a single line. I'll lead the way through, yes?" The lowbred scoundrel spoke confidently, even though he was making it all up as he went along. He smiled and tried to look relaxed while, in actuality, anxiously studying his companions' faces. The group's wizard spoke up more quickly than the others.

"Are we concerned about creatures of the swamp assailing us as we cross? If we're on the center path, we might be more easily attacked from two sides. Isn't that so?" The older man conveyed intellectual concern without seeming fearful.

"Any time we get hit from more than one side at once, we must assume we're facing some coordinated attack. Do we expect that in this terrain?" Their senior warrior was speaking. He had been accepted as the adventuring party's primary combat planner as he had seemingly served in Bentua's navy. He talked a good game and could handle a boat, at least. Furrowed brows and concerned glances were exchanged in an awkward silence after his question. The group's acknowledged scout felt he'd better speak up.

"Listen, I just spent the morning going ahead on each of these paths alone and I'm still here, right? I didn't come across anything alarming. The swamps seem devoid of life other than insects and slimy plants. There was no sign of predators but I'm sure we'll be ready to defend ourselves should one appear. Are there any special precautions we should take before continuing?" He looked to the wizard and their veteran as he spoke.

"I can have my best damage spell at the ready. I think it's a fair bet that most creatures living in wet terrain should be especially vulnerable to fire." The spell caster portrayed himself as having a practical side that the party seemed to appreciate, almost as much as his claim to have fire magic. As for himself, the rogue was more than ready for a demonstration of any power that the caster might have. Thus far, the wizard seemed to be nothing more than a source of wind. The veteran warrior once more spoke up, further establishing his position as their tactician.

"We should all have weapons ready as we travel our chosen path. Father, have you anything in particular that might be good against swamp dwellers?" He addressed their priest of Aerdos, who apparently was less concerned than the others about the proposition of a pitched battle in the wetlands. He seemed more interested in smearing shades of white, gray, and black on his face. Indeed, he held a small mirror in his left hand and applied a soot-black smear as he spoke.

"My castings are specific to the situation. I have nothing special for a swamp." He was a bit too truthful, perhaps. "I assure you, I shall use my Lord's power for whatever situation may arise." The group was slowly getting used to his grim demeanor. His deity was mighty and feared across Maera like none other. Having a cleric of the Dead God in tow while seeking riches in an ancient ruin had seemed clever to the group. If he could do more than deal with encounters with the dead, it would surely be a bonus.

The twins chimed in with their normal dimwitted perspective. "We're ready for anything," said one, between bites of a whole smoked fish. He spoke with his mouth full. The pair seemed to eat constantly.

"Anything at all," the other chimed in, bread in hand. The two had a grating way of adding mindless prattle to an otherwise serious conversation. The youngsters frequently finished each other's sentences or reaffirmed what the other had just said. At first, the cutpurse thought they were simply a bit nervous but he had begun to realize that they were imbeciles.

"Uh, sure, okay. You two are ripe and ready! We got it." The robber didn't give a shaved slug what they had to say. Ignorant fighters were meat for the grinder, in his opinion. If they survived, he might have to relieve them of the burden of their share of shiny once they'd returned to town. "We should be sure to stay in a staggered formation as we continue, yes?" He looked to their war veteran to support his suggestion and wasn't disappointed.

"Aye, let's string out in single file." That said, the veteran assigned each of them a place in line, establishing a marching order before they proceeded. The group accepted this and the thief thought they needed to continue with a more focused and disciplined plan. It had taken too long to agree on their basic tactics. He hoped they'd make good progress from now on. Thus, the thief pressed on at the head of their line, his bow strung and held in his off hand, his walking stick testing the ground as he advanced. He was happy with himself, feeling more like an actual Way Maker, at least in his own ever-deceitful mind. He had no idea of the numerous egregious mistakes he'd already made, nor the terrible consequences such poor planning might bring upon them. The group proceeded with their venture, oblivious to the risks they were taking.

The party lacked a map for the Valley of Ruin. Their wizard claimed to have diligently tried to find out more about where they were headed. He said there had been a distinct lack of eyewitness or historical accounts of the region, especially the swamps that blocked their access to the city ruins proper. The caster took this, and the sparse mention of the area in the research literature he claimed to have scoured, as a good sign that the ruins and surrounding countryside had not been picked clean by marauders, adventurers, or other organized attempts at retrieving all that was shiny from the region. With that limited measure of information, they had ventured forth from Bentua to the small mountain range known as the Dragon's Teeth and entered the sullen valley beneath those peaks. Their only map, which they agreed was the most commonly accepted and used map of the continent of Caan, called the area The Havens of Doom. The rogue chuckled and shook his head. *Map makers, how they loved dramatic names!*

On their one-hundred-and-fifty-mile journey from the realm of the seafarers, they hadn't had to deal with anything hazardous. They'd taken a small skiff and run the coast most of the way. They'd set ashore before dusk two days ago, after passing two broad streams feeding the river, then marched the rest of the way. They made a good camp alongside the rushing water and had gotten an early start. A long day's march had brought them to the edge of a marsh. Another camp, without a fire and under more nervous circumstances, had seen them safe until morning. There'd been wolves; none could say how many, but a few arrows had scared them off.

They'd also seen several small wyverns, which seemed abundant in the area. Such creatures, however, were merely monstrous leathery buzzards, according to tales the thief had heard. More arrows had easily dissuaded those flyers at a distance. The twins expressed disappointment that their swords hadn't tasted blood and the scoundrel was half hoping there'd be something to kill soon. In his limited experience, warriors had to satiate their bloodlust regularly, as some might get surly and then readily turn against allies if foes weren't in good supply. He wanted no part of that! Such were the thoughts on his mind as the human hoodlum strode slowly and with exaggerated false confidence into the yawning, musty reaches of the ancient swamplands.

The terrain had climbed steadily, if not dramatically, from the sea as they followed the river east towards the ruins. Once they reached the shadows of the mountains, the aerth crested in a ridge and then fell away in a gentle slope. They could make out what seemed to be the start of ruins at the furthest edge of their vision as they surveyed the vale from the ridge. The area was heavily shrouded in a persistent mist, which limited what they could see. The party hoped that the haze would dissipate as they continued. The six resumed their march, carefully negotiating their way down from the ridge through random areas of crumbling rock and with much perceived peril, entering the gullet of the Dragon's Teeth.

As they proceeded, it became clear that the ground in the valley was mainly flooded, forming a daunting fen. The area was morbidly quiet and still, other than some percolating of gases and the odd, irregular disturbance in the water. There was a prevalent stale odor of slow death in the air, a robust smell of rotting plants that hung over the place. The pleasantly cool, salty wind that had followed them from the western seashores had waned. Now it had nearly forsaken them. Its clean scent had been appreciated—but what little remained was a taunting reminder of that briny sea breeze. The ground rose steadily on the north and south edges of the valley. It fell slowly away as they advanced east into the dish of that vale. Clouds shrouded the nearly vertical mountains that surrounded the area.

As the party continued, they lost the westerly wind altogether. They slowly realized that the dale had its own weather and the air was cloaked in a light but persistent drizzle. The place was a lattice-work of decomposing vegetation. They passed the point to which the cutpurse had scouted alone earlier. He felt ill at ease. He was wet and his tunic stuck to him. His matted hair dripped as he nervously looked from side to side.

Something moved to the north on his left. He was pretty sure of it, even if he had only caught sight of it for a moment out of his side vision as he'd turned his head. He was more accustomed to peeking around street corners, peering through windows, and looking down dark alleys at night than scanning terrain. This swamp walk was beyond his ken. Whatever he'd seen, it had been large, slick, and just above the water line.

He couldn't make anything out clearly but then he saw it again. Some bulbous, humped figure slid through the murky ooze of the bog. He didn't mention it to the others as it was just a glimpse and gone quickly. He didn't want to seem jumpy. Instead, he watched as they slowly advanced along the main path through the fetid quagmire.

Their warriors were sinking a little in their heavy armor as they stepped. Footprints were visible in the damp aerth and water pooled in them after they'd passed. The boots of the group made soft, sucking noises as they trod. Metal clanged against metal and there were other sounds from the improperly secured, excessive equipment of his companions. *Poorly secured, noisy kit!* His mind reeled. It was another topic about which the others had chosen to ignore his advice. The robber was unused to making anything like their constant din as he worked. It heightened his high sense of vulnerability.

When he saw the lump of a creature a third time, he noticed it was moving away from the group to the north and east, at a decent clip. He stopped to watch. By the time his fellow travelers followed his gaze, the creature had effectively left the area. "Huh," said the scout, "that was big. Guess it lost interest in us." Any actual trained scout would have immediately emphasized a sighting of a large denizen of the morass. A real Way Maker would also have been concerned at the apathy he saw in the faces around him. Shouldn't their veteran have been worried that such a large creature was out there? The rogue chalked it up to the drab, life-sucking weariness of the place, as even he couldn't deny that it affected him a bit. He started moving forward once more, determined to raise the alarm if he saw anything like that again.

As they proceeded, the path was not the even and predictable thoroughfare he'd hoped they'd find. What had been an actual alluring ancient roadway at first now narrowed, broadened, constricted, and widened again. Portions of the roadway had broken and fallen away into the swamp. What remained of the path was tilted and slick with moss or rife with loose soil and overgrown vegetation. That made for dangerous footing and caused them to take far longer to traverse the marsh than the pad-foot had anticipated. He soon realized that he'd lost all sense of time. Eventually, they took a well-earned break. The criminal used the opportunity to try to tie down the warriors' equipment in the group so then it wouldn't slap against their armor.

The veteran shooed him away while drinking from a skin. The twins were less cordial as he reached towards them. "You better think again," said the one brother, "you might wish that you still had that hand later, thief!" They were eating, of course. The second grunted his rude and unneeded approval of the sentiment but with his mouth full, it was impossible to understand him. Shaking his head, the robber left them alone and squatted up front. He chewed on some jerked meat and kept to his own company as he was the only person he could trust.

He was lost in his thoughts when the shout came. "Hey, hey, hey, HEY!" It was one of the dimwit brothers who had fallen back onto his arse. He grabbed his leg and pointed at a single slimy, dark green tentacle wrapped around his ankle. His brother quickly pulled his sword from its sheath and neatly sliced through the wet, serpentine appendage with an unpleasant squelching sound. A good length of the limb was briefly visible as it retracted into the water north of the path with a small splash. It was the diameter of a man's wrist.

Its dimensions hinted at the size of whatever it was attached to, although there was no sight of it. The group drew down in response.

Their veteran pulled steel, their wizard prepared a casting, and the one twin worked to get the other up off his arse. Their priest began chanting. The scoundrel dropped his walking stick, nocked an arrow, and went to one knee. He carefully scanned the watery fen, looking for any hint of an attack to come. What he saw instead as he looked behind them were bubbles.

There were dozens of them, bunches! They were spread out, covering a wide area of the swamp, from north to south, but primarily to either side of the path. They floated through the air, moving slowly, lazily, towards the group. They ranged from a staff's length above the water to as low as its surface. They seemed to rise from dark patches above the waters that looked like vegetation. Most of the bubbles were about a foot across. They had an oily, unwholesome look. They didn't seem to be a threat so much as an unsettling oddity. What was disconcerting was the lack of a discernible breeze to carry them. As the bubbles came closer, they floated around the group.

The six exchanged confused, anxious looks. The veteran was the first to speak. "Loose an arrow," he said, "let's see what happens." The scout let fly a shaft. It pierced the nearest bubble wafting past them. It popped, and its moisture fell to the water below with a faint hiss. The group looked to the north and south as many bubbles floated by, then they exchanged glances, and as they did so, the wizard pointed and shouted.

"By the split tongue of Saet! What's all this?" As a group, they turned to see a strange and startling sight.

Frothing forth from several, then many spots, were masses of bubbles. They stuck together, forming a veritable wall, and ranged from only a few inches wide to several feet across. In the span of a few short heartbeats, the western horizon suddenly filled with bubbles and, all at once, they slowly began floating towards the party!

The situation seemed bizarre and they didn't know how to react. Was this some kind of attack? Were they in actual danger? The rogue looked to his peers to gauge their reactions as he was unsure of his own. He then looked east, as his instinct was to resume their march, accelerating towards their goal on the far side of the swamp. He was startled at what he saw there.

The bubbles that had already passed them had, somehow, come together to the east, effectively blocking their path! They simply hung there in the thick fetid air, unmoving now, as if awaiting the party. He was dumbfounded and then he realized that he alone had noticed this new and deeply troubling development. He gaped in both directions alternately, astonished by what was transpiring.

He turned back to the group and after a few more confusing moments, he found that his nerve had left him. "Well, this is pretty damned unsettling!" His remark was met with nods and various exclamations of agreement but no one looked his way. The rest of the troupe seemed fascinated by what was transpiring to the west. "We can't head back, eh? And I don't think we dare attempt to go forward." He had tried to sound steady, but the thief recognized the alarm in his own voice. That was when they turned and saw that their way further east was blocked.

"What in the Nine Frozen Hells? How did that happen?" Their wizard seemed a bit upset by recent events. "How did they merge? How are they just floating there?" Their thief looked at each of his comrades in turn as the mage spoke. Only one of them was calm—their priest. A quiet and methodical man, their Aerdos cleric had lifted both hands to the sky and was chanting in some strange tongue. The man's face, which he had painted black, gray, and white, suddenly seemed to be a frightening mask of death. It felt eerily appropriate to the moment.

The scoundrel felt trapped and fought the instinct to distance himself from his peers. "What in the world is this? Has anybody ever heard of such a thing?" As he spoke, he nocked a new arrow, feeling a strong need to do something, anything. All the while, a swarm of foamy bubbles was slowly approaching. They definitely wouldn't skirt the path and party this time.

"Why are you asking us? You're the damned Aerth Walker!" The wizard's response had an accusatory tone that hit him hard. There was a lengthy and uneasy silence as more nervous glances were exchanged. When the silence was broken, the cutpurse felt that the veteran warrior's voice had never been so welcome.

"They're just floating bubbles! Stone up!" His chastisement of the group seemed to steady their nerves, and the party settled into a defensive posture as the bubbles swarmed towards them. They now floated high and low, some as big as a man and small bubbles that you could catch in your palm. The western sky was full of bubbles! The spheres were strangely mesmerizing as they advanced on the group. The thief counted them as they approached but stopped after a bit. There were hundreds!

Several group members, still holding their weaponry, abruptly seemed to decide to give up their ground and began moving east. The twins and the wizard were headed away from the fen's approaching bubbles and towards those awaiting them to the east. Their holy man was busy chanting and unaware of his surroundings. The twins went to push past the priest, but the veteran had moved to stand between them. He was apparently concerned that a casting might be ruined if the twins bumped the cleric. The youngsters sought to go around. One of the brothers stepped a bit too far aside in his rush. He slipped on the edge of the path as it gave way beneath his outer foot and his outside right leg slid into the bog, boot deep.

There were loud voices and foul language as the fighter struggled to keep from flopping into the water altogether. The other twin emptied his hands, dropping his shield and thrusting his sword into the soft aerth of the path. He grabbed his twin's breastplate through his tunic and quickly switched to a grip under each of his twin's arms. He struggled to drag his sibling out of the marsh, as they were both substantially encumbered by their heavy armor and kit. The twin stuck in the muck awkwardly swung his sword as the first bubbles arrived. Their distinct pop coincided with shouting as the full and present danger to the group was revealed.

The sword blade had been coated with the wetness of the burst bubbles and it had begun to smoke and hiss. The first twin had to drop his dissolving sword into the marsh as they dragged him out by his shoulders from behind. He was free! The sight of that sword melting had an adverse effect on his brother, who bellowed in a sudden panic. "I don't understand! What is this? WHAT'S HAPPENING?"

Their mage had deduced the obvious answer and cried out, "ACID! THE BUBBLES ARE ACID!"

The commotion that ensued was a blur of confused emotions and wasted activity. The scout watched it unfold, at least for a short while. Their elder warrior had drawn two blades but the second twin slipped suddenly on the wet ground in his hysteria and slid off the path into the marsh. The soft mud threatened to suck him deep into the bog under the weight of his armor. He tried to twist and rotate onto his front to crawl out of the mire. His legs, however, were held by sucking mud, nearly up to his knees. He almost fell back horizontally. With a mighty effort, he managed to stand up in the muck, slowly sinking further as he struggled, all the while shouting for his comrades to help him. "I'M STUCK! HELP ME! GET ME OUT OF HERE!"

The first twin had watched in confusion as his sword began melting. He'd dropped it and started pulling his second blade when his brother flopped to the ground and slipped into the water. He quickly decided to grab his brother instead of drawing more steel, left his blades sheathed, and looked to the veteran to aid him. "Help! I need help here!"

The older warrior cursed loudly but moved immediately in response to the drama unfolding before him. He thrust his weapons into the soft aerth of the path and yelled, "Grab an arm!" He reached the trapped twin in two great strides and secured a steely grip with both hands on the man's right arm. The free twin had ahold of the sinking twin's left arm. Between them, from behind and above, the two began exerting considerable strength to drag him back out of the muck. They struggled mightily, as their cause was severely hindered by the same treacherous footing and encumbrance that had caused the incident. Their efforts ended as they both slipped and lost their balance, falling back. That ruined any chance they had to continue pulling with coordinated power.

The veteran had nearly fallen flat but recovered enough to take a knee. As the free twin began to slide towards the mire, he let go of his brother and ended up sitting down on the path, fortunate that his lost grip hadn't resulted in a worse outcome. As the fighters tried to regain their feet and reached towards their trapped compatriot, they gasped as one.

The first large batch of bubbles had arrived.

The twin had sunk further into the mud after their attempt to extract him from the marsh. He was now knee-deep in water and who knew what else. The muck poured into his boots. He had started trying to free his right lower leg from its high, tight leather prison when he saw small bubbles floating just above the water reach him. A cluster of them landed on the back of his gauntlets. As the bubbles burst, he gawked as the leather of his gloves was eaten away. He then gaped in terror as the flesh melted, and he screeched, "GAAAAAAAAAH!" He straightened up, holding his bloody hands before him. The party watched, transfixed in horror, as many bubbles, large and small, burst against his exposed face, armored body, and the soft leather of his leggings. An acrid stench rose from his hissing remains.

The robber reeled as he watched the man's face suddenly deconstruct into a palette of red and other hues of ooze, effectively boiling. Within seconds, he had transformed into a nightmarish visage, half solid, half liquid. There was a toxic fume produced by his ruination, as his nose, chin, and eyes, in turn, melted away. The sounds he made as he dissolved were positively inhuman and caused the thief to empty both hands and clap them over his ears. For the next several seconds, the rogue remained immobile, engrossed in the most frightening spectacle he had ever witnessed.

The reaction of the others was more dramatic. The veteran staggered away from the man as it became apparent it was over. He snatched his weapons out of the aerth and began to roar, as much in frustration as in fear. The man started whirling his weapons in a murderous arc in front of his body, splashing a wide area with acidic bubble juice. *Those swords aren't going to last long,* the scoundrel thought. The remaining twin had sprung back to his feet, then stood watching as his brother quickly turned from a howling man into a squishy mass of bloody meat that fizzled and sputtered long after the echo of his final wail had faded.

While that nightmare transpired, masses of bubbles continued towards the group. Each of them, in turn, had to determine how best to protect themselves from a horrible fate. The more frantic each of them became, the more bubbles seemed to rush towards them. There was something unnatural about it. The bubbles seemed to be moving at the will of some arcane force rather than floating naturally. They slowed down and they sped up. They changed direction. In the grips of a terrible wash of fear, the thief observed the mayhem and concluded that it was his very inaction that thus far had spared him a horrendous death. He thought to shout to his comrades, urge them to cease the folly of their useless reaction to hell's bubbles. Just as he gathered his breath, it occurred to him that shouting might draw the bubbles to him.

The rogue held his tongue and remained motionless, witnessing the harsh results of an initial lack of truthful disclosure amongst their group, resulting in faulty planning and preparation, leading to their party's unnecessary peril, made worse by the lack of coordinated response to the hellish danger. As things grew worse, his base personality took over. He whispered the same words over and over— "Not me!"

He watched as his companions fell prey to the acidic bubbles produced within the swamp. The twin, overwhelmed by watching his sibling perish so frightfully, had trouble doing more than simply weeping and blathering at the prospect of his own death. He tried to escape from the path in desperation, trapping himself waist-deep in the mire of the fetid marsh. Then he was swarmed upon by bubbles great and small. He liquefied at a pace that seemed almost merciful. The noises he made in his frightful demise were surreal.

The veteran bellowed in his fear and outrage, then shrieked at the horrid dissolution of his hands. He stood aghast and stared at the bloody stumps, aqueous flesh running down his arms. He helplessly swung those stumps in front of his face in an attempt to hold off the inevitable. The acid turned his outstretched arms into a fizzling mass of gore. The warrior looked directly at the scoundrel, eyes wide in horror, as he was fully denatured by a vast collection of bubbles that engulfed him in a caustic grasp like some ghoulish hand straight from hell.

Their mage didn't succumb quickly, casting several *Force Strike* spells, eliminating the larger acid belches as they approached him. He cast *Shield*, using it to take out a swath of bubbles. He couldn't, however, guard himself on all sides at once. Soon the spell caster was overwhelmed by a particularly aggressive patch of foam that seemed more arcanely influenced than those that came before. Though there was less hissing and popping than when their armored men dissolved, the wizard's robes eventually writhed in the final, ghastly spasm of his awful doom.

That left only the cutpurse and the shaeman of Aerdos, who had stopped his chanting at some point. The priest had remained effectively motionless throughout the entire duration of the calamity. It seemed that he had been deep in concentration as he performed some ritual. The robber, however, hadn't noticed any effects of a casting coming to the group's aid. The remaining pair locked eyes for several long heartbeats. The grim man spoke. His voice was quiet and barely audible, his face like a visage of death itself.

"The Lord of Death demands His due and will let only the most passionate of His servants survive this place." Although his words were hard, the thief saw empathy and even concern in the priest's dark eyes. "Are you willing to pledge the remainder of your mortal existence to Aerdos and grant Him the keeping of your immortal soul once you leave this world?" The rogue hesitated for only a moment before rushing to the feet of the cleric and falling to his knees before him, clutching at his dark gray robes.

"Yes! Yes! Anything! Just save me from this place!" He was pathetic and disgusted himself, whimpering like a child. His voice trembled in his fear as he continued. "What must I do? What must I say to enter the grace of the Dead God?" He wept as he finished, burying his face in the caster's woolen garb. The priest's response was steady, and he seemed pleased with the scoundrel's complete and utter supplication.

"Worry not ... I have successfully communed with the servants of Aerdos and they have instructed me on what we must do to appease Him. We shall exit this place together, in the grace and sight of ..."

That was as far as the servant of the Dead God got in his speech.

Just as the cutpurse began to regain his shattered self-control and sought to stand back up, there was a blur of motion. He was knocked back and prone. He looked around, trying to discern what had just happened, resting on his back and leaning on his left elbow. It was a surreal scene; the air about him was still populated by bubbles, large and small, floating aimlessly now. Scanning to his left, he saw a tremendous toad sitting in the muck on the surface of the swamp. Its head back, it slowly sank as it choked down the old man, whose limbs protruded still from its ghastly maw. Three sudden gulps and the cleric was gone, devoured whole by that awful amphibian.

Left alone, the robber found himself bereft of hope, possessed of nothing but panic, which washed over him in sickening waves. He gasped, drawing in huge breaths of the foul air, his eyes seeking any solution to his continued nightmare. All that remained of his group were the caustic heaps of still sizzling meat that ran and oozed into the fen. There was part of a boot here, a piece of cape there, a few swords sprouting awkwardly from the soft, wet aerth. The stench of the party's destruction still hung heavy in the air and, all around him, those accursed bubbles remained. He reeled in mute mental agony as he saw that tiny swamp denizens had already emerged from the fen and were sucking up the liquid remains of his companions! He bit the back of his gloved left hand, seeking to muffle screams that came unbidden.

He didn't know how long he'd remained there, cowering alone in the dank marsh. Eventually, he regained a small measure of calm and muttered under his breath. "No, not me! Not me, too! I pledge myself wholly unto You. Hear me, feared Lord of the Dead! Let me serve You still in this life. I can be useful to You. I will be useful!" He felt a glimmer of hope as his Oath of Faith filled the hollow void of the noiseless swamp, even spoken at such a low volume. "Hear me, Aerdos! I will seek Your servants and pledge my life to them! Just allow me safe passage back to town, any town! I will be useful to Your servants. I will be faithful to You from this day forth. So do I swear, upon my very soul!"

There was nearly no sound at all. There was no further massing of acidic bubbles as, eventually, the airborne doom sank to the level of the foul marsh and burst upon its slimy surface. Was that mere luck or the result of his continued quiet? Perhaps it was a sign of the favor of the Dead God? The rogue slowly found the courage to return to his feet. He squatted low, surveying the fen. He was genuinely miserable, saturated by the ever-present mist, as well as his sweat, drool, and urine. He saw no sign of imminent threat and cautiously began to creep back the way they had come. The lone adventurer snuck past the horrifying remains of his companions, going so far as to break a personal rule by not rifling through what was left of their possessions.

It was getting to be late in the afternoon by the time he reached the edge of that accursed fen, and he took stock of his situation. He was alone but still possessed much of his weaponry, most crucially his bow, as well as his stash of provisions. He was unharmed, knew his path, and still had a dozen arrows. His mental state, however, was still fragile. He had felt a powerful sense of self-loathing after he'd broken down when facing the sheer terror of the fate that had befallen his group. He was able to put it out of his mind and continue, if barely. After all, no witness of his behavior had survived. He set the thoughts aside, relegating them to the dark and remote corner of his mind where he packed away memories of the most wretched things he had done in his life.

He had to make his way back to Bentua, which was no easy task for a man alone and in the wild wilderness. Any true Way Maker would have been secure and in his element. The city thief took a few moments to attempt to summon forth the same false bravado that had earned him this job. His usually reliable ego, however, failed him. It seemed he couldn't fool himself, no matter how much a boost of confidence may have helped him in that challenging moment. In the end, the cutpurse could not deny it—he was in real trouble.

He determined that the best route was to make his way west to the coast. While approaching the area, he followed the tracks their group had left beside the river in the long grass. He reached the previous night's campsite, which was now just a heap of ashes in a used fire ring. A skilled tracker, which he was not, would have noted concerning signs of animals around the camp. As no fire fuel was left there, he decided that the fire pit afforded him no security that would deter an encounter. His fate depended on the favor he had earned with Rhal over the years or perhaps even on intercession from the Dead God, whose name he had pleadingly invoked earlier. He deemed that his chances of surviving any encounter alone were low if a fight did come.

He jogged along, determined to get as far as he could while the light lasted. He was concerned about his lack of skill in piloting a boat but he pushed the concern aside. He'd have to do his best when he faced that task. Meanwhile, he chose to push on without rest, counting on the ample light of a moon nearly in full phase. He was reasonably confident in his ability to negotiate the wild in Sealon's light but would have to stay fully alert.

It went pretty well for an hour or more—until the howling began. At first, it seemed to be only a single wolf, which was threatening enough. In the next few minutes, as its calls were answered, it became clear that he was being cornered by a pack of perhaps the most commonly encountered predators on Maera. He was surrounded quickly. It didn't take long for him to decide what to do.

The wayfarer took out his bow and backed himself up to the river. Then he thrust his remaining arrows into the aerth around him for quick and easy access and squatted, preparing to build a fire. He had a strike flint and a bit of dried moss for a starter. The problem was he had no real fuel. He carried a tied bundle of twigs and small branches but nothing that would last long. The traveler hadn't seen any place to make a better defense as he had jogged from the swamplands, so the spot he held would have to do. Using the river wasn't an option—he couldn't swim. The dark gathered in the distance as he prepared to fight off the pack, which was surely inching closer on three sides concealed in the long grass. If only he'd thought to cache firewood and other supplies in defensible spots along their route just in case they had to retreat to the coast after some unforeseen and unfortunate misadventure.

Possessed of admirable cunning, the lead wolf held its pack back and awaited the night. Humans were such easy prey when alone and deprived of their advantages. A professional Aerth Walker might have possessed a charm of Aethair, Goddess of the Hunt, that the wolves may have honored, for these were not evil creatures. After all, the pack wasn't starving, having had good luck in recent weeks during their hunts. An easy meal, however, was something they would not pass up without good reason. The lead wolf waited until the night cloaked the fangs of its killers, then sent them in all at once.

It wasn't really a fight and was over quickly without wolf blood being spilled. A final analysis of the venture was harsh. The whole party had been killed in various and avoidable ways. It was the worst kind of failure, one with no survivors, who might at least share a cautionary tale with others—a helpful warning that might prevent such incompetence from being repeated.

A few days later, the lingering smell of blood on the grass drew the attention of a recently fledged wyvern. It glided, heading east over the river on its way back to its family's nest atop the highest peak in the area. The sun was rising and its crepuscular hunt had failed to fill its belly. It flew down and looped around. Once confident that there was no danger present, it swept to the aerth, landing where there was an area as wide as its wingspan, marked with a dark red stain. It knew it was in the range of a pack of plains runners and smelled their markings all around. The pack had returned twice daily to the scene while running their range. It sniffed about tentatively, finding a number of items but nothing much to eat. The beast didn't recognize the scent on the equipment but came upon it again, more concentrated, when it located a fresh pile of scat. The feces were cord-like, with remnants of bones in them. The young wyvern choked down the scat and flew away, unaware he had just had his first whiff and taste of man.

*Want to experience more of Maera? Visit **www.maeraworld.com***

THE TACTICAL USE OF FORCE
IN STRATEGIC LEGEND CREATION

On Heathmoor's twelfth day, in the Japari calendar year 2437, an urgent session of the Council of Paellar convened in the Kingdom of Rumorga. Those present were Armon Sarason, King of Rumorga; Graeth-N'throk Shaan, Chancellor of the Realm; Gruntaal of Gaerd, Elemental Master of the Aerth; and Fellimaar of Paellar, Elemental Master of Fire. The meeting began with an address from the monarch.

"I have summoned the council to gather this day, for we face imminent invasion. A naval force of some two-hundred and fifty ships is approaching from the north, their point of origin the continent of Provos. I have had direct contact with the Wondrous Maiden thrice daily over the past week regarding this fleet. Her dragons have used all due stealth while following the dark armada across the Great Northern Sea. The fleet carries a force of the old foe, Aeres, to our shores. I am told that this force is primarily comprised of beastmen, judging by the odor on the wind. These forces have been provided with transport and are supported by the daemon-lord Brunthym and his allies, who are devotees of Loekii."

The king paused after each sentence, allowing time for his council members to digest the information. For all their wisdom, the elemental lords still struggled with the dwaerven language at times. The situation under consideration would be acted upon at the request of the realm. But it would be officially mitigated under the auspices of the council and the king was obligated to use the realm's language. The nation's first bard and Court Historian would record the matter thus, for posterity.

"Celeste offered us the service of her dragons, as they have no love for this foe. She also suggested that perhaps this was an opportunity which we could turn to our distinct advantage." Again, Sarason paused for effect.

"Any and all defense of our shores, as you well know, has always been gladly entrusted to our Chancellor, Graeth-N'throk Shaan." He nodded his head in respect of his audience and took two steps back, allowing the excellent land dragon to come forth in a fluid motion that belied his tremendous power and size.

The Chancellor of Rumorga was also the Grand High Priest of Aarn, God of Fire, on all Maera. Graeth-N'throk Shaan was not only a gigantic, fire-breathing, armor-plated land dragon but also a maena-wielding master of whirling death who was an absolute nightmare to any foe of the realm. He was a ten-thousand-year-old internationally accomplished diplomat who spoke many languages and had sources of geopolitical intelligence across Maera. As he took a step forward, the sound of his stone-hard claws on the polished floor of the council chamber would have been genuinely frightening to virtually any creatures other than the beings that were present.

Gruntaal was, unhappily, the appointed Battle Lord of the Aerth Elementals that resided primarily in the volcanic soil and rock of the Isle of Rumorga. Many of his kind dwelt there, as an elemental affinity existed between the aerth and the fire residing deep within it. Gruntaal enjoyed the warmth of Paellar found in the volcano; it made the transition of his physical form easier, quicker, and almost pleasurable. He stood in the service of Gaerd in the meeting of the Council of Paellar simply because it was his turn to represent his kind in an official capacity at this time. If Gruntaal was to be truthful, he decidedly resented having the responsibility at all, and during a scenario such as this, that duty weighed heavily. He would go along in his role, supporting the plan to defend the isle, although it was a crude display of power he did not condone. However, the aerth was solid, and the aerth was steadfast. The aerth could be counted on, and so could Gruntaal.

Fellimaar was the long-standing Battle Lord of the Fire Elementals of Paellar on the Isle of Rumorga and oversaw the volcanic resources of this region. The mountain was a tremendous stronghold of his kind and he served in his role with great pride, befitting his status. Few Lords of the Eternal Flame held more sway on Maera, and he was proud that Graeth-N'throk Shaan had heeded his advice and seemingly taken it to heart. Fellimaar stood eagerly in anticipation of finally having an opportunity to impress upon all mortals just what kind of power his kind wielded and that they were ready to use it.

Graeth-N'throk Shaan communicated loudly and clearly. He did not form words as he lacked the physical means to do so. He instead projected his thoughts. Each listener's mind imagined his voice in a way their consciousness could perceive and accept. "After analysis of the threat, I have classified it as a scout in force. I estimate that perhaps as many as fifty thousand troops are ready to be landed by the fleet. They have no aerial support and can only hope to land on the beaches west of the mountain, as the reefs along our northwestern shores prohibit landing there." Each council member heard the Chancellor in their own language, which made him easy to understand. His input was strategic and was not recorded.

He continued, "I must agree with Lady Celeste; this is a rare opportunity. Handled properly, we can produce a stunning, utterly devastating result that will provide more than victory. It can turn into a legend, a brutal cautionary tale, which may prove invaluable in the millennia to come." He paused, shifting the angle of his massive body so then he directly faced the elemental lords.

"I believe that we are best served by annihilating this enemy and in the most demonstrative way possible, using the power of aerth and fire at our command." He paused dramatically, allowing Gruntaal and Fellimaar to react. Both did so emphatically. First, the Fire Lord flared brightly. So enticed, the aerth elemental pounded his massive fist on the floor. Each spoke oaths of power and aggression in their god's name. All turned to King Sarason, who had not reacted in any way.

"All right, then," Sarason decreed in his famously dulcet voice. "It is said, and so shall be done. We, the Council of Paellar, agree. The Chancellor, no doubt, has a well-considered plan in mind that he would like to share with us. I feel it shall fall upon enthusiastic ears." Sarason was a Daellus devotee but believing in peace does not preclude the defense of the realm. The dwaerven king knew well that his indomitable Chancellor was perfectly suited to implement such a plan.

Blood-red sails on the four masts of each ship dominated the horizon. They had once formed an equidistant lattice on the open seas but now they swarmed for a beach landing. Each ship's hull and three decks were a dull black, slathered in a fire-resistant stain made with the blood of the Kaetarrae. They formed a daunting armada and were now in sight of their target, the black volcanic beaches of the Isle of Rumorga in the Bay of Asprid. The ships had been constructed through much sacrifice and expense, using rhoanswood for extraordinary strength. The ships were designed to hold large amounts of cargo and deliver it safely over great distances of open ocean in a beach landing. Under a highly demanding schedule, the vessels performed brilliantly.

The fleet had been comprised of two-hundred and eighty ships but at last count, that number now stood at two-hundred and fifty-eight. Fewer than one in ten lost was acceptable as they crossed the open ocean. This result was better than any outcome she could ever have desired. Admiral Caena Kiers of the Privateer Fleet of the Theocracy of Saestis felt confident that she had fulfilled her duties more than adequately. She thanked Loekii under her breath.

"Praise our Mistress, may She ever reign. Honor Her might, may it be sustained. Always give praise when you say Her name. Her worship shall ever be our gain."

With her prayer completed, Kiers kissed her sapphire ring and whispered, "See me!" As the shore rushed to meet them, the Admiral felt it was time for Commander Adren Duennar of Aeres to take charge. Her work was nearly done.

The assailants expected that the dwaerven defenders of the Isle of Rumorga would be well-prepared for their landing. The intelligence-gathering capability of this foe was well known. The Commander here, Lord Duennar, was a heavily honored Blood Reaver in the Grand and Ancient Order of the Supplicants of Ven-Dahr. The Order was a highly active branch of the Fury of Aeres on the continent of Provos, and Lord Duennar was a Hero of the Order. He was having difficulty containing his excitement. "Too damned much poxy," he muttered under his breath.

His Blood Reaver campaign helm as Commander of the invasion force depicted the twisted face of a blood daemon of Aeres. When combined with the black and red lacquered field armor he had donned for the landing, Lord Adren Duennar looked the part. He gazed left at the Admiral, standing handsomely in the garb of her command. Once again, he felt an unpleasant but undeniable envy of her.

She wore an ornate blackened steel chest plate with matching greaves and sleeves. Her leather under armor was soft, flexible, and comfortable and her purple cape caught the wind. Kiers' hair was shorn right to her skull on the sides of her head but formed a wave atop it that crested forward above her forehead. Her hair was so black that it looked almost blue in the daylight. She wore a sapphire piece of folded cloth wrapped around her forehead, keeping any sweat away from her eyes. Her obsidian skin, meant for the night, seemed almost darker in the daylight. Her delicate features somehow gave her angular face an intense, even harsh look. She had a nasty blade scar that started above her ruined right eye and ran to beneath the cheekbone. A blue eye patch denied the Commander a look at the worst of that wound.

The Admiral possessed an iron will. She was utterly calm and highly comfortable in her skin and in her command. Kiers, as she preferred to be called, was admired and feared by her sailors. She was harsh and cruel, which the crew respected, and dealt decisive punishment to any who failed her. In short, she was a true representative of her nation.

Today was the culmination of the lifelong pursuit of a dream. Finally, Lord Duennar was right where he wanted to be after a career dedicated to the Order. He was the tip of the mighty spear of Aeres! He surveyed the dwaerven island as they approached with the wind

behind them. It was peculiar that the steam clouds constantly emanating from the volcano billowed west over the coastline in direct
defiance of the steady breeze. "No doubt the work of that wretched
king of theirs," he said to no one in particular. "No matter, we're
already here!"

The fleet provided for his task had traveled over a thousand
miles in less than ten days across the open ocean with little incident.
To be sure, the blessings of Parsaedos, negotiated on their behalf
through Aerdos, had allowed much of that success. But the contin-
ual monitoring of the enthralled beastmen aboard the ships had been
crucial and was very impressive. Each hold contained two-hundred hate-bred beastmen of Aeres who could barely tolerate being
whipped onto the boats. Without the Supplicants to cast *Enthrall*,
the troops would have ripped each other into bloody bits in minutes.
But here they were, after nearly ten days and with no food, having
been in full thrall the entire time. All of this was utterly amazing to
Lord Duennar, who feared the beastmen terribly. He knew what the
creature's capabilities were. The fleet would beach its every ship
before opening their under-decks. The Commander meant to be well
out of the way as the beastmen's enthrallment was ended.

This fleet was obviously too small and had too little support to
make much of a dent in the dwaerven defenses. His orders were simple; they were to take and hold the beaches in the shadow of Mount
Altabor. They would hold them long enough for the maena-wielding
Supplicants of the Order to open a Dread Portal to Provos, through
which the mighty daemon Brunthym's powerful armies were prepared to pour.

The concern had been getting across the ocean and arriving
with the fleet fully intact. With that in mind, this mission was already
a success, to a large degree. His beastmen would undoubtedly be

enough to hold these beaches for the few minutes the shaemen required to complete their task. Dwaerves were not known for quick action! Duennar would then be honored to turn the beachhead over to a greater daemon lord of Aeres! That spectacular moment would be the climax of a life devoted to serving his God. Lord Duennar could then go and seek a good death in battle if that was indeed to be his fate, as he had always prayed it would be.

Graeth-N'throk Shaan found Sarason on the balcony that the King favored, overlooking the Cauldron of Aarn at the heart of the mountain. After over four-hundred years, the dwaerf had grown accustomed to the heat that kept him from this ledge when he had first joined the great dragon so long ago beneath the ancient Steaming Mountain.

"It is all arranged then, Graeth?" asked the King.

"Indeed. It will be terrible to behold, my friend, but very quick. A lesson remembered for some time, I would imagine," replied the dragon lord.

"Yes, already I can see it ... terrible, indeed," mourned Armon. "I will be in the Chapel of Light if you need me. Carry on, my old friend."

The dragon walked away, eager to be done with it all. Graeth-N'throk Shaan had endured much in his one-hundred centuries. He had slain innumerable enemies in the name of God and homeland, war pacts and other obligations, self-defense, and glorious aggression. Through it all, he regretted little, being the product of a warlike folk. He had little taste for slaughter without at least bloodying his claws.

Armon Sarason was an avid Daellus worshipper and advocate of peace. The Chancellor deeply respected Sarason's reluctance to spill blood and did whatever was needed while fulfilling his role as Protector of the Realm. One might expect some measure of conflict in a relationship between two who were so distinctly different. From their first meeting centuries ago, the dragon had just understood, as he had quickly sensed the vibrant aura of the young dwaerven prince. As he grew to know him, he'd realized how much help the dwaerf could be when next the Aeglain chose to test the resolve of the mortals of Maera. Fallen Gaelthar might still be with them had the alliance been closer and worked together more readily at Gaedennon. Ah, such thoughts were maddening! But he had sworn it—a lack of understanding and cooperation would never again be their downfall.

Graeth, as only Sarason called him, climbed to the mountain's crest. He took his time, for he had some to spare, risking no misfortune along the way. He could have coordinated things from elsewhere but the dragon wanted to see it all as clearly as possible. He crested the summit, found his chosen plateau, and looked back down into the extraordinary yawning maw of the mountain.

The massive volcano of Mount Shahir, or Altabor as the dwaerves called it, was entirely under the control of the two elemental forces of aerth and fire. Thus, it fell to Lord Gruntaal of Gaerd and Lord Fellimaar of Paellar to manipulate the mountain. Their cooperation forged the Council of Paellar and their continued benevolence allowed Graeth and the Fraeraam nation to share the Isle of Rumorga with their dwaerven allies. As the leader of that nation, he stood alone in the massive plume of steam from the mountain, eagerly coordinating the realm's defense. Such was the terrible reality that the enemy invaders faced on that ebony beach. There was no measure of exaggeration in saying that such a proposition was not only daunting but, arguably, suicidal.

Lord Duennar could see the beach before them. They were just beyond the break of the surf and beneath the great steam cloud of the mountain. The soft black sand was smooth and unobstructed for hundreds of paces to the north and south. It was just fifty to a hundred paces on the black sand to the rocky base of the hills beneath the mountain. There was no sign of any life, let alone defenses. The island looked, to any casual observer, to be uninhabited.

"Let it begin!" hissed the High Master of the Ven-Dahr. His Supplicants were becoming impatient. They desperately wanted to begin their ritual casting as it would be a great accomplishment they had built up to their entire lives. Lord Duennar understood but his considerable experience warned him that something here was very wrong. He knew in his warrior's heart that some awful fate was waiting for them on that exotic-looking black beach. However, there was nothing to be done. Their force was not subtle in composition.

The armada finished riding the waves into the shoreline in the final glorious moments of their long and daring journey. Large iron-wood posts, shaped like fangs, had been placed on either side of the bow and slid into heavily reinforced iron sleeves. The posts were set forward to strike the beach first, sparing the hull a portion of the impact of the collision. Among the first to reach the sands of Rumorga, the fleet's flagship landed dead center on the beach. More than a hundred ships rested on either side of it. Lord Duennar had already climbed to the top deck of the flagship. He gave the order and the Prime Supplicant thrice sounded the Horn of Fury! Upon that signal, his shaemen, three assigned to each ship, threw open the doors and hatches to the hold. Then they broke their spell, releasing the beastmen from their thrall!

It was initially subdued with a few strange grunts and chittering sounds emanating from below the decks. Then a great noise emerged—the sound of two hundred confused, starved, maniacal beasts twitching back to life and sounding their fury! The noise threatened to break him and several salty sailors in view cried out, clapping their hands over their ears as the howling reached an awful, nearly deafening crescendo. The fetid hosts of the Blood God Aeres had awoken!

The Prime Supplicant stepped up next to Duennar, again blowing his massive Horn of Fury. Next, he bellowed, his voice impossibly loud, amplified by his maena. "COME FORTH, FOUL THINGS OF FURY! COME FORTH, ACCURSED BEASTS OF WAR! SEEK OUR FOE … REND THEM TO BITS … TODAY YOU TASTE DWAERF!" Lord Duennar felt his hot blood coursing. His left eye twitched spasmodically.

The noise from below took on a new and truly frantic tone. Then, from every hold access, poured the ravenous beasts of the Blood God! They were horrible to behold as they surged forward, a veritable wave of foulness. This ship carried half-rams, their thick horns curled back and spiraled against their great skulls. They had the head and legs of a ram; their torso and arms seemed human and were thick with muscle. The fell creatures carried war spears. Their horizontal yellow eyes bulged wildly in their massive skulls, tongues wagging, teeth bared. The foul things that lived on their hides had thrived for ten days while their hosts were enthralled. The parasites had produced rancid excrement that was caked on the beastmen's fur, and it created a fetid reek beyond description. The very sight of them was truly horrid. They rushed forth, leaping over the ship's sides into waist-deep waters and onto the sand past the ship's bow. The stench from their flesh crawled into Duennar's skull, threatening to bring forth the bile he had already tasted in his mouth. But he was a seasoned veteran of many campaigns and would not succumb to his disgust. Instead, he clenched his teeth tightly while all around him, even seasoned sailors retched.

In a few minutes, the ships had emptied, spewing their foul cargo ashore. The troops swept up the beach in their thousands, flooding the sands with their swelling numbers. Badger beasts, half-boars, dog beasts, and half-lizards spewed forth in huge numbers until the sands were thick with them. The Supplicants of Ven-Dahr, led by their Primus, issued forth behind the beast-men. Commander Duennar joined them, battle helm donned. Then—absolutely nothing happened. They were an army without an enemy to fight. Realizing what great jeopardy that put them in, Lord Duennar barked orders to the Primus.

"Order them forward, up the hillsides, towards the mountain!" he shouted. The Primus seemed to understand the situation and as his Supplicants began to prepare for their casting, he again blew the Horn of Fury. Duennar scanned the terrain for any sign of the enemy but saw nothing to indicate any defenses.

"TO THE HILLS! SEEK THEM OUT! FIND THEM! ROOT THE DWAERVES OUT OF THEIR HOLES!" the Primus shouted. While he had seen this kind of maena on battlefields before, Duennar had no idea how each type of beastmen heard the voice of the Primus in their own language but it was apparent they did. Roughly half of the Supplicants had left their ships and massed in front of the flag-ship. The spell casters formed a circle, perhaps sixty feet across, halfway up the beach. The rest stayed behind the beastmen, who had begun to clamor up the rocky foothills. It was then that they heard the first rumble.

"Quickly, begin the casting!" Duennar commanded. He removed his campaign helm, terribly worried and confused by what he thought he had heard. His concern was mirrored in the unprotected face of the Prime Supplicant, who was looking directly at him. "Do it! Do it now!" Duennar shouted.

The Primus nodded and the ritual began. The establishment of a Dread Portal is an intricate, arduous task. The casting can be lengthy, depending on the worship. For the Grand and Ancient Order of the Supplicants of Ven-Dahr, this was a particularly challenging mastery of maena. Still, the intensity of their preparation matched the task. Thirteen members of the order had been specially prepared for this day, this assault, this very moment. The small group separated themselves from their brethren's throng, stepping into their peers' circle.

The first Supplicant stepped forth, removing his blood-red robes. He turned and faced the sea, naked before his deity. His head was shaved, his torso covered with the scars of many sessions of penance and flagellation, most self-inflicted. He had been emasculated, detaching him from the pleasures of the flesh. The Primus raised a unique staff for all to see as he shouted to the rabid members of his order.

"LET US BEGIN THE SUMMONING WITH OUR BROTHER'S SACRIFICE!" The Supplicants responded in one voice.

"OUR BLOOD SERVES THE BLOOD GOD! IN AERES' NAME, LET THAT BLOOD BE SPILT!"

The Staff of Summoning had been created for this casting with precision great and grim. It was made of rhoanswood and had been blessed and stained with the Blood of the Innocent. One end bore the classic spear blade of Aeres, while the other was festooned with long red feathers from the infamous blood vultures of the Saeshaam Desert. The unrobed disciple before him began reciting his Litany of the Blood God, asking his deity to recognize his faith. Soon the Supplicant had finished his prayer and four of his trusted brethren stepped forth, grasping him tightly by his wrists and ankles.

The Primus stepped forth and in one sweep of the spear end of his staff, he expertly split open the abdomen of his disciple. Intestines spilled forth onto the black sand as the circle of Supplicants began chanting.

"BRUNTHYM ... LET HIM COME! BRUNTHYM ... LET HIM COME!"

The distinct smell of blood and viscera had already filled the air with their horrid fume. The Primus rotated his cruel staff, skillfully lifting the intestines while simultaneously wrapping them around the spear. He slowly turned the living guts, foot after reeking foot, onto the ceremonial staff. Slippery and glistening, the intestines slithered forth from the Supplicant, whose visage evoked a beast being slaughtered as he suffered through the ritual. Reciting the Incantation of Summoning, the Primus of Ven-Dahr stepped several paces back towards the surf, pulling out more innards as he went. He then swept his spear's tip in a large sweeping circular motion, the entrails dangling all the while.

"BRUNTHYM ... LET HIM COME! BRUNTHYM ... LET HIM COME!"

The Blood Chant of the Supplicants continued while their leader did his work. The Primus had completed the first step of the casting. The disemboweled disciple's body was dragged to the circle's edge on his back. His feet faced the circle. The Primus removed the gore from his staff. The second sacrificial acolyte came forth and he willingly removed his robes. Then came a great rumbling as the very aerth beneath their feet shook and the black sand danced.

The rumbling went on for ten heartbeats or more. All on the beach and the foothills above were left shaken and frightened. Stepping up onto the bow of the fleet's flagship, Admiral Caena Kiers watched as the army of beastmen faltered in the grip of panic. She didn't hesitate for a moment.

"REMOVE THE LANDING POSTS! SPREAD THE WORD! GET US OFF THIS BEACH!" she cried. Her crew leaped to action. They grabbed their pivot sweeps, a dozen men to each, and started pushing the high end of the landing spikes forward, helping to slowly extract the bows of the fleet's ships from the beach.

Of course, it was too late—the chaos had begun! The primordial threat of the quaking aerth sent the creatures of Aeres into a new kind of frenzy. The beast-men voiced their uncertainty openly, raising in unison their foul grunting, heinous chittering, and unnerving barking voices to the sky. Their morale broken, the beastmen had already stopped seeking their foes and had instead begun to scramble back down the hillsides, back towards the sea, attempting to return to the ships. Another such disturbance would rout the force altogether!

The Prime Supplicant had no choice. The beastmen would rip them to shreds in their maddened fear and confusion. He stopped the summoning, ruining the maena, and sought his Horn of Fury. But it was at that very moment that the defensive plans of the Council of Paellar began to unfold in earnest.

Commander Duennar foresaw a horrible fate as it began to rush towards him. The Primus fretted over his decision. His shae-men, still amidst the troops, had already lost control of their beast-men. The Commander's concern about using the creatures of chaos had come to full fruition—they were about to be ripped apart by their own army! Duennar had begun backing up as these thoughts raced through his mind. He was not panicked, for he had seen and done too much for that. But he dropped his campaign helm and slowly backed across the summoning circle as the next sign of their doom sounded.

From his rocky perch above, on the plateau of the volcano's rim, Graeth-N'throk Shaan had been watching the invaders' advance. He had kept count of the timing of his counterattack in the back of his mind the whole while. It was utter perfection. Just as the half-rams, the enemy's best climbers, had leaped up to the halfway point of the hills, the percussion quake hit. The dragon lord reflexively bared his fangs as he watched the panic set in below. As the foe began to retreat, he flexed his chest and throat and let loose his most vigorous battle roar. It blasted from him for a full three to four seconds. It rolled to the beach below from atop the mountain, echoing his fury.

An unbelievable roar crashed upon them from on high, like nothing most had heard before. The monstrosities of Aeres were undoubtedly unprepared for it. Commander Adren Duennar knew what unthinkable nightmare had caused him and every other creature there to wince, clapping their hands over their ears and ducking as if expecting an actual physical blow from above. The mighty sound had been amplified considerably by the hot, wet air that flowed to the sea from the mountainside.

"Dragon rage," he muttered. "There's nothing else like it." Many thousands of eyes desperately searched the mountaintop. There they settled upon a giant armored land dragon, his broad skull crest in full view, silvered scales offset by his fiery red chest. Seconds later, the boom of that roar still echoed across the rocks and up and down the beach. Then came the response to that terrible roar.

Struggling with her sailors to back their ship off the shoreline, Admiral Kiers had been struck full-on by Graeth-N'throk Shaan's mighty roar. It caught her mid-task, unaware. It was impossibly loud, knocking her to the deck. She gazed at the mountain, scanning for the source of that thunderous boom, and saw at the top what could only be a legendary Rumorgan Fire Lizard!

"Mistress, spare me! What a monster!" she proclaimed aloud, kissing her ring reflexively. "What next?" All too soon, she had her answer. The aerth shook again, a low rumble now, followed by the sound of crushed stone. The noise was coming from the mountainside and she did not have to look for long to find the cause. She watched in disbelief, herself and her crew all still and silent now, as large holes began to be punched out of the cliffs above the hills. From each hole, appearing up and down the entire beachfront, there came creatures that were things of myth.

Seemingly made of rock and roughly the shape of a hugely thick-bodied giant, the creatures had to be the aerth elementals from the tales of her childhood. Slow-moving but immensely strong, the monstrous beasts climbed out of what seemed to be cave openings and lifted themselves above those caves. As the invaders watched, enthralled by the sight of walking, and climbing stone, the creatures phased into the cliff face, one by one disappearing entirely.

Within the inferno that was the main lava chamber of Mount Shahir, Lord Fellimaar of Paellar, Elemental Master of Fire, had gathered his fellow Fire Lords. He led them in a frenzied dance to honor their God Paellar and superheat the vast reservoir of molten aerth inside the mountain. He wanted the magma as liquid and hot as possible for the day's lesson. Gruntaal and his kin should have their task completed at any moment. He was just awaiting Graeth-N'throk Shaan's ... Ah! There it was! The signal!

With something akin to glee, Lord Fellimaar commanded his brethren to attack. He took the route that led to the center of the beachhead so then he might strike at the heart of the invading force. He swam in the magma, a hot flare point in the matrix of the fluid stone. It was a rare and exhilarating experience riding the slag to the end of the tube and he took mere minutes to reach the cliff face.

Caena Kiers had secured an enormous payday for herself on this trip. She had done a great many dangerous things in her thirty years of life on Maera, many of them professionally. In short, the draevar was seemingly agreeable to even reckless risks if enough coin hung in the balance. However, as stakes went, this endeavor had suddenly entered the realm of the ridiculous. If land dragons and even aerth elementals were allied with the dwaerves, what else were they about to encounter? After the immense stone beings had melded into the cliff and vanished, there was a pause of several minutes in the action.

The Admiral and her crew returned to the task at hand, removing the ship from the beach. Their work slowed as they were stunned by what they had witnessed and heard. They were still making progress when the beastmen, most of whom were retreating towards the beach, suddenly went wild. The creatures wailed pitifully, making sounds that she had never heard before. It was more than unsettling, as if they were reacting to something only they could sense.

It started at the far ends of the beach. One at a time, and with a sudden great whooshing noise, the caves revealed themselves to be lava tubes, as liquid aerth now flowed from them! It issued with such force that it exited the tubes horizontally and spewed directly onto the beastmen as they fled in abject terror. Dozens of lava tubes flooded the hills with molten death that destroyed everything in its path!

Kiers backed away but in all her horror, she watched the fantastic spectacle unfold. First, the hills were engulfed and then it became clear that it would not stop. Now she stood transfixed in disbelief, the aerth fire spreading down the beach, engulfing the troops as they fled in their thousands. Then she saw them within the lava flows! Swimming within the solid wall of aerth fire, effectively riding atop it, there seemed to be human-like shapes—shapes themselves made of elemental flame, mixed in with the flood of lava!

Commander Adren Duennar spent his last mortal moments trying to flee while being overrun by his own troops. He was half right about his death. It would indeed occur this day on the black sand beaches of Rumorga. He just never imagined that he would become part of that beach. The beastmen he so feared swarmed all around him, utterly panicked, ignoring him completely. The wave of lava was upon them so quickly that, upon attempting to get to the flagship, he did not even reach the water. He was not killed so much as utterly destroyed. At least there was someone who remembered him to this day.

Lord Fellimaar was riding the center of the wave of lava that flowed inexorably toward the flagship. He was in his element, literally, and having a glorious time of it. As he crested the front of the wave he rode and maximized his flare. He saw before him a human that seemed differently dressed than any other. Dressed in elaborate plates of red and black, the human seemed to him to be a commander. Fellimaar rushed excitedly toward the man from behind.

As hot as lava can get, a fire elemental's maximum flare is often more searing. In the final few moments of his mortal existence, Adren Duennar was embraced by Maera's Elemental Master of Fire. He died very suddenly with a look of both crazed fear and tremendous surprise on his face. As his body was vaporized, his brain boiled in his skull so quickly and violently that his head quite literally exploded. Lord Fellimaar found it both surprising and uniquely entertaining, and it was, to the day, one of his favorite tales to relate to his comrades whenever war stories were told.

Caena Kiers was the only one amongst her shipmates who seemed to understand that death was indeed upon them. It was already too late to save her ships or her sailors. When that realization came over her, she dismissed further concern about it. After that, she had not thought beyond her own self-preservation. Her nimble mind raced. Many leaders may have chosen to go out with their men. Caena Kiers, however, was not ready to die, not yet. She was in the good graces of Loekii to be sure, if such things mattered. A death such as this, though? That might consign her aether to Aeres, God of Blood and War. It was also possible that Aerdos, the God of Death, would glean her soul should she perish thus. By the nine frozen hells! The dwaerven gods, or even Aarn, might harvest her energy should she die in such a misadventure. That would not do— no, not at all. Who amongst the living knew what happened when they died? Did the gods keep their flowery promises to their mortal worshippers? Why, in truth, would they? All maerans lived and died utterly at the mercy of the Aeglain! Caena Kiers felt no need to find out. She never had before and certainly felt no such compunction on that day! No—she must live!

The mantra of the Loekii worshipper was, at best, seen as curious by those outside the faith. Caena was no fanatic but a purist. Family, certainly, was essential as long as the dynamic was healthy. Her nation and duty were vital, at least while they served her equally in return. Her god? She, above all others, knew Caena's heart, surely. Self, it was her own self that came first. She did not deny that simple truth. That philosophy had kept her alive through many things, strange and terrible. It was who she was, at her deepest core—a survivor. Still, as doom rushed toward her, she devised a scheme to cheat death. Could it even be done? Would it work? She turned and ran, as she had no choice but to act. She sprinted up the decks from the bow towards the stern. All the while, her mind desperately searched for a better solution. Her cabin lay before her. There was no place else to go.

It wasn't that she saw her path to survival clearly but she kept going. Caena never gave up and never stopped struggling. It was an imperative that had served her well countless times. That habit benefitted her in her current circumstance and at another level that she did not yet perceive. Instead of diving into the bay like many of her crew, she bolted into her quarters. She knew the sea would be boiling in mere moments. While she did not see the lava reach the water, Caena heard the steam created as it did and then the screams of her crew as they were cooked alive on the deck behind her. She slammed the cabin door closed as the billowing steam came at her, throwing the bar down for reinforcement.

She nearly tripped over a large bucket of water as she turned and chose where to hide from the steam. She quickly doused herself, dumping the sea water over her head. Caena dove over her bed and into the corner of her cabin, only to land adjacent to Sari, her cabin lass. For a moment, the warrior's fierce gaze met the wide and panicked eyes of the child. She had only that instant to make her choice. Caena shouted, "COME HERE!" She grabbed the terrified girl and curled into a ball around her, shielding her petite body.

Steam blasted the cabin as it billowed out into the bay. It was the manifestation of a vast amount of energy, creating a deafening roar that seemed endless. The cabin portals, which were no more than wooden shutters, burst open under the intense pressure of the expanding clouds of searing heat. The pair screamed in unified terror as the steam rushed in to fill the room. Caena felt the right side of her face blister, switching her focus from their fear to new and terrible pain.

King Armon Sarason prayed to Daellus in his private temple, which he had named the Chapel of Light. He suffered still, bathed in the experience of the invaders, as his empathetic sight missed nothing. The Ruler asked his god to forgive this violence in the name of future peace. He searched for a way to find some good in the horror they had unleashed. His mind was attuned to the Stone of Power that was the source of so much of his strength. It showed him a glimpse of how he might grant a small measure of mercy that day, a way that would also serve the future. He felt the presence of Graeth down the hall well before he arrived. When he heard the claws of his Chancellor, he stood and exalted the beautiful Altar of Peace before him. The King turned towards his dear friend; his mind was already made up.

"It is done, then?" He received a nod. "Did we achieve the desired effect?" Armon asked.

"Spectacularly!" answered his Chancellor. "We believe none survived."

"Precisely two survived and it must remain so," said the King. "Please see to it. Bring the ebony warrior to me. I sense compassion dwells still within her. I shall await you on my terrace."

"As you command," the dragon replied. The indomitable warlord understood that Sarason's heart was pained, even though their foe had been so deserving of immolation. Graeth loved him for that heart and constantly struggled to be worthy of it. He sensed Armon had more to say. He queried, "Sire?"

"Mind the child, my friend. She has a worthy purpose yet, as well. Her mind must not suffer further."

As always, Graeth knew he could trust Armon's sight and wasted no more words. He nodded his assent and pivoted, ready to make his way to the beach.

As Caena returned to reality, she was nearly overwhelmed by searing facial pain. Her visage had been further ruined; she saw it in the stare of Sari. The girl looked at her with tears in her pale eyes. The Admiral sensed her gratitude and the fear of how she looked. "At least it's the right side," said Sari.

They shared an ironic chuckle but the levity couldn't last. It was quiet now, the kind of noiseless lament that eternity reserved for a field of battle saturated with death. Caena heard her own heavy heartbeat thumping in her ears. She concentrated on her breathing and slowly calmed herself. What else would befall them now that the invasion had been so utterly crushed? At best, she would forever be a captive. What of young Sari? Would the girl be spared such a fate? Rumorgans were Daellus worshippers who valued peace above all else, it was said. How did the justice of such a nation manifest? Time to find out.

The pair stood and looked about the cabin. Condensed water had left it wet. Wisps of mist clung to the corners and edges of the room. They removed the bar, which she imagined had kept the intensity of the explosive burst of steam from scouring the chamber entirely, saving them. She kissed her sapphire ring in thanks for her miserable life. "I feel Your gaze, Mistress," the privateer offered with a grimace.

As they stepped onto the deck, the smell of boiled meat filled the humid air. The swollen, cooked remains of their crew mates surrounded the two. Caena hugged Sari to her waist. "Look at them, girl. See what the elder folk of the world are capable of." Better if the child saw the truth, knew what she had been spared, and felt the gratitude their goddess was owed. That was when Caena's breath left her. She saw an absolutely monstrous beast striding on the black sands, approaching her command ship. As the massive land dragon already held her in a menacing stare and there was nothing she could do for her crew, the draevar summoned her pride and stepped slowly to the prow of her vessel.

She pushed Sari behind her as the terror came near, within the reputed range of its breath attack. Had she survived being steamed so that she could be broiled? Caena stiffened her spine and wondered why it did not kill her. She thought of several things to say, but her mouth was parched. In the end, she failed to summon words. As she quietly awaited its judgment, she wondered if the dragon could speak the common tongue of Maera. Graeth-N'throk Shaan was unaware that the scales bordering his mouth appeared to the ebony captain to sneer at her. Taller than any dwaerf, the female was slender, athletic, and her skin black as pitch. The Chancellor found the woman's appearance to be fascinating. He lowered his head slightly and tilted it to the right, his gaze unrelenting. He did his best to choose his words correctly.

"I bid you welcome to Rumorga."

So it was that Caena Kiers, Admiral of the Privateer Fleet of the draevar Theocracy of Saestis, and a ten-year-old, were the sole survivors of the doomed invasion of Rumorga in the Aelvae year 2437. The Chancellor took her to the private mountainside terrace of King Sarason. The balcony offered him a view of the beaches of the isle. He enjoyed standing there and catching the westerly winds. It happened to be the area above which the immolation of the invasive forces had occurred. The super-heated lava flows had left a wide area of beach covered in a crusted shell of newly forming volcanic stone. Hissing black rock and glowing outbursts of liquid fire continued to produce plumes of steam that lingered over the field.

The flagship of the enemy was somehow the sole vessel still intact. Only in that spot did the beach remain, a corridor of sand bifurcating the new lava field. No sign remained of the invading army. Even their bones had been consumed. The dwaerf stood, his hands clasped behind his back. Armon rotated slowly to face his captive. Caena felt the monarch wore garb beneath his regal station. She also noticed that he wore no armor. She was unimpressed, as it was common knowledge that much of the spoils of Maera had long ago found their way to dwaerven coffers. The king's youthful, unwrinkled face belied his long white hair and beard.

The eyes of Armon Sarason mesmerized her. In future days Caena's memory of the meeting was limited to his words and a series of impressions about her host. His handsome face reflected strength as well as understanding. She came to feel that he genuinely grieved for those lost that day, although they had sought his ruin. She sensed a nobility of purpose and genuine gentleness of character. She felt that he understood her and deeply empathized with her existence. Caena felt all these things, though they were unspoken. He chose empathetic words to begin. "Horrendous events have brought us together."

Caena had met rulers before, individuals with tremendous power. She'd also met the leaders of various religious factions, the principal figures of immensely influential organizations. She had known her share of truly charismatic individuals who exerted their will upon others by sheer force of personality. Caena had planned military incursions with warlords, shared council with guild masters, feasted with diplomats, and kept the company of generals. However, nothing in her broad experience had adequately prepared her to enter the aura of King Sarason. "If you feel well enough, we have a mutual interest to discuss, Caena Kiers." She was unhappy that he knew her name, yet she felt at peace with it.

Although large, Sarason was not physically imposing like other dwaerves she had met. He was a far cry from the reavers of Kharak-kaar! Sarason carried himself as a young dwaerf yet was the founder of the dwaerven kingdom and was over five hundred years old! He spoke slowly in a mellow tone, carefully choosing his words. He had a pleasant way about him, and she enjoyed his voice. She realized she was smiling at him and snapped back to her usual scowl. She wasn't angry about that. She should have been angry.

"You have survived a terrible ordeal today. I intend to see you and your charge sail away to safety." He was not at all what she had expected. The longer she spent with him, the more she felt a growing, tactile sense of arcane power that seemed to radiate from his body and through hers. It was soothing and bathed her in a rejuvenating warmth that confused her. She had difficulty concentrating and even felt a little wobbly on her feet. What kind of being was this? What was being done to her?

At first, she could not fathom what the dwaerven monarch gained by meeting with a foe that had been so thoroughly vanquished. The title most commonly used to identify the king was informal—Sarason the All-Seeing. It was widely accepted that he had earned that name due to the truly impressive ability of his kind to gather information. This idea had been bolstered in Caena's mind by the incredible response to their attempted invasion. Now that she stood in his presence, she realized that the appellation might be literal. "You must be tired. If you need rest, I would not be slighted." He was being kind to her! Why be kind? As always, the sentiment confused her. She did feel exhausted, though. It had been a howling bitch of a day! Her arms felt heavy.

She realized that the dwaerf was looking right through her. Caena had only once encountered Daellus maena in a weak, useless caster. Here was the pure energy of the God of Peace! The swashbuckler began to understand how attractive Daellus worship must be to the vulnerable of the world. Here now was the embodiment of empathy and forgiveness. King Armon Sarason thrived on the pain and wrongdoing of others. As she struggled to stay on her feet, Caena realized that she must speak on behalf of the child. "I need to know that Sari will be safe," she managed. She shook her head, weary and confused. As Sarason stepped forward slowly, she couldn't move. He placed his right hand on her left cheek and smiled widely.

"The child is safe." She was tired. "There is nothing to worry about." She felt clumsy, off balance. "You're both in my care." He kept on smiling at her. "Your pain is gone?" She nodded; it was.

"There's nothing to worry over." She knew it was true, deep inside. That knowledge was emotionally overwhelming—a deeply visceral realization.

She felt at one with him as he continued to stare at her. Her deepest emotions and innermost motivations were laid bare before him. Caena closed her eyes and suddenly felt dizzy. "We're going to come to a fine agreement, you and I." Caena Kiers drifted away on a warm, gentle breeze. She sat happily, her feet in a lovely pool of water. She looked at her toes, splashing playfully—a child's toes. She had found peace.

Some months later, in the time of the Sweeping Rains, the privateer drained her flagon and pounded it down emphatically on the dark wooden table. She had the full attention of those sitting around it. After all, they were just men, and she was damned entertaining! It had never been her way to talk so much, but she would honor the deal she had made with Armon Sarason. She needed his magic to protect her.

"And that, my fellow ale whores, is how I survived the doomed invasion of Rumorga." The five were left speechless, for a few moments at least, while she stood and gathered herself. She leaned forward, both hands before her on the table, and allowed herself a sly grin.

"With that, I bid you all good fortune in your endeavors." She snapped her fingers loudly, seemingly for emphasis, her left hand on the odd charm hanging around her neck. Nobody but her noticed a slight burst of arcane energy. No one ever did. In a few minutes, they wouldn't remember her, just her story, and that it was true. The veteran swept from the table, swiftly crossing the room towards the exit. Nine ales in, and still she had her wits about her! "Kiss my perfect ass!" she murmured. She had to rotate her head to see the whole room with one good eye. No one sought that frightening gaze. It was a shame, she thought, that she needed the scorched scar to verify her tale. Confident there was no threat there, she slipped away.

"Well, that was a heaping pile of dwaerf scat," spat Haerald of Taelin. "And us, buying her drink until she finished? We're fools, all of us. Damnable fools!"

"I, for one, believed her," replied Jaemus of Landale, standing and preparing to take his leave. "You all saw that scar. Face like that, that burn scar? What I heard was plain truth."

"Ah, you believed her, did you?" said Haerald, incredulous. "A small towner like you? You'd believe anything!" The group tensed noticeably, as such words were often enough to provoke blows or blades.

"Aye, a small towner I may be. But we have an old saying where I come from," replied Jaemus. "'Scars are important—they remind us that the past really happened.' Yeah, she was there, I'd say." With that well said, he walked to the bar, ready for female company. Caena had stepped outside by then. The rains haunted Sneedon's Landing again that night. She carefully looked the street up and down, then stood in the downpour for a bit longer, pulling the hood of her cape over her face.

"Let's be off, then!" she said, seemingly to the rain.

Sari clamored from the small roof above the door porch of the tavern and leaped deftly down onto the cobblestone. She caught up quickly, staying to the right side and just behind her mistress. The draevar corsair looked toward the teen with her habitual sneer.

"Aye, Admiral," said Sari.

Together, the pair strode through wearying rain in the good cheer and the welcome company of those who walked still amongst the living, if only undeservedly and by some kindness of fate.

"In such ways, through the grim march of history, do the wise and truly mighty make tactical use of the circumstances of war to forge wisdom into strategy and make enduring legends come alive in the hearts and minds of mortals. For, artfully met by intellect, aggression may be a particularly useful tool."

— The Book of Ilmarae; A Treatise: 'On Mortal Reasonings for War' Chpt. 7 – Chronicled by Nagara, Son of Ilmarae, as recounted by The Seer.

*Want to experience more of Maera? Visit **www.maeraworld.com***

THE REACH OF
SHAERRA'S HAND

It was a world gone mad as an utterly shocking and truly dreadful turn of events had given Aerdos, the God of Death, free reign. Now, the vile Minions of Hell roamed unchallenged across the land. The very ground itself had been corrupted, overwhelmed by the sheer volume of death-maena released. The aggressive invasion of death in such magnitude into a beloved, celebrated sanctuary of life represented a tremendous affront to Kuraile, the God of Life. But this was the dynamic—life and death in constant flux. And so, the lush parks and lawns of Limrin's famously beautiful capital city writhed in a terrible new energy that pulsed through the aerth in waves, causing the vegetation to dance as if to some sinister heartbeat. The change couldn't be more drastic and there could be no doubt that this was death's day.

The mere touch of its rubbery skin on that cursed grass filled the newly-summoned greater devil with intense energy. The Arch-Devil Cestanos himself had blessed the forces of the Dead Lands, sent them forth in his name, imbuing them with the unholy, righteous power of Aerdos. That energy was tactile and intense, overwhelming yet, at the same time, somehow surreal. For any living creature that encountered that maena, it meant a horrible death in the clutches of a primordial evil so strong that it threatened to corrupt the translation of one's life force. It was raw aether, flowing directly into the flesh of any being that contacted it. To the tentacule's physical body, the Maeran form of an other-worldly being, that energy was intoxicating and indulgent.

The tentacule was native to the eternally frozen Planes of Hell, the hopeless Land of the Dead, diabolically refined through many tests of viciousness throughout the vastness of time and on many worlds. It was a type of devil that was most useful to Aerdos, for its adaptability made it effective in nearly any environment. If need be, its epidermis and other organs could quickly and instinctively alter to whatever new conditions its new locale dictated. On this infamous day in the history of Maera, the Hosts of Hell had been summoned to the human Kingdom of Limrin on Maera through a Dread Portal. Having left the relentless cold of Hell to roam in the temperate climate of the continent of Maerisna, the extra-planar, or Inaeran, immortal devil known as a tentacule transformed.

Tentacules are likened most often to the marine creatures widely known as starfish. The tentacule is much larger, measuring up to twenty feet from the tip of one appendage to the end of an opposite arm, as they are called. They are said to have a varying number of appendages. In Hell, they have eight; on Maera, they have six, typically twice as long as the center body mass of the tentacule is broad. Likewise, in Hell, the tentacule had an ice-blue hue to its epidermis while on Maera, they were known to adopt a pinkish tone akin to human baerbaraan flesh. It was not an aesthetic alteration but a change that indicated a difference in the thickness and texture of the epidermis, a reaction to the atmospheric conditions, that semi-aqueous bath so specific to each world. It was atmospheric pressure that caused the adaptation and it allowed the devil to maximize its physicality in this new world.

So it was that, upon passing through the gate to Maera, the tentacule lay flat on its central mass with its beaked maw facing upwards. Two of its eight symmetrical arms began to wriggle violently, seemingly convulsing, until they tore away from the creature's body altogether. Both limbs flopped to the ground, still writhing. They slithered, snake-like, to that horrid beak at the body's center. There each was devoured whole and, in turn, reabsorbed into the mass of the monster. The creature's core swelled and morphed in response to that added mass. Each of the six remaining limbs thickened and grew a bit longer. The transformation of the devil continued as its arms simultaneously re-centered their location as they radiated from its core, each extending from seven to roughly eight feet long. After the limbs were equidistant from one another, the tentacule shuddered through various internal changes, adapting to Maera's reality.

Next, the limbs began rippling rhythmically, rapidly twitching from their tips to the body, which became more and more frenzied. The arms flexed simultaneously, lifting the horrendous being suddenly up off the dead, yet grotesquely energetic, turf. Its outer epidermal layer quickly and suddenly sloughed off as a new sublayer of tissue that had adapted to be more suited to the conditions of its current location was exposed. The creature devoured the shed skin, still quivering and oozing, in a heap of its own vileness. Now actually a pale pinkish skin tone instead of its former icy blue, the tentacule appeared to be various shades of gray while on Dead Ground. It began lubricating itself by exuding a thick, shiny ooze from epidermal glands throughout the entire surface of its body. Once covered in a thick sheen of its skin's protective excretions, the devil reared up on two arms, easily overcoming imbalance with sheer muscularity. It needed to test its readiness, for it was time to hunt.

The terror sent a pulse of concentrated energy out from its central brain, amplified by the ganglia in each of its arms. The power traveled in all directions in a wave of unseen force that a specialized portion of its complex mind was adapted to detect. That region of its brain had adapted to this thick, soupy atmosphere quickly and could now sense life within the radius of its pulse energy. Life interacted uniquely with the pulse, causing a ripple in its surging power. The last tragic victims of the fall of Limrin fought desperately on in pockets of defiant, if hopeless, attenuation. There was still abundant life here. After using its impressive ability, the fiendish tentacule headed for the nearest life force, using the most direct path.

At first, it moved tentatively, lurching forth on the tips of its arms, which had stiffened to travel at speed. Each of its appendages tapered to a conical tip that could support its entire weight, if held rigid, while it traveled. That same tip trifurcated into three equal, supple, but powerful digits that afforded the beast impressive dexterity. Each arm possessed its own neural ganglia and could thus act independently, yet they cooperated fluidly under the command of its central brain. The tentacule had modified itself to achieve maximum efficiency on Maera, and now it applied itself entirely to the task for which it had been summoned—eliminate all life encountered!

Once the devil began moving, it quickly found its balance, taking air into specialized ducts along its skin to increase the girth of its arms, allowing for more stability at full velocity. Each individual arm had control of the texture of its skin, able to harden or soften it in an instant as needed. It continued to send out its life-detecting pulses, homing in on its target. The tentacule began cartwheeling, rotating around its center core and pounding along on its arms, each, in turn, making directional changes on the fly as required to maintain its balance. In this way, the devil could cover a long distance at a shocking speed. It was quite a sight to behold, for the raw power displayed in its movement was immense and savage.

Although it had no discernible eyes or ears, the awful beast moved with alarming agility and unerringly approached a pocket of human warriors, desperately delaying the inevitable. They were surrounded and would be overwhelmed yet they persisted in their futile resistance. It was not evident if the tentacle had any capacity for higher reasoning. But even if it had the aptitude for such thought, it may have found these actions perplexing. It certainly sensed that the life it now approached was small in number but disproportionately strong. Something was adding to the life force in that group and that terrible devilish entity now found it tremendously enticing.

Kalestaen Elderstar had lived a long life, even for an aelf. As a youth, he had walked happily amongst the mighty laembin grove of the Aelven Lands and swam in the rivers of the Balkael Forest. Kal was the only child born to his family in his generation. That was not unusual amongst their kind, and he enjoyed the full attention of his parents. He was also encouraged to seek encounters with other adults in his community. He learned to balance the aelven yearning to be apart, in the wild, with the expectation that he be a member of society. As a youngling, he showed an excellent aptitude for learning, studied the natural world, and gladly invested his young mind in theology and history, amongst other things. All the while however, his youthful heart found most delightful whatever time he spent alone and in quiet solitude beneath the famous laembin grove of his homeland.

Kalestaen began training his body at a young age, striving to discipline his aelven physique. His natural slenderness and agility were honed into endurance and speed. In the way of his people, he learned to trap and subdue his foes, training with staves and other non-lethal weaponry. Out of necessity, he also became proficient in using the traditional aelven bow and the sword and shield. As a young adult, he met his great love while strolling within the laembin grove, and they were heart-coupled in the faith. Together they brought several new aelven lives into this world, an act of great worth to their families and community. Known as Kal by those closest to him, he fathered his children with proper diligence and saw them well-raised in the worship of Kuraile of the Laughing Eyes. With pride and satisfaction, Kalestaen Elderstar witnessed his progeny integrate into aelven society along paths that would make each of them useful to the aelven people. He often celebrated his good fortune and contentment by walking long beneath the stars and the broad golden leaves of the elegant trees of the Aelfward.

Kal delved deeply into the knowledge amassed by his nation over millennia, achieving expertise and true usefulness in multiple academic disciplines. Eventually, if not inevitably, Kalestaen Elderstar became a teacher and disseminated the knowledge he had gathered unto himself in service of his nation's youth. In a long career as an academic, he served his community well. But he persisted all the while in his affinity for the gray, delicate bark and wonderfully proportioned branches found only in the woods of his homeland. Indeed, his time amongst the laembin grove brought him closer to Kuraile, for it was within the majestic trees of the wood that so many of his kind found eternity. In time, Kalestaen Elderstar pledged himself to the benign service of the God of Life and became a leader of his people. He administered the holy sacraments of the worship and gave his guidance freely to all who sought it. In time he advanced through the ranks of the church, not by design but on the merit of his character and extraordinary ability to be helpful and apply his energies to the greater good. Although the centuries had begun to fly, Kal, when possible, spent what time he could 'neath the laembin canopy with his beloved.

As a High Priest of Kuraile, Father Elderstar excelled in his many duties. He had lived many times a length of life that might be considered a great gift to a man. For centuries he had served his people in varied ways, always with success and in the joy of being useful. So useful that he was given the charge of a staff of mighty maena, crafted by the finest aelven artisans from the wood of a laembin stem felled in a sudden flash of destiny by a stroke of lightning. With their skill and the blessing of their creator, the wood was transformed into a magnificent Staff of Life that housed the recalled spirit of the laembin tree that the bolt had disrupted. Once it dwelled again within the smooth wood of the Staff, that spirit became emboldened with the righteous power imbued in it. Then the Staff and the priest were joined in service to life through the Ritual of Bonding. And so, Kuraile of the Laughing Eyes was well pleased.

The Staff of Life allowed Father Elderstar to truly understand the relationship of the aelven people to their ancient homeland. For, in possession of the Staff, his senses were enhanced and he was thereafter able to interact directly with the spirits of the woods and witness in plain sight the aether of his distant kin living on in the laembin trees. Like all aelves, he had grown up with the stories of his ancestors, how they had eventually passed on to dwell forevermore as one with the land. Even in his youth, Kalestaen had felt deeply at peace in the woods and the laembin grove in particular. He had always felt a special affinity for the life force he sensed there. Indeed, all aelves felt it but Kal sensed it more profoundly and realized it. It had always been an intangible thing, more spiritual than physical. But it was undeniable, something that had always distanced

Kalestaen from his peers. They each had their path and a haven that was their special place, which was typical, an aelven norm. Kal had always felt drawn to the laembin grove of the Aelfward and now he knew why.

Kal had achieved a new and deeper understanding. Spirits long gone from his folk found a higher state within the laembin trees, translating into a new life form that lived on. One single, magnificent, ancient organism, the fabled grove of laembin, actually stemmed from a single core of roots, each identical to the others. Unique to this holy place, the grove was a vast network of sentient life, sharing its aether in symbiosis with the former aelven inhabitants of the forest. As the huge laembin grove of the Aelfward was interconnected, one life duplicated over and over; it formed a spiritual community living within the foliage of the Balkael Forest. Its aura was the energy Kal had always sensed. The trees were the aelves—the aelves were the trees! Aelven children had been told as much through the ages but it was a different thing altogether being able to walk the woods with his staff and to be a part of that marvelous amalgam of life.

The relationship Father Elderstar had formed with the Staff of Life had changed him. The things it had shown him, the understanding he gleaned from living with it, was a gift of knowledge that had altered him forever. He now had the wisdom to grasp what the Aelfward was, what it fully represented, and the importance of its mere existence. It was knowledge well-earned and understanding that was profoundly transformative. Armed with such a gift, Father Elderstar thereafter deemed it most useful for him to volunteer in defense of the Balkael Forest, which he loved so deeply. In coordination with the nation's military, he pledged his service under King Frenastis, the only national leader in the history of the Aelven Lands.

The Aelven King wielded full authority over all defensive measures in the aelven homeland. He was undoubtedly the oldest and quite possibly the wisest of the children of Kuraile, and his great personal sacrifice in leading them was appreciated by all. No one else seemed eager to take on the endless responsibilities and labors involved in his duties. The contacts beyond the realm he had built over eight-thousand years were invaluable, making him one of the best-informed individuals on Maera. It was that expansive knowledge that so uniquely qualified Frenastis Faern to be the leader of the aelven people. It was his very willingness to sacrifice so much of himself for the good of his kind that made him such an admired and beloved King. Kalestaen now truly understood that sacrifice. To stay for so long in his aelven form, under such stress and with the tremendous responsibilities of his duties, was a sacrifice that was counter to the nature of most aelves and difficult to comprehend. In his new position as a High Priest, a Caretaker of the Faith, and a Carrier of the Life Staff, Father Elderstar began to understand the role of an aelven King and appreciated his liege all the more.

So it was that after decades of learning the intricacies of the defenses of the aelven woods, Father Elderstar had gained a great deal of expertise in theoretical warfare. War theory is an arena of academia to which the elder races have a particular affinity, for attacks against any kingdom as ancient as the Aelven Lands were extraordinarily rare and nearly always thwarted before they were even launched. Caretaker Elderstar showed an excellent affinity for war theory and became an intricate part of the decision-making process of the realm's defense as he, once again, proved very valuable to his people.

Thus, it came to pass that Caretaker Kalestaen Elderstar was asked to be a liaison between aelven-kind and the humans of that great depository of hope, the newly-formed Kingdom of Limrin. The King, Frenastis himself, had requested it of him. The Caretaker understood the importance of that request and took his acceptance very seriously. He made a solemn vow to do what he could to foster a love for nature and a proper understanding of life in the men of Limrin. He honored that vow. For over two centuries, the aelf spent most of his time helping to establish that young nation and their worship of Kuraile. His term of service was nearly at an end when death came to Limrin. Never did he imagine, in all that time, that his duty would come to such an end.

When word of the attack came, Caretaker Elderstar was at a prayer service with a group of locals. Many left, seeking shelter in their homes. Others stayed with the aelf, who had always served them. As he sought information, it became clear to Kalestaen that something was very wrong indeed. The sky to the east was darkening in a way that was foreboding and offended him somehow, gnawing at his mind in an awful way. And, as soldiers retreated before the onslaught, Kal saw their faces and the terror that each of them wore like some nightmarish mask. Then, he reached out with his staff, trying to sense what he could in the east. He was heavily rebuffed, repulsed in a way so foul that it brought bile to his mouth. That was when he knew that something genuinely horrifying was happening and that he must flee, saving any he could along the way. But to where, he thought, could they escape?

Father Elderstar was a war theorist, not a warrior. In his great peril, his mind oddly went to a vague memory of an aelven veteran of many battles he had interviewed long ago. The warrior had survived a terrible massacre. When Kal asked how he had managed it, he explained it thus. "When things go that wrong, panic sets in. A herd mentality takes over. Mistakes will be made. You must remember that your enemies will always concentrate on massed targets. If you want to live, you must be smart, practical, and follow one rule. Never run with the group!"

That account of desperation had chilled him when he heard it. But the sudden and unbidden memory of it made all the difference on that fell day. While the vast throng of humanity fled south towards the border of Limrin, Kal instead headed north to the Monument of Shaerra's Hand. *Never with the group*, he thought. He could have tried, like so many others, to get to the southern reaches of the kingdom when all hell broke loose. All such folk could hope for was some miraculous appearance by rescuers from the dwaerven-held lands of Throgar, which encompassed the territory on either side of Kaeran-taar, the mighty bridge that spanned Ae-Gaeltor, the great Aerth Wound. Kalestaen was a realist and knew just how many times in aelven history their allies had saved the day—and how many times they had not. As mighty as the dwaerven people were, a quick military response was not their strength. He could put no hope in the thought of such a miracle that day.

When the dead came, insanity seemed to surge before them. Kalestaen found that the mind of a human is not equipped to face such a fate. Even hardened veterans faltered before the doom that came for Limrin that dread day. Wherever he went, Caretaker Elderstar and his Staff of Life were a beacon of calm and hope to the humans in his charge. Unable to do more, Kalestaen provided them with what peace he could, for there were many, and they clung to him in fear and panic. All the while, he continued to push north and thus avoided the largest part of the enemy's forces.

When planted, the Life Staff of Kuraile, which Caretaker Elderstar held in his firm grip, repelled the dead ground which sought to engulf them. The Staff allowed him to cast a *Live Ground* spell of a variable area of effect, pushing back death's aggressive presence. If he planted the Staff in the aerth and concentrated all his power through it, and if the conditions were favorable, the radius of effect could be maximized to become profoundly impressive. He could carry it or ride with it at a moderate pace and still maintain an effect. If he rode at top speed or ran, that radius was reduced. Its area of effect was spherical, and its very presence had the significant secondary effect of giving those around him a palpable sense of calm and well-being. Under the current circumstances, that aspect of the Staff's power had never been more crucial.

The ground was dead. It writhed as if in mute agony and its vile spread would have enveloped them save for the Life Staff. On that fouled turf were myriad swarms of the dead, agitated and milling about, charging in at odd intervals only to be repelled, for they began to dissolve within the radius of the Staff. As they approached, its presence pained them and the wretched creatures screamed in their suffering and frustration. Their tortured howls reached a crescendo as he called to the group, took up his Staff, and moved slowly northward. The aelf gazed around and witnessed the dead melting in the aura of his power, all the while throwing themselves at the living in a desperate attempt to bring them down. *How these poor souls must suffer,* he thought, *to exhibit such aggression in the presence of the staff!* He knew that he must continue to try, against all odds, to get north to the Monument of Shaerra's Hand while the attention of their foes was still unfocused. Before long, he feared, their group of survivors may be all that remained in this area. Then the weight of their terrible enemy would wash over them.

There were perhaps two dozen warriors within his radius of protection and disturbingly few civilians with them. It troubled him greatly when he considered the dreadful fate that had befallen the vast majority of the citizenry of Limrin. Still, he sought to steel his mind against such horrifying considerations. He remembered once more the words of his king when he was asked to become a Caretaker. Frenastis had advised him, "By taking on this work, you must acknowledge that there may come a day when you have to do your best to salvage whatever you can. There will be ample time later for you or others to debate whether your efforts should or could have been more helpful elsewhere." He had often thought of that statement over the decades and always imagined it was merely a political prognostication. As such, he had felt that the caution of that message had applied to several other situations he had faced in two centuries of service to Limrin. The aelf was left stunned by the stark reality of how well that warning seemed to pertain to this day.

As had happened earlier more than once, a cry went up from the rear of their group as they started taking losses in their attempt to flee. Father Elderstar once again planted the Life Staff in the aerth and as its radius of effect increased, the loud shrieks of the dead rang out once more as they were repelled. They were mainly facing weak creatures of hell, newly dead, that shambled forth with varying degrees of flesh left on their bones, animated by the sheer evil will of the Dead God. It was their more powerful masters, the beings that massed and controlled the dead, that were the more significant threat. They were now arriving in greater numbers, adding to the menace of the forces surrounding them.

The real tipping point, which the aelf most hoped to avoid, would be the arrival of devils, great otherworldly beings who wielded power that could oppose that of the Life Staff. Immortal beings such as these were inevitably part of any Aerdos invasion of this scale and it was just a matter of time until the arrival of such a being would mark their last stand. It was up to Father Elderstar to lead these few desperate survivors still further north to reach the power place of Kuraile, the Monument of Shaerra's Hand. Unfortunately, the priest calculated that their chances of achieving that goal dwindled with each passing moment. As he made that dread computation, he felt intense trepidation. It was like an ever-increasing weight on his chest. As he contemplated that feeling, which was an awful and new experience for him, he wondered at the power of it.

Father Elderstar had met a human woman here in Limrin years ago. He remembered her well. Her face aged and heavily wrinkled, her eyes a deep and lovely brown. Her face had a unique character, and she was approaching the end of her life when he met her as part of his work within the community. She was a lifelong and faithful Kuraile worshipper and had reached her seventy-seventh year. By all accounts, no small feat for a human. She had lived a long, wonderful, and fulfilling life and they met as she readied herself to pass on to her next existence. Her name was Waelma Younger and they had engaged in meaningful dialogue during her final weeks as she came under the care of the Order. Kalestaen had helped to ease her passing, and Waelma had made quite an impression on him.

Waelma had touched Kalestaen deeply with all of her human confusion and fears. The priest had developed much empathy for her but, in the end, he had to admit that he had great difficulty grasping how she must have felt. She was dying and knew it, and even with her faith, which was substantial, Waelma still felt great despair at the loss of her life. So, she fought to live as long as possible, to hang on even though the aether was clearly calling her. When she finally went on, she had asked for him. Waelma thanked him for his kindness and for being there for her. "I only regret that I can never repay you in kind. Though I suppose, when your time comes, one distant day, someone will be there for you?" She gave him a weak smile, and then he gave way to her family so she might pass. Now, with a heinous death suddenly looming before him, Kalestaen Elderstar's mind, for some reason he couldn't fathom, went to the memory of her and her last hours on Maera. The aelf looked around at the humans in his charge, at their faces. Even the powerful influence of the Staff of Life did not entirely dispel their terror and could not fully comfort their minds. Father Elderstar struggled to stay focused and resolute. He had to push on.

The tentacule had reached another pocket of resistance to the inevitable wash of the dead over Limrin. The intoxicating influence of the death swarm was upon it and it was moving at top speed. It could do so for hours in the state it was in, constantly invigorated by the dead ground's pulsating energy. That power came over it again and again, feeding its frenzy. It wasn't a being that functioned beyond when it had been roused from its torpor. Although an age-less immortal, extra-planar entity, the tentacule had no memory of the past, no sense of its existence. It was kept perpetually in a state of stasis and only awakened when needed to do hell's worst. The killing was all it knew and was allowed to experience and its only purpose. The tentacule was an irredeemable murdering monster, a foul mingling of the aether of many beings who had thrown their mortal existence away, committing crimes most foul, setting them-selves on the irrevocable path of damnation. The very worst of the mortal plane came to Aerdos, and their raw aether was congealed into creatures such as the tentacule. There was no escape when such a being came for you. It was a natural force of the universe, there to claim your essence.

It came upon the hapless mortal denizens of Limrin in the open. It seems they were all heading in the same direction, directly toward the devil. It was not some slathering daemon. It worked quickly and with efficiency. There was excitement as a hunt culminated in death but no real pleasure was taken, just life. No lingering fear or pain was dealt, only death. The humans used what tactics they could, forming a circle around their woman folk and offspring, bunching themselves together against the unknown hell-spawn that approached. The ground alone should have been enough to take them over the time that had already transpired. It sensed, now that it was close, that one of them, the elder in the center of the group, was wearing a powerful Charm of Life. She clutched it to her withered chest as she wept and prayed. Her prayers went unanswered, engulfed as they were by the mighty evil at work all around her.

The nightmarish devil spun into action in the air above its victims so quickly that it made a faint whirring sound. Screams accompanied its run, then shrieks in turn. It might have sensed their horror if it knew the ways of mortal minds. Another type of devil may have enjoyed it. Indeed, there were cruel creatures who would have found it a rich bounty. The tentacule took no pleasure as it struck, fully intent on its attack. It landed with all its weight upon the group, bringing the wriggling mass to the aerth beneath it. Each arm of the terror was spread wide and now wrapped with a terrible embrace around whatever limb, torso, or head it touched. Two small rows of tooth-like spikes arose on the inside seam of each of its arms and found wicked purchase in the flesh of the bodies beneath its bulk.

The beak of the wretched devil clacked in a moment of hesitation, making a horrible chittering sound as its grip tightened. Then the tentacule raised the total weight of its body slightly as the wailing, moans, and cries of its victims filled the reach of its assault.

And in one sudden, fantastic feat of raw physical power, it flung its muscular mass into the air while rotating as it squeezed along the length of its limbs. The resultant crushing, lacerating, and rending of bodies left the immediate area flooded with large and small chunks of quivering man-flesh, accentuated by gouts, droplets and, finally, a fine mist of blood that marked the tableau—a spectacular ruin of the life that had been.

The hellish scene of evisceration and mutilation started to settle as the riot of tattered meat that lay in a heap soaked the aerth. Covered in the red foulness of its own creation, the tentacule rose, making an awful squelching sound. It chewed a mouthful of woman as well as the Charm of Life she had worn. Swallowing the gore, it reared up on three limbs and screeched savagely at the gray sky above—a sound that was the horrible manifestation of triumphant Hell come to Maera.

Its homicidal intent fulfilled, the devil sent out a powerful pulse in search of more life. The energy surge echoed back to it and it pivoted sharply, taken aback by the strength of the life it sensed. It twitched, visibly, offended by the sense of it. The tentacule tweaked thrice more, sharply, animated by an overwhelming desire to kill. It rushed away as the fetid dead poured in behind and the feasting on the pile of flesh began. The horrid devil accelerated to full speed, awash in the rampage of death manifest about it in all directions, rushing towards the concentrated life force it had sensed to the north.

Father Kalestaen Elderstar, Caretaker of the Faith, First of his Order and Primary to Kuraile in the human Kingdom of Limrin, had nearly reached his goal. He had made it north to Monument Park, a place of unity in the Faith unlike any other. It was crafted by his folk from the Aelven Lands of Maerisna, along with the northern

Kingdoms of Golaidris and Japarandir. King Silverstalk and even Dantilles collaborated with his ruler, King Frenastis Faern, in the design of the gardens and the breathtaking monument that made it famous. If the park represented the pledge of the elder races of Kuraile to be a positive force in the story of man, the Monument of Shaerra's Hand surely promised the protection of those ancient peoples.

The silvered, shining metal of the monument flashed brilliantly in the clear sky above it as it was still free of the sphere of death that was inexorably engulfing the Kingdom of Limrin. After their great tribulation, the group of survivors managed to reach the park proper, only to find the globe of power that emanated from the monument dwindling rapidly in the face of the overwhelming aggression of dead ground on all sides. The mighty memorial was a sanctified power place of the God of Life, bestowed with a permanent and abundant radiance of maena of Kuraile. It was a beacon of hope and a promise of everlasting life to the faithful. To a disciple of the Dead God, it was an insult, a great affront, and a blight on the land.

As Kalestaen stepped into the protective circle of the monument, he felt its power surge through the Staff and him as well. He felt revived, refreshed. He took a head count. Thirteen, just thirteen, had survived the journey, and none were warriors. He had failed to protect all but a few of his followers. They had entrusted him with their safety, lives, and aether as the kingdom crashed all about them, and he could do nothing. He felt his heart pounding, felt his chest tightening. He felt everything all at once. He felt too much and couldn't process the loss. Now that he had time to relax, all the thoughts and emotions he had blocked out came flooding back in a sudden rush. Father Elderstar fell to his knees as tears welled in his eyes.

The physical exhaustion, compounded by the mental stress, enveloped him, threatening to overwhelm him. He felt his strength, his core, crumble. It was just too much. The other survivors milled about nervously, all eyes on the aelf, their leader, their savior. They had never seen him upset, let alone like this. Slowly they all huddled around him, trying to comfort him. The humans, the handful that remained, women and children and a few older men, knelt with their hero. He was not some shining knight nor a great international leader of legend. He was not even a man, not one of them. He was an impossibly ancient and incredibly aloof being as alien to them as the beasts of lore. He was kind, to be sure, and he had always seemed to care. However, to those surrounding him, he was like a magnificent bird that had floated above them just out of their reach, somehow too beautiful and perfect for the human world. In their great need, he'd been with them. The aelf had stayed with them and faced all the horrors of that day head-on in their protection. Father Elderstar had given his all to save them. Against all odds, they were still alive, and at the monument.

The priest was on his knees, head down, leaning heavily on his staff, and many of the humans reached out to him, touching his robes. Perhaps they sensed his wavering, for he had never been more human to them, and they lowered their heads in empathy. At that moment, although he was on the brink of being consumed by his despair, Kalestaen heard a voice from his past. *"So, now it's your time, and here I am, after all,"* said Waelma Younger. Kal looked up and saw a face, younger now and luminous with health. While he had only known her as an old woman in her time of dying, Kal knew it was her. *"Come, Child of Eternity. He of the Laughing Eyes has one final task for you."* So it was that staring into the eyes of a phantom of faith whom only he could hear, Father Elderstar regained his strength and carried on.

It was a seminal moment in the history of that faith for, indeed, there was one defining trial yet to overcome. Kalestaen arrived at this moment by following his own unique experiences in life, by a path only he had walked. He was delighted that Waelma was there for him. As he marveled that it was she that Kuraile had sent to him in his time of great need, it had given him a true measure of desperately needed comfort to see her. He went first to one knee, then rose again, leaning on the Staff. Kalestaen whispered under his breath, "Surely, all good things come to us through Him," smiling wryly and shaking his head in amazement. His tattered resolve was renewed, and he assessed the situation. The sphere of resistance to the many horrors that sought them was shrinking. He strode quickly to the silvered statue of Shaerra's hand, holding her famous sword Aetherail aloft like a mighty spike that impaled the sky. His people doggedly followed him across the last expanse of live turf.

He touched the metallic sheen of that beautiful statue in disbelief, for he had feared he would never make it so far. "God of My Fathers, Giver of Hope, Maker of Life ... see Your servant now in his terrible need! I beseech You, grant me Your eternal might!" He turned, right hand still touching the monument while his left held the Staff aloft. The humans knelt around him again, touching his robes to connect themselves with him physically as if they required a tether to their faith which he provided. The collapse of the radius of protection the power place offered against the unabated encroachment of dead ground continued as the Priest of Kuraile sought to push the established limitations of his capabilities by tapping into the previously unrealized potential of the Staff of Life in his care.

Now came that dread Reaper of Life, known to both men and aelves as Cestanos the Cruel, Arch-Devil of Aerdos, Populator of Hell. He who had called down the appalling corruption of the human Kingdom of Limrin. It was his day of greatest triumph and Cestanos rode on a massive, rotting ox that pulled a torturer's cross that was mounted on two wheels. Upon that x-shaped device writhed Targor Temrael, Crowned Prince of Limrin. He was not in physical distress, bound only by rope, but his state of mind was another matter. Drool foamed from his open mouth and his eyes were wide with abject horror. His head snapped to and fro as he fixated upon one abomination after the other, an observer of the atrocities of the hell-spawn that surrounded him. Sweat poured from him and gibberish issued from his lips. Sanity had long since fled his consciousness. It was now replaced by the realization of the future he faced.

"Let the terror wash over you, mortal ... swim in it!" The words came from the fetid maw beneath the rider's black helm and echoed in his captive's skull. Cestanos allowed himself to enjoy Targor's torment. It was an indulgent pleasure but one well-earned. "From this day forth, that terror shall sustain you. Let it sweep you away, for it cannot be resisted, and you have no way back now. Wallow in the dark dream that your foolishness has wrought! Bathe in the anguish of the fallen while you witness the death of your nation!" After he spoke those final words, the Devil-Lord cackled in heinous laughter that stung Targor like a hungry whip and gave him over to a whole new dimension of nightmares.

The vanguard of Cestanos swept west from the Dread Portal from which they had poured, like some gurgling confluence of aetherael agony and fleshy putrefaction. At their furthest reach, the dead ground that preceded them stopped fast at a barrier of raw maena enforced by the Church of Kuraile, the God of Life.

The energy emanated from a titanic monument to some long-dead she-aelf whore who had laid down her life in the service of Limrin. *Surely,* he thought, *only man could make such fools of the elder races!* The resistance was the cause of great consternation amongst the dead, who swarmed, thick as a carpet, over the land. But it had been expected and, to the devil's current knowledge, no survivors had reached the temporary haven it offered. The vanguard pushed on toward the monument. When it was close, they fanned out to ensure it was surrounded.

Cestanos, Devourer of Hope, used his otherworldly maena to reach out to the live ground that radiated from the monument. But, as he pushed forth with his energy, he hesitated. He sensed some new, unforeseen development at the power place of Kuraile. Pure malice welled within his black heart as he sensed the presence of a priest of the Living God and, much worse, the Staff of Life he carried!

Although they were able to traverse the natural world, no low-level dead creature could hope to survive for more than a few minutes while on live ground, which countered the dead ground of Cestanos most efficiently. The Arch-Devil's ability to sense life told him that the Staff had reached the memorial and that the Staff's power had been fully activated. Cestanos quaked with outrage, which he channeled into the summoning of all of his most powerful servants to him while he began to emanate his strongest maena-thrall. Lesser devils flew, hopped, ran, and slithered to him with the worst intentions. Their leader urged them to rend, tear, shred and devour their pathetic, hapless foes in the circle of life-maena surrounding the monument. Devils care little what befalls them. The enslaved dead care less still. So, upon the urging of their Master, the minions of hell rushed forth to the Staff of Life and its wielder.

As he spoke, his voice filled the minds of his slaves. "FORWARD NOW, MY RANCID SLAYERS, MY REAVERS OF MEN! RAVAGE THEIR FLESH AND TOGETHER WE SHALL SUCK THE MARROW FROM THEIR BONES! DRINK DEEP OF THEIR AETHER AND ENSLAVE THEM IN HELL! THEY DARE MOCK US IN THEIR FEEBLE RESISTANCE AND OFFEND US AS THEY TRY TO CLING TO THEIR PATHETIC LIVES! GO FORTH TO FINISH OUR HATED FOES! BRING THEM THE SUFFERING THAT THEY DESERVE!" Their minds bludgeoned by his order to advance; the dead flung themselves ahead in a fervor that was terrible to see. All the while, the focused and incendiary rage of Cestanos sent forth force waves of maena that battered the sphere of protection around the aelf and his Staff, causing the imminent collapse of that defense to accelerate.

Cestanos watched as his dead flushed across the interface, so raw and tangible now, between death and life. All of his intensity and rage mattered not, for the Staff drew strength from the monument and it was now evident that the mere activation of the Staff amplified the religious monument's reciprocating power. The increase in power seemed exponential and Cestanos looked on in disbelief as the dead melted away in the circle of life. Even as it had collapsed when faced with his fury, the life sphere now expanded in a sudden surge, and then another, and another. His lesser devils now fell and faltered in their approach, having gotten little further than halfway across the defending ground. The vanguard of Cestanos and his devils was no longer enough. If his forces failed to take the monument, life would linger for an undetermined span here. He concentrated all his efforts into one massive and desperate push of maena against the life circle, willing a surge against it by all his forces from every side and all angles.

The tentacule approached the circle of life at full speed from the south. It had murdered many humans caught in various stages of exposure to the dead ground that was now virtually everywhere in Limrin. The tentacule could sense Cestanos, although it had no ears. It could feel the powerful maena that the Arch-Devil was emanating and that power's push against the sphere of resistance. Unlike his Master, the tentacule could not determine the source of the life-maena nor what bolstered it. It could only feel pulsating, baleful energy that filled it with an insatiable hunger to kill. Continually refreshed by the dead ground it traversed, the devil only gained strength as it rushed forward, cartwheeling in its killing frenzy.

The tentacule had existed for an untold length of time in its service to the Arch-Devil Cestanos, who favored the hell-spawn, it being such a perfect killing machine. Few creations of the Aeglain were more efficient or effective in their service to their creator. When all others failed him, Cestanos knew that a tentacule would eliminate whatever it was that had vexed him. So, although the vast bulk of his forces dissolved, howling, as they tried to cross the final few paces of open, live ground to the Staff of Life that opposed his will, Cestanos knew the tentacule would succeed. However, as it breached the barrier at the monument, the tentacule's senses reeled in mute, ragged agony and its body began to come apart at the edges. Its epidermis lost its integrity and its advance slowed as the strength in its limbs began to fail. It had just a few seconds left to exist and flung itself at the aelf, his followers, and that accursed Staff.

Father Kalestaen Elderstar placed his right heel against the Monument of Shaerra's Hand and leaned into his pulsating waves of maena. Never had he wielded such power! The monument drew from the Staff and the Staff fed the monument in a cycle of energy building toward some mighty crescendo. The dead had breached the defensive radius and the circle of defense had shrunk and threatened to collapse at any time. As he struggled to make a final stand, the aelf stood leaning with his Staff in the protection of his remaining followers, who shrank to the aerth beneath him and to his sides. Kalestaen was not meant to perish here, not this way. He was to take his place amongst the laembin spirits of the aelven lands so that he might find his next state and translate beyond his current existence. It seemed impossible to fulfill that dream now, as no help was coming. Death was closing in all around them, and the source of this hellish nightmare would soon engulf them.

Father Elderstar shook his head, trying not to succumb to despair as he contemplated the end. He looked across the open aerth that separated him from the dead and saw them flooding into it. The dead shrieked in unfathomable suffering as the power of the life force of the monument utterly undid them. It was then, in all that horror and through all that hellish screaming, that he once again saw Waelma Younger's face before him as she touched his hand. *"There are worse fates than being a hero of your faith,"* she said. Having heard that and looking into her eyes, he realized what he was meant to do.

He must infuse the Monument of Shaerra's Hand with the full energy of his life force, his followers, and the maena of the Life Staff. That might bolster the strength of the power place, thus denying the enemy a total victory. The aether of his followers and he would hopefully pass into the monument to add their will to the area's defense. Perhaps, one day, they would be freed to go to their reward should the region be taken back by the forces of good and the appropriate maena cast on their behalf. Father Elderstar smiled at Waelma and then closed his eyes in concentration. He had been taught that a Staff of Life could expend all of its energy in a single explosive moment under the most extraordinary duress. Kalestaen focused all of his remaining power on the visualization of this intended result and called down the attention of Kuraile of the Laughing Eyes. He felt the power of the Staff, his mind, and the Monument of Shaerra's Hand all meld together and he held that sensation for as long as he could. Then, all at once, he suddenly gasped.

The tentacule leaped through the air, reaching out with all of its limbs. It was mere moments from coming undone entirely but would be able to strike first. The hideous beak on its underside chittered wildly as it altered the flexibility of the tips of its arms. The bottom of its fleshy appendages, each of which was controlled independently, rippled in toothy expectation. As it arced closer to its targets, the tentacule was suddenly sucked closer to the aelf, as if some mighty vacuum had formed at the base of the statue. All of the air, energy, sound, and even light in the spherical protective area of effect of Father Kalestaen Elderstar's maena drew instantly into the Caretaker's body—and then exploded outward in a silent force wave that engulfed the entire circle.

The tentacule never had a chance to perceive what had occurred. It was blasted out of the mortal plane of existence, as were all the other dead obscenities that had most recently flopped, flown, slithered, hopped, or run into the fray. The dead ground was likewise cleansed in that stunning blast of force which was like a tremendous white flash to anyone who had witnessed it. In that instant, Father Kalestaen Elderstar, the Staff of Life, and thirteen humans passed from their reality as they were ensconced within the Monument of Shaerra's Hand. When the explosion was finished, washing away any sign that the unholy filth of Aerdos had ever approached the artifice of Kuraile, all of the dead nearby had been blown back with a great many of the wretched travesties relieved of their abhorrent existence.

Cestanos felt the touch of righteous Kuraile sear his dead flesh as he was forced back by the spectacular outcome of the encounter. His impuissant fury was unparalleled, fueled further on by the insane, cackling laughter of Prince Targor Temrael on his cross of submission. How that still-mortal fool suffered at the hands of enraged Cestanos as a result of what transpired was beyond all imagining. The Arch-Devil, suddenly rendered wholly ineffectual, watched as that blast's consequences multiplied all too quickly, as a sky-high column of pulsing white light exploded from the tip of the sword held by Shaerra's Hand. The monument's power tremendously increased and spread great hope, for that luminous beacon was seen at enormous distances from the fallen nation of Limrin and promised that some measure of resistance to that region's new reign of Aerdos yet remained. That massive outpouring of life-maena then cascaded to the aerth, outlining a spherical boundary of life surrounding and entrapping the dead ground that had yet to fulfill all the sinister machinations of the being known as Cestanos or any other servant of evil.

The gentle breezes that waft through the primordial Balkael Forest of the Aelven Lands still frolic among the golden leaves of the pristine laembin grove of that mystical realm. There are those who, by some wondrous means, can perceive the lyrical whispers of those legendary vessels of life. To this day, carried on those dancing zephyrs for any finely formed, tapered aelven ear to overhear, echo the haunting, melancholic yearnings of the woods for a favored son named Kal to return home and take his promised place amongst the aethereal spirits of the laembin trees. That Hero of Life remains still in the Wastes of Limrin within the Monument of Shaerra's Hand, where his jealous vigilance helps deny the hell-spawn of Aerdos their final victory over that once beautiful realm.

The love of Kuraile's aelven folk for those devoted to life and goodness amongst humankind has neither failed nor should it be disputed. And so, the dawn of each new day brings light to the heart of darkness, where hope dwells eternally in the service of the Living God, leaving the shredding teeth of evil to gnash in ineffectual frustration at the renewing of the light. Meanwhile, in the verdant perfection of the Aelven Lands, the immortal laembin grove awaits with infinite patience and tangible longing for the joyous return of their valiant son.

*Want to experience more of Maera? Visit **www.maeraworld.com***

THE LESSON OF THE
RAVAGED MAN

A sailor by trade, he was used to self-denial. Even so, he had to admit that he'd gone too long without a woman's touch. He was a handsome man who seldom struggled to attract female company. He'd had a rough stretch of lousy fortune of late and was drunk, which was a particularly bad idea for one in his circumstance. He'd caught the eye of a demonstrably aggressive young warrior in town with friends, celebrating some successful venture. She sported several severe campaign scars in a way that showed her pride in them. He liked that in a woman. Be who you are! The buxom brunette was seemingly from Vaerogar, a matriarchy located west of the Kingdom of Soltaern, on the north shore of the continent of Maerisna. She was loud, she was curvy, and she was brazen. In other words—she was spectacular!

It was customary in her nation for women to take charge; again, he loved it! That was, however, precisely why he had to go. He was already too far into their intermingling. She had insisted that he drink with her, had even dropped coin in her pursuit of his attentions, and so she followed him as he attempted to leave. He used the back door and thought she hadn't noticed as, at the time, she was engaged in a casual bout of leg wrestling. He wondered if she'd engaged in the activity merely to throw a leg high in his direction, but instead of enjoying the view, he'd bolted. Her words stung him, letting him know he had failed in his bold exit strategy.

"Leaving like that, all sly and such … and without even a word of good-bye?" Saerano was half-disappointed, half-irritated by his shitty behavior. He was in the stinking alley behind the tavern, apparently badly in need of a piss. He'd thought he was away clean, so he had decided it was safe for a splash and shake. Left arm above his head, hand on the wall, right hand doing the deed, she'd caught him with his spike out. He tried to come up with a retort but his stream surged in a most distracting way. Instead of words, his response was a sidelong sneer that came off as lascivious. Saerano didn't mind. She wasn't offended at all if it was just a matter of him being soppy. There were damned few men who could match her drink-for-drink and her chosen meat had already been at the bar for an undetermined length of time before she'd arrived. Besides, she was an expert at ensuring that a man deep into his brew still met her needs. She had no worries.

"Awww … did we have a bit much to drink?" She sauntered in his direction, head tilted to the right in a way that she knew flattered her. By the time the man had finished, Saerano had gotten a look at what he'd be working with. She decided it was worth her efforts and sidled up to him as he sought to compose himself. He grunted as she filled her weapon hand with him. She put herself solidly between the brick wall and her new acquaintance. This fellow was less bulky than the type she usually sought out but she found his light curly locks and sparkling eyes irresistible. "No worries … I'm just going to slide right in here. Don't get skittish, beautiful." She thought about it for a moment, then sought to ease any awkwardness her aggression had caused. "There we go … my friends call me Saerano. Let's be friends, yeah?"

A scar through her lip made her smile crooked. It was cute and disarming. "Janes—I go by Janes," he managed, as he didn't want to invite the ill omen of kueting unnamed. Resistance was futile at that point, as she was on him. Saerano's banter was charming. She had alluring features, and she smelled strongly of ale and sweat. All of that worked for him! He signaled his assent by pulling down her trousers. Her grip was unrelenting and she guided him into her. They moaned in unison. She was excited and ready to go, and she showered him with an intense barrage of wet kisses on his mouth, face, neck, and ears. It was his ears that got to him. They were ridiculously sensitive and such attention drove him crazy. She sensed it and pressed him. They were already tightly coupled, she against the wall and he standing, bearing a good deal of her weight. She wrapped both legs around him. He was grateful that she wore little armor but found himself struggling to manage it. Saerano was broad-hipped, big-bosomed, and a decidedly healthy woman. He found himself in a haze of indulgent physical pleasure.

"C'mon now, Janes ... let's get a good lather going!" Saerano was more than ready to work out some frustrations. Although her group's venture had been a stunning success, she would have to wait about a week for her share to turn into coin, as her companions sold what they had found. She'd been told her cut would be a small fortune, more than she'd ever seen at least, and she was admittedly a bit giddy. She had a nice rush from the poxy she'd been offered before entering the tavern. Tankards of ale had dulled her sharp edge and she'd been left with excessive energy to burn off somehow. Now that gorgeous had snapped out of his stupor, he was performing admirably, and she was starting to think that they'd have to get a room together for a few days to get to know each other better.

"Oh, that's nice. Right there, just like that!" She felt odd but was enjoying it. Then she giggled and felt foolish. "I don't know how but you've got my whole body tingling." That remark caused some unexpected turmoil. Janes suddenly stopped humping and stared hard at her. He looked at her hair and saw that it was standing on end. He raised his right hand, reaching to touch her left earlobe. They lost their balance and Saerano started to slip down the wall. Her bare arse dropped towards the ground. His finger contacted her ear with a distinct, crackling spark as she protested.

"Oh, shit!" Janes was in a sudden panic and struggled to disengage. Neither of them had finished, so Saerano tightened the grip of her legs. This wasn't over! Janes was fighting to get free and shouting at her. "LET GO! You don't understand! No, no, no, no, no, no, NOOOOO!" His eyes had gone crazy and he looked above them in a frenzy. Saerano was growing angry. What in the nine frozen hells was going on? What was Janes doing? As he continued to push away from her, the air around them in the alleyway exploded in a deafening, thunderous roar, accompanied by searing heat and a blinding flash of blue-white light!

Bockscar Janes had learned the telltale signs of a strike. He had known that they had just a few seconds to separate but Saerano was strong as a horse. The lightning arced into the alley from above, striking them flush, and sending a massive charge of electricity surging through them. He stiffened, his limbs spasming in excruciating, involuntary muscular contractions that wracked his core. He was still inside her, and while he was somewhat used to such hits, she'd never experienced anything like it. Saerano convulsed wildly in a spasmodic fit. She began bashing her skull against the brick wall behind her, showing an alarming loss of control. She cried out, spewing the foam that filled her mouth all over him. He bellowed along with her. The pain was ridiculous! She thrashed and writhed as waves of erratic contractions tortured her body. Finally, her bowels and bladder emptied in a sudden rush of foulness, adding to the unmistakable charm of their surroundings.

Janes stared into the dead face of Saerano. Her eyes bled and she was no longer lovely. He carefully pulled out of her and slowly slid her across the wall towards the tavern door to avoid setting her down in a puddle of her excretions. This was a new torment. He had experienced different kinds of weird and wild lightning strikes, but nothing like this! He looked down at himself. His spike was as hard as iron, seemingly a side effect of the blast. Static discharge still popped and crackled here and there about him. In disbelief, he noticed that there was smoke swirling around his spike! Janes breathed deeply, seeking to control himself, and blew out big, ragged breaths. He stood, then squatted before the dead woman's body.

Little curls of smoke played in Saerano's hair and emanated from her kit and clothing. Her chin was on her chest, her arms and legs were splayed out, her back was to the wall, and her bare arse rested on the pavers. It was a damned shame. Janes squatted further, lifting her chin. He looked into her wide, vacant, bloody eyes. Her clothing had burst apart at the seams in several places and there were smoldering holes in the bottom of her boots. There was absolutely nothing he could do for her. He let her chin fall back to her chest and quickly rifled through her items. He came away with a tiny bag of uncut gemstones and a palm bag filled with silver. He pocketed the gems and coin and backed away, pulling his pants up. He checked his kit, then turned and jogged out the alley into the streets beyond as quickly as the iron between his legs would allow.

As Janes left the rank odor of the alley behind, he realized that he stank of singed hair and smoldering clothes. He slowed down and joined the throng of life that wandered Bellost. He realized something was off as he got random stares while trying to blend in on the street. Jancs paused for a few moments after escaping the body in the alley behind the bar. He looked at his reflection in a storefront window. His curly hair was wilder than usual. He was pale and sweat wet his brow. Janes felt dizzy and achy. His head pulsed, there was a distinct ringing in his ears, and his teeth hurt. The right side of his face and neck felt as if they were burning.

Unfortunately, he knew that feeling. His reflection revealed the truth. His neck, jawline, and the lower right side of his face were inflamed. Raised red fern-like lines stood out on his skin. He closed his eyes, feeling dizzier now, and shook his head. His long streak of terrible luck hadn't changed. Janes knew from experience that the pattern on his neck and face would at least fade to a pale white over time as the scarring became permanent. It seemed like his entire body was covered by reminders of his curse. His joints and muscles ached constantly, and the strike brought on a flare-up. His pain increased as he continued towards Barterer's Way. Soon Janes realized that he couldn't continue. He needed to find a place to sit down for a while.

The bolt had coursed through Saerano, it seemed. She'd certainly gotten the worst of it. His clothes, at least, had survived the blast. Of course, one of the first things he'd conceded to the curse was his style of dress. You did not want to be sweating and you didn't want to be wearing tight clothes if you were struck by lightning! He knew not to carry metal weaponry or armor, as such equipment made things much worse. There had been times when the metal that he carried fused or melted. He had stopped wearing jewelry long ago. Even carrying coin was unsafe. There was a foul taste in his mouth. He was passable in public, which was his primary concern.

He slipped into the Clever Marten, a pub at the corner of Caretaker's Run and Barterer's Way. He found a small table, attempting to blend in as he tried to get it together.

It had been nearly a year since the vengeance of Kraekus had been called down upon him. He had been at home in Ithil-Bane when he found himself embroiled in a situation that, in retrospect, had to be described as deeply regrettable. He had been struck by lightning the morning after the incident. The strike was immense and inflicted pain upon him such as he'd never encountered. It came suddenly, under a clear sky, and threw him from the street into a fruit stand. His injuries were extensive and it seemed a miracle that he had survived. Brutal though the hit was, it was only later that Janes discerned that something truly daunting and more persistent had begun.

He didn't know that the assault would continue until after the second hit, weeks later. That strike left him aghast, for it was then that Janes began to fully comprehend what had been invoked. Priests at local temples he approached about his dilemma suggested that he had been cursed. He was told that the actual words used were important, but he didn't recall hearing any casting being spoken. Not one of them could do anything on his behalf, and several loathed even discussing it; so feared was Kraekus, the Lord of Lightning. The lack of intercession was upsetting and Janes decided that he must make a pilgrimage to Harab and the largest church of Kraekus that he could find. There he would beg forgiveness for his transgression. The clerics could at least direct him that way and he booked passage on a ship for the City of Paellor, the capital of Harab.

Once in Harab, Janes was turned away without relief by the worship of Kraekus. He was told that his body had been marked, illuminated by what they called "arc light"—an arcane sigil visible to any true believer. That sign singled Janes out as a targeted foe of their deity. Such a mark, they said, was a sure sign of retribution to come. It could not be mitigated. His sins could not be forgiven, as apparently a direct appeal to the demigod Himself had set the arc light upon him. His punishment was the full measure of the immortal's judgment, manifesting in the harshest terms. Indeed, at that moment, Janes realized that Kraekus might slay him at will, at any time. Instead, the demigod seemed eager to torment him, to enjoy his suffering as he skittered across the aerth like some insect, trying to avoid being stepped on.

Imagine knowing that such a being had noticed you and desired your slow and torturous annihilation. The feelings that washed over Janes were overwhelming! He felt tremendous fearful helplessness, for who could hope to survive the wrath of the Aeglain? The proclamation of impending doom that he received from the worshippers of Kraekus made the second strike even more terrifying, as the full consequences of the hex became clear. The clerics warned him that further distancing himself from where he'd been cursed was useless. Janes responded by fleeing in a blind panic.

He wasn't assailed sailing upriver to the west on the River Throrng and deep into Harab. He disembarked, acquired a horse, then sought to flee the wrath of Gaelthar's tempestuous second son. However, it soon became apparent that the priests had been prophetic and that the eternal sky was ever watchful. A storm gathered as he rode and seemed to shadow him as if in pursuit. Soon, the very skies were alight with thunderbolts. The inevitable, vicious strike that came claimed the life of his mount and sent Janes sprawling. That third strike was so brutal and massive that it left Janes in a state of semi-consciousness and wracked with seizures for weeks. Only the kindness of strangers saw him through this new crisis.

Oscillating back and forth between oblivion and convulsive consciousness, Janes was cared for by a gentle and kind priest of Daellus in a small farming village. The cleric devoted himself to caring for a stranger his parishioners found in a gully on the roadside. He ministered to the stranger's many wounds, honoring the way of his worship. Slowly, he brought him back from the brink. Janes eventually regained his wits and strength. When he could, he fled, his mind full of thoughts of what harsh reprisal the saintly priest might face for daring to help him. In so doing, he had unwittingly taken the next step toward his ultimate fate.

Janes wasn't a wise or even an educated man, but he knew the lessons that any child of Ithil-Bane was taught. Human free will was both a burden and a gift, as a man's choices might doom him to the judgment of one or more of the Aeglain. Such a man would be the greatest of fools to think that he could escape the torments of an immortal by merely ending his life. Suffering decreed by a member of the Aeglain, manifest in the punishment of one's mortal form, no matter how severe, could always be worse.

If a full measure of anguish wasn't extracted from him, if the deity did not glean enough satisfaction from his pain, Janes' punishment might continue after his death—unbound by the limitations of time. Only intervention by another god might protect a mortal from such an ongoing fate. Thus, a large part of Janes' suffering was the horrible and specific knowledge that, once Kraekus had singled him out for retribution, all he could do was endure whatever the immortal decreed he deserved. Janes could only cling to the hope that his persecution would eventually end, along with his life.

Thus, the panic that had overwhelmed Janes was terrible as he felt there was nowhere to run, no place he could hide. He feared that his fate was sealed and that he could only await further torment under a vast and darkening sky. Several weeks passed while Janes wandered the wide world. He was constantly aware that the heavens could spew forth his immolation at any moment. The waiting was perhaps the worst part of it. The days were interminable, stretching out as each successive moment was filled with the awful anticipation of what would surely come. Just as he'd started hoping the curse had dissipated, the sky fell on him again.

The fourth strike found him at a crossroads, the blast coming without warning on a clear and cloudless day. He awoke as pass-ersby found the roadway littered with bodies. All had survived, but only he was awake. Perhaps his body and mind were becoming accustomed to the abuse. His clothes had exploded, his skin was scarred, and his mind was in a state of turmoil like he had never experienced. It seemed like blind luck that there had been no deaths and in the ensuing days, he went into a deep depression. He was haunted by the concern that all whose path crossed his, no matter how casually, might suffer the retribution that he alone was meant to bear. Janes began to pray to Kraekus, appealing to Him directly. That may have seemed strange but he begged forgiveness, praying for his curse to end and that he might return to some semblance of ordinary human existence.

No absolution came.

Janes' waking thoughts were a wide array of spectacular anx-ieties. He was always concerned, not just for himself but for those around him. Everywhere he went, he imagined the destruction that would ensue should he suddenly be subjected to another strike. In his mind, he conceived the mighty titan looking down upon him from some distant thunderhead and his gaze was ever turned towards the sky. It was too much and he entered a period of denial. He determined he needed to stay indoors, hiding away where he couldn't be easily detected. His plan was predictably short-sighted but his mind was made up. Surely, he reasoned, such a damning malediction couldn't last forever! He would outlast it.

In Paellor, he'd encountered folk who could see his curse about him, true believers to whom the manifestation of his so-called arc light was visible. He couldn't stand their gaze upon him, for it was as if they could see his guilt and judgment filled their eyes. There can be no doubt that such an experience only added to his desire to be alone. While his coin may have been a bit melted, its value remained. He overpaid gladly and so he found a quiet hamlet at the western border of Harab with a relatively comfortable place where he could lay low. There he experienced a few extraordinary weeks of relative peace. In the end, however, he learned that a roof doesn't necessarily stop a lightning strike. Just as he began to think that he might have escaped further torment, the judgment of the dark heavens crashed through the very ceiling, bringing the place down around him!

Janes survived, as he had four times before, but several innocent people died in the ensuing fire as the boarding house went up like so much tinder. The concern that had haunted him, the precise thoughts he had put aside so forcefully coming to full fruition as an entire family in their beds suffered a horrible fate, entirely because he'd sought to avoid his. The undeserved suffering of that fell night left Janes wallowing in his curse. It dashed his attempts to deny reality and reinforced the knowledge that he must endure his agony alone. Although he faced the tribulations of an uncertain future in a constant state of trepidation and awful anticipation, he realized that he must push on without involving others in the wrath of the gods.

The Lord of Lightning had proven to be a cruel torturer, seemingly insensitive to the perils of the innocent, suffering or even perishing in the wake of His wrath. Janes spent his days cowering under the oppressive anger of the heavens, constantly moving, never daring to stay in one place for long, lest those around him suffer. Janes trekked the wilderness, at one point finding a remote cavern in which he sought to live like a hermit. Kraekus, however, would not be denied his retribution. All too soon, large, angry storms began to coalesce in the area around the cave. Massive fits and frenzies of blazing lightning increased in frequency, finally zeroing in on Janes one night.

Blue-white heat filled the area around the mouth of the dugout. As Janes watched in horror, bolts from above electrified the cavity itself, somehow dancing into the cave he had assumed would protect him. Deafening thunder reverberated in the tight space and Janes was thrown off his feet. The entire area was blasted asunder and portions of the cavern collapsed around him. Although much of the cave survived, Janes was left stunned and confused. He wouldn't have believed lightning strikes could get any worse but it had happened. The sheer size of the conflagration that had filled the hollow was impossible to forget and Janes had to acknowledge that he no longer felt safe there. He was, in fact, too afraid to even venture outside to seek the meager roots and berries that were keeping him alive.

When the skies cleared, a thinner, more haggard Janes fled the cave in desperation, seeking concealment once more amidst the obscurity of the tiny villages and hamlets along the border of Harab. He had deceived himself, imagining he could hide from immortal attention. However, his memory had begun to fail him, a symptom of the continued damage from the wrath of Kraekus. During that stretch, he endangered all around him, for his sleep was so disrupted by his various afflictions that his mind was genuinely unsound. Headaches constantly assailed him. He was easily distracted and unable to concentrate. His personality had changed and Janes no longer thought of those around him. Instead, he wallowed in wretched selfishness. Janes was woefully befuddled without a reliable sense of time, place, or even himself.

He led a pathetic life of thievery, lurking on the outskirts of any settlements he came across in his wanderings, simply taking what he needed to survive. Lightning punished him during the following months. A seventh and an eighth strike found him, although the hits came at increasingly slower intervals. He frequently prayed, attempting to sway Kraekus with various proposed bargains that he somehow imagined might be acceptable to the immortal. A life spent living alone in the wild, praying to a son of Gaelthar? If the old Janes had seen the bizarre new incarnation of himself that the fates had forged in the crucible of sky-fire, he wouldn't have even recognized himself.

At that point, Janes could not say how many others had been badly injured or died randomly for merely being near him. He thought it through. He could remember several individuals and one incident in particular with three children. The rest were just a blur. Janes no longer felt the remorse or guilt that had once caused him such anguish. He had realized that such victims were merely collateral damage. After all, was it he that flung lightning from the sky? Was it he who killed those folk?

The longer he pondered it, the angrier he became. After the ninth strike, Janes was consumed by rage. It helped to focus his ragged mind, which had nearly failed him entirely. The strike was so intense and prolonged that it caused him to clamp his jaw shut tightly enough that he had a mouthful of toothaches to accompany his ever-present, full-body joint pain. He was no longer on the verge of mental collapse but his body had begun to fail him altogether. Janes' chest hurt and his skin was covered in fern-like scarring from the bolts of sheer energy.

As the tenth strike approached, the pain shocked Janes back to a more conventional state of mind. The repeated hits seemed to cancel out some of the more awful residual effects of the previous strikes. Capable once more of ordinary thought, he sought to be more prudent. He tried to avoid the open sky. Janes had learned that neither being careful nor doing things that seemed clever were effective. So, a sense of desperation grew in him, for he knew that Kraekus was watching and tormenting him selectively, choosing the most inopportune moments to strike. Janes more actively sought to come up with a way to do something about his dilemma.

The tenth strike came, and James' despair matched his desperation. He realized he'd never been struck without a sizable time delay after the previous hit, so he risked a journey on the waves, returning to Ithil-Bane. Janes did not have a sizable tally of friends or a large family upon whom he could rely. Even so, while on the water, he made a list in his mind. Whatever the debt, no matter how small a favor owed, whoever might be of help, he called it in—to no avail. No one in his life could help him. Weeks in the Dark City yielded no new plan and revealed no options or avenues of action that promised any relief. While again seeking the lifting of his curse, Janes turned to any who offered a glimmer of hope. He failed to find anyone capable of such a feat. Janes had bargained with the priests in Harab. Now he sought the counsel of the power brokers of the City of Dreams. No priest or wizard he could access was capable of or willing to take any decisive action on his behalf. Finally, one bold, if improbable, plan came to light.

On a suggestion from a longtime acquaintance in the navy, Janes traveled to Nurn, the land of the gnoams. There he sought the aid of a particular inventor of renown who was said to be able to tame lightning. This kind and brilliant visionary had conceived of a type of cage that could shield one from the terrible bolts of the angry skies. In the end, it proved to be an impossible task. The generous genius was still far from being able to see his aspirations through, no matter the amount of effort the splendid fellow spent on his behalf. As if to cruelly highlight the futility of it all, the gnoam's failure was punctuated by a savage eleventh strike that left him injured and Janes even more despondent than ever.

Quietly, sadly, he arranged passage back to the eastern shores of Caan. Janes figured that he had at least a few weeks before he had to worry about a twelfth strike. On its way, the coast runner stopped in several places and they were scheduled to spend a day in the port of a great tavern town, Bellost. Janes felt depressed. He figured that he could perhaps get away with a day of drink and forgetfulness in Bellost. Maybe ale would numb his pain. A casual conversation with one of his shipmates yielded a tip about one particular place that sounded like a good time. Janes let out a heavy sigh and resigned himself to what meager hopes he could muster.

Bockscar Janes wasn't an overtly evil man. Yes, his life had been defined by a certain moral indifference. He had, admittedly, committed more than his share of regrettable mistakes. As a young man, he'd spent years in the Ithil-Banian navy and had lived to tell the adventurous tales of such a life. When his five-year conscription had ended, using the coin of his duty bonus, Janes had taken a wife.

He had tried to make it work, settling into a job as a day laborer on the docks. He had a roof over his head, enough to eat, and a good woman. Soon a child was on the way, and he had the kind of life that, if a bit boring, was good enough for most men, as they say.

Janes, it seems, was ill-suited for a life on land. Such a sentiment was expected in a country that sailed far and wide. It was a thing that many men of his nation have experienced. He missed the travel and freedom of the seas and yearned to return to the waves. An accidental fall saw his wife's pregnancy end suddenly and tragically. After an appropriate mourning period, Janes chose to leave his wife in their home, supported by his remaining coin. She had family members and friends locally to keep her company. She also had her habitual sewing and her beloved books. So, he struck out, determined to trust his fate again to the briny foam of Maera's vast waters.

Janes made his way north and signed with the Far Coast Trading Company out of Eglair. That outfit highly valued his time on the waves and familiarity with a blade and gave him gainful work aboard ships running goods along the shorelines of Caan. Somehow, that rich and powerful Eglairian company's vessels had a license to run the waves south to Ithil-Bane, north to Harab, west into Gindlorn, and even around the entire continent to tie at the docks of Bentua.

By some clever negotiation of man or grant from the gods, they crossed the southern oceans of Maera, molested by neither storm nor fiend of the depths. Where others dared not travel, the mercantile fleet of the Far Coast Trading Company sought rare spices from around the world, trading them in every port of Caan and Maerisna for vast rewards. For a man like Janes, it was a wonderful life, full of ample reward for honest and exciting work, with plenty of time spent in foreign ports full of strong drink, stronger pluck, and beautiful, exotic women of wonderfully ill repute.

Months passed and Janes enjoyed his time at sea. He earned his wage and the trust to go ashore where he spent the small portion of his pay that he'd agreed to take in coin on himself in drink and other less savory endeavors. Distance and time helped heal his heart and the loss of their child, his son, eventually wore less heavily on him. Perhaps he would put another baby in his woman upon his return home. He became known for doing more than his share, kept himself out of trouble, and became a valued veteran of the Company. When his ship rotated back to Ithil-Bane, Janes was a year older and ready for quality time with his woman in a town he knew well.

Janes disembarked in the rain, the chilled westerly breeze stinging his face as he entered the port side of the Dark City. Men were everywhere, bringing to mind a saying. "The Dreaming City never sleeps," he said aloud, feeling a local's pride in the thriving economy for which his nation was known. As he left the ship, the mate offered him a draught of Bentuan rum for services well rendered. He settled up with the paymaster on the docks and someone broke out a bit of poxy, which gave him a nice surge of energy. The bustle of the docks faded into the distance and he entered the city proper. His wife was no great beauty but her body was inviting, and she'd always missed him badly when he traveled. She was a good girl who kept her mouth shut and never failed to finish her chores. He wanted to sleep in a comfortable bed, eat a hot meal, and enjoy a few good sessions of rough kueting.

Janes arrived home and was surprised to open the door and find the apartment empty. It was day, so he had papers that allowed him to travel under Aarn. It was one of the many perks of being a Company man. His wife would have no such favor with the law. It was illegal to cast a shadow and she should have been home, asleep like everyone else. The older man in the flat above opened a window and called down to welcome him home. The man suggested that he try Balton's Brew, saying that Janes' wife had been seen there of late. That seemed odd and he was confused and irritated by the news. Festering foam! Was she out day drinking? With his coin?

Minutes later, Janes stood in front of Balton's Brew, looking at his wife. Lana sat across from the bar at a table with a man. Each had a full measure of ale in front of them and she was laughing happily, seemingly having a good time. The apparent ease she felt in the stranger's company stung the seaman like the strike of a scorpion. His pleasant sense of anticipation evaporated, replaced by an instant, icy rage. Janes felt a familiar murderous urge that had served him well in battle. For him, it was a substitute for courage. Janes knew from experience that he could do anything under the influence of that emotion.

He paused for a few heartbeats, reasoning it out. In cases of such an obvious outrage, publicly discovered, the law was unambiguous. The accepted customs of Ithil-Bane favored what Janes was contemplating and opportunity encouraged action. In truth, the sailor never thought twice. He went calm as he followed behind a barmaid carrying a full tray past his wife. Janes used the wench to shield his approach as he moved on the fool who'd so badly overstepped the bounds of his marriage. "Aerdos—guide my hand," he whispered as he came up behind his intended victim with merciless and bloody intent.

Janes was good with a dagger. He used weapons infrequently in his duties over the years but was always a willing participant when it was time for violence. Few who knew him noticed the slow, insidious change in Janes, as each time he took a life, he was more willing to do so again when the next opportunity came. The Creep, his fellow sailors called it, for they believed a man seldom ran to damnation but crept toward it, one foul deed at a time. Indeed, there was nothing cruel about Janes' eyes or face. His good looks belied his ability and willingness to do horrible things. He came with stealth upon his foe from behind, easing his dirk out of its sheath in a solid reverse grip. His wife looked up at him, not yet registering any sign of recognition, as Janes pushed his victim's head to the side with his off-hand and simultaneously plunged his double-edged blade into the man's shoulder. Using the clavicle as a guide, he pulled his blade through the meat of the shoulder to his neck, slashing the side of his throat as he withdrew his steel.

His victim moaned as a shocking amount of blood gushed from the nasty wound. Janes stepped quickly aside to avoid the wet. The man fell forward onto the table amidst a chaos of spilled ale and his flailing arms. His eyes rolled back in his head as his body fell heavily to the tavern floor, flooding the timbers with crimson arterial spurts. His wife's screams filled the bar as she watched her friend's murder unfold in a hellish display of Janes's darker side. Hands to her face, she wailed in horror that became terror as Janes stepped forward and dealt with her. He could not abide screeching from either a woman or child, so her caterwauling eased his anxiety. The din ended in a series of gurgles as he freed his blade from 'neath her chin.

The lean seaman scowled as he looked about the place but no one there objected. "Let it be known—the right of a husband has been claimed here," he said in a loud, steady voice. Several patrons met his stern gaze as Janes sought theirs. Most gave a slow nod in acceptance of the deed, then looked back to their own business. Janes studied the body of his victim. The corpse stared at the ceiling, the initial shock in his eyes replaced by the glazed look of one whose soul had left the confines of the mortal world. The man was surprisingly youthful in appearance. Janes had imagined that, should his wife ever seek another's affections, he would surely be an older man. Regardless, fate had proven that any such choice was wrong.

Janes relieved the bodies of their wealth, which was the right of a slayer in the Dark City. The pair each carried a purse and their coin would be useful to him. The dead man wore a cobalt tunic of fine make. His leather kit was of equally high quality. Was it some vague promise of a life of luxury that had lured her into this relationship? He stopped short of thinking about it further. The matter was ended and had been well and decisively handled. As if to punctuate that thought, Janes crossed the room and addressed the barkeep. "Feed that meat to fleshers, for all I care," he said loudly, in a clear voice, for any present to hear. "I offer this for your considerable trouble." He shook a palm bag, fat with coin, dropping it to the bar with an audible jingle. The barkeep nodded acknowledgment without contention.

Having addressed the requirements of Ithil-Banian law, Janes took his leave of the tavern. He went home, cleaned himself up, and rested in bed. He planned on leaving the next day much as he had arrived. There was ample food in the house to satisfy him. He slept through the rest of the day and the following night without incident, his conscience unburdened by his deeds. When he awoke, he prepared a meal to break his fast. Janes left his home with the dawn, intending to leave his old life behind him. The sailor, however, never made it back to the ship that awaited him.

Father Aerald Stevenson of Harab faced many difficulties in his position as the High Priest of Kraekus in Ithil-Bane. Few gods so clearly aligned with good dared serve the public in the Dark City but the worship of Gaelthar's second son required it. All manner of casters ran rampant in the City of Dreams and it was his role to moderate any improper use of his Lord's power. "One cannot abide rules untaught," he'd said upon accepting the assignment. It was a phrase that described his role well. He acknowledged the unique customs of the nation of Loekii as part of the administration of the Will of Kraekus. In so doing, Father Stevenson faced daily, complex challenges that required not only a flexible mind but a keen sense of political proportionality in response to unpredictable events.

Aerald's son Tomas had joined his parents in Ithil-Bane. In his early twenties, he led a life of great privilege. It shielded him from the harsh realities of the world that enveloped so many others at such an age. His future was already assured. His parents sought to offer him as many avenues to success as possible while striving to keep him away from the seedier parts of Ithil-Banian life. He had body men wherever he went, assigned by his father to keep him from any physical altercation, a daunting task in a realm where merely standing in a man's shadow often led to blood.

Tomas was extremely well-educated. His continuing tutelage was bolstered by an eagerness to learn. His father's success led to multiple assignments in their native Harab and many foreign lands. Thus, Tomas had learned firsthand that different points of view were one of the complexities of human existence on Maera. That knowledge had led him to develop an open mind, free of snobbery, and assumed societal superiority seemingly inherent in the noble class of his folk. Such enlightenment at a young age left him isolated from his peers and steeped in profound loneliness. His gentility further alienated Tomas from others, so he was thrilled, perhaps overly so, upon meeting one of a like mind.

Tomas enjoyed frequenting lower wards of the Dark City more often than his standing suggested he might. He did so out of raw curiosity and in search of rare books. On one such venture, he encountered a common woman who reminded him of a lady he had previously known. Her lilting laugh was what first drew his attention. He followed her at a distance, observing that she had an easy smile that complimented her charming exuberance. She was pretty but not the beauty that Tomas remembered his former lover to be. Still, he felt an intangible attraction to her that he could not explain. Perhaps it was his sense of curiosity that ensnared him. He wondered how a commoner could afford prohibitively expensive books. He went out of his way to make her acquaintance.

She had been a shy and private child whose father had indulged her rather pricey habitual reading, bringing her any books he could acquire while sailing abroad. She traded the foreign books to dealers for more standard fare until she was well-read. Janes was a good match for one who was used to being alone, so she became an intelligent but quite lonely woman, unused to the attention of any nobleman, let alone such a handsome young man. She felt innocent joy in his company and, woefully, indulged in an urge for acknowledgment that she badly underestimated.

What resulted was the pair forging a friendship based on their mutual love of reading. While each felt attracted to the other, they hesitated to act. She was married and fully five years his elder, in any case. He was kind and handsome, but she had always been faithful to Bockscar, even when they were still single, and he had sailed away to an uncertain life as a navy man. Tomas sensed her hesitancy and would never have pressed another man's wife, regardless. His upbringing as the son of a priest had hammered such morality home. It was enough to have someone he could meet with occasionally, whose company he enjoyed, to discuss the latest books they had read. He accepted what happiness he found in their shared interests, making sure not to overstep the boundaries separating them.

The two fell into an easy rhythm of biweekly meets at a pub conveniently located for her. Tomas insisted that such conclaves were free of any social demands or difficulties for her. He secured papers through his family's connections that allowed their encounters to occur during daylight hours while the Dark City slept. They selected one of the few taverns known to cater to the daytime workers necessary to keep the metropolis running. There were rarely more than a few people in the tavern at their chosen meeting time, which assured their relative privacy and the superior, attentive service Tomas required. Their latest meeting was a delightful time. They often laughed while discussing a particularly clever comedic offering that Tomas had rightly guessed would entertain his friend.

Aerald Stevenson heard of his son's murder in the middle of a stressful day. The facts were upsetting, and he was confused. Why was his son in a tavern in the town's Fifth Ward? Where were his body men? Who was the woman found with him? Who would want his son dead? What could be done about it? The day was a whirlwind of painful activity. He desperately tried to control his emotions. He largely succeeded, although awaiting the detailed information he demanded was torturous. The answers came reasonably quickly though, as he had made powerful friends in local law enforcement. He scheduled an update for that evening and made the trek home to inform his wife of the untimely and violent murder of her eldest child, their only son.

Aerald Stevenson returned to his church the following day for a briefing on what the investigation he had financed had yielded. The information was as enlightening as it was frustrating. As he had expended copious coin, a shocking number of details had already come to light. No one they'd interviewed had sought to evade the process. Neither was the explanation for what had happened complicated. His son had died while sitting with another man's wife in a tavern the pair had been frequenting. The meetings were intimate enough that his son had bribed his body men to give them privacy. Her husband had come upon them, engaged in an apparent affair, and slew them both. He had openly invoked his right, by Ithil-Banian law, to kill a wife who had strayed and her lover when he found them together.

The man's identity was known, as he'd paid the tavern openly for their inconvenience in removing the bodies. The authorities were not seeking him. The investigative team had recovered his son's body, which was already in the temple being properly prepared. He sent the team back to the tavern to retrieve the woman's body. She had been important to his son. The priest bore down. He had much to accomplish before turning his attention to his family in their time of mourning.

Aerald secluded himself in his private chapel, located directly beneath the metal spire of the cathedral of Kraekus. He communed with the immortal Lord of Lightning, providing the mighty titan with the name of the slayer of his son. He asked for justice. In his heart, he knew that his son had not lain with the wife of another. The authorities found two copies of the same book with the bodies. The bar staff had heard them speaking of shared readings. Aerald's son had died under suspicious circumstances, but he asked Kraekus for justice in the matter born of His flawless judgment and endless wisdom.

As he sat in the Clever Marten in the City of Bellost, Janes was confused and his chest felt tight. He drank ale slowly, quietly minding his own business. His thoughts lingered on Saerano, the wonderful touch of her lips and the potent allure of her flesh. Janes thought of his wife for the first time in ages. He clung to the tattered shreds of his composure but tears ran down his face. His mind drifted, eventually settling on a harrowing memory from months earlier. In his wretched condition, he didn't have the strength to suppress it.

Janes recalled the day he approached the Seventh Ward's massive, ironwood temple of Loekii in Ithil-Bane. It was extremely vertical in construction, one hundred feet tall, and dominated by a steeply slanted roof covered in large, shield-like tiles. The entire structure was painted in multiple coats of a dull black concoction called tungst created by his folk, with which they waterproofed and fireproofed their ships. The monotone darkness of the mixture, when applied to such a tall and massive structure, was highly oppressive, setting a mood that only served to increase his trepidation as he approached the House of the Dark Mistress.

He requested an audience with the ward's High Priestess. Shockingly, he did not have to wait long. Taleth Raegail, having seen him in her dreams, pondered the man's request for mere moments. She strode into her private reception chamber where her attendants had left him to contemplate the company he was about to experience. Just as almost any denizen of the Dreaming City might, Janes found meeting the temple's most favored theurgist of its Dark Mistress entirely and utterly daunting. Thus, as she entered the tall, dark space, his desperation was apparent and on full display.

She ascended the stairs to a central dais made of black stone, her elaborate boots sending echoing clicks through the room. The raw sensuality of her appearance dumbfounded Janes. She threatened to spill out of a deep blue bodice, cinched so tightly at the waist that her body seemed impossibly proportioned. Her black, layered skirts were made of soft and supple leather that flowed as she strode forward. He couldn't even fathom how much work went into donning such attire, let alone how difficult it must have been to wear while attending to administrative church business.

"Come forth, supplicant—submit to my touch," she commanded. Above her mouth, her face was concealed behind a dramatic white and black mask. All her exposed skin was painted white to match, adding a frightening and macabre edge to her costume. Janes ascended the stairs slowly and knelt on one knee upon the dais before the Voice of Loekii. She open-palmed his forehead. Her touch was cold, her tone colder. "I see your sins, Bockscar Janes." She seemed to hover over him threateningly. "You murdered a man you did not know. That is always perilous. In that act, you were sundered from Our Mistress, as you unwittingly dedicated yourself to serving a lesser god, for whom you will now be a valuable tool."

The priestess raised her face as if trying to avoid an unpleasant odor. Her mouth curled into a blatant sneer. "I find your blundering to be … offensive." Affronted as she was, she had already expended a fraction of her daily maena to enter his mind, thus she felt compelled to finish her reading of it and then deliver the Word of Loekii.

"Ah, yes … I understand. Your folly was two-fold, mortal. A more egregious crime was committed, one which repulses Our Dark Mistress. You invoked another to 'guide your hand,' yes?" She removed her palm suddenly as if from a flame. She held the hand aloft, away from her body as she continued. "Did you think such an affront would escape the Eversight of Loekii?" She paused to allow her words of accusation to set in.

"Fool … you shall be granted no intervention here!" Her cold, harsh words pummeled him in their truth and judgment. "Since you seek to compound your weakness, perhaps you should petition the Dead God, whom you asked to condone your murderous actions." Disgust dripped like venom from her tongue as she continued. "Heed my words! Any attempt to seek mercy from the Aeglain will only further the cause of your tormenter! Now … LEAVE ME!" With her warning delivered, the priestess spun dramatically away from him, the sharp metallic edge of her black outermost skirt cutting the air. She strode from the chamber even as her servants showed Janes the door.

Janes finished his ale, dwelling on the day he had been removed from the black Temple of Loekii. He now knew that was the day when the width and breadth of his plight became clear to him. He sat alone in his misery, the events of that woeful encounter still stinging his heart. What happened next may have been sheer chance, but to Janes, in that moment, well, it felt like something more. A stranger addressed him and the deep bass of the man's voice cut through all of the hazy confusion in his weary mind.

"If you don't desire company, I would surely understand, but it looks like you could use a friend." Janes looked up and met the gaze of a man with an impressive beard and long brown hair, piercing dark eyes, and a ruddy skin tone. The handsomeness of his face, when combined with the strength of his tall, thick build and the rich clothing he wore, added to the man's air of authority and personal power. Janes stared openly but no words came.

"I'm Father Henrikson of Gaellus, and this is my acolyte. He has sworn an oath of silence, so I bid you ignore him. May I join you, sir?"

Janes was caught off guard and could barely stammer a response. "Yes, yes … certainly … please, join me." He gestured to the seat to his left. The man walked around the table and took the chair to his right.

"Forgive me but I prefer not to sit with my back to any door. It's a very ingrained habit that has served me well before." He smiled and Janes' mind reeled.

A Priest of Gaellus? Here? Now?

"What are we drinking?" The cleric gestured to the nearest barmaid and ordered a round of ale. What followed was a conversation in which Father Henrikson skillfully, patiently, extracted a heartfelt confession from his new friend. After an undetermined amount of time, the sailor had bared his soul. It was the first time he'd let it all out, the first opportunity he had taken to unburden himself of his woes and the vast loneliness compounding them.

"I did not come across you by mere chance." The priest now seemed to have a confession of his own. "I dreamt of our meeting, Janes. I've sought you out. Gaellus has shown me His will through dreams before, and I believe He has charged me with your redemption." Such a notion stunned Janes. The toxic nature of the dreams of Loekii's brood was well known. Ithil-Banians feared their dreams, and any that came true were certainly not benevolent. Janes was so shocked by the sudden offering of hope he was left speechless.

Gaellus Gaeltharson is the eldest of the three sons of the God of Leadership, the banished standard-bearer for the forces of good on Maera. Gaelthar was lost more than two thousand years ago at Gaedennon, punished for His role in that debacle by Ptalles, Judge of the Aeglain. Gaellus was the immortal that took up that banner in His father's absence and took over the heavy burden of Gaelthar's command imperative. Kraekus was subordinate to his brother Gaellus. Did that mean Father Henrikson could offer the sailor relief from the vengeance of the Lord of Lightning?

It seemed too good to be true but he was ready to take any chance, willing to cling to any offering of hope. A man from a society such as Ithil-Bane does not eagerly seek the aid of others. They live by a harsh word followed by a harsher act. Janes felt disgustingly helpless. He had lost his self-determination. He was weak, a victim. He'd lost everything that made him feel like a man. His life had been taken away from him. The few minutes he'd shared with Saerano had been the first normal human contact he'd had in months. He decided right then and there to trust the Father.

"Redemption, you say?" His voice quivered with hope and doubt. "You can do that?" The priest nodded his head. "What do I have to do?" Janes asked.

After an entire year of loneliness, hopelessness, pain, and mental anguish testing the limits of what a man could endure, Janes felt vulnerable in a new way. He'd spilled his thoughts and fears into the ear of the Priest of Gaellus as much as the nearby drunkard doused the floor with his vomit. So, he sat and stayed quiet, ready to soak up whatever the priest said.

The cleric appreciated the circumstances from which a citizen of Ithil-Bane came. It was a base function of his ministry to hear the confessions of the foolish and the weak, and he felt a constant strong impulse to relieve the burden of the suffering. This wretched man that now sat beside him, he reminded himself, was murderous and unrepentant for his crimes. Indeed, the man did not even comprehend his wickedness. Janes did not see the evil such acts served in the wide world. The sailor was unaware of the misinformation constantly fed to the masses of Ithil-Bane. Through long experience, the priest understood that a state of ignorance such as the young man lived in concisely summarized the circumstances of most humans on Maera. Men, left to their own devices, seldom sought out inconvenient truths through painful introspection.

"Would you be willing," he queried, "to journey with us to a place where we expect to have a religious epiphany? I hope that, if we are exposed to the raw will of Gaellus, He shall see fit to mitigate the terrible judgment that His brother has laid so harshly upon you." Father Henrikson tried his best to be charitable, especially when the opportunity presented itself as his lord's intention. "We are about to journey to meet the manifestation of Gaellus in the wild. Surely our road would be improved by your company."

Janes did not understand all of what the holy man was saying. Mitigate? Manifestation? He had seldom heard such words. He had never been one for fancy speaking, in any case. He hardly hesitated at all, although a year ago, he would never have desired the lofty company of a religious leader. He had some idea of what so-called "good folk" believed, having traveled the world a fair bit. Vessels on which he had worked for the Company berthed in Harab, Gindlorn, and other such places. Janes had not, however, frequently observed charity, kindness, or altruism firsthand. Thus, his confusion was to be expected. The sailor put his trust in the instincts he had always relied on at sea and fell silent altogether. He merely nodded his head in assent.

He spent the night in the comfort of a nearby inn, sleeping in a hammock in a common room. Janes arose before dawn and met his fellow travelers for a hearty break of their overnight fast. When the cleric insisted on paying for the meal, Janes accepted generosity as honest kindness. Clergy members were known to be wealthy and he took the fine clothes Father Henrikson wore as a sign of that truth. Overnight, Janes had pondered his immediate future and accepted being at this man's mercy. He'd readied himself to bear the awkwardness that charity would bring. The cleric had mounts ready and the three rode from town that morning into the wild.

They followed a road going south, which was nothing more than a dirt path. The first few days were ridden at a leisurely pace, a boon which Janes' backside appreciated, for he had never developed any tolerance for a saddle. The further they rode, the stronger his foreboding became. Janes had long ago developed an affinity for storms and could sense them well before they arrived. Premonition would have been a helpful skill under normal circumstances but instead only served to increase his constant state of paranoia. Thankfully, Father Henrikson was wonderfully patient. He had an overtly caring nature and as they rode, it became clear to Janes that the priest was one of the few kind men he had ever met. In his hometown, such interest and gentleness directed towards a younger man would have been seen as physical longing. So, Janes struggled to accept it as something decent, as that impulse was foreign to him. Growing up in the City of Dreams, the lecherous desires of an older man of privilege were a notion all too familiar to him. Although he found such an inclination distasteful, at least he had experienced such motivations.

A man like Janes understood the base things that men did. Benevolence was what baffled him. What makes a man think that what he's learned is more profound than the experiences of another? What could make him sure his thoughts and beliefs are better and more moral than others? Impulses felt by men, a balance of perceived risk and reward, and the cause and effect of decisions were concepts Janes was comfortable with. Morality was a trap, another set of rules typically imposed by those seeking control over others. His people, the free folk of Ithil-Bane, would not allow such constraints to be placed on their aessance. In Loekii worship, sin was anything a man did against his self-interest. Morality made a man weak and thus was a sin.

As Janes considered these things, an old saying of his people came to mind, encouraging understanding in such circumstances. The sailor tried to recall the wording of it. "It's a common sin to imagine that all men are motivated the way we are." It had been a favorite saying of his father's; a phrase Janes had always pondered. Around the time that he'd joined the navy, he had asked his father what it meant. His father had assured him that some people went through their lives pursuing something that they called "noble" aspirations. His father's advice on the subject had stuck with him. "As you travel the world, watch those you meet for signs of such a weakness. When you find it, treat it as the ripe opportunity that it is."

By the fourth day of their venture, a significant storm front had moved in, something for which the Peninsula of Harab was well known. They ate a morning meal just after dawn and drank a celebratory breakfast mead the priest brought to commemorate the day. Janes found being with the cleric calming. Father Henrikson promised they'd find Gaellus in the wild and properly approach the event, making his lord more amicable. "We'll see the culmination of our gambit this very day, my friend. There's no need to travel further. We are right where we want to be!" Janes could feel the lightning in the air and sensed that some significant event was imminent. He should have been scared. Instead, he felt a thrilling sense of anticipation. Would Gaellus Gaeltharson help him?

The priest walked with him out into the open wild, followed at a respectful distance by his silent acolyte. The cleric explained that he would engage in a casting designed to draw the attention of the immortal Lord of Storms. The physical presence of the storm front that would soon pass over them was an integral part of his casting. They would be under his protection as the storm raged. Janes knew nothing of such things and had no idea how to feel about it. "We'll need to prepare you for the presence of Gaellus. It would not do to receive him unceremoniously." He smiled and gave Janes a reassuring pat on his shoulder, a Harabian gesture of fellowship the sailor had encountered before. Ithil-Banians did not touch others so, unbidden.

The morning passed quickly as the priest led them to a sloped hillock that overlooked the terrain as it fell away shallowly to the south. "This will do nicely," he said. "It's time we see about lifting this curse of yours." That remark was heartening. After they shared another draught of the priest's excellent mead, rain began to fall in a steady drizzle. It was warm enough that it didn't bother them. A steady breeze drove the shower from behind them as they stood on the hill's apex.

"This is the place foreseen. The anticipated time has come. The waking dream reveals itself. Bockscar Janes, do you consent to this casting? Will you give yourself to the Will of Gaellus, my friend?"

Father Henrikson looked to the seaman with a solemn intensity. Janes felt light-headed but confident that he was making a good decision. He doubted that Kraekus would hurl thunderbolts at him while he was in such company. His feeling of bravado admittedly heartened him. He was astounded that he was out in the open, braving a full-blown Begaen storm without succumbing to his fears. Due to his nearly constant state of disorientation and confusion over the past several months, Janes had no idea that it was one year to the day since he acted upon what he perceived to be the betrayal of his wife.

"I agree ... may the Will of Gaellus guide us this day!" He committed to the favor of the Lord of Storms and thus, the stage was fully set. After that, Father Henrikson would hold full sway over his mortal existence.

"Rise now! Greet the Storm Lord Gaellus Gaeltharson! Welcome him into your life, Bockscar Janes. Open your heart to His judgment so that He may end your suffering." Janes began to glow in the eerie blue of the arc light as it peaked about his body. He left the aerth, floating upwards into the sky as the rain and wind increased around him. His arms splayed away from his torso, and his head tilted back. Janes opened both his mind and heart.

"I PRAY THAT KRAEKUS MAY END HIS CURSE OF THE OPEN SKIES! I CALL UPON THE FINALITY OF THE FOUR WINDS OF WRATH ... LET THIS BE THE TIME ... LET THIS BE THE PLACE ... LET THIS MAN FACE THE FULL MEASURE OF HIS DEEDS! MAY THE RIGHTEOUS JUDGMENT OF THE ETERNAL SKY ENGULF HIM! COME, ALMIGHTY GAELLUS, GRANT THIS MAN YOUR SIGHT, UNWORTHY THOUGH HE BE! REGARD THIS MORTAL IN YOUR PIERCING GAZE ... WEIGH HIS SINS AND, IN YOUR UNMATCHED WISDOM ... LET YOUR WILL BE DONE!"

The acolyte watched as Janes rose into the heavens while his patriarch shouted against the tumultuous gale in his full voice. The casting complete, he rushed forward to help his mentor overcome his fatigue. The effort of the summoning had exhausted him. The drug-laced mead's effects were spent. They watched together as Janes disappeared into what had become a funnel cloud. Soon, even the man's arc light had merged with the swirling heavens.

The skies had darkened and the roar of the tornado dominated the landscape. Neither man could say later how long it had lasted, lost as they were in the majesty of such proximity to the judgment of Gaellus. For the rest of their lives, they were marked by the experience. However, their clearest shared memories of the day were primarily of the aftermath.

In his weakened physical state, Janes was heavily influenced by the mead. He relaxed, even as he rose far above the plains. He was carried away at the heart of the raging storm, lifted high into the skies above the peninsula, arms spread, blue light dancing about his frame. He felt a wild elation as he fully surrendered to the spell. Suddenly, however, his joy abated as Janes felt the jarring, utterly raw and unmistakable presence of Gaellus Gaeltharson. All that most Ithil-Banians knew about the Lord of Storms was the legend of his piercing gaze. That manifestation was how He appeared to Janes, who was overcome by an all-encompassing vision of Gaellus' disembodied, incredibly intense eyes.

Janes felt his mind laid bare under the immortal's devastating scrutiny. The man reeled; his floundering mortal cognizance transfixed by the unspeakable peril of being so nakedly exposed to the tremendous power of the demigod's consciousness. Gaellus enveloped Janes. The Lord of Storms entered the man's mind and there was an instant in which the mortal was utterly known to Him. That was followed by another moment in which Gaellus rendered his judgment. Who can say how long that span was, as experienced by Bockscar Janes? Indeed, Gaellus had to partially shelter the man's intellect so then it was intact to comprehend his ultimate fate.

Then came Kraekus, Lord of Lightning, to the core of the devastating storm. He'd been invited to the moment by His brother Gaellus and He instantly realized why. The arc light of the man glowing, Kraekus sent a dozen bolts of lightning to savage the man's body in a devastating succession of white-hot agony. One after the other, the bolts of storm energy found him, each delivering a full array of mind-rending, traumatic anguish. Thus, the judgment of the sons of Gaelthar was delivered, the culmination of the Curse of the Open Sky laid upon the man a year earlier. Mind and body shattered; what was left of the man was cast from the heavens back down to the aerth. Janes had been destroyed by the justice of Kraekus and finally released by the mercy of Gaellus. Whatever glimmer of his mortal life remained was brutally truncated as Janes reached the ground. His suffering had finally ended. The example was well made.

In a role of increased prominence and after the fall of His father Gaelthar at Gaedennon, Kraekus had taken up residence within the dwaerven Kingdom of Kharak-kaar. He had claimed the tallest of the Grimmaere Mountains, the sacred peak the bearded folk called the Bosspike, and there He had built His legendary keep—Jaggedoom. From there, Kraekus dominated the mortals of the continent of Provos and influenced all of Maera. His constant fury and arcane power were ever displayed in the vast storms that swept the aerth.

In the forge chamber of His keep, Kraekus stood by a corner of His hearth. There He kept a collection of irons in a hotbox. These rods were linked in their arcane energy to His constant, simmering rage and glowed in their arc light. The demigod chose the iron that represented Bockscar Janes and considered its glow. He pivoted and plunged it into a nearby bath of water. The rod fretted and hissed as steam emerged from the vat. After just a few heartbeats, Kraekus removed it and pondered its jagged, lightning-shaped end. No longer imbued with His power, the iron grew cold, its radiant heat dissipating even as Janes' mortal life ended. Kraekus cast it aside, pitching it into a large pile of other raw materials. There Janes' mortal soul would remain in a type of spiritual stasis as it awaited future usefulness.

Father Henrikson and his acolyte found Janes' remains in a nearby settlement on the slanted roof of a farmhouse. When the pair arrived, a farmer and his sons were removing it from their home. The body was a startling sight. It effectively had to be scraped off of their roof. How it hadn't disintegrated on impact was anybody's guess. It had been carried thousands of strides south by the tornado, first over the rain-soaked plains and then onto the farmer's land over his winter crop. It had been so bombarded that the clothes had been almost completely stripped from the body. It had struck the roof with such force that there was little integrity left to the skeleton. Many of the bones were merely badly broken while others were utterly shattered.

What remained was barely recognizable as human. The hair had burnt off and the eyes had exploded from the face, leaving scorched holes in their place. That face was nothing more than a ghoulish mask of lumpy red flesh. The scorched body had swollen to more than twice its normal size and gave off an odor of cooked meat that made one gag. Tiny stalks of wheat sheared from the fields by the ferocity of the twister had imbedded in the entire body. They had sunk into it like thousands of tiny needles, making the corpse reminiscent of some prickly thistle. Aghast as the two were, Father Henrikson and his supplicant took charge of the remains, praising the farmer and his sons for their efforts. The body wasn't fit for travel, so they buried it in the nearby woods without a marker and with little ceremony.

The two could never put what they had seen out of their minds. The story they told upon returning to their community was so vivid, the graphic details so awful, the description they gave so horridly

surreal, that the tale spread across Caan like wildfire. For generations uncounted, parents would tell the story to frighten rebellious
children into a proper reverence for the Aeglain. The foes of the
sons of Gaelthar were filled with foreboding upon hearing it. Even
the draevar, known to be well-hardened against such terror, trembled. It fed the endless well of fearful helplessness mortals feel
when confronted with the forces of the aerth and sky that ever rage
around them.

Father Aerald Stevenson never truly recovered from the loss
of his only son. He and his wife tried to birth another but they were
no longer young and failed. It was a heavy burden to bear, one inad-
equately assuaged by the death of his son's killer. However, as he
became known by the locals of Ithil-Bane as the invoker of the Curse
of the Open Skies upon one of their ranks, Father Stevenson found
great success in his post as the Dark City's High Priest of Kraekus.
From their point of view, he had come to their town and suffered.
He had reacted not as a weak outlander but as they would, given
the power to do so. Somehow such an act made him one of them,
adopted by their city, and that dynamic persisted in their wicked
minds. He managed to instill quite a useful fear for his deity in the
nobles of the metropolis, a success that never failed to serve him
well. The legend of Aerald the Invoker took on a bit of life of its
own in the end.

The story of the malevolent doom that claimed Bockscar Janes
eventually secured an aggressive hold amongst those with a strong
storytelling tradition. The Maergen favored the telling and the story
was particularly popular with the survivors of the fallen human
Kingdom of Harab, ever counted high up on the list of enemies
of Ithil-Bane. The multitudinous baerbaraan tribe members of the

continent of Maerisna, known to prefer colorful stories, developed quite an affinity for it.

The Lesson of The Ravaged Man, although a story that had originated in a far-off land, became a favorite of Aeres' people. Perhaps this was due to the immense sway that the sons of Gaelthar hold over the furthest western plains of the continent, where the storm season so torments those humans. Their children are known to make frightening little dolls out of old rags soaked in human blood. The pups impale the figurine with many slender twigs. They then take the dolls into their beds, where they brave the dark of night. They hold their talisman tight to guard them while they sleep, believing it will protect them from the still-suffering spirit of The Ravaged Man, whose tortured howls, they say, can be heard on the dreaded storm winds that ever haunt the furthest tenacious edges of humankind's reach.

Want to experience more of Maera? Visit **www.maeraworld.com**

HE WHO SERVES
THE BALANCE

Alone he walked the lands of Maera, striding ever forth with the purpose of the power he served. There was nobleness in his purity of duty. He was aged but not bent. His old, ragged brown robes covered all but his bare feet. His walking staff was seemingly a large, oddly shaped branch from some dead tree, gnarled as his beard. His pupils were milky, making his blindness obvious. He toiled slowly but managed a steady pace. His weary face was sun-kissed and the deep lines in that face suggested an exceedingly long and challenging life. At a glance, he would seem naught but a roaming beggar. He stopped, lifted his head, and straightened his back. Just then, a large raven flitted to his left shoulder and gronked but once, loudly. The old man answered aloud.

"I agree. It is time."

The raven stepped sideways as he raised his staff. The bird touched wood with its beak. The bird blurred strangely and merged with the staff. That done, the raggedy man whispered to the dark and bled forward into the night, vanishing with a faint wink of emerald light. He phase-walked to his destination, an act of great power that few could duplicate. He arrived at his destination nary a moment hence, again with a brief, titillating flourish of viridescent energy.

His appearance had transformed as he traveled. Where previously he was the blind and lowly Pilgrim, he was manifest now as the Delight of Spring, one of his best-known forms. In this new and powerful expression of faith, his garments were rich. His clean, fresh robes were green and white, trimmed with silver and gold wire lattice. They were accented by his great snowy beard, now twice braided and decorated with emeralds. His long flowing hair swept away from his vibrant face, and his eyes flashed like jade. His staff was now polished ironwood, sleek, dark, and beautiful in its simplicity. A ball of green flame burned at its spherical tip. Here was the Wanderer in the Wilderness, the Arbiter of the Scales—this was the Grand Master Druid of Maera, carrying the great Staff of Balance—this was Bartolame.

It was nigh the aengel hour, fewer than four such measures 'til the dawn. The waning moon sunk in the sky. A low fog thickened the chill air. It was the Eve of Grace, and Bartolame stood alone at the border of the ruined land of Limrin.

That kingdom had once been a shining beacon of interracial cooperation, for the human nation had been closely aligned with the aelven folk. Together, the two peoples produced a beautiful country, one rich with many gardens, parks, and other expressions of nature, as well as new and exquisite styles of architecture. It was like a wondrous dream but it was too good to be true. The enemies of Kuraile are great indeed and with the full ferocity of their hatred focused on that symbol of unity and good, evil found a way to corrupt it.

The dream was shattered as Aerdos, using deceit and great treachery through his minions, caught the kingdom unaware. A Dread Portal opened to the netherworlds and the innumerable Legions of the Dead poured through it. *Dead Ground* was cast, befouling the very aerth and bringing destruction and a tremendous loss of life in a crushing blow to Limrin and the forces of good. Once a place of much beauty and repose, it became a horrid stain on the face of Maera, where the most dread forces of evil held sway. Thereafter, very few dared venture anywhere near the region.

No sound of life was heard there and an unnatural silence gripped the darkness. No beast hunted, and no bird or insect flew, for this was where nature and the unnatural met. Where so many others would have found this disturbing, Bartolame felt only a sense of grim purpose. He leaped into a whirling dance of power, spinning the staff in a precise pattern that left a trail of verdant fire as glyphs in the air. A witness would no doubt have been shocked as the raw physicality of it belied his apparent age. The casting was inherently complex but he finished quickly by striking the heel of the staff to the aerth with a crackling of energy.

That was merely the start of his casting.

He began to walk, a powerful march that saw him place his staff on the aerth at the end of each long, measured stride. He stayed within six feet of the line of death that defined the Wastes of Limrin so then the emerald flame of his staff left a sustained parallel line on the grass just to his side. The Dead Ground writhed in its search for a life force to drain. It seemed now to sense the power of that fiery line and shrank away from it. He strode ahead quite quickly but in complete control of the power he wielded. Such speed was crucial, for he must complete the circle he traced before the light of dawn.

Bartolame accelerated, walking now at an inhuman speed, for he had many miles to go. His was one continuous casting that would take perhaps three hours. Far beyond the ability of mortals, the spell was possible because of his symbiosis with the staff. Possibly the greatest of such vessels, it carried the combined souls of They Who

Had Come Before. Thus, after his last day of service to the cause, Bartolame would join his fathers in that eternal artifact. One day he would meld with them, forming the Grand Master of the Balance, and serve the next Grand Master Druid. But he would not rest yet. He was up to speed. Now it was just a matter of sustained concentration. That was when the voice started.

"Why do you bother to come here year in and year out? Why make us your enemy, old man?" it began. The speaker's voice dripped with taunting contempt. Bartolame knew that voice, having faced this challenge many times and still, it filled him with a familiar sense of clinging dread.

"Do you really think that you can continue this farce? How much more can you give and for whom?" It had the haunting quality of a disembodied presence, yet the voice stung him like a physical assault.

"How do the fleshlings reward you for your efforts but with their continued foolishness and constant selfish betrayals?" Not only was the voice disturbing in its words but the very sound of it seemed to attack the mind. It sought to fill the head as it unleashed doubt and psychic terror.

"For each moment you spend in their defense, they reward you with a lifetime of ignorance and insolence." Potent was the voice that had led young Prince Targor to ruin centuries earlier, the voice of the dead embodied. Bartolame further steeled his mind, knowing that distraction could not be tolerated.

"You will not finish, old fool. The task is beyond you now; you are no longer what you once were and you shall falter." He could hear its breathing but pushed on, half expecting to smell its breath next.

"What the wickedness and weakness of humans have wrought here shall spread, devouring all the aerth. You know this in your heart, for Loekii's spawn is the world's bane! Their precious free will has decided the matter." He understood how lesser beings fell prey to such tactics, for the relentless assault tested even his enhanced will. He allowed himself one long moment to imagine the effect on a less protected mind. It was simply inconceivable!

"Your bid to stem the inevitable is wasteful, for none can reverse what has already passed. None have even attempted it. Why should this task fall to you?" The voice continued to pry at his mind from every angle, searching for any frailty, hungering to find any doubt.

"Step twice to your left and join us, my old foe. There is no need to be forever alone. We understand power and how to use it, and we would welcome you. Come now to your deserved rest, for all things must end. Come, walk with us."

That voice continued, constantly invasive, seeking weakness, searching for any purchase in his mind. It found no such place, for if Bartolame himself had any deficiency, the Staff of Power did not. The merging of the Great Druid and that staff created a tremendous force for neutrality, which was fortunate, for this foe was mighty indeed. The dark entity chiding Bartolame was none other than the Arch-Devil Cestanos who held sway here with the Nosduh Stone of Power. The preeminent leader in the worship of the Dead God, Aerdos, this wicked creature was the being most responsible for the destruction of Limrin and so it was now his to rule. And that vile being was not accustomed to facing such strength, such resistance to his will. His venom continued to spew forth, unceasing, as the dawn neared. The druid continued to ignore it.

Bartolame approached his starting point again with time to spare. He finished the spell with a flurry of motion as he had begun. He spun his staff in the final gestures that closed the circle. When he brought the staff down to finish the spell, it struck the aerth with an explosion of energy and a clap of thunder. The space between his marked line and the dead ground was then illuminated in a pale green glow. Bartolame surveyed his work, clearly a great success. He seldom endured such a long casting with such continuous use of power, but this ceremony was necessary. The Ritual of Renewal was an annual event that kept the Wastes of Limrin from spreading further, infecting more of the aerth and increasing the sway of Aerdos over the region. As Maera's Grand Druid, he must not allow any further imbalance between good and evil. He had done well tonight thus far to ensure it. Next came the difficult task of greeting the dawn to fix the barrier in place for the coming year. With no thought of delay, he flashed green once more and disappeared, reappearing with another effervescent surge in the bowels of the beast.

He had transformed once more and was now manifest as the Flame of Dawn. His robes were a bright and fiery red, culminating in a hood with two floppy, symmetrical peaks. There was no adorning finery, no complimentary colors. His beard was a trimmed shock of white, forming a neat wedge beneath his ruddy face. The staff was now twisted, charred, and burned with the righteous flames of Paellar, Giver of Light. He was thus materially prepared for the ritual that would mark the culmination of his work as the Eve of Grace ended.

Bartolame was standing in the center of the vast gray and toxic Dead Ground that had once been Limrin. Here the very foliage moved of its own volition. The air was stifling somehow, as if thickened by the evil that plagued it, distorting one's vision. Walking on the aerth here sapped a being's very life force, impeding the voice and disrupting the hearing. It was said that it felt like being underwater. Everything was more difficult, somehow slowed down. Eventually, one's mind would reel until, finally, life draining away, there would be a succumbing to the waste. There was a circle of live ground here, some fifty yards across, surrounded by a swimming sea of horror. There had been a beautiful public space there when Limrin lived, built around an inspiring monument that was an extraordinary architectural accomplishment. So slender and beautiful, tall and reflective, it rose to the heavens in breathtaking splendor. Known as the Monument of Shaerra's Hand, it was still magnificent though enveloped by death.

Made of highly polished silvered steel, it featured a female forearm holding a slender, dazzling sword aloft. It climbed one-hundred and fifty feet into the sky and depicted the weapon named Aetherail, the Spring's Blade. It had been wielded in great fame by an aelven heroine, Shaerra Naedeen of Golaidris, in defense of Limrin. More importantly, for Bartolame's purposes, the monument was a great power place of Kuraile, God of Life. Thus, the vile Dead Ground could only surround it, not subsume it. By combining his power with the strength of the monument, he could set the *Ward of Containment* for another year.

As he sought to clear his mind in preparation for the task to come, he heard the moaning. The Dead had sensed his presence. They were massing at the edges of the circle, hungry for his life force. Ghouls, death walkers in all stages of decay, ghosts and ghasts, things that slithered, things that flew, and all manner of devils, lesser and greater, groaned and wailed in the torments of the lost. As horrible as that cacophony was, the sight of it was shockingly terrible. So he looked away, concentrating on the gleaming metal.

Paellar was nigh, so he climbed the stone stairs of the vast, round base of the monument. He reached the plateau upon which the giant statue rested and began his incantation. This task was much more verbal and less physical than his previous work. He placed his bare right hand on the sleek steel, resting the staff in his left hand against it. He spread his feet shoulder-width apart, spoke, and sensed his power gathering. As the casting climaxed, he shouted to the heavens.

The sun crested the horizon at that moment, the first rays of the new day striking the top of the monument's great blade. His elemental power significantly increased and strength filled his body. All at once, he gave all of that energy to the monument. There it would be stored to radiate over the next year. The dead, as one, shrieked and fell back from the Circle of Life. Perhaps they somehow sensed that its tremendous power was renewed. He stood leaning against the statue, more than a little spent.

"Curse you and all your kind!" came the voice, loud and full of rage. "I will have my day and we shall taste your flesh in the end! You will come to us in time; all come to us in due course of time. And, oh, how we shall enjoy your company." Then the horrid presence was gone. Weary but grateful that his task was accomplished, Bartolame allowed his mind to wander.

Maybe I will take a few hours to myself, he thought. He straightened his back and stretched, then greeted the new day with a silent prayer. He did not linger to admire his work but allowed himself a grin of measured satisfaction as he blinked away, leaving only his signature emerald glow behind.

As he strolled down the country path, he enjoyed the smell of the wildflowers and took delight in the simple bird song that filled the air. He was in an aelven form now, called the Aerth Father. His staff was ornately carved rhoanswood with a club-like head. He wore only aerth tones, browns, and grays. His attire was casual but conveyed a moderate level of wealth, and his hair and beard were silver. He was rather neatly groomed and as he walked along, he felt anticipation. This form enjoyed mortal pleasures and he felt hungry. He continued down the path until he passed the modest clever homes of the Naelcn. He was in Tharlas, one of his favorite places, and as he reached the fourth home on the right, he saw that for which he had come.

Raena Bottomly was making breakfast while her husband, Baelem, washed up. She was a fine cook and her love truly enjoyed a hearty meal to start the day. Raena enjoyed indulging him, regardless of how round he was getting. Suddenly she had a strange feeling, like a tickle in her brain. She immediately recognized it and crossed their entry room, opening the front door. Sure as sunshine, there he was!

"Why, by all the birds and bees, if it isn't Aellis Gaelean! What brings you here?" she asked cheerfully.

"Ah, this and that. I just happened by and thought I would say hello."

"Well, now, don't just stand there. Come on inside! Breakfast is about to be served and you know I make enough for five!" She waved him in, thrilled to have his company. After all, he was kind, thoughtful, and generous. He always had the best pipe mix around and was ever so handsome. Besides, Aellis and her Baelem got on famously. He told such wonderful stories and every time he "happened by," her gardens burst forth with growth. She would swear to it!

And so, the tall aelf entered the Naelen's humble home, his elder senses tantalized by simple mortal pleasures. "Thank you so much for having me," he said earnestly. "I've had a most wearying night."

Want to experience more of Maera? Visit ***www.maeraworld.com***

THE ALLURE OF
LAUGHING EYES

He led his folk by ship through a torturous ordeal at sea. They sailed to a new existence where they'd be free of the frozen desert of their homeland. He'd not yet seen his twenty-third Day of Life and despite his exceptional intelligence, the task before him had felt insurmountable. While he wasn't the admiral that piloted them north, it was his dreams that they followed. It was upon his insistence that they sailed towards twin dazzling stars in the night sky, stars prominent in his dreams, his visions of a new life. Thus, Dantilles was personally responsible for the lives of thousands. Although he was a prince, he'd never before felt such a weight of accountability.

Dantilles' relief was immense when his people found themselves anchored off the shore of what looked to be the land of his vivid dreams. After many weeks at sea, having exhausted their stores of food and drink, the faith of his followers seemed to have been rewarded. Every father, mother, and child, every sailor and warrior had shown bravery in no small measure by committing to that daunting journey. Each had faced gripping, lingering anxiety throughout the harrowing voyage. As they finally arrived at their promised destination, a more focused and immediate fear replaced the pilgrim's trepidation—the stark terror of the unknown.

Floating peacefully in what they would later name Japar Bay, their ships rocked by gentle waves, the Kraen folk of the continent of Olwae peered warily at something unbelievable. Neither Dantilles nor his fellows had ever seen an array of life such as this! They were unfamiliar with trees, let alone all that grew here. The density of the foliage, and the variety of creatures, from insects to lizards to game, was dumbfounding.

His people were from a continent of impenetrable snow and ice, howling winds, and treacherous terrain. The Isle of Olwae was a grim place, often likened to the hell of Maera, a frozen waste where horrible devils held sway. His father, the king, had provided Dantilles with a large fleet to follow his dreams north and after many weeks of sailing and great hardships, they had finally arrived in an apparent paradise.

Such lands were beyond the imagination of his compatriots, and it was only through years of dreams that Dantilles had come to believe such a place existed. He first took a small landing craft ashore alone, as he must, for he had always been alone in his dreams. The sheer multitude of life here frankly terrified him and his visions did not include the sensations of heat and smell. It took a long time for Dantilles to build up the confidence to touch the bark of one of the massive trees. The textures of that bark, the leaves, and the sheer size and strength of this living thing before him were unfathomable.

Although the Kraen had all gradually experienced the increased warmth of this region as they had sailed north, the heat of the forest itself was astounding. It was so great that steam rose from the very aerth itself! Dantilles had never experienced anything like it. Noise from vast numbers of insects and birds was louder now than it had been from the ship. The sounds of seemingly more fantastic creatures added to the terrifying din. The smells that met him as he stood there were wholly unbelievable.

Prince Dantilles controlled his breathing and took it all in. To continue, he had to gather his courage. He walked to the tree line of the first forest he had ever encountered. He again exerted control over his mind and body, the rigors of his intense arcane training serving him well. He walked into the dense forest and disappeared as his shipmates watched breathlessly.

Dantilles had to brush aside the heavy foliage as he went forward and soon found himself wet with sweat. He felt utterly exposed to threats from all sides, for he could see just a few steps ahead, and his other senses were overwhelmed. Insects swarmed Dantilles, and having never seen an insect before the prince began to panic, for the tiny beasts were bloodthirsty and relentless. Time passed but he couldn't guess how much, for he couldn't see any part of the sky, let alone the sun.

The prince was hours into the forest and nearly exhausted. That was when he saw it. A creature stood perhaps twenty paces ahead, in as clear an area as Dantilles had yet encountered. The animal was unlike anything his mind had ever imagined. It stood on four legs, was nearly waist high, and was as long as a man was tall. It had a thickly muscled body and a long tail and was covered in golden fur, with small round blotches of black all over. It had vicious, sharp fangs, piercing bluish eyes and perked ears. The beast was a predator and impressive to look upon. It was possibly the most beautiful thing he'd ever seen. It stared directly at him, seemingly through him.

Dantilles froze in place, listening to the low, menacing growl it emitted. He had brought no weapons with him, for he was putting his life in the hands of his god. Suddenly the great beast lowered its head and took a seemingly dead animal, nearly as large as itself, in its mouth. It lifted the limp form quickly, and then the magnificent creature turned and leaped straight up the side of a tree and into the canopy of the jungle. Dantilles was dumbfounded, a witness to the impossible strength of that beast, his mouth ajar. He felt intensely relieved and was left wondering what he had seen.

As he was about to step further forward, Dantilles felt an intense desire to turn back the way he'd come, swallow his pride, and sprint to the relative safety of his ship. Once again, he calmed himself, and the moment passed. He reminded himself that this was all his doing. He was here of his own will, alone and lost in this terrifying place. He focused on why he was there and what it had taken to come so far. He had faith and was there out of a sense of sheer trust. This new place, in all its impossible bizarre complexity, existed in the real world. No, he realized, he could not stop now. He closed his eyes, summoning the thought of the perfect being from his dreams, and just breathed. In the newly-found calm that the image provided, he opened his eyes again and smiled.

At that moment, an impossibly beautiful bird flitted about in the air before him. It was tiny and its wings beat so quickly that they were a blur. Its floating body was brilliantly colorful and iridescent. It had a long spike-like beak and the prince realized that he recognized this creature, for he had seen it in his dreams. It had come to him many times, wings buzzing, darting back and forth. So Dantilles took comfort in that one familiar sight and, as in his dreams, he followed it.

His new companion seemed excited, darting forward to lead him, then hovering in place as it waited for him to catch up. Dantilles felt a strange rush of the saturated air around him, an odd turbulence he had to push through. That sensation passed as quickly as it had come, and the prince found himself at the edge of a clearing. His heart leaped as he saw the open sky above him and felt the hot sun on his face. Above a rise in the terrain was a fantastic waterfall, perhaps five times the height of a man. It created a pond that fed another fall into a smaller pool, and beneath that were several more tiered pools, all spawned by the first. Never had Dantilles seen such an abundance of fresh water free of the hold of ice. The prince found his senses overwhelmed again, this time by the raw beauty of his surroundings.

Slowly Dantilles approached the rocky hillside adjacent to the waterfall and those glistening pools. He had dreamt of this place many times but here it was. It genuinely existed. His folk had risked everything to follow him here and now, at long last, it seemed as if that risk was finally paying off. The life of a prince was full of many stressful situations but never had Dantilles experienced the anxiousness that he felt simply stepping onto that shore and walking amidst the teeming life of the thick, lush forest. He had never seen green before, except in his dreams. His language had no word for it. It was beyond his waking experience, and it had been exhausting.

Now he stood before that lovely bubbling waterfall, doused in brilliant sunlight, and the prince breathed in a fragrant mist created by the falls. Dantilles realized that, in his dreams, this was always the moment when he heard a soft voice.

"Yes, my son, I am here."

Dantilles smiled and turned to see before him the only perfect being he would ever see. He felt pure relief wash through him and he suddenly felt his mind spinning. He lost his balance, falling softly onto the grass-carpeted aerth. At peace at last, having seen the smiling face of eternity, his incredible anxiety was relieved in a single moment. Dantilles fell into a deep sleep.

When he awoke, the world was new. The weight of all his fears and weariness had left him. He felt refreshed and his mind was mercifully clear. Bird song filled his ears while his nostrils flooded with fresh, exotic scents. Was this a new day? How long had he slept? A small and fascinatingly beautiful creature floated by, carried on a gentle breeze. Flat and colorful wings beating awkwardly, the tiny being seemed impossibly delicate. On Olwae, anything that flew was frightful, undoubtedly dangerous, or at least waiting to eat your remains. Here flyers were somehow ornamental; it was fascinating!

At the water's edge stood his regal host, facing him. The immortal had adopted a magnificent human form but His ears reached a distinct point. His shoulder-length curls, mustache, and beard were all stark white, yet He seemed youthful. The being gave off a noticeably odd energy, causing the sunlight to distort and interact with Him strangely; simply put, He shimmered.

The deity wore a simple tunic that matched the foliage around Him, with yellow and white accents. It was complimented handsomely by a leather belt, bracers, greaves, and sandals, all intricately made. A large amulet, His rings, and the other finery He wore were gold and silver. His garb was simple, looked comfortable, and seemed functional. The superb quality of all that He wore was apparent. He saw that His guest was awake, and His peaceful face broke into a broad smile. If the prince needed proof of the divinity of the being before him, it was dispelled by the gleam of His emerald eyes as He grinned. *By the Four Furies of the Wind*, Dantilles thought, *they sparkle with delight!* After being transfixed by those eyes for an indeterminate span, the prince suddenly snapped out of his stupor.

Then Dantilles noticed his host floated effortlessly, slightly above the ground.

He moved forward until He was at arm's length. It was then clear that His face was perfectly symmetrical, His skin exquisite, and His features substantial yet refined. But it was His eyes that fascinated the prince. They were green and conveyed more than intelligence and emotion. There was a strangeness to them that Dantilles could not define, something that seemed more than just a bit unnatural. Those eyes, seen in his recurring dreams, so full of life, conveying such peace, and brimming with an abundance of happiness, had bidden him to travel there to meet their gaze. Now those eyes were focused upon him.

"Welcome and well done! Long have I awaited this day. My heart soars to finally have you here and safe, my son." He cupped Dantilles' face in His hands and gently kissed his brow.

And so, the prince ascended, beyond where other mortals reached, beyond his dreams. Together they drank from the pool and Dantilles transformed. His past melted away and now all good things seemed possible. He was with Kuraile of the Laughing Eyes, the Peace Giver, and His Pool of Eternal Life. It was a new day from which all days have since been tallied.

"Rejoice, my son, for you shall live from this day forward touched by neither age nor disease. You will no longer need to take life from plants or animals for sustenance, and sleep will be a sweet luxury to allow you to dream. You and your people, our people, shall truly know peace."

Then they spoke about all manner of things, walking together through that fantastic forest. Kuraile made Dantilles known to the many varied forms of life there, and each creature of the woods they met seemingly accepted him. So, the day passed, and they pushed unto dusk until they finally had somehow made their way to the beach.

Introductions have seldom been more welcome than they were on that beautiful coast as the sun gave way to a starry night. The prince and his folk spent a night of celebration at the tree line, and many did not surrender to a deep, relieved slumber until Sealon, Maera's moon, had ridden the sky towards dawn. The next day, Dantilles slowly led all His folk to the secluded pool, as He had promised, and from which they all drank deeply. Thus, they left behind their land of snow and ice and became known as the Folk of Forever, and they dwell in that holy place even today. Japar, or "joyous," the forest and bay were named, while Japarandir is the kingdom where those pale, well-made children of the Living God remain ever a shining beacon to the worship of life.

Four-thousand and twenty-two years have flowed, like a current in an ocean of fate, since Dantilles became the leader of this new nation. He reigns still, in youthful vigor, over Japarandir. That is the test. Can a mere mortal, one granted practical immortality, retain his young mind? Will that mind become weary with a burden of wisdom and experience that men were never meant to carry?

His folk, of necessity a part of that grand scheme, were named the Aelvae, or "chosen," by Kuraile. They have, over the millennia, slowly morphed into an appearance akin to their god. Thus, they are often mistaken for aelves. The Aelvae have pale skin, rather athletic bodies, and pointed ears, all of which undoubtedly add to any such confusion.

Intellectual and curious, the Aelvae were a peaceful people who sought neither to expand their territory nor interact with or influence other nations. They remained reclusive and reveled in their nation's inherent privacy, while enjoying observing other lands at a safe distance. Their magnificent homeland was a secret, mystical place in which their god Kuraile walked at will.

Perhaps it is natural that these folk became somewhat obsessed with the passage of time. It's thought that the primary Aelvae contribution to civilization is their calendar, used across many regions of Maera. Indeed, Japarandir has come to represent the passage of time more than any other single nation.

Amongst the mighty, the relationship between the Aelvae and Kuraile defines the nature of divine benevolence. These former humans were not Kuraile's creation but chose his worship as a function of their aessance or free will. This acceptance of divine intercession has set a new, higher standard for the behavior of the Aeglain regarding their worshippers.

On Maera, the Gods may walk amongst mortals. In such a world, there are no non-believers. A vast majority of advanced races, those capable of acknowledging and worshipping a deity, worship their creator. It is part of what they are, built into their design. Therefore, aelves are aelves, dwaerves are dwaerves, and the Ourk are Ourk. In time, their maker translates the life force of worshippers from their mortal existence on Maera, for this is the will of the Aeglain. Races committed to Maera represent an investment of their creator's power which that creator then reclaims, either amplified or reduced when individuals have played their part in the various designs of their god.

But if a race has free will, "aessance," as the aelves named it, then they may choose their god, effectively choosing between good and evil. On Maera, these are not words that invoke a vague concept such as morality nor are they words that spark philosophical arguments. Good and evil are strategies to be chosen and tactics enacted. On Maera, a race that has the free will to choose their worship represents a substantial element of chaos in an otherwise appreciably more predictable dynamic. That chaos is declared to have been the intention of Loekii, as She gave Her beloved humans their gift of aessance.

One of the eldest of the group of quasi-immortals that have come to be known as The Sundered, The Chosen, and many other names, Dantilles has perhaps the most direct communication with his liege. Having had such a relationship for so long implies that Kuraile has received whatever he desires from the arrangement. This close relationship with the Aeglain has allowed humans to develop their great affinity for magic over thousands of lifetimes, spanning multiple worlds.

For over four-thousand years, the Aelvae have left virtually no mark on their forest home. They exist peacefully and without need under the forest canopy and the stars. Any who have dared approach Japarandir have never reported signs of human habitation. Those who have entered have awoken later and found that they had lost time. They say they awoke far away from the forest, in a state of confusion, but unharmed. Individuals who have repeatedly attempted to enter the Japar Forest have mysteriously disappeared. Dantilles himself became a mighty spell caster and became fascinated with the stars and was a passionate devotee of life.

In a practical sense, Dantilles had time—time like no previous man. He also had a tremendous source of information as Kuraile's visitations were a daily event. He did not need to sleep but learned to benefit from the time he spent dreaming. He soon realized that dreaming was the key. Even just a few hours spent each night dreaming became quite a lot of time over four-thousand years. As Dantilles learned to use his mind more efficiently, he maximized the gifts he had gleaned.

Dantilles of Japarandir lay down under the stars at the aengel hour, near the Pool of Eternal Life, virtually every night since establishing his realm. Kuraile, his confidant, often joined him and the two discussed the day that had passed. They would then converse about life, muse about the cosmos, or contemplate the mysteries of mortal and immortal existence. At times, the two might even have stumbled across bits of wisdom together. It was a constant source of wonderment for the God of Life to discover what heights could be reached by a human mind when unburdened by the crushing knowledge of its mortality. Kuraile's time spent with His Aelvae child was indeed rewarding as He was always intrigued by the results of this experiment.

As for Dantilles, with only the cycle of Sealon to ground him in any measure of reality on Maera, he was a warrant of the forest. He was a brother to the sky, a partner to the winds, and a daring witness to life. He was a child of eternity who once dreamt that he was mortal. As such, his mind sought and found many intriguing new diversions, just as he made new acquaintances.

Dantilles soon learned to communicate with unicorns, the faerie folk, the residents of the forest, and even the trees. Then, he realized that there were other, even more powerful and elusive creatures to encounter if desired. So it was that the Aelvae leader soon befriended dragon-kind.

Madrain, the Elemental Goddess of the Wind, created dragons, Her favored spawn. She granted them aessance; thus, they were free to worship, think and believe as they chose. In this way, dragons diversified until each of them became unique. They vary significantly in size and are capable of casting all three types of magic: maega, maena, and manaera. Dragons fight as masters of the Whirling Death combat style and possess a wide variety of breath weapons. Dragons are known to live for centuries, sometimes millennia, and are also known to be highly unpredictable, which makes them an even more dangerous encounter.

Over many centuries, Dantilles has cultivated a close relationship with dragon-kind, which seems only natural, as the Aelvae and dragon-kind share a mutual history of personal life experience through aessance. The life of Dantilles is, in fact, perhaps the single most significant expression of aessance in the annals of Maera. Thus, the dragons pronounced that the prince was a draegal, or a great friend of dragon-kind, a title granted to very few. This is not achievable in an average human life span, for dragons are long-lived, intelligent, and cautious. Such recognition usually takes centuries to earn and dragons have indeed found themselves an ally in Dantilles, one with a unique point of view. One who can communicate with every nation leader pledged to the Gods of Good, for he knows the mind of Kuraile like no other.

Ruling Japarandir is considered one of the least demanding of all monarchies in the history of Maera. Dantilles had many citizens who willingly assisted him in any way they could. Free of the need to eat and effectively immortal, with no need for sleep, each individual Aelvae was encouraged to do whatever they found fulfilling. Their society quickly evolved into more of an intellectual collaboration than any standard nation. Dantilles had the luxury of exploring his interests and, as a result, he became one of the greatest astronomers in Maera's history. He has also engaged extensively in many other pursuits.

As a draegal, Dantilles began to influence the rest of Maera heavily. Dragons soon began appraising him of critical geopolitical intelligence from all of Maera, daily. His relationship with dragons slowly matured over the millennia and Kuraile Himself has displayed distinct pride and satisfaction at how diligently His Aelvae leader applied himself to securing the safety of Maera. Dantilles' worship of Kuraile and devotion to good, so bold and inspiring, indirectly convinced the world's aelven and dwaerven peoples to trust men. They worked with the tribes of humans that inhabited the southern continents of Maera to form the hugely successful Kingdom of Gindlorn and its sister Kingdom of Limrin—may their dead find peace.

So it was that dragons from all over Maera visited Dantilles during the aengel hour each night. Amongst them were the most potent and intelligent dragons, roaming high and far across the skies of Maera. They gathered precise knowledge of the activities of many nations and the disposition of their armies and navies from great altitudes, at which they went undetected. They assumed a non-threatening humanoid form as they landed, which was one of the greatest compliments any member of dragon-kind could bestow upon their host. The prince greeted them each night, often joined by Kuraile or other fantastic creatures. Dantilles listened to these benign masters of the winds nightly, soaking in the information they had to offer.

Often their discussions turned to astronomy, for dragons are fascinated by the stars, just as the prince was. After the dragons returned to the sky, Kuraile and Dantilles might talk until dawn and then watch the sun rise beautifully over the Lundain Mountains. After many centuries of information gathering, Dantilles had a fully functional knowledge of the realms of Maera, even those far to the north on the continents of Provos and Thrunde.

Kuraile and Dantilles had millennia to discuss the wisdom and restraint that was prudent when striving to determine whether the dissemination of geopolitical intelligence was helpful or if such magnanimity would do more harm than good. Maera's history provided many instances that detailed how useful information meant to help those in need, when used poorly, yielded bad results. It soon became apparent that to have the ability to be helpful to the allies of good, Dantilles would need to change his personal goals. To do good, the prince would have to become the best-informed individual on Maera.

Once Dantilles accepted this hugely burdensome responsibility, he shared his intentions with his allies: dragons, aelves, and dwaerves. With Kuraile as his partner, no one expressed concerns, as the God of Life was beyond reproach in His judgment. Kuraile provided all the life on Maera that made up the incalculable biomass supporting the advanced races: every plant, every insect, all creatures of the air and water, all fungoid life, and a great many organisms yet unknown to the more intelligent races of Maera.

So, it came to pass that Dantilles of Japarandir perfected a system by which he gathered more crucial intelligence about the world than any other life form indigenous to Maera. He often fielded requests from some of Maera's strongest leaders and most advanced minds about crucial geopolitical situations. He developed the wisdom necessary, backed by nearly daily discussions with Kuraile, to determine how much information to disseminate and to whom and when.

While ruling Japarandir never demanded nearly his full attention and he was known throughout all of Maera as the king of that great realm, Dantilles was still the same young man he always was. He was still the young human who believed in his dreams, took up those dreams and, at risk of all, tried to make them a reality for himself and thousands of his fellow citizens that dared follow him to a new and better life. He was still the young man who, despite his terror, insisted on walking alone into the jungle of the new world they had discovered. He was still the young man that entered that jungle without weapons with only the trust that he would meet his God somewhere within that forest, for he had boldness born of faith and the will to see his dreams through to startling reality.

He is now four-thousand and forty-five years old and has spent a tremendous amount of time dedicated to educating himself so that he might help not just his nation but all of Maera. When needing important advice, or making a critical decision requiring accurate geopolitical intelligence, many of the most powerful leaders on Maera have turned to this young man for the information they so ardently need. Once introduced to Dantilles, a daunting task typically arranged through mutual friends, an open line of communication is often established and vigorously maintained. Dantilles is happy to provide allies with what they need to be the best rulers they can be.

All around Maera, Dantilles is imagined to be some aetherael spirit, living in a mystical realm, sitting on an ancient throne, and wearing a golden crown. Instead, he is a starry-eyed dreamer with perfect clarity of conscience and soul. He lies on soft grass by a waterfall-fed pool during the aengel hour, looking up at the stars with his friends, enjoying every minute of perhaps the most extended life a human has ever lived. He has filled many roles over the fading millennia: dreamer, prophet, leader, and liege. He has been called the Child King, the Favored Son, the Vessel of Grace, the Pilgrim of Peace, and even the Guardian of Forever. Those who know him best have known him since the start, have watched him grow great and powerful while marveling at how he was the same. Those who love him most, those who followed him to their destiny, those who have entrusted him with their eternity, even the God of Life Himself, who may love him most of all—those blessed, happy souls, call him what they have always called him, what he has ever been to them, and seemingly ever shall be. They all call him, quite simply, their prince. In truth, in his mind, he is ever the daring lad who could not resist the allure of laughing eyes.

Want to experience more of Maera? Visit **www.maeraworld.com**

SO MANY KISSES!

Saeven was exhausted and he felt that his work was finally through. Of course, that was not his decision to make. He was confident that he had extracted every bit of information the object of his attention could offer. In fact, the man had been blathering nonsense now for quite some time. The Honorable Renton Maas, Master of Law and renowned nobleman, was no more. In his place was a whimpering, quivering mass of ruined flesh and tattered nerves. He was stretched over the Wheel of Loekii, bound by cruel hooked steel, and at his mortal end. It was a testament to the torturer's exquisite, perhaps unmatched, skill that Maas was still alive.

The draevar lord's charcoal skin glistened with perspiration as he removed his long, tight leather gloves and placed them on his prep table. His cobalt hair slicked back with styling wax, looked even more dramatic, slathered with his sweat. He crossed the chamber to the lever on the wall and enjoyed the feeling of sensuality that such complete control over another gave him. His work always enticed his lascivious instincts—his slaves would pay a heavy price for that tonight. He looked back wistfully at his plaything as he pulled a lever, causing an acidic wash to dump on Maas from above. It carried away all the blood, sweat, nasal mucous, drool, urine, and feces that had obscured the vivid details of Saeven's exemplary efforts at the price of an agonizing burn in every single wound on what was left of the nobleman's body. As Maas experienced a shocking new

247

torment, he tried to scream but only an inarticulate squeak emitted from where his lips had been. Lord Saeven smiled deliciously— what a delightful indulgence! These men of the south were weaker than those on Provos upon whom he had earned his awful reputation and, as an erudite artisan in a baerbaric land, he took his enjoyment wherever he could. He motioned to the slave children attending him. They rushed to sweep the floors and wipe the room's surfaces clean, sloshing the vile excretions of Maas' traumatized body into the drains on the cold stone floor.

Lord Callus entered the chamber from the eastern wall as if on cue, followed by his small prancing dog. The seamless secret panel shut cleanly and silently behind him, leaving no hint of its location on the black wall of the chamber. Saeven struggled to conceal his intense physical desire for the Chancellor of the City of Dreams but felt certain Callus could sense it. His liege graced him with a smile as he approached the tragic devastation of Renton Maas. "Has our guest had anything to add to his previous admissions?" Callus inquired.

"No, my Lord," replied the torturer, "Just gibberish as cognizant horror replaced reason." The perfect human specimen Saeven knew as Lord Callus was tall and massive yet possessed the light step and uncanny agility of a jungle cat. His tanned skin emphasized his stunning muscularity and his chiseled features showcased his devastating beauty. As he spoke, Saeven felt his knees weaken. His dog barked loudly several times. Its plaintive, high-pitched yelps brought horribly violent thoughts to Saeven's mind unbidden. He tried desperately to banish them, fearing Callus could see his mind.

"Quiet now, Baby!" The Lord chastised his pet first, then addressed the draevar Lord. "I appreciate the thoroughness of your efforts, Lord Sinn. Can you maximize his awareness for me? I fear I do not have his attention."

"Yes, Lord." As the torturer complied, the diminutive beast yapped again as if he was offended that the draevar approached his victim. Saeven made the mistake of looking at the dog, which only caused the barking to increase and become more aggressive. Lord Callus snapped his fingers, and his pet fell silent, sitting at the feet of his master obediently.

"Any more of that, and Daddy won't share!" His warning quieted the dog for good, who seemed adequately chastised. Using a unique sifting device of his own design, Lord Sinn powdered his prey's body with poxy, focusing Maas' consciousness by adding one more layer of suffering to his wracked form. Callus watched carefully as slow recognition entered the face of the fallen judge. He put his hand out when he saw the man's terror and knew he had been identified. "Your findings?"

Saeven quickly produced a small, leather-bound book from a pocket inside his tunic. He handed it to Callus, who flipped through it with disdain. "It is disappointing, isn't it?" He was speaking to Maas now with open contempt. "A lifetime of self-serving, double-dealing, petty treacheries, and pathetic machinations, all come down to this?" Callus took the opportunity to lean in, being sure to make eye contact with his quivering enemy. "By all the failing gods, you are worth even less to Her now than you ever were." Callus shook his head with dramatic disdain. "In any case, as you go to your eternal reward, be assured that I will make the most of your confession's usefulness. At least you can enjoy knowing that the next man to occupy Lord Sinn's valuable time shall understand that your words put him here."

Lord Callus stared into the helpless man's disfigured face as if assessing the damage done to it. The corners of his mouth turned down, and he circled the judge and the Wheel he was on, hands clasped behind his back, seemingly satisfied. "Release his bonds and leave us." His command was said in such a flat, final tone that Saeven rushed a bit in complying. He cut the wires to the hooks as quickly as possible and let the man loose. Then he tilted the Wheel forward, letting Maas slide to the black stone floor in a heap. He looked to Lord Callus for any sign of further instruction, but when no signal was given, Sinn rushed to exit the chamber at the heels of his slaves. He would have to return later for his kit. As the chamber's western door closed behind them, the large room was suddenly ominously private.

Lord Callus squatted in front of his prisoner, who could not even straighten himself in the face of his destroyer. Men in such situations often asked after their families, begged for a merciful end, or prayed to their gods as doom prepared to engulf them. Renton Maas did none of those things.

He could hardly imagine what had befallen his kin and wanted no details. He knew that begging one such as the Chancellor would only be met with even more cruelty, and Maas had no energy to debase himself. And to whom, exactly, would he pray? Loekii had forsaken him, that much was clear, and would claim his aether and do with him what She pleased. He shuddered at the thought. His mortal existence had now been starkly divided into two distinct experiences: forty-two years of success and privilege, followed by ten hours of horror, psychological trauma, and indescribable agony. Wretched and beyond exhaustion, Maas just wanted it all to end.

"I fear that I have no more time for you, as much as I could enjoy your company further," Callus explained. "But I, more than any other, know what you go to next. As your perception of time drastically shifts and you slowly begin to appreciate what eternity is, know that I will never forget you and shall always enjoy this time we had together."

The Chancellor stood up abruptly and pivoted back towards the door through which he had entered the chamber. His feisty little dog stayed behind but stood up and watched him go. Its small tail wagged in eager anticipation. The secret chamber door opened silently inwards as Callus neared and as he passed through it, he loudly snapped his fingers.

The dog turned to face its prey. Its low growl slowly changed into a louder, deeper, and more guttural sound. That change was accompanied by a tremendous stench that somehow made its way into Renton Maas' crushed nostrils and assailed his senses. He choked at the utter foulness of it, vomiting blood and saliva onto the floor as he struggled to lift his head.

It is impossible to convey the disorienting confusion and raw visceral terror that came over the man as he watched the tiny dog violently morph into a vast, shambling thing, the very sight of which gripped him in a spasm of revulsion.

It was a pulsating blob of oozing putrefaction, covered in tentacles, mouths, and eyes. It slavered menacingly, seemingly enjoying the man's reaction. The mortal known as Renton Maas had never imagined such an unfathomable nightmare and realized that his suffering had just begun. The daemon slowly, inexorably, took the man in its tentacles and lifted him up and towards its body. Dozens of eyes drank in the mortal's last moments on Maera, and the man somehow found a final shred of strength. As many mouths began to devour his convulsing body, the man let out a long, uniquely inhuman screech.

Callus paused a few steps past the open doorway to appreciate the glorious sound that he might remember and revel in it in the future. Renton Maas had used his considerable influence in the Dark City to oppose his advancement over the years. The Master of Law had chosen to throw his political weight behind the plot to subvert Callus' achievements. He had even been involved in an attempt to assassinate him. A thousand such deaths were not enough for Maas.

It took a disappointingly short time for the daemon to ingurgitate Renton Maas's mortal form, claiming his aether for Her. The daemon was directly linked to the eternal halls of torment that were the afterlife of Loekii's creations, from which it had been summoned to Maera. The man translated and joined his kind in everlasting suffering while Callus paused, halfway across the room, his back to the door. He whistled once, a quick, piercing blast that had the desired effect. The small dog trotted to him and he turned back to see it. He squatted down and it jumped into his awaiting arms. Callus stood back up as Baby licked his face vigorously. "Oh, my!" he said, laughing happily as he spoke. "So many kisses for Daddy!"

*Want to experience more of Maera? Visit **www.maeraworld.com***

RUN THE WILD

Ch'kaarl took a moment to ensure he was centered, his breathing under control, as well as his heartbeat. His footing was stable, his stance allowing for the transfer of power that his full draw required. His body's lean was dramatic but so practiced that he was comfortable, and the security of his grip was sure and relaxed. His form was made possible by the tremendous energy he could generate in the curvature of his spine and the other features of his formidable physical build. Both his finger positioning and his draw were sound. His aim was rarely an issue and it was with quiet confidence that the warrior achieved a smooth release. Ch'kaarl's rhoanswood shaft flew true, and its steel arrowhead found flesh with a distinct "Thwack!" that his keen ears registered even at such a distance.

His target went down, blood gushing from a massive intrusion in its middle that, upon Ch'kaarl reaching it, seemed even more devastating than it had at a distance. Indeed, the arrow had passed through the man, entering low on his back and at a slight downward angle. The archer could smell the man's viscera, which his shot had massively perforated and exploded forward onto the aerth before the wretched creature. The K'haap warrior was pleased to be able to retrieve his arrow from the grass well beyond his prey. Its shaft, nearly as thick as his thumb, was still serviceable, as were its fletching and head. He took a few moments to wipe the human innards off it on the grass and looked down the length of the shaft. It was still sound and so he returned it to the quiver on his back, which his amazing arm length facilitated.

The hunter turned his trophy onto its back. Upon close examination, it was apparent that it had not been killed instantly and had crawled a bit before dying. The baerbaraan was typical of its kind on central Maerisna, being well-muscled with rather pale skin darkened only by daily exposure to Aarn. It had blue eyes, and its blonde beard was shortly shorn. Its shoulder-length matching hair was pulled back and tied. Its life story was told in blood tattoos on its naked torso. They revealed that it was but a pup. The manling wore loose pants tied with rope at the waist and soft leather foot coverings. It carried no shield and little other than a spear, a simple axe, and a hunting knife. It most likely had been seeking, as the baerbaraan called it, hunting for a trophy.

Ch'kaarl used his long dagger to make a vertical slice through his victim's tattoo line near its terminus, signifying to any that found the body that its slayer understood the rituals of the baerbaraan folk and the implications of what came next. Ch'kaarl removed the middle finger of the man's stronger hand while splitting it to the wrist. He wrapped his trophy in a cloth square and tucked it in a belt pouch. The ruined hand would not serve this man in its next life, and its aessance would have to be repurposed. At least, that's what its folk would believe, which was the point. Such primitive beliefs set these men apart in their ignorance, making them perfect tools of the Blood God.

The K'haap had been at odds with the human baerbaraans of Maerisna for decades and while that might not justify mutilating the dead, Ch'kaarl had no issue with it. He knew what would be done to his body should the circumstances one day be reversed. He searched various scents carried on the westerly breeze but detected no hint of other men. These fools ran alone on the plains as often as not in an attempt to prove their cunning and fearlessness. Of course, it was only the fact that their vast numbers had flushed out so many beings indigenous to the region that made such an exhibition of ludicrous bravado possible. It was just how far this unskilled baerbaraan was from home that made the encounter alarming. Ch'kaarl realized that his safe return to his base to report all he had seen was now more vital than ever. If the folk of Aeres were seeking this far north, their audacity had increased. That would not play well with his chieftain K'thraekus or the other battle lords in the Land of Baelthas.

The large caninoid, or canine-humanoid leaped energetically to the top of a small rocky outcropping nearby. The terrain here was typically flat and it was the highest ground nearby. Ch'kaarl focused with all of his considerable sensory perception on the open plains to the south, east, and west. He leaned with his muzzle far forward, like the fearful carnivore he was, and reveled in the feel of the wild on his face. He relied primarily on his fantastic sense of smell, using each nostril independently to home in on any odor, determining its direction unerringly. By doing so, he could smell a foe as far away as an hour's sprint, with the favor of tempestuous Madrain, Goddess of the Winds. Ch'kaarl would utilize this advantage many times each day as he traveled towards the Tower of Baelthas. Thus, he could maintain the level of stealth required to dominate anything he chose to meet while avoiding most encounters altogether. So, he began his trek west, skirting the death zone known as the Burnt Lands to the north, his safe path relying heavily on his ability to remain unde-tected by most creatures of the wild.

Ch'kaarl stood a head taller than a robust man and was slender yet thickly muscled in his shoulders, arms, chest, and thighs. He was an impressive jumper and runner with superior speed over short and long distances. His endurance was tremendous, allowing him to cover vast stretches of ground in shockingly little time. But he was more than just an impressive physical specimen. The K'haap were the chosen of Ilmarae, the God of Knowledge. He spoke and read the elder tongues, being highly educated, and took compensation for his service to Baelthas in general access to the eternal library of the Tower of the Emerald Twins. It was in the hallowed recesses of that fabled aetherael place that Ch'kaarl of the K'haap had learned the terrible truths of his reality and the fell fate of Maera that he now risked his life to change. This privileged information led to his now inveterate opinion on the viability of the human baerbaraan tribes of Maerisna. He could foresee no future in which these tribes of man shook off the yolk of Aeres and became anything other than a force for evil.

Ch'kaarl estimated that he was roughly one hundred- and fif-ty-miles due east of the eastern shore of the Inlet of Shandrael, a piv-otal point on the map of Maerisna. From that point, a line could be drawn directly northeast to the Burnt Lands that separated the Lands of Baelthas from the open plains of the continent. It was that imag-inary line that the forces of Ilmarae defended from incursions from the Plains of Shatal to the south. It was that line that the caninoid runner needed to reach before he could expect any support. The trick would be to skirt the treacherous desert to his right. It was known as the Anvil of Aarn to some but as the Burnt Lands to most. That dread desert promised any who entered an epic struggle to survive and added a chance of a fearful encounter for all who laid eyes on it. Thus, Ch'kaarl chose to travel well south of that place of death.

Were it not for the stress of his purpose; the K'haap rover would undoubtedly have enjoyed the day. Aarn held the aerth in His warm embrace as the westerly wind lavished gentle caresses upon him from the eternal sky. Ch'kaarl reveled in the blue above. He rejoiced in the feel of the grass between his toes. The perfume of wildflowers on the breeze intoxicated him. He would have loved to linger in that experience and place for a long while. But the waking world was demanding and there were many miles to be run before he could indulge in such luxurious notions. The bloody Age of Man was upon this world like some slathering beast at the throat of reason. Ch'kaarl imagined his role was that of armor, a steel collar encasing the vulnerable gullet of Maera against the savage folk of Aeres and Loekii. He hated the humans for the part they played in the tawdry tragedy spewed from the wretched mind of the Mistress of Deception. What a rude instrument man was—so ignorant of the truth, so selfish in their desires, and so wicked in their willingness to take part in the ruin of the world. Their mere existence threatened all other life. It was quite a time to be alive, an age of high adventure with the opportunity to do great deeds. Such bold aspirations were refused by Baelthas' master archer, who could not walk the wide world in peace or self-indulgence while such a threat prevailed.

He started at a light run, a pace he could maintain all day. It afforded him enough awareness of his surroundings to support his nimble mind and its capacity to foresee danger. Few dared rush the wild without his vast experience, for threats abounded on the expansive grasslands of Maerisna. Most mortals who strode the aerth alone did so with dangerous hubris, confident in a false sense of their ability to cope with what they might encounter there. Most of the challenges of survival actually lay in the early detection and subsequent avoidance of danger. With such a measure for success, having to use one's weaponry meant a failure had already occurred. For one such as Ch'kaarl, his mastery of going unseen was invaluable, more precious than his skilled evasion or prowess in battle.

He felt he could avoid detection altogether in most cases, and thus Ch'kaarl felt assured that he could manage such a run.

Typically, the K'haap faced danger wearing a coat of fabric, a type of armor called a cumber, sewn in layers, that covered his arms, torso, and below, extending past mid-thigh. It was cinched at the waist by a belt from which he hung various pouches, bags, and other kit. It was lightweight and comfortable, providing a surprising amount of protection from slashing attacks and many penetrating combat modes. Even battering attacks mostly failed to do more than bruise a wearer of a quality coat of layered sewn armor. Ch'kaarl's was of exceeding excellence, having been custom-made by Greshann artisans to his size. If combat were a foregone conclusion, he would use a raindrop shield in tandem with his longsword, which he wielded one-handed with ease and no loss of control.

Ch'kaarl had decided to travel without his custom gambeson or shield. For a pure scouting mission such as this, the K'happ carried only his great bow and quiver of two dozen shafts, his long dagger, a war club, strangle cord, throwing sharps, and a robust manx paste, his favored venom. He relied on his mastery of destra, the legendary hand-to-hand weaponless fighting style of the tall wolf, which made full use of claw and tooth. His sheer reach, strength, and speed were enough to devastate most other tall-walkers or bipeds that he might come to face. Such a conflict was typically resolved so quickly and surely that he rarely took any damage or received a blow at all.

At real speed and during emergencies, his bow and quiver could be a hindrance that he might abandon to range freely. He often went on all fours when unencumbered and could maneuver in a shockingly effective way that caught all but the most experienced opponents off guard. Once his claws found purchase on a foe, his victim rarely had even basic competency in dealing with an enemy such as he. In such scenarios, Ch'kaarl did not disengage until it was over. The sheer animal ferocity of the K'haap was seldom survived to be spoken of and so their ability to leave men shredded to bloody tatters was feared and seen by many as an almost mystical thing. Superstition ruled the belief structure of the human baerbaraan culture and victims of K'haap warriors were often attributed to waers, those legendary shape-changers that were becoming a more and more frequent danger across Maerisna.

Ch'kaarl had taken care to slather himself with the greenish-yellow dye he carried in powder form, which he mixed with the moist soil he had found under an overturned rock that dawn. It was a blend of his own creation that gave a clever coloration to his fur. When combined with the green cloth tunic and dull brown leather items he wore, it had the desired effect of hiding him well from all but those with the sharpest of eyes which sought out motion specifically. If his senses or intuition gave him a sudden warning as he ran through the grass, he threw himself flat, allowing the greenery to envelop him as he gathered more information. This way, Ch'kaarl could avoid the vast majority of unwanted encounters and influence the outcome of any chosen confrontation. And so, he spied on many creatures at a distance during that morning's run, both predator and prey.

The first half of that day passed without incident. There were signs to the south of the passing of a massive herd of loarn, a linchpin herbivore species that shockingly outnumbered every other grass eater on the vast plains of Maerisna. They were passing to the east in such numbers that a disruptive haze filled the sky above them that could be seen from miles away. As the day went on, the haze grew larger. They were drifting north towards him or perhaps the herd was getting wider as it went along. Either way, the beasts seemed to be trailed by every predator on the grasslands. The K'haap was grateful for that, as they certainly drew unwanted attention from his run. As evening approached, a swoop of manticorae, as a group of such creatures is called, floated lazily above the herd, attacking intermittently. The K'happ decided he should adjust his chosen path slightly northward to avoid the threat of running too close to the herd and the possibility of encounters with pursuant hunters. Ch'kaarl continued his run, carefully watching for crepuscular predators, which were plentiful here. Before nightfall, he came across a lone ancient tree.

It was a dengael tree, which generally grew only at the edge of the desert. Ch'kaarl had never seen one so far into the grass. It was smooth, tall, and thick with a large canopy shaped rather like a mushroom. Its trunk was devoid of branches, all of which instead emanated radially from its crown at a slightly vertical angle. Its greenery was comprised of many smallish spade-shaped leaves that stood upright, reaching for the sky. At its base were heavy, convoluted roots that showed prominently above the ground. The roots formed a broad base that looked like the tentacles of some giant sea creature.

The K'haap knew better than to spend time in such a place. The tree drew the eyes of every being in the area. But, as he lingered overlong there, he felt oddly safe under the dengael tree. His muscular body relaxed and his burdened mind knew peace. He broke from convention, taking his ease in the twilight and resting his back between two larger roots. It seemed to him that it was almost as if they edged closer, enveloping him in their strength. Ch'kaarl smiled at the notion, this long runner, this fierce hunter, this reaver of men. He let his tongue wag freely from his mouth like a carefree child. For a short span of his life, the deadly warrior was as one with the aetheric perfection of that massive, ancient life form, as together they drank in their solitude, silently celebrating the starry array of the universe under a vast, darkening sky.

A new dawn marched slowly across the sky as Aarn began His solemn watch over the aerth. The night crept away before it, like a sneak thief with a full take. Ch'kaarl was wide awake and full of resurgent energy. He felt no tightness in his muscles, none of the soreness he had expected from the previous day's exertions. He couldn't remember the last time he awoke so refreshed. He ran his hand slowly over the smooth bark of the dengael tree. The leathery gray surface seemed warm to his touch. Ch'kaarl had experienced many moments of wonder interacting with natural and arcane forces. He felt sure that both were influencing him during his time under the dengael tree. So it was that he spoke in a quiet, thoughtful voice before he took his leave. "I thank you for sharing your strength with me, aerth-father. May water come to you, may neither flame nor lightning ever find you, and may the gods favor you through a long and peaceful existence."

Wishing peace for another was a profoundly generous sentiment, especially among the K'haap. They were broadly polytheistic by tradition and used the aessance and respect for knowledge granted to them by their creator, Ilmarae, to revere the four elemental gods in particular. The wise know that few wish for peace more than the warrior, especially one who fights with an obligation to protect one's people and a sense of moral duty to one's world. Ch'kaarl was such a warrior, and the scirocco, that aged temperamental sentience that dwelt in the mighty dengael, sensed his brave heart and felt an affinity to his keen mind. Primordial energies swirled within the windswept nature of the being's unconventional intelligence. It had difficulty aligning its consciousness with the thoughts and speech of mortals. Thus, it was only with concentrated effort that it expressed its emotions through the veil of its vision of the world. "We shall meet again, child of the Brooding God …" the scirocco said in its hollow, haunting voice, so like that of a man, yet even more like a desert wind. Then, as Ch'kaarl continued to jog away to the east, it added quietly, "… should you last."

He was able to avoid several encounters as he went along his way. Some he could not avoid. There were wolves in the morning, no longer a common sight now that the baerbaraan had ranged so far and wide on the plains. Comprised of varying shades of gray, white, tan, and even black, the clever beasts strode the aerth with inherent pride. Ch'kaarl quickly realized that he must deal with the pack, who numbered over thirty, and walked over a large area as they kept several body lengths apart. The K'happ made himself fully visible and stood his ground as they approached. He spread his arms wide, making himself as large as possible. The lead wolf, quite an impressive specimen, stopped and sized him up. The wolf made eye contact but broke his gaze before Ch'kaarl had to be aggressive or make any further warning. The predators had no wish to face a K'haap, a race that frightened them, especially with a banquet just a few hundred paces south. Indeed, there were no empty bellies in that region of the plains that day. Thus, the pack went on its way east without incident, shadowing the herd.

As he progressed in his run that day, Ch'kaarl passed several prominent terrain features. The first was a patch of stones that broke through the grass, forming a small hillock. As always, he took advantage of the opportunity. Ch'kaarl looked long over the lay of the land from the high ground. He was concerned about finding deep long scratches in the largest of the stones—brambler sign. He quickly determined it was a large specimen in the health of its prime. The biped carnivore had left tracks that indicated it had moved south at a rapid pace, no doubt to hunt the herd, which was still clouding the skies in that direction. The herd could be days in its passing. The most extended mass of such life that Ch'kaarl had seen took six days to pass him. The manticorae were still visible, swooping to the attack from the dusty skies above it. As he watched, he realized that the herd was closer to his path than the previous night. Manticorae, a brambler, the widening herd—all increased the risk of his run. Therefore, he again adjusted his route, running closer to the Burnt Lands.

At midday, he saw a wyvern flying higher than usual above the grass, skirting the edge of the desert to the north. It was easy to evade its sight in the waving growth of the grasses. A few hours later in the afternoon, he heard a commotion to the south. He saw the manticorae falling from the skies, pierced by arrows. They quickly flew off rather than counterattacking whoever assailed them. Ch'kaarl made himself small in the grass and observed. The herd of loarn had continued to widen and was just a mighty bow shot away. The desert was not much further than that to the north. He saw the source of the arrows and realized he was stuck in a narrow grass strip just a few hundred yards wide, a swath between a notoriously deadly desert and an entire company of Ithil-Banian Marines!

Ch'kaarl was all alone and being approached by over a hundred of the most feared troops on Maera. He had nowhere to hide except the grass around him, which, in his imagination, was growing shorter and sparser with each passing moment. He rolled onto his back and stared up at the sky. The blue expanse above him was clear and quite lovely. A single, wispy cloud drifted slowly to the east, riding upon the westerly wind. It moved gracefully and seemingly cautiously as it crossed the azure vastness above. Deliberately but inevitably, it made its way across the sky and off to the east. Calm again, he rolled onto his front and turned himself around.

He could hear voices in the distance. Ch'kaarl crawled on his belly slowly, deliberately, making progress back the way he'd come, only closer to the edge of the desert now. Eventually, he felt safe enough to turn. The unit of men had either split the loarn or, more likely, skirted the back end of the herd. They were shooting the manticorae for sport! Or so it seemed, although they had not stopped to claim any portion of their victims. Ch'kaarl watched and he listened and was shocked at how loose the tongues of the Ithil-Banians were. Of course, they were certain no one could overhear them, so he picked up a good deal of information from the rather boisterous men in a short span.

It seemed that the marines were marching to a meeting at the edge of the desert. They had draft horses pulling a large heavy wagon. Its iron-reinforced bed was built quite low to the ground, and its design hinted that it could carry a massive payload. Some of the men were joking loudly about the supposedly heinous terrors of the Burnt Lands that they were about to face. Those troopers who rightly feared the region's beasts were being brutally mocked as cowards by their peers.

The unit's Commander seemed to be oblivious to the chatter. He, and a second individual that Ch'kaarl took for a dark spell caster, were on horseback, riding slowly alongside their formation of marching troops. It looked as if their four draft animals were expected to pull quite a load. As the wagon wheel ruts in the aerth betrayed no weight heavier than the wagon itself, Ch'kaarl deduced that the transport was empty but they intended to add something bulky. That certainly piqued his interest. The troopers slowly passed him, continuing towards the desert. They were traveling north and east, apparently looking for a specific place where they would rendezvous with another group. Ch'kaarl had the wind in his favor, so although he believed that he could have skirted the Ithil-Banians and continued on his way, the K'haap determined that he should stay with them at a safe distance and witness their activities.

That required him to scramble low and on all fours through the knee-high grass. He carried his bow in his first hand. His quiver was strapped across his chest laterally instead of on his back. The caninoid was well practiced in this mode of motion and low-crawled his way along, the whole while keeping roughly a hundred paces away, slightly to the south and east of the Ithil-Banian troops. By doing so, he maintained a discreet distance from them, as he kept within earshot. That allowed Ch'kaarl to gather that they were expecting to reach their rendezvous point later that day and be met there the following dawn.

Whatever it was that they were picking up, their Commander considered it to be extremely deadly. He was named Doage and addressed their spell caster as Eiger. The pair were definitely the thinkers for the group, and the warriors in their charge were terrified of them. That much was evident in the way they interacted. Ch'kaarl overheard one such exchange that made a real impression on him. The incident began when an argument followed the taunting of a less experienced trooper by one of the more vocal veterans. The Commander apparently had finally heard enough. He rode over to the man with a sudden directness and spoke loudly so that all might hear.

"Tell me, Besser, was it your intent to seek my attention as you spewed your constant stream of maak? Because my attention is what you now have." He leaned forward in the saddle as he spoke. His voice dripped with venom. As the man named Besser came to attention, his Commander slowly dismounted, implying an awful purpose. "How much of my attention has your mouth earned you?" Doage's semble covered everything but his eyes, but he could be heard without speaking loudly. "Let's see, shall we?" As Commander Doage slowly walked up to further address the trooper known as Besser, the man's sergeant rushed to his side from the front of the formation. He formally snapped to attention before their Commander with a sharp 'click!' of his boot heels.

"As foul as this one is, he is one of our best with the spear, sir!" The man was willing to risk the wrath of his superior to lessen the punishment of his trooper—an impressive show of nerve. "With your permission, I will see to the administration of discipline, Commander!" He spoke quickly, loudly, and with an energetic crispness that convincingly conveyed respect. There was a long, tense, awkward silence as Commander Doage stared the trooper up and down, taking stock of his worth. When he answered, it was with an air of finality that was as measured as it was dramatic.

"See to it now, and leave the lash soaked! Let lacerated skin attest to my lack of tolerance for any more foolishness during this assignment!" Then he raised his voice so the rest of the troops could all hear him, without a doubt. "If I am forced to deal with any member of this unit again during this venture, I'll take bits and pieces of them for our Mistress so that we'll all remember our time together in this land!" His voice contrasted starkly with the silence that followed. Then he turned back to Besser and locked eyes with the man. "I hope you're smart enough to appreciate your sergeant, soldier. Not every platoon leader would stake their hide, gambling on your welfare." He then turned to the sergeant. "Praise the Goddess with your work." That final remark was said with an eerie calm that chilled the archer. The K'happ couldn't see the Commander's evil grin but he was sure it was there.

Ch'kaarl watched as the sergeant chose men from the troops and had both Besser and the man he'd taunted stripped to the waist and held firmly by the arms. Then the lash came out and the K'haap saw firsthand the punishment that had spawned an infamous Ithil-Banian saying: "Rest your tongue—use the lash!" The man known as Besser was a veteran of years of military service and had spent time under the lash. His wickedly scarred back was a testament to the heavy yoke these men bore under the cruel command of a brutal master who valued them only for what they could do for him and the horrors they would inflict on others they met. Commander Doage ruled his men with the threat of Loekii's backing. It seemed enough to strike fear into the hearts of any of these humans, no matter how hardened they might be.

It might seem harsh to some that the target of Besser's abuse received the same vicious treatment as his marching mate but Ch'kaarl saw the wisdom in it. Indeed, although he suffered much, rarely having been shown such treatment before, the younger man took the punishment without complaint and bore his pain well. Once they had experienced torment together, side by side, the older man seemed to gain an appreciation for his younger comrade. As the pair tended to one another, each applying poxy salve to the other man's wounds, they were left to develop a new bond in their pain. As Ch'kaarl pondered the strangeness of the human mind, the words attributed to the Jaan Brothers as they declared their intent to rule the Dark City together came unbidden to the K'haap's lips. "Life is suffering. Let us at least suffer together!" He muttered under his breath, shaking his head in morbid understanding.

The rest of the day passed without incident as the troopers settled down noticeably. To the archer, it seemed that the humans gleaned comfort from the pain of their comrades. He found the notion unnerving. The K'haap had no problem staying undetected and alongside the unit. They traveled at a slow but steady speed. It seemed to him that they arrived at their destination early, camping by a flat rocky area adjacent to the first sands of the desert known as the Burnt Lands.

The heat of the central portion of that desert was so severe it had been named the Anvil of Aarn by those that lived there. It was said to be like an oven and was reputed to be an incredibly unforgiving place. The Burnt Lands stretched for hundreds of miles on the southern side of the mighty Taeragorn Mountains. The Ithil-Banians had camped right at the edge of the widest portion of it, where the sands reached furthest into the rest of the world like some vast hand of creeping death, forever searching for new victims. Ch'kaarl knew better than to enter that dread place.

The camp was set early and the men settled in for a long night, keeping a bonfire lit at all times and relying on their numbers to keep them safe. It worked well and the night passed without incident. Ch'kaarl watched them from a safe distance and listened for any more information he could gather. The men pitched body-length personal tents just a few feet high and slipped into them for a peaceful night's rest. The troops swapped stories around the fire and shared food and drink. Other than gaining a better understanding of the men, who talked about certain topics in particular, as any soldiers tend to, the K'haap learned scant else about their mission. The dawn came soon enough and the camp broke early in preparation for their planned meeting. Just as Aarn crested the eastern sky, the watch reported creatures approaching from the northeast, from the heart of the deep desert.

Ch'kaarl felt gratified to be in an excellent position to view firsthand what turned out to be a contingent of the seldom seen lizardfolk of the Burnt Lands, widely known as the Angkhaar. A cursory count yielded maybe sixty of these new arrivals, and they were quite a sight, draped in their loose-fitting pale fabric shattras. The word shattra means 'veil of deception' in the ancient language of the dead, the tongue spoken by this race of Aerdos worshippers. If the information yielded by Ch'kaarl's ongoing studies of the lost deities of Maera was accurate, then they were a race of beings from a bygone age. They had been converted from the service of their creator Saet, who was lost to them when He was banished to the Void after Gaedennon. That made the Angkhaar extremely controversial amongst several religions and few did business with them. Many thought the Angkhaar were dangerous, enigmatic, and untrustworthy. In person however, and as a group, these tribesmen looked more mysterious than frightening, at least to Ch'kaarl's mind. The men of Ithil-bane obviously desired their wares more than they feared their presence.

Perhaps the most intriguing thing about them was that they had brought their pets. Three monstrous scorpions that were the color of sand flanked them. They were massive creatures with a thickly armored outer carapace that blended in with the desert. Their clacking sounds were unsettling but each was handled by one of the Angkhaar, who seemed to have tamed them. At the head of their column was their leader and beside him a spell caster with a strangely shaped staff. The troops marched alongside a massively built cart, goading on the gigantic, large-headed saurian that pulled it, and hemmed the lizard in with their spears. There was a massive rectangular shape on the low bed of the cart. A rugged-looking tan leather tarpaulin covered it and that weathered skin hid whatever was being given a wide breadth and being shown a lot of respect. Clearly, the Angkhaar were there to deliver whatever was in the cage to the Ithil-Banians.

Commander Doage approached the sands, accompanied by his first man, Eiger. It seemed the Angkhaar would not step onto the grass as their leader and spell caster awaited the approaching easterners. Words were exchanged in low voices that the K'haap could not make out. There were nods, exaggerated gestures, and signs of greetings exchanged. In a few minutes, the reptilian wizard gestured towards the cage, and the four walked over to it as the tarp was pulled back, slowly and carefully, with the butt-end of the spears of several lizard troopers. It was then, only with abundant caution, that the four peered under the tarpaulin and into the large cage beneath it to inspect whatever was inside.

Ch'kaarl risked getting too close, straining to see just what it was that the reptilians had caged for delivery to the men, but he could not get a glimpse of it. All four observers instinctively stepped back quickly from the cage as a sudden sharp noise emitted. It wasn't particularly loud but that sound! It was a noise between a call and a shriek, more hateful than angry, and Ch'kaarl had never heard anything like it. He felt the fur on his neck and back raise involuntarily.

Commander Doage seemed well-pleased that the Angkhaar had kept up their end of the bargain. He moved to have his easterners begin the delicate transfer of the ponderous cage from one cart to another. With the Angkhaar assisting, the Ithil-Banians soon had their cart adjacent to that of their counterparts. However, their captive soon took exception to the noise and commotion around it, even though the tarpaulin blocked any view of the tall-walkers around the cage and carts. Hostile, horrible yowls and screeches began to emit from beneath the tarp. The commotion, in turn, agitated the giant lizard harnessed to that cart and began to panic the draft horses of the Ithil-Banians. Ch'kaarl watched from the nearby grass in expectant fascination as the animal handlers on each side of the exchange tried to calm their beasts. The wizards, who functioned as interpreters for their Commanders, stood apart, having an animated discussion about the situation, which was rather quickly threatening to become untenable.

At this moment, Ch'kaarl briefly considered loosing a single arrow from concealment, straight through the tarp and into the cage, just to see how much chaos he could unleash. He shook his head, quickly dismissing the crazy notion. But he'd briefly considered it. In the end, Ch'kaarl did nothing more than watch while an agreement was reached and the handlers responded to new instructions from their leaders. As a solution, they simply exchanged draft animals, managing to rig the harnessing they required. Soon the men prepared to leave, hauling the cage on the desert dweller's cart and leaving their own behind in a straight swap. Once this was accomplished, the man known as Eiger produced what looked to be a large, heavy book that was carefully wrapped in dark cloth, and eagerly received by the Angkhaar wizard. After unwrapping and briefly examining it, undoubtedly, to verify its authenticity, the spell caster began nodding and bowing at the waist, apparently delighted with the tome.

The Angkhaar had come to the meet with Aarn rising behind them, something Ch'kaarl had anticipated. What he didn't foresee was the buzzard that suddenly flew in from the same direction, unseen by the K'haap until it had nearly landed on the cross-strut of the strange staff, the odd design of which suddenly made sense. It was a bird perch as well as a wizard's staff!

The carrion eater cried aloud twice, bobbing its head in Ch'kaarl's general direction. The reptilian wizard pivoted and spoke to Eiger. Then both casters and leaders turned as one, and Commander Doage pointed his way. The buzzard danced on his perch excitedly, nodding its head and emitting a loud, drawn-out hiss. Heads turned amongst the troops of both nations, fingers pointed, alarm cries were uttered, and a great many eyes focused in Ch'kaarl's direction—and just like that, the favor of Rhal was lost.

The K'haap was a conservative-minded warrior who relied, whenever possible, upon the intellect he'd been born with and diligently sought to enhance throughout his life. For years he had honed his skill with bow and longsword, training his body as he had his mind, seeking perfection in his mortal form. At the moment of perhaps his greatest peril, Ch'kaarl could fully comprehend his situation, weigh his options, and act without the hesitation that might have hindered a less prepared individual.

Commander Doage scanned the plains to the east. As far as he could see, there was a sea of knee to waist-high growth of green-to-tan grasses. He squinted against the newly risen sun and watched as a single large figure suddenly stood up, a dark blur against that burning light. As he tried to make out the details of the being, who seemed larger than a man, Doage realized that the creature had the largest bow he'd ever seen and that he was aiming it—at him!

Eiger stepped forward, placing his hand on Doage's chest, and stepped up by his side as he pushed him back in a protective gesture. The wizard had begun to cast a spell, speaking in his arcane tongue, defending Doage with an invisible *Shield* born of arcane force. The archer turned his hips slightly to his right, releasing an arrow that sped straight through the leather tarp and into the cage it concealed, where it found flesh with a heavy 'FAP!' A series of things then occurred in such rapid succession that it was enough to take one's breath away.

An unholy screeching erupted from inside the cage, which began to rattle and shake with a terrible energy that suggested it might soon burst. The sound of dragging chains and metal-on-metal was so loud that all eyes, human and Angkhaarian, were drawn to the sudden racket. Thus, they were staring as one as the distinct and unmistakable wrenching of shattering iron issued forth from the cage so loudly that the reaction of those watching was to stand aghast at the implication of that sound. A moment of silence hung in the air. Doage used that moment to quickly swivel his head back towards the archer, whom he saw sprinting at a tremendous pace directly away from them through the grass. Before the Commander could react to that sight, he heard a further fantastic racket. It was so frightening that few who heard it would ever forget it. As he turned back to look upon the cage, he saw the tarp being ripped to shreds from behind the bars of the enclosure, and for the first time in his life, Commander Doage laid his widened eyes on a raegaar.

The monster was large but so lean that its bones were visible beneath its smooth, moist-looking blood-red hide. Its head was huge, supported by a long neck, with great round, black eyes. Its slathering jaws overflowed with what seemed like an impossible number of slender teeth, long and sharp, so that its visage was truly horrid—and that noise!

It was otherworldly, like the shrieking of an animal set aflame. The creature was kinetic, so frantic in every movement that it was as if it had just come out of some long stupor and realized that it had been set alight! It had broken the chains that held it down and shredded the tarpaulin in mere moments, and now it was seeking freedom. It screeched and threw its entire weight against the cage, which was heavy blackened iron and had clearly been crafted to resist tremendous strength. Even so, against the raegaar's frenzy of tumultuous rage, it was clear that the cage would be utterly ruined in mere moments.

The Angkhaar reacted quickly and efficiently to their credit. They had not been idle as they faced a long day's journey ahead of them back through the Burnt Lands. Already their great lizard had been harnessed to their new cart and it was first to react, letting out a hiss of its own and pulling away from the caged raegaar. Its handlers rushed to calm it and regain control of the beast with spear staves, shouts, and placating gestures. Their leaders retreated from the Ithil-Banian Commander and their spell caster hugged his prize to his chest as they went. His buzzard had already taken to the air. Their great scorpions had started to scuttle nervously side-to-side in anticipation of battle or flight. The Angkhaar troops were still nearby but were already as good as gone, slipping back towards the desert they called home.

The Ithil-Banian horse wranglers desperately sought to regain control of their panicked drafts but could barely keep from being bludgeoned by a flurry of thrashing hooves. Their four horses were only partially lashed to the Angkhaarian cart and began pulling away in their hysteria. That lateral pull west, combined with the baerserk rampage of the raegaar, caused the cage to slide and then topple off the cart to the east. It fell onto its side with a resounding crash. Things were quickly getting out of hand as the powerful horses fled, dragging the wagon off while the raegaar started forcing its body, arms first, through the southernmost, and now horizontal, bars of its enclosure. Commander Doage started to back away from the cage alongside Eiger, shouting orders for his spearmen to approach the cage. The pair then attempted to get their riding horses under control as the men they had assigned to hold their reins were struggling mightily in their task.

Ch'kaarl concentrated on his breathing and on maintaining his running form. He was a tremendous sprinter, his powerful legs propelling him forward at a remarkable pace. He could maintain his top speed for minutes but quickly felt he had run long enough to be out of bow range. The warrior judged that he must also be unreachable by any spell. The reprisal attack he had expected as he ran had never come, judging by the noises behind him, his single arrow's effect had been simply stupendous! The K'haap launched his body at full speed, diving headlong onto his belly, arms extended before him. He slid to a stop on the grass, then scrambled to turn his body. Ch'kaarl quickly raised himself onto all fours to catch a glimpse of the mayhem he had caused. As he took in the scene, he could hardly believe his eyes.

The Angkhaar had pulled back towards the desert in an enthusiastic retreat. They had adequately controlled their creatures and seemed to possess no inclination to give aid to the easterners now that they had fulfilled their side of the bargain that had brought them there. Meanwhile, the Ithil-Banians had a true calamity on their hands. Reluctantly, the marines stepped up with spears and shields and moved to encircle the cage. Inside it was a monster straight out of some twisted nightmare! It is said that no one forgets the first time they see a raegaar, and that saying proved prophetic. Suddenly, and perhaps for the first time, the hardened marines faced something they feared more than their leaders—the mighty scourge of the Burnt Lands, aggression incarnate!

The horror's bony, protruding spines along its back accentuated wickedly hooked claws, each like a small black scythe. Big, pitch-colored eyes, dull and emotionless, contrasted with a cruelly toothed, oversized maw. Its bloody-hued hide glistened with an ooze it produced when agitated. Its slender build belied its incredible strength and speed as it thrashed about, seeking its freedom. The human's tangible fear of the heinous beast seemed well-founded and their masters, now astride their unnerved steeds, faced a real challenge merely controlling their mounts. Then things quickly got immeasurably worse.

With a sudden, sustained, and enormous effort, the raegaar grasped a single bar in its mouth. With all four clawed appendages, it lifted itself, so then it bore most of its weight on its long, curled, and muscular tail. It transferred all its weight forward, using its mass to bend the bar to ruin. It immediately repeated that tactic with terrible speed. Soon it had mangled a second bar and wrenched it out of place. Next, the raegaar forced its muzzle into the gap it had created, rotated its body sideways, and started bending bars above and below with all four limbs. Commander Doage shouted an order to his men in a plaintive tone, filled with raw desperation.

"KILL IT! KILL IT NOW! DON'T LET IT BREAK FREE!" His company of spearmen seemed momentarily stunned by the command. These were soldiers used to slaying helpless creatures with cruel indifference. They did not relish this kind of fight. Then one man cried out in raw aggression and leaped forward to bring his weapon to bear. Others soon followed the trooper's lead, and in moments a dozen men sought to kill the savage thing while it was still caged.

Spear thrusts bounced off the face and thick, leathery hide of the monstrosity as it defied death. The raegaar shrieked in a rabid response. Its writhing was so frantic and fast that numerous other attacks against it simply missed their target. Finally, it could force its weight forward sufficiently to squeeze itself through the bars. With a screeching howl that seemed to shatter the air around it, the raegaar burst forth from its prison, claws, and teeth bared!

The exotic hellish terror was FREE!

The sight visibly shook the spearmen around it and its shriek weakened their knees. Spear thrusts were attempted by multiple marines, whose sergeants led them bravely in the endeavor. But, now loose, the dexterity of the creature was wholly evident. Its massive head bobbed quickly to and fro, for it could switch its focus between individual targets at a much higher rate of speed than a man could. Then it advanced, swatting away the Ithil-Banian spears mid-thrust as it went. Several spears tested the raegaar's hide but their strikes failed, for its thick and loose skin repelled most attacks. The monster whirled south and as it did so, it swept its tail across the soldiers to the north and east of it. It was surprisingly long once uncurled and the power in that tail caught them off guard, forcing several of them back and even knocking men to the ground.

Then the raegaar screeched and rushed forward, engaging the easterners so quickly and viciously that it was amazing to behold. Trained veterans of years of brutal military service seemed to stand no chance against this gruesome foe. Claws slashed flesh to bloody ribbons and teeth found ample meat to rend to horrid shreds, each attack occurring so fast and with such a burst of energy that a mist of blood began to fill the air around the beast. The raegaar momentarily paused its rampage, as if for effect, as it breathed deeply that blood-misted air. That seemed to throw it into an even greater state of frenzy. It emitted a joyous barking chortle that was an assault on the ears and minds of its hapless prey. Commander Doage turned to the right in his saddle, shouting at his spell caster.

"DO SOMETHING!" Doage yelled, sounding exasperated. The wizard turned, looked at his commander, then back at the rae-gaar, and again at his boss. Eiger nodded curtly, pivoted around, and unleashed his most powerful magic on the beast. A column of billowing fire issued from the skies ten paces above the monster in a twenty-foot-wide circle that blasted the area in tremendous heat like a furnace. The fire burned for three long heartbeats and the force of it pushed the raegaar towards the ground. As it waned, the men closest to the raegaar ran screaming, their tunics and leather aflame. Others nearby reeled, falling back away from the area of effect. The raegaar crouched low at first and Eiger's hope that he had done real damage to the fiend swelled inside his chest. Then those hopes were dashed like an infant's head against stone.

The raegaar had been protected by its oozing skin, an adaptation that helped it survive the extreme heat it faced daily, running the Anvil of Aarn. It had, apparently, suffered no damage from the spell's effect. It hissed aggressively, swinging its head back and forth, still low to the ground as if searching for something. Its gaze fell upon Eiger and Doage on their horses, safely back and away from the fray. The creature fixated on the wizard. As unbelievable as it seemed to the spell caster, the raegaar screeched and came right at him! Spears were thrust at it from three sides as it pushed towards the wizard, whose horse reared dangerously in response to the threat. The riders needed both hands to stay in the saddle and their mounts sounded their panic while rearing up. Ch'kaarl contemplated using arrows to take down their horses. Then he saw his first shaft, though broken now, was still lodged in the meat of the raegaar's left rear thigh. The K'haap felt a small measure of concern that the monster might, if able to track him, next seek out the archer who had wounded it. That apprehension was enough to keep him hidden. Better to let things play out as they would. It was in Rhal's hands now.

He watched as the creature went about its fun and that was the right word, for the raegaar seemed to revel in its butchery. Many men surely thought themselves brave, even daring. Yet in Ch'kaarl's experience, humans were as self-deluded as any of the creations of the Aeglain. They knew fear, certainly but in the wildly convoluted expanse of their minds, many thought they knew the limits of it. Indeed, their imagined terrors were far more significant than those found outside their minds. The K'happ knew, however, that when running the wide world, one always had a chance to encounter things that redefined terror in one's mind. He looked on in utter morbid fascination as the easterners shared such an experience.

Horror was painted on their faces like a contorted mask. Shouts of aggression and calls to arms had been replaced by louder cries, those of the eviscerated and mauled. The awful noises men made as they died were like a chaotic accompaniment to the death song screeched by the raegaar. Ch'kaarl had heard tales of the ferocity of the raegaar. He had heard of their ability to wreak havoc against any number of foes. But the sheer physical capabilities and raw capacity to terrorize opponents displayed by this beast had never been conveyed to him in terms that did it justice, regardless of how harrowing those tales might have been. Seeing it with his own eyes made Ch'kaarl's fur bristle and left him feeling both threatened and shocked, although he was in no immediate danger from the glossy blood-red juggernaut.

Suddenly a chorus of voices rose from the south as the rest of the easterners charged towards the battle. Once the combatants realized that reinforcements were on the way, the raegaar was opposed with greater zeal. The entire contingent would certainly contain and then impale the monster on their bladed staves. Eiger and Doage struggled to back their mounts away from the raegaar. Their troopers rushed between them and the ravening beast. It seemed to the K'haap that the easterners valued their wizard and commander highly, for they threw themselves into spectacular peril to shield their leaders as the pair distanced themselves from nearly inevitable, horrible evisceration.

Ch'kaarl realized this was likely his best chance to distance himself from the brawl. He secured his bow and longsword on his back and side, respectively. He ensured that his quiver was set across his back and the rest of his kit was properly stowed away on his person. He quickly went through his mental checklist: dagger, water-skin, war club, left hip pouch, right hip satchel, bed roll across his back, provision sack, and poison cache. All he carried was still in place.

He turned away from the battle, rose from all fours, and stretched for a moment. Then he sprinted due east for a distance and at a pace that no unhorsed human could ever hope to match. When he was finally fatigued, Ch'kaarl slowed his run, and eventually, he was merely jogging. He stopped, turning to look behind him, but saw nothing giving chase from the west. He scanned the sky to see if the conflict was drawing the attention of any fliers in the region, but he saw nothing about which he was concerned. Ch'kaarl stood with his hands on his hips and caught his breath as he considered his options.

The K'haap imagined that whatever their losses, the Ithil-Banians would put the raegaar down eventually. Their sheer numbers were enough to assure that outcome. With their mission an utter failure, their Commander would be looking to save his own life, as whoever had dreamed up the task would not be pleased. There was little else the man could do but pursue the archer who had caused him such trouble. They may only have had two horses but Ch'kaarl imagined that there would be an attempt made to exact some form of vengeance upon him. It seemed the nature of these humans to fear, hate and then destroy those they met. That predisposition would be far less of a problem for life on Maera if Loekii's spawn weren't so insistent on encountering everyone else everywhere.

His evaluation of the situation led him to conclude that the Commander would send his wizard and whoever was his unit's champion, or perhaps their best tracker, to pursue him. The archer could not foresee a scenario in which his superior bow range would not ensure his victory if an attempt to take him ensued. He thought it especially unlikely if the order was to take him alive. He believed that to be the most likely command under which such a hunt would proceed. For such an aggressive plan to be implemented, the Commander would need to be sure that there was a decent chance that his spell caster could succeed. So, Ch'kaarl determined that he must not underestimate the wizard's capabilities should he detect pursuit. With that in mind, he decided to retreat to a known point, which would give him a tactical advantage.

So it was that the K'haap warrior headed south to the rocky outcropping where he had, just a day earlier, found the brambler sign. A change, of course, was wise in case of pursuit and the vantage of that low ledge would allow him a chance to scout before continuing. He intended to return to the great solitary dengael tree to spend another night in the relative safety of its roots. By doing so, Ch'kaarl was conceding an entire day to avoid a continued encounter with the Ithil-Banians, which he felt was wise. In any case, while the K'haap had to acknowledge his desire to rid Maera of such beings, the information that he'd gathered during this scouting mission, specifically his account of the easterners being present in the region, far outweighed his predatory inclinations. "You will have your way some other time," he softly promised his tall bow, which he had affectionately named Iyla, lightly running his long fingers along her artfully-crafted belly side.

The familiar ledge held no surprises for him but neither did it yield much to see. There was no additional brambler sign and it was apparent that the great herd had passed to the west. Ch'kaarl saw no sign of the pursuit he had feared would come. The area seemed particularly quiet, so he did not tarry and moved along. Thus, the K'happ warrior made his way without contention back to the massive dengael tree, where he'd enjoyed a refreshing deep rest just two nights earlier. He once again found himself running his palm along the smooth gray bark of the tree's roots, admiring the majesty of the mighty life form.

"Somehow, regardless of what brought me back, I find comfort in your company," he said aloud. "Perhaps you'll allow me to spend another night with you under the eternal sky?" As he fell silent, the archer placed his hands shoulder-width apart on the huge root that lay before him, placing his forehead against the wood in a gesture of open supplication. It seemed to Ch'kaarl that a barely discernible shudder passed through the ancient tree as if affirming his heartfelt sentiment. As the evening came upon them, the pair shared a few peaceful hours as the warrior watched for any sign of what evil the children of Loekii might have conceived.

The riders Ch'kaarl expected never came. Nothing at all happened and the light finally failed. Aarn retreated from the sky quickly as if pursued by the encroaching dark. The sky was crowded with a magnificent display of stars, filling the K'haap with a welcome and familiar sense of wonder. Once again, he experienced the calming effect that resting amidst the roots of the dengael tree seemed to provide. At first, he frequently rose to scan the plains for any sign of avenging easterners, aided by the keen predatory eyes Ilmarae had given to his kind. The gentle breeze carried no scent that caused concern nor did the sounds of the night alarm him. Eventually, several hours after the dark had fully embraced the sky, the caninoid slipped into a restful slumber, the likes of which he seldom achieved while alone and running the wild.

He awoke suddenly and with a strong sense of trepidation. Ears, whiskers, fur—all of his anticipatory triggers had been tripped. In a heartbeat, his acute senses had fully focused. Something was wrong … there was something near … some … thing. He realized that he was holding his breath and his body trembled perceptibly. As a survivor of many dangerous encounters, the K'haap was not fearless but had learned to manage such fright. In doing so, his hands went to his sword and scabbard. Slowly, ever so slowly, the warrior rose to his feet, his breath now coming in long and measured inhalations. His sense of unease was distinct and he turned, gradually searching in all directions for whatever it was that he was reacting so strongly to. Ch'kaarl detected nothing, becoming more tense with each passing moment. He knew that he was in danger. Years of free-running experience, combined with a sensory perception few could match, told him so in the kind of clear warning he never ignored. His teeth showed in a sudden grimace as he turned west.

It was upon him.

Ch'kaarl shrank away from the air above and before him. Something darker than the sky hung in the air, discernible only as an area devoid of light, blocking out the stars. The thing wasn't vast in size and made no sound. It had no odor he could detect and hovered, unaffected by the slight wind, like an animated patch of empty, absolute blackness. The warrior recoiled in revulsion, a stark horror he couldn't comprehend. The void seemed to sway back and forth, inching closer each moment to the archer. Ch'kaarl's usual warrior's composure failed him and he fell backward. He retreated awkwardly, scuttling across the aerth like some kind of giant furry crustacean. His hands reached behind to stabilize him until his backside met the junction of two great roots of the dengael tree. He shrunk further, tucking his legs against his chest, away from the entity that seemed to have come for him. He had no defense against an Inaeran predator. Summoning and releasing extra-planar beings upon the world required rare magic and the K'haap simply had nothing to counter such a threat. It seemed to Ch'kaarl that he had drastically underestimated the Ithil-Banian spell caster. As he cringed alone in the dark, he did not doubt that his miscalculation would cost him his life, and perhaps more.

If he was to perish, Ch'kaarl knew that he needed to do what he could to ensure that his life's energy translated in the benevolent custody of his creator, Ilmarae. He had heard fearful tales of the servants of the dark gods stealing life energy from faithful servants of other gods, even those who were blessed by and in good standing in their worship. The K'happ warrior had never before encountered such a threat and now it seemed that he faced that stark, brutal reality. Ch'kaarl realized that there was nothing to do but reaffirm his grace in the worship of Ilmarae and embrace his fate, whatever came. So, he whispered the prayers of the faithful, kissed the charm that hung around his neck on a leather thong and prepared his consciousness for its translation to energy that would join the collective mind of the God of Knowledge.

The blackness approached the caninoid slowly, a bit confused by the sudden loss of sweet deliciousness. Its pursuit of this quarry had thus far yielded tangible energy that the entity fed on—delightful fear, luxurious trepidation and, disappointingly, measurably less confusion and panic than expected. Now it sensed that its intended victim had purged itself of the emotional banquet that had allowed it to feed, to track this prey, and come upon it unsuspecting in the dark of night. The very lack of physicality that made the entity so dangerous to the denizens of this world now betrayed it. It fluttered and thrashed in the air directly above and in front of the mortal but to no avail. Its attempts to influence its intended victim's mind met surprisingly substantial resistance.

Soon it realized its feast would be less fulfilling than anticipated. There would be no succulent banquet of wildly inflamed base emotions upon which to satiate its ever-increasing hunger. It shook in sudden fury at the notion, for even under the Inaeran's most potent invasive attack, the maeraan resisted being overwhelmed by its primal instincts, those powerful survival pangs that the being so desired and found so satisfying to ingest. At least there would be that most splendid of moments—that instant of sudden realization that its very essence was being taken and the rush of thrilling satisfaction that accompanied fulfilling its purpose.

At that moment, a hot wind seemed to swirl from the desert to the north. While it arrived suddenly, it felt somehow eternal, as if it had always been and always would be. It was as if the desert itself had arrived on that searing dry gust. The wind became a spinning whirlwind of withering heat. It wound tighter, more fiercely, while engulfing the dark being in an unnatural storm of lashing, biting force. Although the raw physicality of the event did not affect the Inaeran, there was a potent psychic component to the assault.

There was a brief interaction between the summoned darkness that merely temporarily roamed the skies of Maera and a being that had swirled through the atmosphere of that world since Madrain had first endowed it with life so long ago. It was a brutal decisive encounter in which the scirocco destroyed the intruding entity, banishing it to the plane from which it came. So overpowering was the assault that it lasted mere moments. The dark could not resist the inevitable outcome. Meanwhile, Ch'kaarl had faded from his reality into another place, perhaps some alternate existence devoid of sight, sound, and any other familiar thing.

He had disappeared.

A gentle breeze was the first indication of reality returning. Ch'kaarl blinked, turned his head, and saw a deep purple butterfly with white dots and black edges to its wings. It sat above him on the root of the dengael tree, resting on the smooth, gray bark. As the warrior watched, he had to concentrate on focusing his vision. He felt odd, out of touch with his body. The butterfly suddenly rose and flitted away on a fragrant zephyr that smelled familiar. Ch'kaarl rose slowly, carefully. He was unsure that his limbs would function normally. He eventually stood to his full height and stretched for a few moments. Aarn revealed that he was facing west. That much, at least, was readily discernible. The odor he recognized was a blend of wildflowers that he realized was reminiscent of home. *Could it be?* he marveled. "Am I in the Land of Baelthas?"

He had spoken aloud without thinking to do so. He recognized the sky and the flora. All told him he was in the region under the control of his liege. As he looked around, Ch'kaarl wondered how he had gotten there and how the dengael tree was with him. Was he deluded, under some effect of powerful magic, or perhaps in his promised afterlife? He somehow felt comforted that the mighty tree was still with him. He placed his hands once again on the skin of its root at shoulder width and rested his forehead on the ancient being's cool bark. "Well," he smiled as peace filled him, "at least we have one another, yes?" As if in acknowledgment, the leaves that filled the canopy of the oddly shaped wooden giant seemed to him to shimmy of their own volition.

Ch'kaarl saw that it was still early in the day, although he could not say what day. The thought of leaving the dengael tree irked him, somehow. So he sat down with his back to the pocket formed by the convergence of its vast roots. Now that his mind was clear, he took the time to consider all that had occurred in recent days. Once he had analyzed current events and pondered his unlikely survival, including the unexplained and miraculous relocation of himself and the tree hundreds of miles to safety, Ch'kaarl knew that a serious attempt must be made to communicate with the dengael tree or the spirit that dwelled therein. His expertise on the creatures of the wild was far greater than his limited knowledge of energy beings. He knew trees could harbor the spiritual essence of aelves and other more mysterious entities. He had never heard of dengael trees being sentient but he imagined it was possible. So it was that the K'haap took his ease leaning against the comforting roots of his host while trying to make contact with the consciousness within the tree that he credited with saving his life.

The warrior aligned his posture and crossed his legs. He strove to free himself of tension in his body. He had learned long ago that such a passive physical state assisted him in clearing his mind and forming memories and even increased his ability to comprehend and process complex information. It also connected him with his spirituality and gave him an inner peace that he had found other beings could sense. This personal ritual had helped him in the past to communicate under stress and primed him when seeking the counsel of others. Ch'kaarl concentrated and sought the intellect of another. He opened his mind to the benevolence he had felt in the company of the dengael tree and the powerful sense of comfort he had experienced sleeping beneath it. He made his waking mind a conduit of his energy, seeking any flow of consciousness that might reciprocate his offering of peaceful contact.

The warrior's personality was firmly based on his worship of Ilmarae, his creator, the God of Knowledge. His lifelong desire to learn and his long training in gathering information had served him well all the days of his life, and it did not fail him on that eventful day. The voice that came to him was disembodied and while he knew that he'd never heard that arcane medium before, it somehow seemed familiar. While it conveyed an undeniable message of peace, Ch'kaarl also sensed tremendous strength.

"You need not fear me, plains runner," the voice echoed. "Have I not demonstrated where my sympathies lie?" The K'haap had met and even spoken with the tree folk of Maera's forests on more than one occasion. This was something else.

"I thank you for coming to my aid," Ch'kaarl began. "I am in your debt." The caninoid drew a deep breath. He'd have to do better than stating the obvious.

"Yes," the windswept words answered, "but I have no need of perceived obligations." The sound of the voice was like the aching of loneliness and it made the warrior feel a sense of genuine empathy. "For too long have I ridden the sky alone," the desert spirit continued. "I have wandered the vast seas of sand, above the ever-shifting dunes. I have swirled amidst the soft stone of the forgotten caverns of bygone eons." There was a regretful sadness in the eerie timbre of the words, heard yet unspoken. "While I sought dalliances with the vortices and eddies of the wastelands, I chose to ignore the age of the dragons. In their turn, I eschewed the glory of the ascending aelves and looked away as the dwaerven folk rose. While I couldn't help but watch the encroachment of man across Maera, I did so with arrogant indifference. Even when Ptalles acted to save this world, I did nothing, choosing instead to cast my lot with the burning silt of Aarn's Anvil."

The entity's narrative enthralled Ch'kaarl and he quietly listened with the respectful silence he felt his apparent savior deserved. He was starting to realize that he might be privy to an unprecedented moment and have a unique opportunity to further what was quickly becoming a new relationship with an emissary of a race of ancient and elusive beings that haunted the Burnt Lands. The K'haap warrior actively strove to project his most empathetic mindset and allowed that emotion to dominate his waking mind, as it seemed that the being with whom he was communicating could perceive it. It appeared that this was indeed taken as encouragement by the scirocco, who continued to share its mind with Ch'kaarl.

"My folk have sensed a change in the world. We have heard it on the wind, tasted it in the sand, and felt it in Aarn's light. I see it in your mind, in your apprehensions and fears, in your doubts and beliefs. Where once my kind stood separate from the mortals of Maera in the time of our world's greatest need, I cannot bear to avoid a role in the troubles of this age. I would remain isolated no longer." The caninoid listened intently, feeling that his silence was not only polite but also that it conveyed his acknowledgment of the harsh reality that the being described, and its accuracy in doing so. The ancient melancholy entity continued his oration.

"We met under circumstances that some might call fate. In truth, I have strategically chosen where my companion tree has manifested. Together we have explored beyond the traditional boundaries of the desert, testing the greener world's reception of my kind. This is how you came here now; on the ground you find familiar but to which I am a stranger. I would ask you, Child of Reason, shall I be made welcome here in the Land of Baelthas?"

Ch'kaarl was not in the habit of speaking on behalf of Ilmarae's manifestation on the continent of Maerisna. The Emerald Twins were known to be His incarnations in the mortal world and although the K'haap warrior had been in His presence on more than one occasion, he had never before served as a diplomat for Baelthas. However, in such a matter, he felt confident that he could speak for his liege to some degree. He rose to his feet, turned and faced the dengael tree's trunk, palms held out wide.

"I'm certain that you will find that Baelthas will welcome any sincere offering of a peaceful discourse," he said in a humble generous tone. Then, as the K'haap imagined that the ways of mortals were perhaps mostly unknown to his new benefactor, Ch'kaarl submitted a notion for consideration. "I will offer my name in friendship if that pleases you, as it is the custom of our land and, as your guide, I will thereafter be at your service." He bent at the waist and adopted the pose of a modest suppliant. Ch'kaarl awaited acknowledgment with no small degree of trepidation as silence ensued, leaving him concerned he had overstepped. In a few moments, however, he was reassured.

"Names … yes, let us observe the rituals of your folk. I have been called a 'scirocco' by the dwellers of the desert." The moment was a bit awkward, but the warrior was pleased by what he perceived to be much progress.

"Wonderful! I shall address you as 'Scirocco,'" said the archer. "I would be honored if you used the name my people gave me. I am Ch'kaarl of the K'happ nation from the Isle of Raluuk and I would be pleased to introduce you to my lord, K'thraekus of the Greshaan, and then to our liege Baelthas. In their stead, I welcome you to these lands." The warrior was on unfamiliar ground, exchanging ritualized greetings with a member of an unknown race. He was, nonetheless, pleased with the outcome of his efforts, as a response was quick.

"Ch'kaarl, it shall be. Surely, you honor your kind with your noble way, loyal Servant of Ilmarae, and I would be honored to call you 'friend.'" Scirocco continued, and now his voice, previously so ominous and hollow seeming, conveyed just a hint of relaxation as he spoke. "Would it be acceptable if I take us to the tower of your liege?"

The K'happ warrior realized that suddenly appearing in the vicinity of the obsidian tower of Baelthas might be a bit daring, as most of the region's conventional defenses would be breached instantly by such an approach. He pondered the idea for a bit, remaining quiet in the now certain knowledge that his new friend indeed had some level of access to his mind and would sense his concern. There was a long pause before he finally answered.

"Although, as a warrior, I find such drama a bit … alarming. I also see the wisdom of directness. Certainly, you would be risking more than Baelthas in such a sudden appearance within an area so firmly under His power. I would sanction such action so long as I may assume responsibility for it. So, I must insist that you do so only as my guest and at my direct behest. Would you allow me to speak for you when we first arrive and make the appropriate introductions?" Ch'kaarl surprised himself with the realization that he had just assumed the mantle of diplomat and ambassador for the

Land of Baelthas. It felt to him that he was overstepping and he had real concerns that perhaps his friend Scirocco could detect it, even though he had attempted to seem confident in his statements regarding the matter.

"Agreed. I will take us there now if it suits you," Scirocco said. His voice still had a quality that made Ch'kaarl think that only he could hear it and that, while not only incorporeal, it was also somehow distant and ever crept along the verge of an arcane echo. Scirocco continued, "I shall rely on your courage then, friend and what I have seen of your mind and heart."

With that said, the elemental scirocco of the Burnt Lands translated himself, Ch'kaarl, and his ancient tree to the heart of the Land of Baelthas. Scirocco accomplished this feat after interacting with the desert for over a millennium and adopting a massive dengael tree as a base from which it operated. It had merged its aetherael energy with the physicality of the tree. By doing so, Scirocco disciplined its mind to insert itself into the tangible world. By exerting its tremendous will, it extended and mastered its reality. Through a seemingly random meeting with a plains runner, scouting for the Lord of Knowledge on Maerisna, the spirit had stepped forward from the obscurity of its existence. It accepted a role in the struggle to determine the fate of all of Maera.

The Tomes of Knowledge noted that Ch'kaarl of the K'haap people brought into the fold of Baelthas a mighty new ally in the struggle to maintain the balance of power on Maera. It was also recorded that the master archer of that land was thereafter heavily relied upon by the region's defensive commander, K'thraekus of the Greshaan, in matters of diplomacy. At times, he acted on behalf of the region as an ambassador of that faction. It is said that the experience of bringing the scirocco to the Word of Ilmarae further transformed the warrior. He grew more focused on his worship and thus his reward for his efforts was indeed remarkable.

Ch'kaarl was later asked about the legend spawned by his actions while reconnoitering the edge of the Burnt Lands at that fateful time. The K'haap warrior's response served to increase the esteem in which he was held. He revealed his growth in the worship, speaking in a way that added to the lexicon of the faithful. "I can only attest to the glory of Ilmarae, whose every gifted word is truth. I cannot hope to relay what transpired to you further than to say that I was indeed there, for truth is ever elusive in the minds of mortals—and who am I to claim to possess it?"

*Want to experience more of Maera? Visit **www.maeraworld.com***

THE BAD-BAD

The day had been long and Basta was weary. Shielding, as they called it, was a demanding profession in which the twins were on the rise. He and his sister were deeply embedded with a wealthy merchant's family who were desperately trying to survive the realm's transition to its newest Chancellor. They'd been given the lucrative assignment of protecting Graetchel, the pride of House Laeyon. Now fourteen, she was a young woman and was not the miserable charge they had initially feared she'd be. Born into a soft life of protected luxury, she'd still somehow managed to turn out well, if wildly spoiled. The pair attributed this to her intellect for, while she was quietly obedient, her cooperation seemed born more of a savvy appraisal of her surroundings than any supplication to her breeders. The two gave her credit for that. Graetchel, as it turned out, was easy to shield and even somewhat likable.

The twins had been waiting for their day off patiently. Each Day of Fortune, or Rholm, as men called it, their charge was fully locked down and they were allowed a day away from the house. They were given walking papers, a benevolent expense considered an earned bonus in their position, allowing them to stroll the streets as the population of Ithil-Bane dreamed. They spent such days visiting various popular establishments in the lower and middle wards where they enjoyed drinking and engaging in other more distracting enthusiasms.

It was nearly dusk, and they were spent. Sheen was an aggressive gambler, and a successful run of jux had fueled their day. They were headed home, the remains of her winnings in hand, but they took a slight detour. Sheen had to squat and squirt, and they entered a fully shadowed alley to provide her some chance to avoid prying eyes. There she found a grating that led to the underflow of the streets. Basta stood to watch over the alleyway, which was seemingly empty, as a standard precaution. He patiently waited while his sibling saw to her business, but in overhearing her stream, he realized he had to join her. "Nine hells! Now I have to spray!" he said, not even trying to hide his irritation.

"Stop your pathetic whining, you dangle-balled crack-lapper!" Sheen spat at him, grinning wide in her amusement. Like many twins, the two were more than close. They often stole each other's words and regularly partnered in thought. They saw things the same way, even if she was a bit more tightly coiled than he. They certainly didn't coddle each other! Basta chuckled as he dropped his leggings below his cheeks and let loose the fury of his spike. Abundant drink fed the strength of his flow in the way only it can. Thus, the pair splashed the alley in a decorative tribute to a day well spent in irreverent and dramatic hedonistic pleasures.

Basta placed his second hand on the brick before him and sighed. He'd spent hours tilting back ale and watching Sheen play while he feaked with some random tavern meat with a taut belly and soft skin. What was her name? He shook his head but already, the information had faded from his mind. There was no denying it. They had needed a day like this!

There had been persistent rumors of a plot to kidnap Graetchel, which they had taken extremely seriously. A number of the noble houses of Ithil-Bane had seen their eldest blood-child taken, with the intent of forcing their families to accept a woefully disadvantageous re-ordering of the hierarchy of the ruling class of the metropolis. Basta was a bit unclear on the strategy involved. Capitulation seemed a better option, at least to his common mind, than the wholesale slaughter of the household, which had occurred in several instances where families had resisted. The twins found themselves in a perilous position. They could only hope that they had hired into a family whose worth the new Chancellor deemed sufficient to tolerate their defiance.

That made for a nerve-racking workplace. For weeks, the pair had served through all hours under very tense circumstances, helping the Laeyon family keep up the veneer of a smooth relationship with the new and brutal administration of Lord Callus. The everyday dangers of the Night Realm dictated that private tutors were the norm for the children of noble houses. That meant that Graetchel rarely left the family apartments except to attend her beloved dance lessons. The twins had therefore expanded their duties to include escorting different family members to and from their various appointments, as well as participating in household security overall. They were amongst the most capable warriors employed by the Laeyons which had made them increasingly valuable. However, the twins truly did not get on well with the family's Head of Security, under whose volatile command they had squarely fallen. This dynamic added to the considerable tension they had been subjected to recently.

"That's my grate." The voice came suddenly, creepily close, jolting Sheen. She'd just finished her squirt and was still squatting. She looked to her left and saw a child, perhaps ten years old, standing just a few feet away. The majority of denizens of Ithil-Bane went about without care for their unwashed state. However, she was immediately struck by how genuinely grimy the boy was, thoroughly blackened by what looked to be soot. He stood still as death, with his arms at his sides. His dark eyes locked onto hers in a focused emotionless glare that was unsettling.

"Hell's whores, boy! You startled me. Let me have my privacy!" She stood and started to look for Basta but thought better of it. The rum and fatigue quickly cleared from her mind as she held the child's gaze and spoke aloud. "Brother—you seeing this?" Basta was only a few strides to her right. He had closed his eyes and was deeply lost in his thoughts. As she spoke, her voice loud with wariness, another voice reached his ears.

"That's my wall you're pissing on." It was a girl's voice, and he turned his head left to see a youngster standing just out of his reach. She and her tattered clothes were blackened from head to toe. A mass of tangled brown curls mostly concealed her face but she was a tiny thing and couldn't have been more than eight or ten. Several other children, small and just as filthy as the first, emerged from the alley's walls. They crawled out of ground-level horizontal apertures with rectangular wooden flaps that swung outwards and upwards. In his mind, he blamed all the day's drink for the fact that he had not taken note of the openings earlier. By the time he pulled up his pants and tucked away his spike, the little kuetlings had multiplied like rats!

"Uh … yeah! I'm seeing a lot right now!" he called back to Sheen, at a volume that betrayed his growing discomfort. He quickly rotated and put his back to the wall. He took his eyes off the first child for just a moment as he took stock of their situation, which was deteriorating rapidly in his judgment. Then he looked back. The girl seemed to have stepped a bit closer in the heartbeat that he'd looked away. Basta could scarcely believe it. In less time than it took to maak, they'd gone from being alone in the alley to being nearly surrounded by a hauntingly calm, ever-increasing mob of ankle-biters! He had heard of gangs of thieving street scabs roaming the alleys in search of hapless victims but only in The Deep End or perhaps in The Dank—never in the middle Wards! Not to mention that they were hard-edged and not some soft merchants who had stumbled away from their shields. What in the frothing seas of doom was going on?

"You squatted over my grate!" the boy said slowly and with a malicious edge. Sheen didn't like his tone one bit and drew down hard. With her hands filled with double-edged steel, she struck her favorite combative pose, the scorpion. She wasn't going to let some hellion's spawn kuet with her!

"Is that so?" she demanded. "So what? I'll squat wherever my tender bits tell me to. What's a little kuffe like you going to do about it?" There was something truly odd about the child. He smelled of slow death, diseased, the way that so many of the poorest in the city did. He had some intangible otherworldly quality in his gaze that made her skin crawl. Her instincts never failed her and they told her not to take her eyes off the imp. She used her peripheral vision to see it was getting more crowded in the alley. "Basta ... what are we doing?" she shouted, openly agitated.

Basta turned to his sister's voice. "We meet in the middle!" he replied. As he turned, the girl suddenly rushed to him. The little wretch wrapped her left arm around his right thigh and stabbed him with her right hand! She held a palm's length carpenter's nail and went into a frenzy, snarling and fighting maniacally to drive the iron home, again and again! In the flurry of attacks, she punctured his leg several times. He was unarmored and reflexively protected his groin and inner thigh. However, she effectively savaged the meat of the big muscle at the front of his leg. Blood ran hot down his skin and the wounds she'd inflicted burned like fire.

Basta grabbed her by her hair with sudden violence he had seldom used on a creature so small. He used her weight against her, slight though it was, twisting her head hard at the fulcrum of her neck. Basta felt her break and yanked her away from his leg as she went limp. He cast her towards the others, who paused their advance and looked down upon her body. She lay there with her little head turned backward. As one, his diminutive attackers scowled. He had expected to produce fear but instead, when they looked up again, their young eyes seethed with a terrible burning hatred that was shocking. He drew both of his blades and started to shuffle towards Sheen. The grubs from hell followed, circling.

Sheen shifted her stance to broad blades but kept the boy locked in her sight, holding her second arm out towards him, her blade pointing towards his little, round face. She began moving toward her brother, slashing widely in the area directly to her right with her heavy hand. Sheen glanced around nervously, seeing what she quickly determined to be more than forty of the little stains hovering all around her. "Back-to-back!" she called out, but they were on her before she could take another step!

The Shabott twins had seen twenty-four cycles of the seasons come and go during their time on Maera. They had remained intent on being there for one another through all that. Simply put, the worst things that had ever happened to either of them occurred when they were separated. Thus, it was just as much blind instinct as a spawned strategy that saw them working to come together.

Basta had been bloodied already. His ruthless retaliation against his assailant only seemed to feed the fervor of his attackers.

He had lost a good measure of blood and faced a severe challenge in employing all his practiced balance, hard-earned strength, and speed to fend them off. Basta went straight to his most deadly attack mode, hydra, without considering the children he was using it on. It had been developed for use against massed, unarmored foes, against whom it was devastating. One thrust, one kill—Basta used his blade points to slay and his weapon's heavy guards to stop the advance of his foes. He didn't even attempt to keep a running tally of how many he killed or wounded as he went. His energy expenditure was spectacular but using the traditional street fighter's long and short daggers that the twins preferred, Basta was well-served by his steel as he fought back a charging press of vastly inferior foes.

Sheen stabbed and slashed her way toward her twin. She stabbed any that grabbed onto her and, when she could, slashed those who tried to advance on her. The violence she did to the children would surely have upset some but it didn't bother her. She had always hated the foul offspring of others. She wasn't frightened by the bizarre and unprovoked attack, eerie as it was. She had been the target of an abundance of assaults during her span. It was their remorseless aggression and the way that they ignored their losses that alarmed her. Were they all drugged? She was sure she had slain at least five of the fetid little rodents by the time she backed up to Basta and they had shown no signs of stopping. Her brother breathed heavily, the huffing an injured man does. Just then, it all suddenly stopped.

The swarm of children had been well-thinned by the twins' proficient use of their finely edged steel. That might suggest that the problem was getting more manageable. Unfortunately, the mob continued to grow steadily during the attack and now numbered nearly ninety. Still, when faced with the proposition of taking on the pair's fully united defense, the swarm of little maaklings backed off. They stood perhaps two strides away and completely encircled the twins. The pair stood their ground and sought to control their breathing and rest their over-taxed muscles as they maintained a defensive posture, points out. Alternately glowering and growling, the mob seemed to have had enough.

"I'll toss them my winnings," Sheen proposed. Basta didn't object to her plan, although he had staked half of her bets. While he loved coin as much as the next man, Basta was not enamored with it as a possession. He knew with certainty that what truly gave coin value was what you could buy with it. At that moment, buying their lives sounded pretty damned good. She used a softer tone, forced herself to smile, and nodded her head to appear agreeable. "You want a little shiny, don't you? Would you like that?" she asked aloud, projecting her voice so that all could hear her offer. "You'll have to share but I'm sure I have enough for you."

The boy who had first approached her, whom she had slashed viciously shortly after the onset of the violence, came to the front of the fetid mob. Somehow, he ignored the slash that had splayed open the flesh of his upper arm. With a growing sense of trepidation, Sheen noticed a subtle and sinister swirling of dark aether around the boy's eyes. "You're bad," he said.

"Bad!" another boy repeated.

"You're both bad!" said a little blonde girl.

Soon all the children had added their voices to the denouncement of the twins. "You're bad!" they proclaimed. "Bad-Bad!" they insisted. "Bad-Bad!" they agreed. Their young voices soon synced into a strange chorus of frank hatred and roiling accusation. "Bad-Bad! Bad-Bad!" Now, it seemed to the twins that the children had joined in speaking some manner of dreadful incantation. "Bad-Bad! Bad-Bad!" they continued.

An inky, heavy mist seemed to rise from the cobbles as the mob of urchins continued their chant. "Bad-Bad! Bad-Bad!" Shadow swirled about their tiny ankles and rose between them as they spoke with ever-increasing energy. "Bad-Bad! Bad-Bad!" The children stood staring and chanting, obviously building towards some fell crescendo! "Bad-Bad! Bad-Bad!" The twins looked about like trapped animals, sensing that something truly horrid was about to unfold. Basta pushed his back against his sister and Sheen ground her back into his. The twins realized that the children's chant had ceased and a foreboding silence had replaced it.

Then the Bad-Bad came.

The twins watched, frozen in fear, as the air swirled and condensed amongst their foes. They somehow knew it was quickly thickening aether that rushed towards them, all at once, from all sides. Some*thing* drew deep, rich energy from the wretched mass of street scabs, lavishing in such base and raw emotion. The dread darkness swept in upon the twins, enveloping them. They were lost in it, drowned by it, violated as it fondled their flesh and knew their minds. The mob of children lowered their voices as the reckoning of the dark did their bidding. Soon, the Bad-Bad they had summoned coalesced into what they knew as the Dark Mother.

She attacked the pair as she formed, drawing strength from the Shabott twins, devouring their aether as their mortal forms fell to the cobbles. There they lost control of their bodies and began to convulse. Effectively paralyzed, they were doomed to helplessly witness the foulness that manifested in that alley. Naked, save for a black shroud that seemed to float about her, the children's adoptive dacmon was nearly whole. Her form was slender and her hair a deep auburn mass that swept about her pale shoulders. Sheen spasmed, for she could see the being's skin, which seemed to have melted. It was viscous vileness, like some milky puss, translucent and oozing. The ruddy strands of her muscles clearly showed beneath that horrid pooling purulence. Then Basta moaned as he saw the awful entity grin, lavishing in the pleasure of feeling the twin's anticipation of their imminent doom.

"Come to me now ... come to Mother!" The wispy inhuman voice of the dark terror was indescribably torturous to hear. Its unholy, melancholy song swirled in one's ears and echoed hollowly in the mind. The twins lay amidst it, their bodies the actual source of it, as it fed off their maddening suffering. Sheen vomited in her mouth, struggling as she choked on it. The children rushed forward as one, reaching out to the Dark Mother. They smothered the twins further as they massed about the Mother like some fleshy bandage placed on an open wound. The children hugged together in a circle, forming a dome about the entity's waist. In turn, she touched each of their heads in a gesture of recognition of their devotion, an understanding of their pain.

"They hurt us!" one cried.

"They killed Janie," wept another.

"They cut me," complained a third.

"Make them pay. Make them suffer!" others said.

"There, there now ... it will all be alright. They'll pay. Soon, they'll all pay! All that abandoned us. All that betrayed us. All those who failed to wipe away the tears of a child. All that turned away from an outstretched hand and failed to help us. Oh, yes, my

children! They'll all pay soon enough. Now play for a bit while Mother dances."

With that said, the Dark Mother swooped away from the twins, leaving them to her children. As the entity vacated their immediate area, the pair were left in her shadowy residue. They quickly regained control of their weakened bodies. Sheen spat out her spew and the pair tried to recover but it was too late—the mass of tiny bodies was upon them! The Dark Mother danced, sweeping to and fro, as if following a pattern, spinning and floating in circles with her arms out, seemingly in the close and formal embrace of some long-lost partner. It was as if she was dancing in a ballroom that only she could see, to the music of an orchestra that only she could hear, the whole time floating on the aether just above the cobbles. She relived the most vivid memory of her former life, which was macabre and haunting to behold. All around her, the children who could not reach their victims were entranced by her phantasmal performance.

She danced away, up and down the alley as, nearby, her children fell upon their hapless, twitching victims, bringing their hatred to bear. They used their terrible iron nails to peel away the skin, to remove eyes, ears, noses, and, eventually, tongues. Then the true horrors began, for nothing goes to waste in the realm of Loekii. The children feasted on the pair who were still alive through much of it. Slowly, the mass of screeching flesh that had once been the Shabott twins fell silent. The sounds of their agony and terror were replaced by a quieter rending and tearing. Only after far too long of a span did they finally, mercifully, succumb to death. The horrid feast continued long after they were gone.

All the while, the Dark Mother danced as if to the cries and screams of the twins. With each moment of their epic torment, it seemed as if she became more solid, her skin slowly flowing, regaining integrity, and returning to its original perfection. Indeed, as Mother danced, it was as if she was transformed again into the fantastic beauty that she once was. In the waning of their victim's last moans, she wore her gown again, her hair an elaborate work of art, her face painted in the way of her day. Through the offering of the twin's abundant suffering, the Dark Mother was finally whole again and she shimmered in the arcane glow of her vast and perilous beauty.

Her little ones, mostly satiated after the ravaging of their victims, turned with bright eyes and bloodied faces towards the wondrous form of their Dark Mother, remade. They chewed on their last mouthfuls as they grew excited, having now seen the results of their work. The Mother saw the devotion on their little faces and gestured, waving them in and smiling back upon them, her lustrous visage stunning in its perfection. She stooped low and hugged as many of them as possible as they clung to her dress and filled her arms. She positively beamed as she held them tight and announced in a low, calm voice that was now melodious and distinctly human.

"It is our time now, children."

Want to experience more of Maera? Visit ***www.maeraworld.com***